UNGUARDED

UNGUARDED

JAY HOGAN

VINO &
VERITAS

HeartEyes
Press

For my family who read everything I write and keep saying they love it all, blushes included.

1

TAI

"Hey!"

The passenger window rattled in its rust-eaten frame, jerking me awake.

Son of a bitch.

"Piss off," I grumbled and rubbed my knee, cursing the hand brake before hauling my leather jacket back around my ears in a futile attempt to maintain some body heat, because holy shit, this place got cold at night. The jacket was a typical Dion gift—soft as silk and screaming money, it hit all the right fashion and aren't-I-a-great-boyfriend notes, without doing a fucking thing toward actually keeping me warm. Mind you, who knew Vermont hit blue-balling temperatures by the last week in September. My piercings were sporting fucking icicles.

"Hey!"

Goddammit.

I kept my head buried and flipped off whoever it was, doing my best not to expose a single inch of unnecessary skin. The fact my fingers still worked was an unexpected bonus since I couldn't feel a thing south of my knees. An attempted toe-curl only confirmed my fears.

None of this was helped by a pair of painted-on leather pants, less than a whisper thick but which hugged my arse in all the right places; a multi-colored silk scarf with just the right amount of fabulous and minus a single drop of warmth; a neon pink fishnet shirt that drew all the boys' attention to my perky nipples but whose holes could've let a complete Iditarod dog team through with nothing but net; and a pair of pink canvas sneakers minus socks.

But it wasn't like I'd planned to bolt from the ninety-degree dance floor of Both And, one of the inclusive clubs my fuckwit boyfriend owned, and wake up in arse-crack, bone-rattling icy Vermont, newly single and minus a home.

Single.

Wow.

Could I get a hell yeah?

Quickly followed by a what-the-fuck-have-I-just-done?

Yeah, mostly that last one, since Dion was no doubt curled up in our, *his* bed in *his* soulless but ever-so trendy and *warm* Boston loft, with one or both of the sanctimonious twinks I'd caught him sandwiched between in his club office. On the other hand, *I* was here . . . somewhere just under the Canadian border and a memory foam mattress short of comfortable.

But shit happens.

Motherfucking, Dion-shaped, cheating, lying, three years down the drain, toad-wrangling *shit* . . . to be precise.

He'd be laughing his arse off if he knew I'd spent the night in a car. *"But what if you break a nail?"* was his standard snotty comment whenever I tried anything that might get my hands dirty. *"This amount of pretty doesn't need to think"* was another favorite he used with his arsehole mates who regarded me as an amusing dalliance if they even acknowledged me at all. That was apart from the times they were trying to convince me to fuck them behind Dion's back.

More rapping on the window. "You need to move. You can't park here."

A blatant lie, considering I'd been parked here for about six hours. Six ball-chilling, regretting-my-life-choices, uncomfortable-as-shit hours.

"I need you to open up, sir, right now."

The tone finally caught my attention, and I peeked out from

under my jacket, only to wince at the uniform. *Fuck.* I wouldn't be buying a lottery ticket any time soon.

I popped the seat upright, managed a quick check in the rear vision mirror, and *holy shit*, I looked even worse than I felt. I scrubbed at my face and dropped the window just enough to exchange a few words without exposing the poor man to an unfiltered serve of morning breath. Not to mention I smelled like a drag queen's tuck after a pride parade. *Don't ask me how I know that.*

"Yes, Officer?" I mustered the best law-abiding look I could, considering my outfit screamed rent boy more than respectable rural-Vermont citizen. But whether it was my obvious exhaustion, ludicrous attire for the climate, or the tear-carved ravines in my cheeks, the officer's severe expression softened. It clearly wasn't his first rodeo.

He gave a puff of a sigh that misted into the car and the corners of his eyes crinkled in a sympathetic half-smile. "License and registration, please?"

"Oh, sure." I patted my jeans and desperately tried to think where I'd shoved my wallet. Nothing in either of my pockets—no surprise there since a fucking ant couldn't fit inside without donning some shapewear. Nothing in my jacket either. *Shit.*

The officer's brows crunched. "I'm gonna go out on a limb here and guess you're not a Vermont local?"

"No. I drove from Boston last night." My gaze swept the car. *Where in the hell had I put it?* I spied the glove compartment and remembered. But as I reached, the officer's hand went to the gun on his hip.

"Whoa." I raised both of mine in the air. "Sorry."

"Slowly," he said, his hand hovering.

I did, *very* slowly.

"You have an accent."

"Yeah, I'm originally from New Zealand." The glove box popped open and I carefully retrieved my wallet and papers and handed them over. At least Dion had put the piece-of-shit car in my name.

The officer flicked through and eyed me up and down,

clocking my state of relative undress. "If you slept in there, you're lucky you didn't freeze." He arched a brow. "You're a New Zealander living in Boston, then?"

"Yeah. I was born in Dallas while my dad worked for an offshore oil and gas company, so I'm a US citizen. But I grew up in New Zealand. Came back about three years ago. My passport is at the back."

He took a look, then returned my wallet. "You working in Boston?"

At fucking up my life? Absolutely. "Not at present."

"So, what brings you to sunny Burlington?"

Is that where I am? Also, excellent question. I thought about fobbing him off with some cock and bull story but decided against it. He listened politely and nodded in all the right places, barely flinching at the leaving the ex-*boyfriend* part, which earned him some credit.

"Hell of a night, by the sounds of it." He frowned. "Are you in any danger?"

"Not in the way you mean."

He studied me for a minute, then gave a brief nod. "Okay, well this is a dedicated one-hour parking lot, and although I appreciate your situation, you need to find somewhere else to park while you . . . sort things out, understand?"

Only too well. "Right. Sorry. I'll get out of your hair. Can you point me in the right direction, maybe?"

He studied me for a minute, then sighed. "If you want to park for more than a couple of hours for free, you'll need to head that way a few blocks." He indicated further along the road. "And here's a tip for nothing. There's a great bakery in the Church Street Marketplace about a hundred yards from here, The Maple Factory. Head down this street and turn left. The street's closed off to cars for a couple of blocks; you can't miss it. And you won't have to sell your soul to get a maple cruller that'll fill you up until lunch."

"Thanks." The small kindness had fucking tears welling in my eyes. Jesus, I was a mess. "I'll get out of here."

He gently slapped the door of my car and said, "You do that.

And take care. There's a good hostel in town if you need one. And get yourself some warmer clothes while you're at it."

"I will."

He slapped my door once again and headed out of the parking lot.

I steered my death trap of a Civic toward the free parking and cursed my arsehole of an ex yet again. Dion drove a fucking Mustang, and what had he given me to do his club errands for him? Twenty years of rust and goodwill all wrapped up in a metal can and bumping along on a dubious set of balding tires. On a more positive note, it had spent most of its life parked at Dion's club which meant I'd had a getaway option after barging in on his cheating arse. So, I guess there was that.

The Marketplace turned out to be an attractive three or four block outdoor pedestrian shopping and dining mall, and clearly the heart of Burlington's downtown. I found The Maple Factory easily enough and the maple cruller lived up to the hype. I was still licking my lips five minutes later as I leaned against one of the massive stones that spotted the Marketplace, and tried to defrost my brain.

Although still a month away, Halloween was already alive and well in the town with a banner advertising something called Nightmare Vermont strung across the Marketplace. Oversized pumpkins crowded retail windows, fighting for space with well-dressed scarecrows and cutesy witches and ghosts, all designed to reel in the kids and empty the parental wallets.

I snorted. The last Halloween event I'd attended had been a clothing-optional private party in one of Dion's clubs. As far as I was concerned, clothing was never optional, no matter how much Dion wanted to parade me around buck naked in a collar for all his mates to see, and the argument had been protracted and nasty. But it was one of the few times I hadn't given in and I'd won. The treat basket at the entry door had held a selection of weird and wonderful sex toys to make use of during the night. And the trick part had come in avoiding Dion's handsy mates who'd apparently decided I classified as one of the treats whenever Dion wasn't around. G-rated, it definitely wasn't.

Nightmare Vermont looked a whole lot more fun.

Standing and shivering in little more than fifty degrees, I really, really needed to do something about the threat of encroaching hypothermia. There was just one tiny little problem. When I'd tried to pay for the bakery cruller from my own tiny account, my card declined. For a second, I'd just stared at the machine, my gut clenching. Then when the credit card Dion had given me for emergencies was also declined, I just knew.

That fucking son of a bitch. He'd cleaned me out. In my very first week in Boston, when I was all starry-eyed over this sophisticated man who seemed to worship me, I'd handed Dion my bank details and pin so he could transfer money when I needed it, or so he'd said at the time, and I always kept a spare debit card in the loft. I may as well have bared my fucking throat to his blade.

Which currently left me the three hundred dollars he'd stuffed in my wallet the night before—my damn pocket money for the club—and that was it.

A snort of disgust broke my lips. Jesus Christ, had I really become *that* guy?

Unfortunately, yes. Twenty-seven years old and some dude's fucking paid-for arm candy. Pathetic meet just plain embarrassing.

It wasn't that I needed him, not really. I'd been more naïve than anything. I'd trusted him. Believed I was loved. Believed this was it, the big romance, the be-all and end-all. Believed it enough to follow Dion back to Boston after his holiday in New Zealand. Believed it through the first time I'd caught him fucking some guy in our bed a year later. Believed the apologies, the promises, the dance of a future dangled in front of me. No need to have friends of my own—we were a couple, right? No need to work—he earned enough, right?

No need for monogamy—it's not like I could just up and leave, right? How the hell would someone like me survive without him?

6

Motherfucker.

It had been so easy to simply close my eyes and believe. Pretend I didn't notice the smug looks and pitying smiles his mates sent my way. On some level, I'd known. They said you always did.

Which left me leaning on a rock worthy of a Flintstones movie in the middle of an outdoor shopping mall in a town I'd only just learned the name of, my nipples frozen to my goddamn mesh shirt, and mulling over my foolishness. There was a lot to mull.

I was broke, homeless, alone, and fucking freezing. A quick sweep of the nearby shops revealed a well-known outdoor supply brand that I couldn't afford to buy a pair of socks from.

A rainbow flag in the window of a bar next to The Maple Factory caught my eye, and I glanced up at the sign. Vino and Veritas. The next-door bookstore sported the same flag and the two shared one entry. *Huh.*

As I was studying the book display in the front window, lights flicked on inside and a cute guy wearing a brown beanie, flannel shirt, and looking pretty damn country delicious—a gay varietal not frequently seen on the club floors of Boston—appeared through the doors carrying a sandwich board advertising some book thingy. He put the board in place and did a bit of a double-take when he saw me standing there staring. Then his brows raised as he clocked my outfit, and his lips quirked up for a second before he nodded and disappeared back inside with an audible chuckle.

Great. Winning friends and influencing people.

I continued my vigil, ensuring the rock had zero chance of a sneaky escape for another five minutes while I watched Mr. Beanie getting the bookstore ready for customers. But casual interest quickly turned to burning need the minute I saw him warm the espresso machine.

Fuck it. I could afford a damn coffee, maybe even two. How much worse could things get? Not to mention the place had to have heating. I pushed off the rock and made a beeline for the front door.

The coffee was delicious and the heating toasty. Which left me, an hour and a half later, deftly avoiding Mr. Beanie's—Briar, according to his nametag—slightly concerned gaze as I continued to take up space on one of the sofas located close to a heating vent. I even had a book in hand to look the part—about what, I couldn't tell you.

The idea he might throw me out seemed a little extreme for a man who looked, if not quite understanding, at least curious.

Like he knew I had nowhere to go.

Like I had *Fucked Over By My Lover* tattooed on my forehead in big fat neon letters.

I'd have been mortified if I weren't already too busy freaking out about being homeless and broke.

My phone buzzed in my pocket, again, and I pulled it out to confirm what I already knew. Message 993 from Dion. I'd only bothered scrolling through the first dozen or so he'd sent the night before, before muting and pocketing the thing.

But this latest one caught my attention.

What the fuck are you doing in Burlington?

Shit. I flicked to settings and turned off location services before I texted back.

In case you didn't get the memo, we're done. Piss off.

You're such a fucking drama queen. It was a mistake.
Didn't mean anything. I'll take you to Pierre's to make it up to you.

Fucker. I texted back.

How is a restaurant going to make up for cheating on me, again? We're done. Over. Finished.

I canceled your card.

I know.

You don't have any money.

I'll be fine.

Don't be a child. What are you going to do? You need me.

Like a hole in the head. Stop texting me.

I pocketed the phone without reading his reply, but the anxiety ate at me. I didn't like that he knew where I was, and the phone was under his account. Could he log in and switch it to lost mode and locate me? I had no freaking idea. I needed to ditch it, like I should the car, but I needed somewhere to sleep and I couldn't afford a new phone, not yet. The car was in my name so he couldn't say it was stolen, but the phone was a problem.

Dion had never been physical with me, never hit me. It was more that I didn't trust myself not to cave and let him take me back if he found me. Because he was right. I had no idea how the fuck I was going to survive with no money. He was clearly pissed I'd walked away. And even though I'd told him we were over in no uncertain terms—cue an accurate shot to his head with the glass of Glenfiddich I held while he was still balls-deep in a twink —he'd struggle to believe I'd actually leave.

Which reminded me, I needed to find somewhere to be tested. God knew where the hell Dion's dick had been and whether or not it had been clothed at the time. Motherfucker.

"Can I get you another coffee?" Briar collected my empty cup and wiped the table.

My gaze shot to those lovely eyes and the gentle smile beneath.

"Cold enough for you?"

I rolled my eyes and glanced to the heavy gray sky, ripe with rain, brooding over the city. "Do you really need an answer?"

His smile broadened. "Figured as much." He perched on the other sofa and studied me. "I'm guessing you're not local?"

I snorted. "What gave it away?"

"The accent, closely followed by the shirt." His gaze lingered on my chest. "Don't see that shade of pink around here very often, and certainly not at nine on a Thursday morning."

My turn to laugh. "But it goes so well with my sneakers, don't you think?"

He chuckled. "Definitely not local. If I had to guess, I'd say Boston city slicker."

"Touché. You're good." It was hard not to like the guy.

"Yeah, well, I'm an old Springfield boy, myself. Up here they call guys like us Massholes."

I snorted. "They might not be far wrong. But if that's part of the City of Burlington's welcome patter, I have to tell you, it needs some work. And to answer your question: New Zealand for the accent; Boston for the last three years. Drove up last night."

He studied me in silence. "I'm going to go out on a limb here and say it wasn't planned."

I stared out the window and watched as a pretty woman in her forties drew her coat tight across her chest and laughed to whoever she was on the phone with. "And you'd be right." I turned back to face him. "Suffice to say my love life took a sudden dive. And why I'm telling you *any* of this, I have no idea."

"It's my disarming personality," he deadpanned. "You never had a chance."

I narrowed my gaze. "I'll bear that in mind." My eyes landed on a stack of *Out* magazines on a nearby bookshelf and then lifted to the dark interior of the wine bar. "Is that a gay bar?"

He shrugged. "Inclusive. Same with the bookstore. There's live music some nights, if you're interested."

I shrugged. Hard to see me having money to waste on that. "Cool. And about the clothes thing? There wouldn't happen to be a thrift shop somewhere close?"

He nodded. "Head that way a block." He pointed up the mall. "Take a left, walk two blocks, and you'll find The Wardrobe. Claudia should still have some jackets this early in the season, but I wouldn't wait. There'll be a few people headed that way after this cold snap. And while you're here—" He pulled a card from his pocket and wrote something down before handing it to me. "These are a couple of hostels in town . . . just in case."

I stared at the names on the card, then pocketed it, wondering how the hell this had become my life. "Thanks. And sorry if I've overstayed my welcome. I just—"

"Stay as long as you like." He pushed to his feet. "How about hot chocolate? We do a really good one."

"Oh, I can't aff—"

"On the house."

My cheeks fired hot. *Well, shit.* "In that case, thank you."

"Your welcome. I'm Briar Nord, by the way." He offered his hand and we shook.

"Tai Samuels."

"Well, Tai, in case you decide to stay awhile and maybe sample some more of Burlington's renowned hospitality—" He gave a cheeky smirk. "There's an unemployment office on Pearl Street just up the road from the thrift store."

We locked eyes for a few seconds and I felt very *seen*, like this guy knew something about the mess I was inside. "Thanks. You never know. You don't happen to need someone around here? I can make a pretty good coffee."

He shook his head. "We're good at the moment."

Shit. "No problem."

A few minutes later he delivered a steaming mug of excellent hot chocolate and the world looked a bit brighter. The idea of running home to New Zealand was tempting; my parents would make sure I got there, but it also felt way too much like admitting defeat.

Mum and Dad had thought I was making a big mistake with Dion and tried to talk me out of it. Turns out they were right. But I liked living in the States, and I wasn't ready to leave. There was a whole country outside Boston that I hadn't seen. Maybe I'd go home eventually, but I didn't want it to be with my tail between my legs. I just had to work out how I was going to manage that.

I kicked off my sneakers, curled my legs beneath me on the sofa, and watched the world pass by on the other side of the window. People didn't seem to hurry in Burlington. They ambled, strolled, moseyed, even drifted, but rarely rushed. It was kind of cute.

Which was why my attention was quickly drawn to an attractive man in an outdoor coat that wouldn't have looked out of place summiting Everest. He was armed with a cat carrier and a troubled expression and headed for the bookstore at a veritable canter.

And he was also, not to put too fine a point on it, fucking gorgeous—every harried, tousled, flustered, mouth-watering inch of him. A little taller than my five foot ten, he looked to be in his thirties with unruly blond waves that caught in his lashes and dipped to his collar, a pale, almost peaches-and-cream complexion and a strong frame, not heavily muscled just . . . solid. The kind of body that could easily cage you against the wall if you were inclined to allow it, which, for the record, I would, in case the question ever came up.

Just, damn. I swallowed a hit of hot chocolate and sighed. The morning had taken a turn for the better.

The man hit the entrance to the bookstore like a cyclone, sweeping inside and straight up to the counter, draughting two old ladies in his wake, both of whom looked a little surprised to have gotten there so fast. Briar greeted the handsome man like he knew him, but try as I might, I couldn't hear a damn word that passed between them. A minute later, Briar pointed out back and the man with the carrier disappeared down a hallway.

I scooted around in my seat and put my back to the window to watch for his return. Not that I was creeping on him or anything, but it wasn't like I had other more pressing matters to attend to, and hey, gorgeous guy. Merely appreciating that fact had me feeling somewhat normal for the first time since I'd left Boston.

Behind the counter, Briar caught my eye and arched a brow.

Busted.

I batted my lashes innocently and he chuckled. If the guy wasn't gay, I'd eat my hat. I may not have much to brag about in my arsenal of life's attributes, but good looks, a cheeky disposition, a truckload of snark, and an accurate-as-fuck bullshit barometer got me through most of life's challenges, other than Dion. There, my bullshit barometer had hit a glitch. Or maybe I'd simply not wanted to hear.

By the time the good-looking stranger reappeared with a yowling gray cat in the carrier, Briar was knee-deep in customers, and Mr. Gorgeous was left hopping from foot to foot looking antsy. His gaze swept the shop, landed on me, and paused.

Huh. I sucked in a breath because, damn, if I'd thought he was easy on the eyes before, it was nothing compared to having those baby blues focused exclusively on me. And when they dipped to my mouth for a long second, I deserved a fucking gold medal for not stripping on the spot and asking him to fuck me over the science periodicals on the table next to me. But the way my luck was running, any chance of the guy batting for my team was frankly zero to none and I needed to not add another shit show to my day.

I glanced away and acted as . . . ungay as I could, which, let's face it, was a complete waste of time so I glossed my lips instead. Never said I wasn't complicated.

Seconds later, a pair of jean-clad legs appeared in my line of vision and I looked up to find a pair of china-blue eyes studying me. Fuck me, the man was beautiful. Not classic cover material. No killer cheekbones or hard muscle or bedroom eyes. More disheveled cute, with a side order of endearing nerd and a shy smile. Never thought that was my thing, but I was sold.

"Could you keep an eye on this little one for me while I duck to the bathroom?" He placed the cage with the mewling cat on the floor at my feet.

Fresh soap, musk, and something vaguely antiseptic drifted between us, and I forced my gaze down from all that creamy skin to the moth-eaten feline glaring up at me. "Sure." I cleared my throat. "But you realize it's in a cage, right? I mean, it's not going anywhere." I arched a brow pointedly.

A flush of red brimmed at his collar, and oh god, dimples. "*She,* and yeah. It's just that she's a bit stressed as you can probably tell from the noise. She might be quieter away from the desk and if she can see someone."

I held up my hands. "Hey, no problem. *She's* safe with me."

He almost sagged with relief. "Thanks. It's been a day."

Tell me about it. "You're welcome. I promise I won't abscond with . . ." I raised a questioning brow.

He shrugged. "Your guess is as good as mine. Briar found her out back this morning. She was all tucked up in her tummy and not really moving, so he called me to come get her. I'd say she's been on the streets for a bit, but she let me pick her up easily enough, so maybe someone's missing her. I'm a veterinarian. Emmett Moore." He offered his hand.

His clasp was warm and dry, and if I held on a little longer than necessary, no one could blame me. "Tai Samuels. So, Emmett, you're her knight in shining armor, at least for today. Tomorrow she'll likely hate you for even presuming she needed rescuing, but that's women for you, right? Or so I'm told. I wouldn't know much about that . . . as it happens." *Holy fuck.* My gaze slid away in pure mortification. I didn't ramble or get tongue-tied. *Ever.*

"Okaaaay." He looked at me sideways. "Well, I won't be long."

He disappeared in a flash of blond waves and denim, and I stared down at the cat who had quieted somewhat and was regarding me with considerable distaste through a pair of piercing blue eyes.

"Hey, don't get all hoity-toity with me." I wagged a finger at her. "Unless your arsehole boyfriend threw three years of your life down the toilet by playing guess-whose-dick-is-where with two twinks, a truckload of lube, and Mariah Carey playing through his office speakers, you have nothing to complain about."

A mournful yowl rang out like fingernails down a blackboard and Briar threw me a concerned look while several customers covered their ears.

"Dion, if you must know." I answered what I presumed was the cat's pressing question about the name of said arsehole boyfriend. "And yours?"

Another yowl and I peeled my brain off the ceiling for the second time. "Tom, you say? Well, I hate to be the one to break it to you, but with that name, he's going to be a bitch to pin down in your part of the animal world."

She flopped on her side and turned those mournful eyes my way.

"Yeah, tell me about it. Men, right?"

We sat in blissful silence, and I finally risked poking a finger through the grill. After a few seconds of suspicion, she gave it a wary sniff, then jerked back.

I narrowed my eyes. "No need to be rude. You're a shampoo and spa day short of presentable yourself, so I wouldn't get too judgy there."

Her pinched blue eyes dulled and I remembered Emmett said she might be sick.

"Okay, so I admit you might be having an equally crap day," I said softly and waggled my finger. She took another sniff and let me scratch her under her chin. I felt oddly worthy. "But at least you'll get to sleep in a warm place tonight."

"Depends if the shelter has a place for her." Emmett reappeared beside me.

"Shelter?" I withdrew my finger and gawped up at him, because of course I did. "But aren't you taking her back to your —" I waved my hand around. "—clinic thingy."

He bit back a smile. "Yes, for now. I'll take a look at her, treat her for worms and fleas, get her vaccinations done, and then see if she needs some antibiotics or other treatment. But essentially, she's a stray, and as much as I'd like to, I can't keep every stray I get handed. We've got a good shelter in town. They'll do their best to home her. Anyway, thanks for watching her. I guess I should be getting back to the clinic."

"Oh, right, sorry. Well, it's been nice to meet you, Emmett."

"You too, Tai." He stared at me for a second as if he was about to say something else, then smiled and left, crate in hand. He stopped at the counter briefly to speak with Briar and then headed out without a backward glance.

I sank into the sofa and watched his back all the way up the street and around the corner. There was no denying the man looked good either coming or going.

"You okay?"

My gaze shot sideways to find Briar standing there with a knowing smirk on his face. I scowled. "I have no idea what you're talking about."

15

"Sure, you don't." He grabbed the empty mug and wiped the table. "But I get it. Emmett has great . . . attributes."

Huh. That answered that. I looked a bit closer. Briar was a handsome man. He didn't do it for me like the vet did, but he was cute. "He does indeed."

"I thought I'd check if you were thinking of hanging around Burlington for a bit?"

I shrugged. "I have no clue what I'm going to do past hitting that thrift shop very shortly, so all avenues are open. Why?"

His gaze swept the bookstore, then slid to the Marketplace outside before landing back on me. "Do you like animals?"

I arched a brow. "Excuse me?"

"Simple question. I saw you talking to the cat, so I figured maybe you liked them?"

What the hell? "Sure, I like animals. Doesn't everybody?" I mean, I didn't *not* like animals. I just hadn't had much to do with them other than an old Collie my parents owned who died when I was four.

"Oh, well, that's maybe good news." Briar's cheeks pinked. "Because Emmett, the veterinarian you were talking to—"

"Emmett of the . . . attributes?"

Briar rolled his eyes. "I'm going to regret this, aren't I? Yes, *that* Emmett. Well, his receptionist left him in the lurch this morning and he needs help. He asked if I knew anyone who could look after the front desk, answer the phone, maybe help wash a few dogs for the groomer—"

Wash a few what?

"—just for a week until he can get a new person, and for some reason I thought of you."

"Me? You did?" I was kind of gobsmacked. "And this is because I just scream animal management skills in my pink net top and leather condom trousers, right?"

He snorted. "No. It's because you scream 'I need the money with few skills to offer.'"

I gave him my best eye roll. "Everyone's a fucking comedian."

He paused and looked me over. "Look, forget I said anything." He turned to leave.

Shit. "No, wait, please. You're right. Obviously, I do need the money. And for what it's worth, I am trustworthy. A week's work would help a lot, you have no idea. Not to mention give me some time to get my head around . . . a plan."

He studied me for a moment. "So, you're okay about the animal thing, then?"

I waved his concern aside. "Pffft. Not a problem."

I needed my head read. I knew nothing about animals other than they smelled, had nasty teeth, shit everywhere, merino sweaters were the bomb, and chinchilla fur made great ear warmers. Not to mention I couldn't always be trusted to wash my own hair let alone another creature's. But regardless of all that, I needed a job, like really, really needed one, and Briar might've just saved my life.

Oh, and the vet was crazy hot, so yeah, there was that. Maybe I'd fuck it up, but I wasn't exactly in any position to turn the opportunity down. How bad could it be?

Briar looked relieved. "Good. I figured it could maybe work out for you both. I'll call Emmett and let him know to expect you, but you'll have to take it from there."

I was so fucking grateful. "Thanks, Briar. I can't believe you did this."

"Well, you seem like you could do with a break, and Emmett's a good guy. He's had a hard time of it since his wife died four years ago, and he has a cute kid."

Most likely straight then. Eye candy it would have to be. "I'm just grateful for the chance."

He nodded crisply. "Good. And if you do decide to hang around, you're welcome to join our romance book group, Booklovers."

I bit back a smile. "Romance books?"

His jaw set. "Yeah, romance books."

"Okay, well, that's . . . cool." *Holy crap.* "Can't say as I'm a great believer in romance though, so I wouldn't hold your breath."

2

EMMETT

"So, what the hell happened with our esteemed receptionist?" Ivy kept a secure hold on our newly rescued cat as I had another feel of her tummy. "I had to cancel half my grooming appointments. Tanya was bringing her two Samoyeds this afternoon and there's no way I can handle those on my own. My arthritis is killing me in this damn cold. I'm too old for this."

"You're sixty-two, woman. Little more than a spring chicken."

"Pfft. A spring chicken with a rooster neck, crow's feet, pig jowls, and knees like a baby elephant. I'm a damn one-stop petting zoo."

I snorted and handed her the apron to protect her during the X-ray. "You're beautiful."

"Stop blowing smoke up my ass and tell me about Carolyn. Fool of a girl."

"You know as much as I do—a message on voicemail to say she'd decided to walk the Appalachian trail with her boyfriend, starting today."

Ivy shook her head in disgust. "It's fall. What the hell's wrong with that girl? Is this the same guy she's known for all of three weeks?"

"I'm guessing."

"Good lord, she's asking for trouble." Ivy held the wriggling cat in place while I whipped around the corner to take the X-ray.

Then she cradled the cat in her arms and cooed gently in her ears before returning her to the kennel room.

At five foot nothing Ivy was about as tall as she was wide, with a wit as dry as the Sahara, a take no prisoners attitude, a low tolerance for assholes, and a heart big enough to fit a universe or two. I'd taken over the lease on the building just after her husband died, and since then she'd become almost a second mother to me and grandma to Leo.

We helped her with any heavy lifting or washes she couldn't manage, and she lent a hand in the clinic when she could. But canceling grooming appointments certainly wasn't part of the deal and I needed to solve my staffing problem and stop fixating on the gorgeous young man in the bookstore.

What the hell had I been thinking?

I should've just left the cage with Briar while I hit the bathroom. But no, I had to make a complete and utter fool of myself. 'Can you watch my cat?' Worst pickup line in the history of pathetic pickup lines.

Who says something like that?

Idiot, sex-starved, crushing-hard, closeted bisexuals, that's who.

But damn, the guy was just so fucking pretty. Pretty like a poppy in a cornfield, albeit a poppy with thorns. Melting brown eyes in deep olive skin and an insolent smile under sleek black hair, long on top and still a bit messy like he'd slept on it wrong. And slick lips from all that damn gloss. I wanted to know what they felt like on mine or wrapped around— No, no I didn't. Or at least, I shouldn't.

And then there was that glimpse of pink net under that leather jacket—so fucking sexy, along with tight as hell leather pants just begging for a hand to glide over the thigh and around the curves of what had to be a spectacular ass. One look and he'd burrowed into that place I kept under careful lock and key and blown the fucking hinges completely off.

For whatever reason, he'd also seemed interested, and I was just ridiculous enough to be flattered, my back still burning from the heat of his gaze as he'd watched me leave. I deserved a fucking gold medal for not turning to get one final look for the record.

Ivy returned as I threw the last of the instruments in the sterilizer, leaned against the examination table and flicked aside the shock of pink hair at the front of her short gray bob. She frowned. "What's up with you, aside from the obvious?"

She was too astute by far. "I'm fine, I just—" I was saved from finishing the lie when my phone blared a familiar tune, which I duly ignored.

Ivy cocked a brow. "Your mother, again?"

I sighed and returned the bottle of deworming tablets to the cupboard. "She's still pushing for the two of them to move here," I grumbled. "To . . . help out." I made air quotes.

Ivy's eyes popped. "Dear god."

"I know, right? The very thought makes me break out in hives. The two of us living in geographical proximity is a recipe for matricide."

Ivy snorted and *'Witchy Woman'* blared again.

This time I answered. "Hey, Mom." I rolled my eyes at Ivy who shook her head in amusement. "How's it going?"

"Fine, dear," my mother's voice soothed. "Your father and I were just talking and if we were to put our house on the market, it would be better to do it sooner rather than later, don't you think?"

"No, Mom. Don't do that. Leo and I are fine, honestly."

"I'm not at all sure I believe you. You were too thin last time we visited, and I don't think Leo should be spending all his after-school hours hanging around at the clinic."

Guilt rocketed through me.

"If we lived there, he could come to us. Plus, we could watch Leo for you when you needed so you could start dating again."

Ivy flashed me a broad smile and I mouthed for her to shut up, because of course I *didn't* date, not even close.

"If I need a sitter I have Ivy or Cody's mom."

"Family is better, Emmett. A boy needs a stable female presence in his life."

"A boy needs love, Mom. And Leo gets plenty of that."

"But what about you? I want you to be happy, Emmett."

"I'm fine. Just promise you'll wait until we can talk about it face-to-face."

She blew a frustrated sigh. "All right. But make it soon."

God help me. "I'll try."

I pocketed the phone and banged my head repeatedly on the examination table. "She *never* listens. The last thing I need is Mom twenty-four seven. I love them both, but man, she's hard work at times."

Ivy patted my back. "You didn't mention losing Carolyn, I noticed."

I turned my head and eyed her in disbelief. "Must've slipped my mind."

She snorted. "Which reminds me, now would be the perfect time for you to get that vet tech you've been talking about, someone who could actually take some of your workload, *plus* a receptionist. We could split the receptionist's salary between us."

"It's not a bad idea." I picked up a cloth and started cleaning the examination table.

"It's a brilliant one. Here, give me that." She grabbed the cloth from my hands.

I nabbed it back. "I'm quite capable, thank you."

She grunted and leaned against the sink as I finished cleaning. "So, how are you going to manage in the meantime?"

Fuck if I knew. "I've called Colebury clinic and asked their vet tech Penley to check with his network and see if anyone might be interested. And I'll place the vacancy online today." The clinic bell jangled and I groaned. "But I'll try and lock in a temp for a couple of weeks to buy us some time."

Ivy patted my arm. "Sounds like a plan. I'll go see who that is, and you check the messages for that call that came in while we were busy."

She left and I prayed the message wasn't from the school. It was Leo's first day back after two days with the stomach flu.

Thankfully, it wasn't. Instead, it was Briar to tell me he was sending someone my way who might be able to help out for a bit, with the warning that he didn't really know the guy.

Halle-freaking-lujah. If the man could answer the phone and hold a cat, he'd be just fine.

Ivy poked her head into the room. "Your next appointment turned up early, and there's a guy here who says Briar sent him over to maybe help? Cute accent." She waggled her eyebrows. "Hell, I'd pay him to stand around and look pretty, but that's just me."

Pretty? Accent? *Oh, hell no*. The guy in the bookstore. It couldn't possibly . . . I followed Ivy to the front desk, cast a glance into the waiting room, and—holy moly. I sucked in a breath and waited for my brain to unscramble.

"Shit." I hissed under my breath.

Ivy wide-eyed me from behind the computer and jerked her head toward Tai who looked more than a little nervous. He smiled and gave an uncertain wave. I smiled back and held up a finger. "One minute," I squeaked and disappeared into the storage room across from the desk.

Ivy joined me a few seconds later. "What the hell?"

"I need . . . I was looking for . . ." *Shit*. I couldn't think of anything quick enough and Ivy eyed me up and down like I'd lost my mind, which wasn't far from the truth.

"This!" I grabbed the nearest thing which happened to be a box of gauze dressings.

Ivy arched a brow. "I'm calling bullshit." She took them back and returned them to the shelf. "I saw two boxes in the cupboard this morning. What's up?"

"Nothing."

She folded her arms and stared at me. "Well, then you better get back out there. We need this guy even if he's even only halfway decent. He's breathing and looks like he could lift a dog; that's all that counts right now."

"He has to be able to work the computer." It was a weak protest at best.

"Goddammit, Emmett. We're a veterinary clinic, not the bloody space station."

"All right, all right." I wiped my sweaty palms down my jeans and took a deep breath.

"You sure you're okay?"

"I'm fine." And I would be. I *wasn't* hiring Tai, plain and simple. Based on the last thirty seconds, it would be a disaster on an epic scale.

I left the room and waved Tai over to the desk, aiming for casually professional and failing miserably as the gorgeous man sucked all the oxygen from the room. He offered his hand, the firm warmth of his grip doing another round of odd things to my stomach as I held on just a tad too long.

His gaze tracked my face, curious. "Hi. Bet you didn't expect to see me again. Must be destiny." He smiled, and all that bright shiny resolve I'd shored up shattered with a simple quirk of those lips.

"When can you start?"

It wasn't till he snorted that I realized I'd said the words out loud and felt Ivy's gaze boring red-hot pokers into my back. My cheeks flamed with the heat of a thousand suns.

Tai bit back a smile. "Perhaps you'd like to ask me some questions first?"

Did I? God, I was behaving like such a jackass. "Can you lift and wash fifty pounds of wriggling dog and hold an animal for examination if I need you to?"

He chewed on his lower lip for a second, and I wasn't going to look, I really wasn't, I—*fuck*. I wanted to kiss him. What the hell was wrong with me? I was a boring thirty-five-year-old father with the beginnings of a receding hairline, a demanding job, and a mouthy ten-year-old with a black hole for a stomach and a mother-shaped ache in his heart that wasn't going to be fixed anytime soon. I wasn't *this*, whatever this was.

"I expect I could cope," Tai finally answered. "Fair warning, I'm not exactly an expert with animals."

"But you think you could manage it? Wash a dog? Hold a cat for injections, that kind of thing?"

His gaze slid away. "If you show me what to do."

The way he said it, I wasn't entirely convinced, but then I remembered the bookstore. In a few minutes, he'd transformed a caterwauling stray cat to a quiet and just plain pissy one. That had to count for something.

"I can teach him the basics," Ivy butted in.

I fired her a glare to which she merely batted her lashes. "What about computers?" I asked Tai. "Can you work an appointment calendar, that kind of thing?"

He stood a bit straighter, and I tried not to drool at the glimpse of pink netting under the collar of his jacket.

"Yeah," he answered, a lot more confidently. "I ran a coffee shop once—did the books for the owner. Nothing complicated. But as long as you're not wanting nuclear reprogramming, I should be okay."

"Just the appointment book and billing."

He gave a firm nod. "Then I don't see a problem."

Thank, Christ. "I'll need you for about a week, including Saturday and any emergency calls I might get. It'll take me at least that long to find someone more permanent. Can you manage that?"

"Yes."

Just, yes? I wanted to ask him, why? Why is that okay for you? Why are you here, dressed in clothes not often seen in a Burlington shopping center on a Thursday morning? Why are you standing in my veterinary practice looking for a week's work? What happened to you?

Instead I said, "You're not American?"

"New Zealander, but I was born here. I've got ID if that's what you're asking?" He dug his wallet from his jacket and flipped it open.

The card looked legit. "So, when can you start?"

He beamed and something unexpectedly warm expanded in my chest. Something I wanted to attach to any number of four-letter words like want, need, kiss, fuck, hold, lick, suck—I wasn't fussy.

"Anytime you want," he answered.

Lord, help me. I dragged my mind from the gutter where it was busy pitching a tent and smacked it hard.

"How about now, if that works for you?" He flashed a coy

smile and there I was, scrabbling around in the fucking gutter again. "Just show me where to hang my jacket and I'm all yours."

He needed to stop. Like really needed to stop.

He shrugged said jacket from his shoulders and I nearly swallowed my damn tongue. *Sweet Jesus.* He may as well have been shirtless. Acres of smooth olive skin slid into view through the wide net of that ridiculous, glorious pink top, and two dark brown nipples stood proud in the cool of the clinic. *Holy shamoly.* It was like something out of a raunchy male online site, not that I'd know anything about that, of course.

A sharp intake of breath came as a timely reminder that Ivy was still at the desk. I spun to find a smirk the size of Grand Central Station on her slightly flustered face.

"Haven't you got work to do?"

"Nope." She held my gaze with barely a blink.

I glared.

She raised her brows.

"If you have a stroke, I'm not driving you to the hospital."

Tai chuckled and I turned back to find him holding a bulging supermarket bag aloft. "If you can direct me to the bathroom, I can change."

"That would be—" *Disappointing.* "—so much better."

He raised a brow.

"Not that you don't look fine as you are . . . of course . . ." I cleared my throat. "But, well, maybe . . . actually, changing would be good." I winced. "I just mean . . . well, I'm pretty sure our health insurance doesn't cover what you're currently doing to this old woman's feeble heart."

A hand whacked me up the back of my head. "Down the hall, last on the left," Ivy directed Tai over my shoulder. "When you come back, we'll complete all the forms we need."

"Thanks. I'll just go . . . change then." Tai stared at me a moment longer, amusement and a million questions dancing in those brown eyes—questions I had no intention of answering.

He'd obviously seen straight through me. Or not so straight as it happened. Could I be more fucking ridiculous? No. No, I couldn't. If I'd screamed at the top of my lungs—pitifully inexperienced, closeted, and repressed bisexual head-case standing right here—I couldn't have made my attraction to the poor guy any clearer.

He left with his bag of clothes, and like the fool that I was, rather than fleeing the scene, I stood and watched the bunch and swell of his ass encased in those sinfully tight pants all the way down the corridor. And then two seconds before he turned into the bathroom, he spun and caught me.

Goddammit.

He arched a brow and disappeared into the bathroom, and the sigh I'd been holding back poured from my lungs in a shuddering gush.

Holy fuck, I was in trouble.

Fingers tapped my shoulder. "You and I need to have a little chat, Emmett."

"Not now. I need to—"

"Yes, now."

So much trouble.

I glanced at my next appointment whose wide-eyed gaze was still locked on the spot Tai had just vacated. I knew exactly how she felt. Bees to fucking honey. "If you could wait ten minutes? We've had a bit of a crisis."

She nodded.

I followed Ivy back into the storage room wondering how this had become my life.

She shut the door and eyeballed me. "What the hell's up with you?"

"Nothing." I shuffled my feet.

"Don't bullshit me. You looked like you. . ." She hesitated and studied me with a shrewd eye. "Well, I'll be damned."

"What?" I flustered, feeling my cheeks blaze again. I straightened the box of printer paper on the shelf beside me and avoided her gaze.

"Bi? Maybe pan?" Ivy leveled the question directly at me.

My skin shrank two sizes on my frame. I tried for a scowl, but there was nowhere to hide. "You know, I'm not sure that particular approach has the rainbow ally tick of approval. Just saying."

"Hah! I'm on the right track, then. How did I not know this about you, sweetheart?" She tapped me on the chest with her finger. "And I'm too old for any polite pussyfooting around. At my age, I might not wake up tomorrow."

"I should be so lucky."

She punched me lightly on the arm.

"Ow." I loved her with all my heart and she damn well knew it. "If I agree you're on the right track, will you leave me alone?"

That got a smile. "What do you think?"

Fuck.

"Exactly." She straightened the collar on my shirt and patted my chest. "So let me make it easy for you. I'm ruling out gay, because no one has ever been more in love with a woman than you were with Lu. It leaked from every sappy pore in your body whenever you laid eyes on that wonderful girl." She waited.

"Not gay," I answered quietly. "And I did love her, with all my heart, you know that. I'm bi, maybe pan; I haven't really thought about that one too deeply. I just know that I . . . look . . . sometimes . . . imagine, you know? And before Lulu, I fooled around a bit with a couple of boys. Nothing serious. Girls have always tended to do it for me more, and no one has ever caught my eye like Lulu did, girl or guy."

"She knew?"

"Yeah." I couldn't help the smile. "She was great about it."

"Good."

"But no one else, other than Jasper, and now . . .you. Not my parents."

She nodded and kissed my cheek. "Well, I'm glad you were able to share it with someone. And I won't say a word. Just know that I love you."

I teared up despite myself. "Goddammit, woman, you're going to make me cry. Was I that obvious?"

She snorted and brushed the hair back from my eyes. "To me, and I suspect to him as well."

"Oh, god, really?" I cringed. Ivy's gaze darted to my ears and I knew they were bright red. "I don't even know the guy."

"Lust is lust, my boy. Now, you'd better get back before your next appointment mutinies. I don't have another client until noon so I can walk Tai through the basics."

I rolled my eyes. "And you'll behave?"

She smiled like a Cheshire cat. "Now where would be the fun in that?"

3

EMMETT

Tai caught on quicker than expected for a guy who clearly knew next to nothing about animals, a fact which had become apparent pretty damn quick. There was no hiding the fear in his eyes during that first hour, but when he began to relax, we got a glimpse of the bright, sassy personality just beneath the surface. It was like someone had pulled the blinds up in the clinic and let the sunshine in.

Ivy rarely had to tell him anything more than once. Things like how to hold a cat safely; how to spray a foul-mouthed cockatiel's feathers for mites; how to get a pill down the throat of a snappy miniature poodle—although that one admittedly took a little convincing; and how to hold a ferret while you took an X-ray to locate the rim of the condom it had swallowed—don't ask. The poor thing was staying the night to make sure it pooped the remaining fragment without issue.

The final client of the morning was a grumbling, overweight Pekingese cross named Charles, with an attitude to rival Genghis Khan and an owner who refused to come in with her dog because she didn't want the nippy little demon to associate her with any discomfort.

Under instruction from Ivy, Tai had the growling, muzzled dog wrapped in a towel and pinioned against his stomach, his expression caught somewhere between are-you-fucking-kidding-me and abject terror.

I told him what we were about to do and he stared at me in wide-eyed disbelief. "You did *not* just say you were going to milk this little guy's *anal glands*?"

I swallowed a laugh. "I believe those were my exact words."

His gaze flicked down to the squirming dog, then back up. "Do I even want to ask why?"

I shrugged and pulled on some gloves. "The anal glands are two little sacs on either side of the rectum. Normally they get expressed every time the dog poops. Helps mark his territory."

"Oh. My. God." Tai rolled his eyes dramatically. "I think I dated a guy like that once."

Ivy snorted while I grappled with an influx of images involving Tai with another guy and that whole territorial marking thing. I snapped the second glove on my wrist like an elastic band, hoping the pain might shock some sense into me.

It didn't.

Tai got his freak under control and tucked Charles firmly back against his stomach. It was the first time I'd ever been jealous of the mutt.

"I know I'm going to regret asking this," he said, wrinkling his nose. "But what happens when things *don't* get expressed, on the whole anal gland front? And I can't believe I just said that."

"Welcome to my world." Ivy appeared from the supply room.

I caught Tai's eye and waggled my eyebrows. He was hella fun to tease. "I'm so glad you asked that question. If they don't get expressed naturally, not helped by poor diet and excess weight, then the glands can block and get smelly and painful. They can even form an abscess that can burst onto the skin."

Tai's mouth dropped open in horror. "Holy crap. And also— another date of mine."

I gave a strangled laugh and realized I hadn't had so much fun at work since . . . well yeah, it had been a while.

"Damn, that's disgusting. The poor thing." Tai lifted Charles to smooch him safely around the back of his ears. "We need to talk about your diet young man," he cooed to the dog who, miracle of miracles, appeared to calm. "Fiber is the key, plus plenty of water and attention to timing. Clean, screened, and fit for a queen." He glanced up with a wicked grin. "Right, Mr. Vet?"

Ivy coughed loudly, while every semi-functioning neuron in my body focused on only one thing that shall not be mentioned.

"I, yeah . . . I guess," I managed to croak. "Although maybe not the screening thing, not for dogs."

Tai lifted Charles to eyeball him. "Safety first."

Ivy joined us at the table. "Okay, you two. Let's get this done so I can spritz the room. Keep a firm grip," she told Tai.

His eyes widened. "This is going to smell worse than I thought, isn't it?"

She wrinkled her nose. "Think fishy."

Tai got a tight hold on the wriggling dog. "Huh? Not my first guess. Okay, I'm ready. I have to say, it feels a little like an initiation."

I flashed him an encouraging smile. "You'll be fine. Now hold that tail up." As soon as the words left my mouth, I knew, and sure enough—

He snorted. "Not the first time I've been told that."

I shook my head, gently squeezed, and . . .

"Whoa." He gave a long blink and jerked his head around and out of the way. "Ewww, Charles. That's some nasty shit right there."

I grinned from ear to ear, pretty much as I had from the minute Tai had walked into my clinic. I was so fucked. Tai was quiet, almost reverent while being shown things but then cheeky when his confidence grew. Both sides intrigued me. It only took thirty minutes working alongside him to understand that behind all that brittle snark lurked a kind, gentle man.

And as for his skill on the front desk? When I snuck out to take a peek between clients, Ivy was in the middle of teaching Tai how to schedule a return visit for the cursing cockatiel and had given me a discreet thumbs-up.

"You'll have to do better than that." Tai paused to wag a finger at the bird. "I've been cursed out by a gaggle of drag queens drunk on tequila shots at a lingerie sale. *Nothing* beats that. I was only supposed to be the *chauffeur*. Turned out that word had a number of definitions that never appeared in any dictionary *I'd* ever read."

The bird's elderly owner hooted with laughter.

Which left me with not a single excuse to simply thank Tai for his help and let him go at the end of the day.

And the last time I looked, giving your boss an inconvenient semi from ogling your ass as you bent low over a cupboard wasn't dismissible behavior—an oversight that someone really needed to rectify with the courts, because that ass should've been fucking illegal.

And that had only been the morning.

Ivy had grooming appointments booked in the afternoon which left Tai on his own. With me.

The two of us working together.

Alone.

Wonderful.

Tai chose that moment to stroll through the open doorway and shoot me one of those spectacular smiles he was prone to pull out of nowhere and which apparently was connected straight to my ridiculous dick. He really, really needed to stop doing that. At least for the sake of my hopeless lustful soul.

This whole foolish crush was so out of character that I felt completely disconnected from my body. I hadn't craved a person sexually in the four years since Lu had passed, and now this. It felt like I'd fallen asleep in the Sahara and woken up in a fucking monsoon, minus an umbrella or rubber boots or any clue how to ride out the storm. And simply jumping in and getting wet wasn't an option. Although it was tempting.

And therein lay the problem.

"That's it until your one o'clock." Tai leaned on the door frame, looking goddamn fucking delicious. He was wearing a loose sweatshirt over slightly oversized blue jeans—which you'd think would've helped, but they kept riding down his hips and . . . yeah, that. But he'd at least added socks to the pair of pink sneakers so I could stop wanting to lend him the spare pair I kept in my office. But from the way my body reacted, he might as well have been wearing booty shorts and a collar and leash. Don't ask where that came from.

"You need anything else?" He stared at me with those smiling brown eyes, giving nothing away but looking like he knew every dirty thought that passed through my brain, because the honest answer to that question would get me in a whole heap of trouble.

"Not right now," I told him. "Take a lunch break. We've got a full afternoon, and Ivy said she needs you for a wash at two. There's tea and coffee in the break room and a fridge if you want to store some food. Feel free to help yourself to the bread and jars of peanut butter and anything else you find there. I keep supplies for Leo to make after-school snacks, but we all make use of it. It's part of the deal of working here."

"Leo's your son?"

I nodded. "Yeah, he's ten going on way too smart for his own good. But he's a great kid. You'll meet him later."

He met my eyes with a thoughtful gaze. "I look forward to it. I meant to ask how things work with Ivy? If I'm helping her, I can't be at the desk—"

"I'll handle the desk while you're busy, and clients know to ring the bell and take a seat. It works fine."

"Okay, well, I might take a walk. Can I bring you something back?"

The offer surprised me. "Thanks, but no. I'm drowning in paperwork and I need to post the position online."

He pushed off the doorjamb. "Then I'll leave you to it."

I watched him leave and got down to work, forgetting all about tempting brown-eyed men with trouble written in capital letters from head to toe.

When he arrived back in my office thirty minutes later, I'd barely made a dent in the paperwork, too busy frowning at the business accounts which weren't looking as healthy as expected, considering I ran a busy and popular practice. A brown paper bag landed on my desk and my gaze jerked up. "What's this?"

"Lunch. Food. You know, that nourishing stuff you put in your mouth to keep your body and mind healthy," he deadpanned. "I figured you to be the kind to not let a silly little thing like food stop your mission to heal the pets of Burlington single-handedly. Also, Ivy snitched on you."

I stared at the bag, speechless and more than a bit taken aback.

Tai nudged it closer. "Go on, eat. I'll be coming back to check." He turned to leave.

"Wait." *Shut. Up.*

He turned with brows raised.

"Wanna join me?"

He paused, looking the most uncertain I'd seen him all day, which got me curious. Tai was ballsy if nothing else, and the hesitation in the flick of his gaze over my face, gave me courage.

I pushed back the chair on the other side of the desk with my foot. "Sit. You brought me lunch. The least I can do is ask you to join me."

The tension drained from his face and he dropped into the seat before putting a matching paper bag next to mine on the table. I pulled a chicken salad sandwich from my bag and took a bite as he watched me.

"I'd hoped you weren't vegetarian."

"Nope." I finished the mouthful and swallowed. Turned out, I was famished. "Too many other things to think about now. Maybe later when I'm not so busy being a dad, but for the moment it's just fuel. And this is delicious, thank you."

He beamed as if I'd awarded him employee of the month. It was so damn hard not to like the guy. I took a slug of water to wash the sandwich down and caught him watching. I nodded to the other paper bag. "You're not going to eat?"

He pulled it close and took out an apple. "I had mine on the way back. I'll just finish this."

How I knew it was a lie, I couldn't say, I just did. The same way I knew it was *his* sandwich I was eating. Not that I was going to call him on it. Maybe it was his way of saying thank you; I didn't know. But as I took another bite and watched him power through his apple as if he hadn't been fed in weeks, I tried to understand why a guy who could barely afford his own lunch would buy one for himself and then give it to a man he'd only known for a couple of hours. I determined to get more food into him before he left for the day.

"So, you're from New Zealand?"

He grinned over his apple. "Are we making small talk, Emmett?"

I shrugged. "Why not?"

"Fair enough. Yes, my family's Kiwi, but my dad worked in Texas for a while as a diver, and that's where I was born. We shipped back to New Zealand a few years later, hence the Kiwi accent."

"Brothers or sisters?"

The question brought a huge smile to Tai's face and I wanted to keep it there. He really was a beautiful man. With long lashes and killer cheekbones, he'd lucked out on the genetic lottery for sure. And smooth skin, with barely a hint of stubble, had me wondering just how smooth the rest of him was, which had me wondering how his skin would feel under my hands, which had me— Nope, not going there.

But it was still those fleeting glimpses of insecurity behind his sass that really drew me in. Tai wasn't nearly as relaxed and easy going as he made out.

Who hurt you?

"I have five older brothers."

I nearly choked on the wad of bread I'd been chewing. "Six boys! Damn. I can barely handle one."

He laughed. "Yeah, but my mum loved it. She's part-Maori from a big family and she was a teacher before she retired. Dad's about as white as they come but also from a large family. They worked as a pretty efficient tag team wrangling the six of us. They barely batted an eye when I came out to them at fourteen, although stealing my mum's lipsticks since the age of seven was probably a decent heads-up. Kids at school were a little less . . . accommodating."

"You got bullied?"

He shrugged carelessly and his gaze slid away. "A bit. I mostly dealt with it by not going to school whenever I could get away with it. I graduated, but the damage was done. No one took me seriously, especially my over-achieving brothers who nicknamed me 'Face.'"

"Face?"

"An A-Team reference?"

"A-Team?"

He stared at me. "Wow. We really have some work to do." He pointed to his face. "This. The single attribute I possess that my brothers think might be worth something. Although I'd possibly add the nickname Dyson to that short list." He winked.

He meant it as a joke, but it didn't feel like it. The smile never reached his soft brown eyes and certainly missed his heart. In its place, something incredibly fragile stole into his expression and he looked like a puff of wind might shatter him.

He twirled the remains of his apple in his hand and avoided my eyes.

"Yeah, families are . . . complicated." I reached for the other half of the sandwich. "My mom couldn't understand why I went the vet route when I could've been a doctor. How were your parents?"

Tai pulled a face. "Dad's always been good—just keeps urging me to think of the future. But Mum can still look at me in that disappointed way mums sometimes do, you know? Wants me to reach my *potential*. Makes me feel two inches tall and about as useful as tits on a bull."

I snorted my drink.

Tai's eyebrows gathered and he ran a hand over his face. "It's my own fault. Mum says I'm rebelling against my brothers. But I also never had a clue what I really wanted to do. So, I bummed around in a few dead-end jobs and ended up finding a guy who had money and voilà." He threw out his arms. "A walking, breathing cliché."

Tai had a boyfriend? Disappointment crushed me. It should've been a good thing, the best. It would force me to get my head out of my ass. And yet somehow it was the opposite.

"Did you two meet in Boston?"

He cocked his head, finished his apple, and three-pointed the core into the bin. I threw him a napkin and he dragged it across his lips. My attention followed like a moth to a flame.

"Okay, so this part is really embarrassing." He squeezed his eyes shut and then peeked out from one.

So damn cute.

"I met Dion at a club in Auckland while he was on holiday. We got on like a house on fire. I showed him around a bit and we . . . *lived* in each other's pockets, pretty much, if you catch my drift?"

I did, and no, it didn't sit well.

"At the end of his time I was foolish enough to think I was in love, that we both were, and so I agreed to coming back with him. That was three years ago."

"He left you?"

Tai screwed up his face. "Nah. He cheated on me twice . . . that I know of. I gave him a free pass the first time; don't ask me why. But catching him in the act the second time—last night in case you were wondering—that was it."

Oh. Ohhhh. "So you left?"

"Like a rocket. Didn't even go back to our apartment, just drove. Which explains why I'm here, needing to earn some money. I'd stupidly given Dion access to my account when I first arrived, so he could 'transfer money to me,' and when I checked this morning, he'd pretty much cleaned me out. May as well have bared my throat to his teeth, right?"

My stomach dropped. "But that's theft."

Tai cocked a brow and shrugged. "It's a little more compli-cated, and honestly, there wasn't that much to take."

"It doesn't work that way. You have to—"

He held up a hand. "Please, don't. It's fine. I'm working it out. Like I said, a living cliché."

"You're being too hard on yourself. Leaving your country to take a chance on a guy is a ballsy move, and he let you down." Plus, I wanted five minutes with the bastard.

Tai looked uncomfortable. "I'm not so sure. My looks got me every job I ever had and all the useless boyfriends I ever needed to fuck up my life, Dion included. I'm just hoping it's not too late to change that. Or that I don't discover they were right all along and that there's nothing uniquely deep and meaningful behind these excellent cheekbones, after all."

He blinked hard and the room fell quiet. "Wow, talk about depressing. Enough." He crossed a leg over his knee and eyeballed me. "Let's talk about *you*. Obviously more successful in the relationship department if all these photos are anything to go by." He reached for the framed photo of Leo, Lu, and me camping at Lake Lamoille, five years before, and smiled. "Nice family."

Then he caught on to my silence and slapped himself on the head. "Shit. I forgot. That was a fucking thoughtless thing to say." He reached over and grabbed my hand. "I'm sorry. Briar mentioned your wife, and I just . . . God, I'm such a jerk."

I swallowed hard. I couldn't tell him he was wrong. That I wasn't quiet about the mention of Lu, but instead I'd been caught by the way his hand felt as it rested over mine, the intimacy of the moment stealing my breath along with something I didn't want to look at too closely.

Then the warmth of his hand was gone and he was on his feet. "I'm so sorry, Emmett. I'll leave you to—"

"No, stay." I slid my hand onto my lap and rested the other where his had lain. "I'm fine. Really. Some days I struggle to pull up a memory of her smile, and other times it's like the car accident only happened yesterday."

Tai's sensitive brown eyes took on a soft edge and he retook his seat. "It's not ridiculous at all. It sounds like you had a good relationship."

My heart swelled and I let the memories fill me. "We did. We met in college. She was training to be an elementary school teacher, me a vet. Leo was six when she was killed in a car accident and our world pretty much crashed around our ears, especially Leo." I felt the familiar sting in my eyes. "It's just not something I think you ever truly recover from . . . losing your mother at that age."

"No." Tai gave my hand a brief squeeze, then let it go, and it was all I could do not to grab it back.

"Were you born in Burlington?" Tai deftly changed the subject. I waggled my hand. "I spent my childhood here, and then my parents moved to Buffalo where Dad got two lakes to choose for his sailing. Mom wants to move back here and . . . help." I grimaced.

Tai bit back a smile. "I'm gonna guess that's your 'yikes' look."

I huffed out a laugh. "Let's just say Mom and I get along best at a distance. Plus, Leo and I are doing okay and I don't want to mess with that. He's an amazing kid."

"I bet he is." Tai nodded. "And not that I know anything about it, but you seem like you'd be a good dad."

His words came as a soothing balm, because lately I'd wondered about that. "I work way too many hours, unfortunately. I need to change that. And I can get a bit . . . distracted."

He laughed and the clear sound blew the dust from the corners of my office. "So I've heard. Like forgetting to eat, missing hair appointments, and losing your car keys on a daily basis?"

I shot a despairing glance to the doorway. "I'm gonna kill that woman."

4

TAI

"Are you Tai?" A slim young kid eyed me from the doorway of the kennel room.

With dark hair and even darker eyes, he looked just like the woman in the photo on Emmett's desk.

"I am indeed. You must be Leo." I reached out my hand from where I sat on the floor next to the cages and he walked over and shook it firmly.

"Dad said to give you this. Said to tell you the four o'clock canceled, so you can take a break." He shoved a plate loaded with peanut butter sandwiches my way, and my mouth instantly watered.

Sneaky, sneaky man.

He'd used his cute kid to make sure I wouldn't turn the food down. Emmett obviously hadn't believed me about my lunch. I tried to feel bad for lying but . . . nope. I was so damn grateful for the job that when Ivy said he hadn't eaten, and added that Emmett wasn't good at looking after himself, it simply seemed the right thing to do. Not to mention, after finding a place in the Marketplace to get myself tested during my lunch break, I'd kind of lost my appetite.

"He said you might share it with me." Leo never even batted an eye, and I swallowed a smile.

I highly doubted Emmett had said anything of the sort since

Leo already had a smudge of peanut butter on his lips likely from his own sandwiches. But to give the boy his due, he'd delivered the line with an enviable straight face. "Absolutely, I will."

He took a seat on the floor beside me and I put the plate of sandwiches between us so we could both tuck in. We worked our way through the pile in a weirdly comfortable silence, watched by a dog recovering from surgery to his leg the day before and the stray cat from the bookstore who I'd been stroking through the cage door.

Leo chewed on a mouthful of sandwich while studying me at the same time. "Why do you wear lipstick?"

I choked on the wad of bread in my mouth and started to cough. *Holy shit.*

Leo slapped me on the back. "You okay?"

I looked up into a pair of dark, worried eyes. "I'm fine." I finally got the ball of sandwich down, stalling for time whilst hoping Emmett had raised an accepting son, because there were a million ways this could go wrong.

"It's not lipstick," I corrected Leo with a conspiratorial wink. "It's gloss. There's a difference. Subtle, I admit, but it's there. And I'm wearing *gloss* because I like it. I like the way it looks and feels."

He studied me for a minute, still chewing. "It's . . . shiny."

"Hence the name, gloss." I grinned at him. "Is that a bad thing?"

He thought about it for a moment. "I guess not. It's just different."

Out of the mouths of babes. "I happen to like different. What about you?"

He thought again. "I guess. But if you wore that to my school . . ." He didn't need to finish.

And oh my god, I wanted to hug the boy. "You're right. It can bring trouble sometimes. I've had more than a few nasty comments."

"Then why wear it?"

"Because I like it. And if it doesn't hurt anyone and it's kind and honest, I think a bit of trouble is worth being me. I don't know what your dad would say, so maybe you should check with him, but I think there are some things worth a bit of trouble. Like being true to yourself."

He swallowed the last of his sandwich and pushed the plate away. "I guess. But trouble sucks big time."

I couldn't hold back the laugh. "Yeah, don't I know it." I leaned back against the cage, my stomach full for the first time all day.

"Why are you sitting on the floor? You got something against chairs?"

Oh, I really liked this kid. Blunt and snarky, my two favorite things. "I was having a conversation with my new friend here." I stuck a finger through the cage and the cat nudged her head for a scratch.

"Is that the stray from V and V?" Leo leaned around for a better look and stuck his own finger through. The cat took a sniff and rubbed against it.

"She's too friendly to be wild, so your dad thinks she's been in a home at some point. But she's not chipped and she's in pretty poor condition, so maybe she's been out on the streets for a while."

"Huh." Leo slid closer to the cage and I moved aside to give him better access as he continued to scratch the cat. "Yeah. She's pretty chill. Most of the strays Dad brings in just hiss and spit from the back of the cage. How long is she staying?"

I shrugged. "I guess until your dad figures she's safe to send to the shelter. And I think he's going to spay her first."

"We should give her a name," Leo stated.

Oh, oh. "Do you think that's a good idea if she's not staying? Maybe you should check with your dad? You might get too attached to her. She's kind of cute, after all." It was a blatant lie, and the fiery look the cat flashed said exactly what she thought of being called cute.

"And you won't get attached, of course?" Leo eyeballed me.

I sighed. "Fair point. I'm a sucker for a pair of blue eyes." *Ain't that the truth.*

"Besides, she needs a name," Leo pressed. "Everyone needs a

name, right? And it'll save the shelter from having to come up with one."

Hard to argue with that. "Okay, kiddo, what are we going to call her?"

Leo spun to face me. "I'm *not* your kiddo."

Whoa. I held up my hands. "Okay. Sorry. What are we going to call her, *Leo*?"

He studied me with narrowed eyes, his jaw working overtime before he finally said, "It's okay. I guess you can call me that if you want."

Huh. I stared at him for a second, wondering what was going on in that head of his. "You sure? Because I don't mind—"

"It's fine." He quickly looked away. "But I get to choose her name."

I sucked in a breath through my teeth, then blew out a sigh. "Okay. You're a tough negotiator, but that's a deal."

He got on his hands and knees and stared into the cage. The cat stared back. My money was on the cat. I was right.

"Wow, she's pretty intense." Leo looked up at me.

I pulled a face and shrugged. "Women, right? What can you do?"

"Yeah, women." It was said with a heavy sigh, like he was just beginning to realize the truth of it.

I bit back a smile. "So, a name?"

"Oh, right." He stared again at the cat who was shamelessly rubbing against the side of the cage looking for more affection.

I obliged with two fingers, digging them deep into her gray fur.

"Sassy." Leo's gaze slid my way sitting over a cheeky grin.

I arched a brow. "Sassy, huh? Should I be offended?"

His eyes went wide. "No, I didn't mean—"

I patted his shoulder. "Calm down, kiddo. I'm only joking. Sassy it is. Kind of suits her. I'm jealous, if you must know."

He looked incredulous. "You *want* to be called sassy?"

I smiled. "Are you for real?" I flicked nonexistent lint off my chest with both sets of fingers. "Pfft. It's like you don't even know me."

He snorted and looked away. "Oh, wait—" He looked back. "So, you'll know about plays and drama and stuff, right?"

I narrowed my gaze. "Because I wear lip gloss?"

"Well, yeah." He frowned. "Kind of. I mean, it's like *Glee*, right?"

I made a mental note for a future conversation about labels, except . . . he happened to be right this time.

"Well, as much as I hate to entrench a stereotype, you're in luck, because I do happen to have a little bit of experience treading the boards."

Leo frowned.

I rolled my eyes dramatically and tut-tutted. "Young people these days. Treading the boards means *onstage*." And okay, it was admittedly a stretch, considering that experience had primarily been dancing the cages in Auckland gay clubs for extra coin, at least back in the day when I was young and wrinkle-free. It was how I'd met Dion. But to be fair, I'd actually aced English and drama at school, the only subjects I'd bothered attending.

"There's this school play coming up," Leo explained, crossing his legs to face me. "*Alice in Christmas Land*. The auditions are next week."

I looked at him sideways. "*Alice in Christmas Land*? I'm guessing they've taken a few liberties with the original storyline."

He stared at me. "Huh?"

"Nothing." I patted his hand. "Okay, so there's this play. I'm going to go out on a limb and assume you want a part?"

"Not just *a* part." He looked at me like I didn't have a clue. "*The* part."

"Oh, *the* part. Alice?" I frowned.

"Nooooo. There are *six* Alices—"

My eyes popped. "Six? *So* many liberties taken."

"Alice can't be the most important part if there are six of them, right?"

I blew out my cheeks. "I'm thinking the right answer to that is no?"

His lips set in a smug smile. "That's what I thought too. I want the role of the Mad Hatter. Everyone knows he's the coolest."

I nodded sagely because he was right. "Absolutely. And you need help rehearsing for the audition?"

He beamed. "Exactly."

"I'm only here for a week, remember?"

"I know. But that's perfect, because the auditions are next week. And Dad sucks at this kind of stuff; plus, he's too busy. Sooooo, can you help? We can be friends, right?"

I studied him for a minute, struck by the fact that yesterday I was getting ready for a night of partying in Dion's upmarket Boston club before going back to our apartment to plan a holiday I wanted us to take in the Caribbean. Twenty-four hours later and I was working in a veterinary clinic, of all fucking things, squeezing dog's anal glands, and agreeing to rehearse *Alice In Christmas Land* lines with the ten-year-old son of an almost stranger I wanted to fuck silly. Oh, and in country-as-shit Burlington, Vermont, of all places. How was this my life?

I should be running for the hills.

Instead, I said, "Of course we can be friends. Bring your lines tomorrow after school and we'll make a start."

"Awesome. Thank you."

"You two look way too cozy."

I looked up to find Emmett watching from the doorway. "And why do I feel like I've missed something?"

"Tai's going to help me learn my lines, Dad. He's been on the stage and everything."

Emmet's gaze darted to mine. "Really? Now why doesn't that surprise me?"

I waggled my eyebrows.

He laughed. "That's very kind of you, Tai. And I'm sure you didn't pressure him at all, right, Leo?"

Leo squirmed a little.

"No, I offered. He was fine," I reassured Emmett. "Although I warned him I wouldn't be here for more than a week."

Emmett said nothing but that crease between his eyes grew deeper. Then Sassy took it upon herself to yowl, which reminded me. "Oh, and Leo had a great idea for the cat."

Leo elbowed me in the ribs. "Wow, thanks for nothing, *friend*."

I shrugged. "Hey, you're the boss's son. That's unfair influence right there, kiddo."

The sharp intake of breath jerked my gaze to Emmett whose face had drained white.

"What?" I looked between Emmett and Leo, who'd gone very still at my side.

Emmett's eyes flicked to his son, then back to me, and I noticed Leo didn't meet them, just fiddled with his shoe.

"His . . ." Emmett hesitated. "Leo's mother used to call him that."

Fuck. I nudged Leo's shoulder with mine. "You should've said something. You want me to stop?"

He said nothing for a minute and then looked up. "Nah. It's fine." His gaze traveled to his dad. "It's just a name, right Dad? Can't be scared of a name."

Emmett swallowed hard and I could only guess at what was running through his brain. I mouthed the word *sorry* at him and he blinked slowly in acknowledgment. "No," he answered Leo, so softly I had to reach for the words. "We can't be scared of a name."

"Cool." Leo got to his feet. "Because we also named the cat."

Emmett pushed the mess of blond waves off his forehead. "The cat? I take it this is the great idea Tai mentioned."

I winced and tipped my head to Sassy's cage. "Sorry."

"I've named her Sassy." Leo needed an academy award for the innocent expression he pulled out of the bag. "That's okay, right, Dad?"

Emmett's gaze flicked to mine, his amusement clear. "Sassy?"

I shrugged. "I can see why you'd think I might have had some influence on the decision, but you'd be wrong. I merely offered the inspiration, right, Leo?"

Leo nodded furiously. "It was all me."

"It's a fine name." I patted his shoulder.

Emmett shook his head in defeat. "Okay, so long as you realize we can't keep her," he warned Leo.

I thought there was fat chance of that going the way Emmett hoped, but I kept my mouth shut.

"Sure, Dad, of course."

Oh boy. Crafty kid.

Emmett gave Leo the hairy eyeball. "Anyway, I came to tell you Cody's mom will be here any second to pick you up. I'll grab you on the way home."

"Thanks, Dad." Leo scratched Sassy one last time, grabbed the empty plate, and paused in front of his father. "I'll just wash this plate and put it away. Earn your respect. Show I can be responsible."

He left and I snorted in laughter.

Emmett looked my way with a shake of his head. "I'm totally fucked, aren't I?"

I smiled. "Deeply and irrevocably. Cute kid, though."

He rolled his eyes and left me scratching Sassy's head.

"I have a wash to do for Ivy in five minutes," I grumbled to the cat. "On my own. That will make a sum total of two times I've ever washed a dog in my entire life, the first being the one she walked me through this morning. How badly do you think I can fuck this up?"

Sassy gave a yowl and turned her back on me.

"Yeah, you and me both, sugar. You and me both." I got to my feet, washed my hands, and headed to The Groom Room.

The client was a sweetheart of a Newfoundland called Betsy who stood there and let me do anything I wanted while wearing a blissed-out look on her cute face. Not an unfamiliar position for me to be in, bar the supplementary hair.

"I think I'm in love," I called to Ivy in the next room. She was finishing a Labradoodle whose owner had a penchant for coloring her dog's hair. Today it was tipped in pink.

"She's a beautiful dog," Ivy called back. "And I'm almost ready if you want to get her out of the tub. Be careful with your back. Bend at the knees like I showed you, and make sure you have an arm around her bottom, under her tail, so she doesn't slip."

I snorted. "In my twenty-seven years, this will be the closest I've ever come to a woman's arse and likely to remain so."

Ivy chuckled. "I'll take your word on that. Okay, I'm done. You can bring her through."

I turned the spray nozzle off and kept one hand on Betsy while I spun to grab the towel I'd left on the chair. It slipped from my hand and fell to the floor. *Fuck.* A whole tower of fresh ones were stacked on a shelf to the side, but it meant leaving Betsy alone for about two seconds.

I eyeballed the dog. "Stay."

She blinked dopey eyes at me. Eyes that promised the world.

"Been there, done that, got the T-shirt," I warned her. "I need you to prove me wrong."

I lifted my hand and turned to grab the new towel and—

A hundred pounds of water drenched me head to foot, most of the washroom, and the entire wall of towels to my left, not to mention the ceiling.

"Goddammit, you promised!" I squint-glared at Betsy who was still shaking, all that long hair slapping from side to side, only adding to the deluge.

Spluttering and blinking furiously, I threw a towel Betsy's way in a vain attempt to forestall a second wave, but it only partly hit the spot and I got another good soaking before I could launch myself out of the way.

"What on earth?" Ivy appeared at the door in time to catch the final wave full in the face. "Shit." She flicked her soaked pink hair to the side, grabbed two towels, and threw them my way.

I flung both over Betsy and then collapsed over her back to keep them in place. She wiggled to get free. "Don't you dare," I growled, wiping my face on the already soaked sleeve of my sweatshirt without letting go. "No more treats for you, you lying floozy."

Ivy snorted, grabbed a towel for herself and collapsed on the chair in a fit of giggles.

"It's not funny," I grumbled. "Look at this room."

"I'm looking." She dissolved into another round. "Holy hell, you should see yourself." She pointed my way with another hoot of laughter.

I turned to look in the mirror, still holding onto Betsy, and groaned. "Oh. My. God." I stared in horror at my hair flattened to my head, all except for one front section swept up into a cringing *Something About Mary* moment. Then the rest of it sank in. Eyeliner smudged across my cheek; water dripping from my chin like fucking Niagara Falls; small clumps of wet dog hair peppered my face—I had to wipe a tuft from my lips; and every piece of clothing I wore was drenched. I was soaked to the skin.

And still Ivy laughed.

I shot her a killing look. "It's not funny. This place is going to take forever to clean, and Emmett needs me to hold a parrot's wing for an X-ray in five minutes."

Which only set her off again, laughing so much she looked ready to pee herself. Two seconds of watching the tears streaming down her face and I couldn't hold it in any longer, dissolving into gasping laughter while Betsy regarded both of us as if we'd completely lost our minds, which was quite possibly the case.

Emmett chose that moment to stick his head through the door and cast his eyes around the room in disbelief. "Holy shit, what the hell happened here? I could hear you all the way down the back." He clocked the up flick of my hair and raised an amused brow.

We smothered our laughter for a second, looked Emmett's way, looked at each other, and broke down again.

A smile stole over Emmett's face and he shook his head. "Do I even want to know?"

Ivy could only hold out her hands and keep cackling. I could barely meet Emmett's eye, terrified I'd snort a mouthful of dog water into my lungs if I did. I simply shook my head and croaked, "No."

"Okay. Well, now that I know no one's dying . . ." He paused for emphasis. "I think I'll leave you two to clean up the mess." He looked at me. "Will you still be okay for Mrs. Jessop's parrot in five?"

Ivy caught my eye and dissolved into raucous laughter once again, while I failed in my effort to avoid a snort and inhaled a solid hit of dog water in the process. While still choking, I nodded frantically Emmett's way, unable to trust myself to speak.

His gaze shifted between the two of us, and he shook his head in complete disbelief.

Which of course only set Ivy off again.

"I'm going to leave now," he said. "Which, under the circumstances, seems the only sane thing to do." He caught my eye. "I'll see *you* in five minutes."

I nodded, barely managing to hold in another round of laughter until he'd closed the door and I could finally give up pretending I had any dignity left and sink to the floor, tears running down my face. Betsy then ended the entire cock-up on her own terms and shook again.

"Go." Ivy shooed me out the door, still chuckling. "I'll get the worst of it cleaned and you can come back when you're done. Damn, I haven't laughed like that in years."

"Thanks." I flattened my hair and left it at that. There was no way to fix the rest without a lot more time. Then I raced to catch up with Emmett, garnering a set of raised eyebrows from the waiting room as I passed.

"Plumbing misadventure," I explained loftily to the Labradoodle's owner. She snorted and smiled broadly, clearly having heard our squeals of laughter.

The parrot was Emmett's last client of the day, and he must've prepared Mrs. Jessop about the state I was going to arrive in, because other than giving me a wide-eyed look, she never said a word as I dripped all over the treatment room, regardless of the towel I'd wrapped around my waist over my wet clothes.

When we were done, I got Ivy's space spic and span again, and the towels in the washer and dryer, while she finished with Betsy. I kissed the sweet dog on the nose before I left. It wasn't her fault she had a clueless attendant, after all.

Emmett immediately sent me to shower in the clinic bathroom. He was doing a piss-poor job of not laughing every time he looked at me, and I wanted to kiss him for that alone. I didn't, of course. Because that would be a bad, bad thing.

To say I was grateful for the chance to clean up was putting it mildly. Not simply because of cyclone Betsy, but because I hadn't showered since Boston. Not that Emmett knew that, even though I was pretty sure I smelled like a fish carcass short of a trashcan by then.

Done with my shower and feeling somewhat human again, I put fresh clothes on, threw my wet ones over the towel rack to dry out, and made my way back out to the quiet waiting room to find Emmett behind the desk going through files on the computer, his forehead bunched in a web of frown lines. I dropped my plastic bag and leaned on the desk. "Did I screw something up today?" I didn't think I had, but—

His gaze jerked up. "Oh, no, not at all. I'm just having trouble locating some paid invoices. Carolyn did all that stuff and I'm kind of lost without her. I can't seem to get things to balance."

"Do you want me to take a look? I did do those café books for a while. I could check tomorrow if you tell me what you're looking for." He said nothing for a minute and my heart sank. "But I totally understand if you'd rather not," I backtracked. "You don't really know me and—"

"No, that would be great, actually." He smiled broadly. "I might not know you very well, but Ivy likes you, which is no small achievement. Besides, I've always gone with my gut when it comes to trusting people, and it hasn't let me down yet."

"Lucky you." I ignored the concerned look he sent me and glanced at the darkened windows of The Groom Room instead. "Has Ivy gone?"

He nodded, still watching me closely. "Tonight is bridge night. And she has to get home and feed and cuddle Derek first."

"Her husband?"

Emmett laughed. "No. Her Bocker. He's a dog. Her husband died about ten years ago."

I frowned. "Okay, I'll bite. What breed is a Bocker?"

"A mix of cocker spaniel and beagle," he explained, sitting back in his chair and running an eye over me in a way that made my toes curl. "He was left on our doorstep after a hit and run a few years back. No one claimed him and Ivy decided to keep him. He's as old as the hills but still getting around."

I scrubbed at my wet hair with the towel in my hands and tried to ignore the heat in those blue eyes as they watched me.

I'd have put money on Emmett not being entirely straight, but if that were true, he also wasn't out. And I had no interest in being anyone's experiment, secret hook up, or *anything* for that matter.

Not after Dion.

Not for a long time.

Besides, Emmett was way too nice with a way-too-nice kid and a way-too-complicated life for me to mess up with any ill-advised flirtation.

"Why the name Derek?" I asked. "Not a popular dog name, I wouldn't think."

"It's the name of Ivy's brother who she doesn't exactly get along with."

I laughed. "Why doesn't that surprise me?"

"Right? She's a firecracker. Anyway, how was your first day?"

I didn't even have to think about it. "Good. Fun. Exhausting. Terrifying. Can't wait to do it again."

He practically beamed. "You must be as crazy as we are, then. But you did well, considering I doubt you've set foot in a vet clinic in your entire life?" His eyes twinkled.

I groaned and rubbed the back of my neck. "I guess there was no hiding that."

Emmett leaned back in his chair and a smirk tugged at his lips. "Pretty much. Which only made how you handled everything that much more surprising, floods aside."

A swell of something like pride bloomed in my chest. I hadn't felt useful in a long while. "Thanks. And sorry if I misled you, but I just really needed the job."

He waved a hand. "No problem. And I know we only talked about you staying till next Thursday, but if you could manage the weekend as well, I'd be grateful. I don't want to hold you back from any plans you might have, but I doubt I'm going to find someone before then."

"You were listening at lunch, right? Me and plans have a problematic relationship. So yes, if you want me for the weekend, I can stay. The money will help for sure. Then I can find out how Leo's audition goes as well."

He nodded. "Then we have a deal. But you don't have to put yourself out for Leo. He'll understand."

"It's honestly no trouble. I actually did a couple of productions in high school. Just don't tell Leo that my adult onstage experience was limited to dancing in booty shorts in a gay club for extra money."

His eyes widened and he swallowed hard.

Bingo.

"You were a . . . go-go boy? Is that the right term?"

"Yeah. It was a second job. Easy money."

"Did you dance in Dion's clubs?" There was an edge to Emmett's voice like he was affronted by the idea.

"Nah. He didn't like people paying attention to me like that. He wanted me . . . close. He was never keen on me working officially at all, although he was okay with me running errands for the business."

Emmett shook his head. "I'm liking this ex of yours less and less."

I ran my fingers through my damp hair. "Yeah, it was pretty unhealthy. I told you, it was my own damn fault for staying."

"That's not very fair to yourself." His voice was gentle.

But I knew I shouldered at least some of the blame. "Maybe not. But I definitely took too damn long to wake up and do something about it. Still, it's done now. And if that's it for the day, I'll be off."

He glanced at the clock and startled. "Yes, go. I need to pick up Leo as well. Which reminds me, thanks for what you did today."

I frowned. "The rehearsal thing isn't a big deal."

"No, the nickname. Kiddo."

Shit. "I'm sorry about that—"

"Nothing to be sorry for. It was just a bit of a shock. But he seems happy to let you call him that, and it gives me some hope."

My heart squeezed for both of them. "Oh. Well, good. Let me know if it becomes a problem though."

"It won't."

We stared at each other for a few seconds before I cleared my throat. "So, what time do you need me tomorrow?"

"The clinic opens at nine." He shoved some papers into his bag and shut the computer down. "That way I can get Leo to school first. But Ivy's usually in by eight thirty."

"Cool. I'll arrive with her."

"Great. See you then. And thanks again. For a day that started out shitty, it ended up kind of . . . great, actually, and that's pretty much down to you."

"Really?" Heat rushed to my cheeks, a fucking miracle for a guy who prided himself on never blushing. I caused blushes, never succumbed to them. Yet another thing to add to my rapidly growing 'what the fuck else can happen in a day' list. "I don't know what to say to that."

"Thank you will do just fine." His lips twitched in amusement.

I was, at the very least, a tasty shade of beetroot. "Then thank you."

He nodded. "You're welcome. See you tomorrow."

"Will do." I ducked into Ivy's rooms to get rid of the towel and then grabbed my bag of clothing and any threads of composure I had left before heading out. I couldn't be positive, because I was too damn flustered to check, but I was sure I felt the heat of Emmett's gaze on my back as I left.

I made my way to Vino and Veritas hoping to thank Briar for his help, or at least leave him a message. In less than ten hours, I'd gone from sitting in a bookstore in Vermont contemplating my hot mess of a life and considering hightailing it back to New Zealand like the loser that I was, to having a temporary job; just enough cash in my pocket to eat and get a few supplies; laughing till I cried over a dog wash disaster; a grateful boss; and the first taste of self-respect I'd felt in a long time.

Emmett was right. From a shitty start, the day had turned out to be kind of fucking great. Go figure.

I might not have anywhere to sleep other than my car, but that was okay too. As soon as I could, I'd ditch it somewhere and tell Dion where to find it. Just looking at it made me feel dirty, and it didn't feel right to sell the piece of junk since he'd paid for it. I wanted nothing more to do with his money.

The sign outside the bookstore was gone, and inside, Briar

looked to be closing up. The wine bar next door had a couple of customers, soft jazz drifting into the mall, but as tempting as it was to grab a drink and drown my sorrows, I didn't have any money to spare for that kind of silliness.

Briar caught sight of me through the window, raised his hand, and made his way outside.

"Thought you'd have gone home by now," I said as he approached. "I was going to leave you a note."

"I *should* be home, but I'm filling in for one of the others. So, how'd it go?" He looked me over, eyes twinkling. "I see you've got a new look."

I rolled my eyes. "Still with the jokes. But to answer your question, I had a great day."

His brows peaked.

"I know, right? A surprise all around. I'm actually staying through next week and the weekend as well until Emmett can get someone else."

Briar looked pleased. "I'm glad it's worked out for you both. But just so you know, he actually called a few minutes ago to thank me. Seems you made quite the impression." He looked me up and down with a smile. "Which wouldn't be unusual for you, I don't think."

I snorted. "One tries. And he's being kind. I was a disaster on at least three occasions. Did you know dogs had anal glands? And that sometimes they have to be squeezed?"

Briar shuddered. "I could've lived without knowing it."

"I know, right? Or that a herd of Newfoundlands could solve the world's water storage problems?"

He laughed and held up his hands. "I don't even want to know. And also, I don't think herd is the right word."

"Whatever. But seriously, Briar—" I looked him square in the eye. "Thank you. It was a very kind thing you did. You saved my day."

His cheeks pinked. "You're welcome. I guess I know a thing or two about life's crossroads. Drop in any time."

I tried to remember the last time a virtual stranger had offered me a hand in friendship or anything else that wasn't sexually related in the last few years, and I couldn't. "I might just take you up on that."

"Oh, and if you're here for the week—" He waggled his brows. "—you'll be around for our next Booklover meeting."

I rolled my eyes. "We'll see. But like I said, romance and I are hardly on a first name basis."

He shrugged. "The invite's there if you want. See you around, Tai."

I left Briar to close up and made my way to a convenience store I'd passed that morning. A hot sub and a soda would be enough to fill me up, along with a few other necessities like baby wipes, a toothbrush, and a disposable razor to take to the clinic with me in the morning.

The bulky puffer jacket, spare clothes, and old woolen blanket I'd purchased in the thrift shop that morning for less than the price of my usual Sunday brunch in Boston would keep me a lot warmer in the car. I'd had to fight my way through a thicket of dusty harvest wreaths and a deluge of unconvincing Halloween costumes to find them, but Claudia, who managed the place, had been very helpful. It was funny, not funny, how fast any concerns about dignity dissolved when being frozen to death was a real concern.

I left the store with the essentials I needed and so damn tired I could barely keep my eyes open. I ate in the dark of the car, then switched on the interior light just long enough to don every single piece of clothing I had before throwing the new blanket over top. I wriggled my phone out of my pocket and considered turning it on, then decided against it. I needed sleep, and a flood of text messages from Dion wasn't going to help with that. They could wait until morning. He could fuck off and die a slow, painful death as far as I was concerned.

Death by twink sandwich. I snorted. He was welcome to it. Because sure as fuck, I doubted he'd be alone. Funny how the idea didn't hurt as much as I thought it should.

I switched off the light, snuggled down, and followed a pair of blue eyes and a head of messy blond hair into a deep sleep.

5

EMMETT

The interior light snapped off in the battered Honda Civic parked at the end of the cul-de-sac and I breathed out a sigh, the warm air condensing in the cool bite of the fall evening.

Another cold night.

And Tai was sleeping in his car.

It hadn't come as any real surprise, not when the guy had barely enough money to buy lunch, but it made my heart ache. Still, I could hardly march down and demand he sleep in the clinic instead, or, lord help me, take him home. I'd known Tai for a little more than eight hours, and I was pretty sure my good intentions wouldn't be welcomed.

But it was still harder than expected to simply turn around and leave him there. He deserved better. And regardless of what he said, he hadn't asked for any of this. He'd trusted in the wrong guy, and yeah, maybe he needed to take a look at his life, but didn't we all?

I tugged the collar of my jacket up around my ears and stood a moment longer, just watching. I hadn't planned to tail Tai, and the whole thing was feeling so stalkerish I could barely stand myself. But when I'd passed the Marketplace on my way to my car, I'd seen him talking with Briar outside V and V and ground to a halt.

Next thing I knew, I was following him, watching the convenience store while he stocked up on whatever shit he needed, and then on to this quiet dead-end suburban backstreet not far from the main shopping area. How on earth Tai found it, god only knew.

I took one last look and then headed back to my car. Tai would be fine. He was a grown man, not that I needed that particular reminder. An image of him standing in The Groom Room, water dripping from his face, drenched to all hell, and with his head thrown back, laughing as if life hadn't just chewed him up and spat him out. So full of fun and promise and heart, and oh my god, sexy as fuck.

Back in my Dodge Ram, I grabbed the wheel with both hands and banged my forehead on it. I needed Tai out from under my skin like right the hell now. The last thing I needed was a ridiculous crush, because that's all it was. My body had come back online like a freight train, and Tai was simply the first to get its attention. But it was only lust. And lust wasn't a good enough reason to risk fucking with my life, or Leo's. It was way too complicated, too . . . everything.

What the hell would he see in someone like me, anyway? He was a cool, hip, gorgeous young man who could have anyone he wanted. Whereas I was, well, a widower with a dad bod, an *actual* dad, a workaholic, chronically over-committed, and glaringly sexually inexperienced—at least with men.

And yet there'd been more than a couple of times when Tai had looked at me and I'd seen . . . something? Interest? Heat? *Whatever.* I was also pretty damn sure he'd guessed I wasn't straight. The drool marks on my chin were likely a dead giveaway. Fuck load of good that was going to do me, because I couldn't have him. I wasn't even going to try.

I texted Leo I was on my way and wondered for the millionth time what Lu would think of our son having a phone at ten, even if it was the most basic of basics. Still, single parent and peace of mind—I'd given up feeling guilty.

Before I stowed the phone again, a message flashed up from Jasper.

Your receptionist bailed on you?

I replied.

Yeah. We managed. Got a guy helping for a bit.

Dots appeared and disappeared.

So I heard . . .

Of course he had. And that was another thing I didn't need—people talking. Jasper was the only person who knew I was bi, until Ivy. Cue one drunken night, Jasper and I commiserating over the mutual loss of our spouses in an almost empty bar, his Michael, my Lulu, and things just got said. We were sick of the whole town deciding it was time we moved on and trying to set us up with dates. The common ground we shared was too fucking hard to come by, and we both needed a safe place to vent.

Jasper was grumpy as fuck and determined never to love again, but we'd been friends since that night, sort of. With an honors degree in keeping people at a distance, it was hard to know just how close we were since Jasper was a die-hard fan of two- or three-word texts max, and about as much in conversation. But beneath it all he was a sweetheart, however hard he tried to hide it.

I texted back.

You heard, huh?

Heard he was . . . pretty . . .

Goddamn small towns.

I hadn't noticed. He's also not staying.

Dots came and went.

Right.

That was all he said, and yet somehow it told me everything Jasper thought in a single fucking word. Right. As in, watch out, don't be reckless, I don't believe a word of what you just said.

Ugh. Enough. I slammed the truck into drive and headed to pick up Leo.

Cody's parents were divorced and he split his time between them. His mom, Ashley, was always pretty chill if I turned up a bit late to collect Leo, although I tried not to make it a habit. She lived in town while Cody's dad, Jon, had moved in with his boyfriend, Brent, on a farm just outside the city limits.

And yeah, I was still getting my head around that. Not that Jon was bi, because although he hadn't waved a rainbow flag, he hadn't hidden the fact either. But it was more that he was so damn comfortable with it. And Cody talked about Brent like he was just another dad. To be honest, I was . . . envious. Especially now that I was on my own again. Especially today.

A certain pair of brown eyes sprang to mind.

And yeah, I was doing really well with that whole 'getting Tai out from under my skin' thing.

I texted Leo from outside Cody's apartment building, and a few minutes later, he appeared with a slight, blond Cody in tow— the two of them laughing and trading comic books as they ran. Ashley waved from the entrance and I shouted an apology through the open car window. She brushed it aside as usual, and Cody ran back to stand beside her as I reversed the truck out of the visitor's parking space and headed home.

"Did you two have a good time?" I glanced at Leo.

"The best." He turned to look at me, eyes alight, and I sucked in a shaky breath at his obvious joy. Days like this were becoming more common than in those first couple of years after Lu died, but I never took them for granted. "Cody says I'm gonna get that part now that Tai's gonna help. He's really cool."

He was. "You know he's not staying, right? He's just passing through." *And sleeping in his fucking car while you're just letting him.*

"Yeah, I know. But it's still gonna help. Let's face it, Dad, you suck at reading lines."

I laughed. "I do, you're right. But I make a kick-ass chili. So, how about we defrost a container for dinner and you can whip up some cornbread to go with it if you've done your homework."

"Cody and I finished it together. But I need you to sign off on the class camp in two weeks. You have to tell them what food you're sending."

My gaze shot sideways. "Food?"

He patted my arm. "Don't freak. I'll make some cookies and muffins tomorrow and put them in the freezer. You don't have to do anything."

Conversation done.

He turned up the music and tapped the rhythm on his knee as we drove.

A part of me breathed a sigh of relief while another part wondered, not for the first time, who the real grownup in the house was? I'd never been the organizer, that had been Lu's forte. I did the yard work while she controlled the inside. Traditional? Sure. But it had worked for us.

Until it didn't.

Since she'd died, both had suffered. The yard resembled more of a jungle than a garden, and I was at least two years behind in pruning the big trees. The inside, although not a disaster, lacked the touch of someone who actually knew what they were doing.

Lu had been a whizz in the kitchen. Me, not so much. And in the depths of early grief, I'd given up even putting the groceries away, moving everything we needed to the countertop in a kind of point and click mentality that minimized having to think or plan. See something you wanted to eat and eat it, cereal mostly—whatever was easiest. Leo had done the same. Far too many months had passed before we actually sat down for a proper meal again. Still, it could've been worse, and I refused to beat myself up about it too much.

Things were much better now, but the remnants of that early grief mindset remained, mostly through laziness on my part. Running a vet practice was hardly a Monday to Friday job. In an emergency Ivy took Leo if I was called out at night, since she lived not too far away, or I could drop him with Cody. During the week, Leo walked to the clinic after school and did his homework in my office until I was done—a state of affairs my mother was obviously less than thrilled about. But Leo seemed fine with it, and I dealt with the guilt the only way I could, add it to the list and try to press on.

I missed more parent/teacher meetings than I attended, had to leave in the middle of sport's games, hardly ever took a weekend off, worked late more often than not, and had the social life of a monk—and that was being generous. It was no way to bring up a child and if guilt were energy, I was pretty sure I could've powered Burlington for a good year or two without breaking a sweat.

Lu would never have chosen this way to bring up our boy, but then Lu was gone, and I'd like to think she'd at least understand.

I'd had sex exactly twice in four years, and neither woman had crossed my mind once I'd left their bed immediately after. I suspected they felt the same. I hadn't been looking for anything more than to feel . . . *something*. I hadn't even wanted the sex, and I'd needed to get drunk enough to not care. It was more to sate the craving that was eating away at the inside of my heart, for Lu —the craving for an actual warm body to hold, if only for an hour.

For four years I hadn't given a fuck about dating. Everything hurt too hard in those deep gentle places I protected from the harsh light. No one had remotely caught my eye enough to let that guard down again. No one. Not until a sassy mouth and a pair of soft brown eyes walked into my clinic just a few hours before.

I didn't get it.

I didn't want it.

Except clearly, I fucking did.

But why now?

Why him?

The one thing I rarely allowed myself to even think about, to wonder about, to want, to imagine exploring, was now the only thing in four years to set my interest alight. And what the fuck was up with that?

I swerved to avoid a car turning into a driveway without indicating and then hit the horn to make my displeasure known. Leo glanced over in surprise. I was usually a pretty laid-back driver.

"You okay, Dad?"

I shrugged. "It's been a long day."

He studied me a moment longer, then went back to singing along with the music while I got my frustration in check.

Maybe I just needed to get laid?

Yeah, right. If that was all it was, then any number of attractive women I'd run into recently would've raised the flag too, so to speak. But none of them had stuck in my mind longer than the few minutes it had taken for me to pass them by.

Not like a certain gorgeous young man in a sexy-as-shit pink net shirt, with snark for miles and a way of getting under my skin like a bad case of shingles, leaving me desperate to scratch the itch while at the same time knowing any move to do that would almost certainly come with a side order of pain I wasn't entirely sure I was ready for.

And wow, I'd clearly put a lot of thought into that.

Then again, Tai was only here for a week. I could keep things under lock and key for that long, surely. After he was gone, then maybe I could think about having *that* talk with Leo and my parents, and Lu's. Maybe. In the meantime, I needed to forget about Tai and focus on Leo. It wasn't like the two of us didn't have enough to cope with, getting through each week, without adding a romantic disaster in the making, on top of it all.

"Dad? Are you even listening?" Leo huffed from the passenger seat as I pulled into the driveway of our pretty two-story black-and-white colonial in Prospect Hill. It had been partly bought with Lulu's life insurance, or what was left over after I'd paid off our remaining tuition debt and anything owed on the clinic. Remaining in the smaller house we'd shared wasn't going to cut it. Too many damn memories. Luckily Leo had been totally on board.

"*I said,* are you still taking Saturday afternoon off so we can go on the ferry?"

I hated the way he asked the question so carefully, like it was a landmine, and I knew he thought I'd forgotten, which I absolutely had. *Fuck.* I did a quick mental sprint through my calendar and figured I could clear it. The accounts could wait. I needed to work on being a better dad.

"Yes, of course," I reassured him with as much enthusiasm as I could manage. "I've been looking forward to it all week." *Liar.*

"Really?" He perked up in his seat. "Cool. So, I've been thinking, we should ask Tai, since he's new here."

A lump instantly formed in my throat, cutting off the air from my lungs. "Tai?" It was more squeak than anything as I pulled the truck in front of the garage and killed the engine.

"Yeah. You know, show him around like Mom used to do when her friends came to visit, remember?"

I remembered.

"Can we, Dad, please? He's really nice."

He was. Nice. Sexy. Lickable and hot. *Ugh.* I found myself nodding before I even realized, as much to hold on to this rare glimpse of my son, so open and happy, as anything else.

Inviting Tai was a minefield Leo had no freaking idea about, but I couldn't deny the pulse of excitement in my veins at the thought of spending more time with him. It could also give me an opportunity to raise the whole sleeping in the car issue. Maybe I could get him into a proper bed somewhere, at least until he moved on. Altruistically speaking, of course.

Because it wouldn't be my bed. No. That would be . . . awesome, amazing, so damn exciting I couldn't even breathe thinking about it. But also, ridiculous, dangerous, absurd, risky, and to be honest, terrifying. Yeah, mostly that last one.

A couple of disappointing teenage fumblings in the dark—one in the back of a parked truck behind the science block of the local high school. And the other in the backyard shrubbery of my best friend's house after an epically unsuccessful party and with his older cousin, no less—did not an experienced man on man lover make.

"That's awesome, Dad. Ask him tomorrow. Promise?"

Jesus Christ on a lawnmower. "I promise."

TAI

"You want me to do what?" My eyes bugged out of my head because there was no way I'd heard that right.

Emmett's pale ears pinked adorably. "We thought you might like to come with us on our Saturday trip, see a bit of the Burlington area?"

Oh god, I had heard right. "*Us*, meaning you and Leo?" We were holed up behind the reception desk whispering to each other.

"Yes." Emmett pushed a wad of papers around the desk, cutely flustered.

I stared at him, slack-jawed, because he had to be joking. The three of us had just shared a friendly lunch around Emmett's desk, Ivy's treat—sandwiches from a café around the corner. And as much as she blustered and tried to hide it, I knew the 'treat' aspect was solely for my benefit.

Sneaky little shits, both of them.

But it didn't stop the swell of warmth through my chest at the thought they cared enough to bother or the relief at putting some food in my stomach at no cost to my dwindling wallet. I'd slept like shit, woke up freezing, although not as bad as the day before, shoved a donut in my mouth for breakfast, and made a beeline for the clinic bathroom as soon as I'd arrived, a bag of toiletry essentials jammed in the pocket of my jacket.

It was hard to digest the sharp turnabout in my life, like I'd fallen down a damn rabbit hole. Only two days ago, I'd showered in a bathroom the size of the clinic itself, with a feast of organic and sustainable lotions at my disposal, fifteen jets, three shower heads, lube, condoms, and a bench in the shower . . . for stuff.

But for all the drastic change in my circumstances, I also felt alive for the first time in far too long. And it had been a good morning in the clinic—no dramas, no anal gland expulsions, no floods, and only two scratches from an elderly cat that didn't like the thermometer shoved up its are. I really couldn't blame her. After all, prep was everything.

But I was getting the hang of things.

After lunch, Ivy schooled me on how to dispense deworming

tabs and flea treatments to any walk-ins so I didn't have to interrupt Emmett, and then I made a start on Emmett's books, locating those invoices he wanted—much more my comfort zone.

Which meant I'd been on my own at the desk, staring at said accounts while at the same time wondering how many freaking texts were sitting unanswered on my phone from Dion, when Emmett approached and shyly asked me to join him and Leo on their Saturday excursion.

"Sightseeing, Emmett? Really? I'm hardly on holiday. And I don't have the . . . time." I angled my body away from the curious stares and blatant attempts at eavesdropping by the two women in the waiting room. One held the leash of a Golden Labrador. The other wore an expression as sour as lemons, and had a tight grip on a carrier which contained something hairless—cat or dog, I hadn't quite determined the answer from the file before Emmett had corralled me.

Emmett hesitated. "It was *Leo's* suggestion, since you don't know the area and all." His gaze slid away. "He wanted to thank you for helping him with his lines." He shoved his hands in his pockets and glanced back to catch my eye. "But only if you want."

Jesus, he was cute. But it was still a bad, bad idea.

"Mmm." I frowned and studied him closely. "So, just to be clear, it's *Leo* who asked me?"

Emmett nodded, looking more than a little flustered. "Does that matter?"

It did. The last thing I wanted was to muscle in on any dad-and-son time or make Emmett in any way uncomfortable.

"How do *you* feel about it?" I whispered and watched his expression waver. *That answered that.*

"I think it's a good idea or I wouldn't have asked, of course."

"Of course." Yeah, I wasn't buying it. "Well, thanks for the offer, but I doubt you want some guy you hardly know cramping your limited time with Leo. You two have fun on your own. Besides, I have laundry to do. Washing Ivy's dogs is taking a toll on my limited closet."

Emmett's brows dipped in a deep frown, which I found curious. I'd fully expected he'd be pleased to have an excuse to dump me, since I made him uncomfortable for a number of reasons I'd already guessed at.

"Laundry, huh?" He sounded anything but convinced. "And exactly how long do you expect that to take? An hour?"

I jutted my chin. "Oh, a *lot* longer. Creases have to be creased, folds have to be folded, all the colors separated. I'm quite particular about my clothes, as it happens."

"Yeah, I can see that." Emmett ran an amused eye over my terrifyingly mundane and sad Friday ensemble. "You must be overcome by the sheer weight of the responsibility."

Huh. My lips twitched as I desperately tried to suppress the grin that threatened to break over my face. The man had game. Who'd have known? I crossed my arms and side-eyed him. "Sarcasm, Emmett? I'd have thought that a little below a well-educated man such as yourself?"

"Oh, something tells me you can handle a bit of sarcasm," he fired back. "And probably a lot more."

I stared at him because, *holy shit,* were we flirting? It sure as hell felt like we were flirting.

Emmett must've realized at the same moment, his gaze darting to the blatantly interested women as he turned an adorable shade of crimson. And damn, I wanted to kiss that blush right into the next century. Emmett's pale skin was the perfect vehicle for every emotion that crossed his heart, and I couldn't help but wonder how a whole host of other feelings might play out on that canvas as well.

"Well, I can't deny that in this instance the sarcasm might be warranted." I stole a quick look at my clothes and summoned a pout. "I get that the jeans are too big and the sweatshirt I wore this morning smells like a university frat party, but I kinda thought the T-shirt was a find." I pulled it out at the shoulders and waggled my eyebrows at him. The T-shirt had *I'd Tap That* printed above the picture of a bucket hanging on a sugar maple tree.

Emmett swallowed hard. He'd taken one look when I'd appeared from the bathroom that morning and nearly spit up his coffee. Ivy had merely grinned and kissed me on the cheek.

The evidence for Emmett being anything but straight had been mounting by the hour.

I leveled a cautionary look his way. "Don't think for a minute you can out snark the snark queen."

He laughed. "Riiight. Well, as riveting as your Saturday afternoon laundry plans sound—" He cocked a brow. "As it happens, it's not *only* Leo who'd like you to come."

And he really needed to stop saying things like that.

Emmett took a breath and leveled me a look. "I want you to come too."

And. Oh. My. God. He had to be doing this deliberately. I crossed my legs.

"But not if you're uncomfortable, of course," he flustered, and I wondered if he'd finally caught on.

"For goodness sakes, go with the man and his son," Mrs. Labrador interrupted. "It's a lovely ferry trip."

I grabbed Emmett by the shirt sleeve and pulled him around the corner into his office for some privacy. "Of course, I'd like to come," I hissed. *You have no fucking idea.* "I just don't want to put you on the spot or, to be honest, put you in a position that people you know might . . . *ask questions*, since I'm—" I took a big breath and let it out slowly. "Well, since I'm *me*, right? I'm hardly a fucking wallflower. I scream gay and not the more palatable kind, at least not for some people."

I left it at that, hinting at what sizzled between us, at what I thought he was aware of, but which neither of us had found the balls to mention.

He considered that for a moment, then calm as you like, smiled and said, "Well, it seems I'm not a fan of wallflowers either."

My brows hit my hairline.

"I know, right?" Emmett looked . . . relieved, if anything. "Kind of a surprise to me too. But if you're okay being seen with me, then I am with you. Deal?"

I closed my eyes and shook my head, unable to keep the dopey grin from my face. "As it turns out, more than okay." *What the hell was wrong with me?* "Beats hangin' around the lakefront looking dodgy. So, thank you, both, for thinking of me."

Emmett snorted. "Yeah, well, it seems I'm a little preoccupied in that regard lately." His eyes widened as if shocked at his own words. "I didn't mean . . . I just—"

I rested a hand on his arm and he practically jumped. "It's okay, Emmett. I'm no threat. Yes, I picked up *something,* and I'm flattered. But I'm not looking for anything here but friendship." *Liar.*

We stared at each other for a long minute, then he nodded and headed out the door with me following.

"You can bring Tina Turner through now, Gemma," he called to the owner of the hairless animal.

"Tina Turner?" I mouthed to Emmett and he grinned.

Gemma carried the crate housing Tina Turner past the desk with her nose in the air, and I swallowed a strangled laugh.

Before he followed her to the treatment room, Emmett leaned my way. "Give me ten minutes, then come save me."

I set my watch.

But I wasn't needed, at least not with Gemma, and by five, with the last client nearly done, it was looking like we might be finished on time, something Leo informed me didn't happen often, read *ever.*

Apparently, fifteen-minute consults were not usually adhered to, surprise, surprise. Emmett was a soft touch and rarely moved a client along until they were ready to leave. Even if said client was just way too fucking flirty and taking up his time in an attempt to wrangle a date. Not that something like that would bother me, of course. And not that it had anything to do with my decision to keep religiously, one could even say *obsessively* to the schedule.

That was just good business practice, right? Nothing to do with Miss Blond and Beautiful of the big green eyes and overly handsy approach, leaning across the treatment table, putting everything on a plate while batting those way-too-cute lashes at my boss slash *just friend.*

Because of course that was *my* treatment table and the woman needed to butt the hell out of my personal veterinarian fantasies, which was a whole other story. But that simple acknowledgment from Emmett that he wasn't as straight as everyone thought and that yes, those heated looks weren't all in my imagination had fucked me up completely. And now, I couldn't get the idea out of my head.

Which had led me to becoming the most efficient receptionist I could possibly be when it came to this particular flirty client, tidying up while she talked, and holding the treatment door pointedly open when her time was done. The blistering look I'd earned as she passed, told me I was possibly not being as discreet as I thought I was, and the snort from Emmett confirmed it.

Too bad. And there was no way the woman was getting any of those deworming tablets free as she paid, something Emmett had said I could do with his clients. I had a business to run. Yeah, yeah, I know.

End result? The last appointment got in to see Emmett bang on time, which had earned me a high five from Leo and another two jellybeans from his stash as we practiced his lines.

The kid was actually pretty good, and I thought he had a fair chance of landing the role. The facial expressions he came up with to go along with the lines cracked me up on more than one occasion. But since there were only twenty-one lines in total, we'd interspersed rehearsing the strange little Christmas play and the Mad Hatter's one song—a deviation which had thrown me for a minute until I got my karaoke on—with debating the relative merits of the various flavors of jellybeans.

Leo was a fan of cherry while I got my crank on over green apple, and neither of us had a good thing to say about coconut, miming fingers down our throat.

Both favorites were, however, somewhat at odds with the unofficial Vermont State favorite that Leo had googled—and yes people apparently studied this shit—which, according to an article in the *Burlington Free Press* from a few years before was juicy pear, followed by orange, and only then maple. *Shocker.* It felt somewhat of a slap in the face for the maple-loving state, but then I guessed you could have too much of anything.

It also came as a surprise to learn that the nation's favorite overall was apparently licorice. Eleven states had that as their number one, the thought of which almost made me throw up in my mouth. That horrendous black shit was closely followed by buttered popcorn and watermelon, go figure.

Emmett popped out from an examination to grab something from the storage room halfway through the fascinating discussion and announced he was a strawberry man through and through. To which I replied we could no longer be friends, even at the risk to my current employment status, just in case any of his nasty strawberry kink rubbed off on me.

Leo had dissolved into hiccupping laughter.

Emmett had simply regarded me as one would an irksome child and then informed me that could easily be arranged. I'd snorted my coffee unceremoniously over the printouts of his accounts, and those pale cheeks had turned an alarming scarlet as he clarified he'd meant the unemployment thing, not the kink thing, and hightailed it back to his client lickety-split.

The last client of the day had been an impeccably dressed young man with a beautiful long-haired white cat and a come-hither, way-too-young-for-me smile directed my way, which I judiciously ignored. He paid and left with a big grin having learned his darling Taffy was indeed pregnant. I followed his back with an amused shake of my head.

"Was he flirting with you?"

I spun to find nothing but honest curiosity on Leo's face.

I tucked a lock of hair behind his ears and shrugged. "Maybe. But he wasn't my type."

"What is your type?"

How about your father? Which of course I didn't say, though it was a close call. "Well, that's actually quite a personal question, kiddo, and maybe a little too old for you right now."

"He was a dork," Leo announced, and I had to agree with him.

Sassy also agreed, offering a throat rumbling growl that said pretty much everything she thought of the pampered feline. She'd woken up in the clinic like a different cat. If not quite affectionate, she was at least happy enough to be held, which only proved she'd been someone's pet along the way. I'd put pics and notices on all the lost animal websites and notified the shelters while quietly keeping my fingers crossed that no one claimed her, because . . . well, Leo.

Those two were a match made in heaven.

Hopefully for all his bluster, Emmett saw the same. Not that Sassy's congeniality extended to Emmett. He'd been given the hairy eyeball in no uncertain terms, likely related to the whole thermometer-up-the-arse thing.

"She's looking better today, don't you think?" I scratched Sassy's chin, her favorite spot.

Leo's grip on her tightened and a deep crease formed between his eyes. "No, she's just happy to be out of her cage. She's not eating like she should, and she was crying when I first went in there. And she still feels skinny. See?"

He grabbed my hand so I could feel along Sassy's ribs, which felt a little thin but not too bad. I studied him out the corner of my eye as I stroked the cat, noting the unspoken plea in those dark eyes. *Damn.*

I sensed rather than heard Emmett leave the treatment room down the corridor. In twenty-four hours, I'd grown an annoying sixth sense about the guy that defied explanation. Or rather, I refused to consider the obvious explanation, because . . . yeah, not going there.

He appeared around the corner, wiping his hands on a towel, all those blond waves riotously askew and with a couple of popped shirt buttons around his waistline that exposed the teeniest hint of dazzling blond hair atop some delicious creamy skin. My mouth ran to dust, and it was only the fact I had his cute-as-a-button son at my side that stopped me shoving the man back where he came from to debauch over that damn electric examination table, between the sterilizer and the X-ray machine. Refer to aforementioned fantasy.

Emmett caught my downward glance and immediately ditched the towel to fix his buttons.

"Tai?" Leo nudged me. "Sassy's still sick, right?" He flicked a hopeful glance at his dad and I refocused.

"Hmm." I lifted Sassy's head and pretended to check her ears.

"She does feel a *little* hot." I had no freaking idea if cats even got hot, but if the amused look Emmett fired my way was anything to go by, I guessed not. Bugger.

Emmett ruffled Leo's hair. "I don't think—"

I shot him a warning glance and his mouth snapped shut. "Okay, let's take a look." He investigated Sassy's gums, and even I knew that was a total crock, then felt her tummy and down her legs.

"Okay, she's maybe a little warm," he said with a credible dose of concern and an eye roll aimed at me.

I swallowed a smile and nodded to let him know he'd done well. He was better at that drama lark than he thought.

"And perhaps she could do with a little more fat on those bones before we call Taylor Donovan over at Chittenden County Shelter. What do you think?"

I flashed him a huge smile over the back of Leo's head so he'd know just how wonderful I thought he was for lying so beautifully to his kid.

"Really?" Leo beamed, then caught himself and threw me a smug look. "See, I knew she wasn't ready."

I nodded. "Yep. You called that one right."

Leo spun back to Emmett. "We should take her home for the weekend, Dad. She'd eat more if she wasn't locked up, right? And that would mean she'd get better faster for the shelter."

Wow, he was good.

Emmett caught my eye and I raised my hands in innocence. *Your call.*

He sighed. "Leo, I don't really . . ."

Oh, come on, Emmett. Hidden from Leo, I raised a brow and summoned my best pout.

Emmett blinked long and slow. "Okay. But just for the weekend."

Yes!

Leo shoved Sassy in my lap and threw his arms around his dad's neck, pulling Emmett down for a strangling hug. "Thank you. Thank you. I promise I'll look after her. And I'll make her sleep at the end of my bed, not by my pillow just in case of worms or fleas or toxoplasmosis, right? I promise."

Toxoplasmosis? What the hell was that? My eyes bugged out on stalks.

Emmett saw and grinned widely. "I never said anything about her sleeping with you." His gaze fixed on me. "And she *doesn't* have toxoplasmosis."

Thank God.

"But I guess she can sleep with you if it's only for the weekend."

"Yes!" Leo practically vibrated in Emmett's arms and I couldn't stop the ridiculous surge of joy that bubbled through me.

Emmett continued to stare at me over Leo's shoulder, so close I could've leaned in and kissed that sappy smile right off his face, if I was that way inclined, which I wasn't.

Nothing to see here.

But then his arm brushed mine and a fistful of butterflies took flight in my chest. Those good intentions to keep my distance were thin enough to advertise the hunger in my heart right through the chokehold I thought I had on it. Goddamn crushes.

Then the asshole had the audacity to mouth the words 'thank you so much' to me, and my damn toes curled in my socks. Lights out.

We eyeballed each other for a few seconds longer, and then he let Leo go and shooed him away. "Put Sassy in a crate and get your stuff packed up so we can go. And don't forget to bring some cat food from the kennel room or she'll starve."

"Woo-hoo," Leo whooped and punched the air. "Can we grab a pizza from Tito's?"

Emmett nodded. "You've got five minutes."

Leo grabbed Sassy from my lap and took off with the cat dangling from his arms wearing a particularly smug expression, leaving Emmett and me staring at each other.

"Well done, *dad*," I said. "Not that you need my approval."

His face lit up a little. "It was a good idea. I don't know yet if we'll keep her, though."

"Riiiight." I chuckled.

The small space between us filled with a soft silence.

"You did a good—"

"I had a great—" We spoke simultaneously and laughed.

"You did a good job, today," Emmett said quietly. "We kind of threw you in at the deep end this afternoon, with Ivy having a full list of appointments, but I just thought you should know."

It was hard to hold his level stare. I couldn't remember the last time *anyone* had told me I'd done a good job. "I appreciate that, and I actually enjoyed it. I'm sorry about that woman and if I rushed you—"

"No, you're not." He laughed.

"All right, no, I'm not." I elbowed him playfully. "And don't look at me that way. You know very well why I hurried Miss I-just-love-a-compassionate-man out the door. She was all but groping you. It bordered on sexual harassment."

He laughed. "And yet my virtue remains intact, all thanks to you."

I pulled a face. "Then you clearly haven't seen the inside of my mind." *Stop. It.*

The heated look he sent could've scorched the damn hair off my arms. And there we were again. Flirting.

Then, as if we'd rehearsed it a million times, we both dropped our gaze and stepped back from the brink.

"You did the right thing. Someone needs to keep me on time," he said flatly, as if we hadn't both just stripped each other naked with our eyes. "Ivy's told me I'm way too soft, and Carolyn was more ornament than use. Although the argument could be made that you were a tad selective in your enforcement." He arched a brow.

"I'm sure I have no idea what you mean." I shuffled the print-outs on the desk into a messy pile and gave him one off the top.

"Did you find anything?" His blue eyes swept the page with a frown.

"Unfortunately, yes." I turned the monitor so he could see. "Quite a number of overdue accounts."

His brows crunched and a concern cut into his expression. "Holy shit. This is four months old. And for $1,200."

I winced, because there were quite a few worse than that. "And unfortunately, it's not the only one." I hated to be the bearer of bad news, but whatever skills the receptionist before me had, one of them wasn't competency. Either that, or she didn't give a fuck about the business, beyond getting paid. Most likely the latter. Because it wasn't that the accounts were a mess, more that no one had followed up on any of the bad debts, and I was quietly horrified that Emmett had been ignorant of it. The man was far too trusting.

His face had drained of color. "How many more like this?"

I shrugged reservedly, not wanting to hit him with everything at once. "I haven't finished yet. I'll know an exact number by tomorrow afternoon, but it's not just a few, Emmett. If you want, I could send new invoices out to the more recent ones and then final demand notices to those over three months? Give them a bit of a scare."

"Final demand notices?" He scrubbed a hand down his face. "Shit. You don't think that's too aggressive?"

I schooled my expression because I was mad as hell at these people taking advantage of Emmett's good nature. I'd only worked for him for two days, and I could tell he'd never turn an animal away *or* press a soul for what he was owed as long as the pets were looked after. But in my mind, if you couldn't afford to clear a bill, the least you could do was fess up and work out a payment plan.

"Your business, your call" was what I eventually said.

He chewed on that for a minute; then his lips formed a thin line. "Okay, do it. As much as I hate it, I can't sustain this sort of loss. Goddammit, why didn't Carolyn say anything?"

I simply looked at him.

"Yeah, okay. But do you know how difficult it is to get good help for what I can afford to pay?"

"Maybe it's worth paying more if it means you can trust the help you get to care about your business. Maybe the investment ends up paying for itself?"

He studied me hard. "Lu said the same thing. I was just too much of a scrooge to listen."

I shuffled the printouts from one side of the desk to the other and straightened my pencils, avoiding his gaze. "Sounds like a smart woman." I suppressed a smile and his elbow dug me in the ribs.

"She was."

"Dad, should I take the food for mature cats or the premium one?" Leo popped his head around the corner.

Emmett turned to answer. "The premium for now. We'll give her a boost."

Leo disappeared back down the corridor.

"Speaking of smart." I lifted my gaze. "How's the search for a replacement going?"

He immediately looked away. "I'm working on an interview short list. A very *short* list. Like just one, at the moment." His face dropped. "None of the enquiries so far have come from someone suitably qualified. And by the way, I forgot to get your number in case there's an animal emergency and I need your help."

I snorted. "That's the worst pickup line ever."

"Oh, I have a lot more where that came from, believe me. Just give me your number."

I opened my hands wide. "Don't have one." I wasn't turning that damn phone on for less than the apocalypse, let alone leave it on.

"You don't have a phone?" He gave an incredulous look and I knew he didn't believe me.

"I'm sorry, I just—"

He threw up his hand. "Don't worry. I can give you an old one to use while you're here.

My jaw dropped. "You want to lend me a phone?"

"I have to be able to contact you."

"What if I . . . I don't know, take off with it?"

"Will you?"

"No, but—"

"Then that's settled. Follow me."

We went into his office and he slapped an ancient iPhone in my hand, adding a squeeze to my arm that may as well have been connected to my dick for the zing that shot through my body.

"I keep it on my plan in case of emergencies, and because . . . well, because I couldn't somehow bring myself to turn it off. It was Lu's." Emmett flushed a deep red, and I wanted to grab him and hold him close. "Crazy, right?"

"Absolutely not." I settled for grabbing his hand and squeezing it.

He stared down at where we touched until I let go, and then looked up. "Anyway, you can call and text on it, that's about as fancy as it gets. But at least *he* won't be able to track you." He held my gaze. "I should've realized; I'm sorry."

Shit.

"And while you're here—" He grabbed a tin from the same drawer and opened it. "I'm going to advance you for the first few days of work. Thought it might help." He put a stack of notes on the table.

Goddammit. Warmth rushed to my cheeks. "Thanks, but I'd rather work the hours first. You might need to let me go. We both know I'm out of my depth. Besides, that's way too much."

"You're doing just fine. And I don't mind paying a bit over the going rate."

"I'm not a charity case. I can wait."

His face paled. "I didn't mean . . . shit. I fucked up, didn't I?"

"No. It was good of you to offer and I appreciate the concern, but I really am fine, and I *really* want to *earn* this."

I wasn't fine and we both knew it, but I sent him a look that dared him to say different. He wasn't so easily put off.

"I just want to help. It's not a gift. It's an advance. There's no harm in accepting it."

"Would you have offered before you knew the mess I'd gotten myself into?" Then before I could stop myself, I dropped my voice and added, "Or if you weren't attracted to me? I don't want your pity, Emmett." I regretted it as soon as I'd said it.

He blanched, and then his cheeks blazed.

"Oh god, I'm sorry, Emmett," I backtracked. "I shouldn't have . . ."

But he wouldn't meet my eyes. "Don't worry. I'm sure you've found it, *me*, amusing."

Fuck. "I haven't at all. Emmett, please look at me?" I grabbed his arm and his gaze dragged up to mine. "I'm flattered. I don't know why I said that."

He shook his head. "It doesn't matter. And just to be clear, I would've offered regardless."

Of course, he would. He was a nice guy. Whereas I was a jerk. My hand slid from his arm.

"It's help, not pity, Tai," he pressed. "And if you weren't so stubborn, you'd see the difference."

"I know, I know." I willed him to understand. "It's just that I promised myself, after Dion, I wouldn't . . ." I dropped my head and drew a shaky breath.

Emmett was at my side in an instant. "Shit, I'm sorry, Tai. I didn't think—"

"What's going on in here?" Ivy slipped into the room in a haze of jasmine scent from the dog shampoo she used and glared at Emmett. "Leo's jumping up and down waiting to take Sassy home and all I can hear is you two arguing. What did you do?"

Emmett's eyes popped. "Me? Nothing! And why does it have to be my fault?"

She stared at him.

"All I did was offer Tai an advance, and he didn't like it."

"I don't want charity," I mumbled.

"It's *not* charity if you're earning it." Emmett ground the words out.

And there we were again.

I almost gave in. Then I remembered Dion and my jaw set. "And I am not stubborn."

Emmett's lips twitched like he wanted to kiss the pissy steel right the hell out of me and I was pretty on board with that, to be honest. *Ridiculous bastard.*

"It *is* charity if it's *too much* money," I said flatly.

"Then don't take it all," he snipped right back.

Ivy threw up her hands. "Jesus George, give me strength." She turned and closed the door, then eyeballed me. "Sit."

My gaze narrowed. "I don't want—"

"Sit!" She held up a finger and my mouth slammed shut.

Emmett snorted until she rounded on him.

"And as for you—" She loomed over his desk. "What was it Lu used to say? As subtle as a fart in a library?"

My turn to snort. But the glee was short lived.

"What the hell is wrong with the two of you?" Ivy hissed. "Get those undisciplined dicks of yours out of your shit-for-brains heads and make room for a few synapses to connect, or so help me god, I'll do it for the both of you."

Her flinty gaze darted between us. Then she grabbed the stack of bills from the desk, peeled off a few to throw back at Emmett, and shoved the rest into my hand.

"Take it, say a polite thank you, and then go distract Leo while I have a few words with the good veterinarian here."

I thought about handing the money back for all of two seconds, then clocked the 'I just fucking dare you to' glint in Ivy's eyes and did as I was told. But I did manage to fire Emmett a shit-eating grin before leaving faster than a rat on a sinking ship.

I got my things together and my coat zipped, then found Leo choosing cat toys for Sassy, and we chatted about the relative value of a feather teaser versus cat nip until Emmett and Ivy reappeared. Ivy headed straight for The Groom Room with a decided flounce to her hips while Emmett's soft smile made my heart tick up, reassurance that I hadn't screwed up entirely. And it was hard to ignore the relief that accompanied the additional weight in my wallet. I owed Emmett an apology.

"You ready for pizza, Leo?"

"Yes, Dad." He jumped to his feet. "Can I take a couple of these toys for Sassy?"

"Sure." Emmett turned to me. "I'll see you tomorrow then. Eight thirty?"

I nodded. "Eight thirty it is. And thank you, for the advance. I'm sorry for being a dick."

Leo sent me a questioning look and I squeezed his shoulder.

"Hard to believe, right?"

Emmett chuckled. "Well, the feeling's mutual. And you're welcome. See you tomorrow." He shooed Leo and I ahead through the door, locked the clinic, and then turned to face me.

"And at risk of getting my head bitten off, again—" He eyed me pointedly. "—I also wanted to say you're welcome to use the shower in the clinic, anytime you want. Working all day with animals isn't always clean, and if you were going out, well, anyway, the offer's there. That's all I'm saying."

He was gone before I could answer, and as I watched father and son walk up the road, I wondered how he knew I was sleeping in my car, because that little charade of his wasn't fooling anyone. I couldn't decide whether to be mortified or just plain grateful.

But with a few unexpected dollars in my pocket, there was one thing that might help. I gathered my jacket around my ears and headed for the Marketplace.

Briar arched a brow and glanced at the clock when I slid into a seat at the charming 1950s-style soda counter that served as the bookstore's coffee bar.

"We close in twenty minutes if you're thinking of another long session cluttering up my sofa and staring out the window."

"Funny guy," I grumbled, tapping my finger on the counter. "Hot chocolate, and make it a double." I peeled off my jacket and laid it on the next seat.

Briar rolled his eyes at my T-shirt and grabbed a mug from the shelf. "Do I need to call your sponsor?"

I cut him a scathing look. "I wouldn't give up your day job."

"You can always take this into the bar if you want. Maybe have a beer after? Listen to a bit of music? I think there's an open-mic session tonight." He plunged the frothing nozzle into the small jug of milk.

"Too tempting to drown my sorrows," I griped.

He arched a brow. "Do I even want to know?"

"Better off not, I reckon."

He nodded. "Excellent news, seeing as I'm a bit short on sympathy this evening. It's been a long day."

"Preach it." We bumped knuckles, and I sipped my hot chocolate and watched as Briar got the store ready to close while I tried to unpick my meltdown.

I wasn't used to kindness, wasn't used to good men who gave

without wanting something in return. But I would never be dependent like that again. I might not have a lot to offer the world, but I could change that. I would change that.

I just needed a plan. And a ticket out of Burlington to some place as far away from Dion as I could get.

6

EMMETT

I dropped the phone on my desk, groaned, and sank back in my chair. I was a walking liability in my own office, my focus completely shot, and four hours of sleep wasn't helping. The previous night had been the first in months I'd gotten home at a respectable hour to spend time with Leo, and what had I done? Spent most of it obsessing over a cheeky smile, wide brown eyes, silky black hair, smooth olive skin, a pair of ill-fitting jeans, and the impeccable ass that filled them. Color me ridiculous and be done with it.

Ivy pushed the office door open and invited herself in. "Are you hiding or sulking?"

I pushed a chair her way with my foot. "Would it make any difference to my chances of ducking the words of wisdom I feel looming?"

She looked a little stung, and I immediately regretted the thoughtless snipe. Of all people, Ivy least deserved to bear the brunt of my bad mood. We were both a spouse down with the scars to prove it.

"I'm sorry. No sleep."

She settled herself in the chair and leveled a look my way. "Nothing to be sorry for. Subtlety is a lost art form in my family. I'm here because I want to know what burr got up your butt today? After our little talk yesterday, I thought we were done with distractions. Do or don't do, right? Shit or get off the pot. Fish or bait. Ask him out or don't."

"Shhh. I get it, I get it."

"Yeah, well, you've called two pets by the wrong name, screwed up a supply order, and forgot to eat breakfast . . . again."

"So that was you, was it?"

"No. Leo told me, but he didn't tell Tai. That man worked it out on his own and made you sit down with some toast before you passed out and before Leo could get there first."

He had, and I'd been extraordinarily touched.

Leo's laughter filtered from the waiting room as he and Tai got up to god knew what out there. Tai had shown endless patience, grinding through the remaining invoices while Leo had badgered him with inane questions all morning. In the end, Tai threatened to have Ivy dye Sassy a bold shade of blue if Leo didn't let him finish, and that settled things.

I picked up a pen and began playing with it. "Sorry."

"Whatever. They get on well." Ivy nodded toward the reception area.

I frowned and rubbed my neck, hoping I didn't look as obvious as I felt. "They do, don't they?"

"Hmmm. And that's a problem, isn't it?"

So, that would be a fail on the not being obvious part. I threw the pen on the desk and rolled my eyes. "Say what you came to and then maybe I can get on with my afternoon."

"The afternoon that involves taking Tai sightseeing?" Ivy grinned.

"Taking *Leo* sightseeing. Tai's coming as *Leo's* invite." I stared her down.

"Uh-huh." Ivy-speak for 'don't even bother.' She shook her head. "So, you being holed up in here? Is that to fret over all the unpaid invoices or because you're trying and failing not to look like you're frothing at the mouth over the poor boy—"

"Man." *Shit.* I blinked slowly and sighed. "Tai's a man."

A sly smile crept over her face. "I'm well aware of that, sweetheart. Just making sure you were as well. He *is* a man, in every sense of the word. A lovely, kind, little-bit-lost but totally gorgeous young man. And you, my dear, are a bisexual man who is completely allowed to look and do anything else you want with that information."

I fired her a warning look and she threw up her hands. "All right, I won't say another word."

"Much appreciated." I hesitated. "I don't know if I regret you knowing about me or am really thankful for the fact that you do."

She nodded. "Makes perfect sense."

I grabbed a pen and doodled on my planner. "He reminds me of her sometimes. Lu." I chanced a look, half expecting to find a shocked expression but there was only a soft smile.

"Mmm. I can see that." She reached for the photo frame and ran a finger over Lu's image. "She was a firecracker. Tai is too. Full of life and not scared to tell you about it. They both march to a different drum, right?"

I snorted. "Yeah. Something like that. I guess it feels good to have that energy around again."

She eyed me for a second. "It is. But it's not just that, is it?"

There was no point hiding. "No. But I'm not sure exactly how much *more* it is, if that makes sense. Two days, Ivy. It's been just over two days and I feel like a ridiculous teenager. My body has taken one look and said yes, I want. But my heart and head have no clue. And in case you missed it the first time—two days. And then there's Leo."

She nodded softly. "These decisions never seem to appear when it's convenient. But you're sounding pretty serious for a guy who maybe just needs to take advantage of an opportunity for a quick fling."

"I'm not some kid anymore. And I'm not really made that way."

She shrugged. "Things change."

"Ivy, please."

She raised her hands. "Fine. So, what's happening on the debt front then? Did Tai finish the list?"

"Pretty much. We're re-invoicing the not so old ones and sending final demands to the others, adding an offer to discuss a repayment schedule."

She arched a brow. "Really?"

"It was his idea," I admitted.

She studied me for an excruciating few seconds. "Well, good on him for talking you into it. You need to be tougher on that sort of thing."

"Yeah, well, there's about forty thousand due that I can't afford to lose."

Her eyes bugged. "Forty thousand? Holy shit, Emmett. How could you have missed that?"

I blew out a sigh. "I didn't check, all right? You know I'm shit at that sort of thing. I handed all that stuff to Carolyn and—"

Ivy's brows hit her hairline.

"I know, I know, it wasn't the best choice, but I hate all that stuff. Always did. Lu was so much better at keeping a check on the accounts. I just wait till tax time and then panic. So, yeah, I don't exactly have any choice but to get tough."

"Is the clinic okay?"

I waggled a hand between us. "If we can get at least half paid up and the rest on payment plans, we'll be fine." I crossed everything I had.

"Damn, Emmett. You need to up your game, sweetheart. Lu would be horrified."

I looked her in the eye. "I don't need the reminder."

"You're right, I'm sorry. Well, if anyone can get a few recalcitrant debtors to pay up, I suspect it's that young man. Between charm and snark, he's got most situations covered." She stood and patted me on the shoulder. "So, put your big boy pants on and go out and have fun this afternoon. Leo's practically bouncing off the walls with excitement to spend the afternoon with you, and Tai looks much the same." She winked.

I rolled my eyes at her. "Tell Leo I'll be there in five." I waited for her to leave, then fired off a quick text to Jasper.

I'm in so much trouble.

He answered almost immediately.

Trouble?

Lean and fit, pretty as a picture, sassy mouth, heart like gold, ass like a diamond, TROUBLE.

Dots appeared and disappeared before his reply finally came through.

Oh. Trouble you want or trouble you don't want?

Do I really need to answer that?

Yes.

All of the above.

More dots.

What do you want me to say?

Oh, for fuck's sake.

How about talk me out of it?

Okay. Don't do it.

Thanks.

Feel better?

Just dandy.

Glad to help. Talk later.

What the hell?

You can't just go. You're supposed to give me advice.

I am and I did. I'm also working on a car.

Give me two minutes. I know how hard this is for you.

I waited him out.

Ok I'm listening.

I took a deep breath.

Leo likes him.

Another long pause.

Leo thinks he's your employee not a potential date.

It was almost the longest text I'd ever had from him, which likely said something about what I was stirring up. The death of his husband, Michael, had cut Jasper into tiny pieces, most of which hadn't found their way back to whole yet. Hell, I knew the feeling, or I had, for a long, long time. Grief blew a gaping hole in your heart the size of the Grand Canyon with no one-size-fits-all roadmap for how to crawl your way out. It was an experience Jasper and I both knew, intimately. It might not have been a lot to build a friendship on, but Jasper had kept my head from exploding off my fucking shoulders on some long, godawful nights.

And so, I understood. Me talking about another guy was hard for Jasper. For a long time, we'd had each other's lonely backs . . . and things were changing.

I like him too.

There, I'd fucking said it.
The longest pause yet.

Has something happened between you?

No.

Nothing?

No. Crazy, right? But he's guessed . . . about me.

It's those damn puppy dog eyes.

Fuck off.

I stared at the empty screen for a bit before the next text came through.

It's a big step.

It is.

You're not out.

I know.

I can't tell you what to do Emmett.

That I also know. But I think I'm ready for . . . something.

And holy shit, saying those words out loud unpacked something big in my chest.

For him?

His name is Tai and yes, maybe. But I hardly know him and he's not staying so it couldn't really be a thing between us, but it means something.

What?

I think he woke me up. I feel . . . ready.

I could almost hear the wheels turning in Jasper's brain.

You know I can't do that again. I . . .

God, the man broke my heart.

I know. But you still remember what it felt like . . . so what do you think?

Long pause.

Listen to your heart. It worked the first time around, right?

It sounded so easy.

Yeah. It did.

And get your ducks in a row. You need to think with your big head too.

Good point.

And Leo . . .

I know. I'll pick my time to talk to him.

Emmett I'm sorry if I can't be . . . I'm just not . . .

Hey no problem. Thank you. Are we still good?

The longest pause of all.
Yeah.

The plan was to take my truck on the one-hour ferry crossing from Burlington to Kent, drive north for a picnic on the banks of the Saranac River in Plattsburg, and then come back via the Grand Isle ferry making it a round trip.

The weather couldn't have been better. The early October sun sat unveiled and high in a crisp blue sky, and although not exactly tropical, the rare lack of wind on the lake made everything that much more agreeable—the deck was packed with people soaking up the views and the sunshine. Leo had struck up a friendship with a boy his own age and the two were sitting cross-legged, bent over a Marvel comic, while Tai and I leaned on the railing, our elbows touching, those two square inches of pressure commanding every scrap of my attention.

"You don't need to shelter me," Tai said above the engine noise. "I'm not cold."

I ignored him. The bulky jacket he wore might've been a big improvement on that first day debacle, but he still didn't have near enough flesh on his bones for my liking. I stayed put.

"I said you don't—"

"I heard you. Deal with it. You weigh about as much as a bean sprout." Without thinking, I tugged his jacket collar up and his eyes popped wide before he scanned the crowd. *Shit.* I dropped my arm, making sure to reconnect with his once more when it hit the railing.

He made no further comment, but his lips quirked up at the corners and his arm pressed a little firmer against mine. I sank down on the hip closest to his, which brought us even closer. We were walking dangerous ground, but I couldn't seem to help myself, and he wasn't exactly running away. A quick glance Leo's way reassured me he was too engrossed in whatever Luke Cage was up to on the pages of the comic to bother with his dad standing way too close to another man.

And as for anyone else who might've taken a longer look at us, fuck 'em. I wasn't holding his hand or anything. People could get over it. It all sounded very brave but mostly because there was no one on the ferry who I knew as more than a familiar face. So, not brave at all, mostly reckless.

But I still wasn't moving and Tai seemed in no hurry, either. And so, we stood like that in silence, gazing out over the lake to the pretty ochre and cream low rises peppered over the hillsides of Burlington city, and beyond that to the stacked rise of the Green Mountains, with Mount Mansfield looking more blue-gray than green in the fall light. North and south of the city, and behind us on the New York side of Lake Champlain, glimpses of patchworked farmland dipped in and out of view with the gentle roll of the ferry.

"It's breathtaking." Tai traded glances with me.

"It is." I kept my eyes on him.

He frowned and ducked his chin shyly, and fuck me, it was adorable. Sassy Tai was a blast, but shy Tai did my damn head in. He'd been quiet the entire way to the ferry, his head whipping from side to side as we drove, reminding me he'd been in Burlington less than three days. With no money and working every daylight hour for me, he'd likely seen nothing his feet couldn't get him to in ten minutes.

I knocked elbows with him. "You were in Boston for three years, right?"

He nodded.

"So, you must have done some traveling outside the city."

Another frown. "Not really. If it didn't have flashing lights, a good back beat, a million sweaty bodies, or reeked of money, Dion usually wasn't interested. We flew to Las Vegas a couple of times, but that's about it."

"At the risk of repeating myself, your ex was a bit of a dick."

Tai snorted. "You aren't wrong."

"So, indulge me a little. Why *did* you stay with him so long? I'm just finding it hard to picture you with a controlling guy like that. You don't seem the type to take that kind of shit. At least you don't in my clinic."

Tai continued to stare over the water, his foot jiggling on the bottom railing. "Fool of a guy ignores boyfriend who is an obvious douchebag because said fool thinks he's in love with him. It's not that complicated." He turned to face me. "Last Wednesday night we went to one of the clubs he owns—it was our usual thing. He checked on his properties most nights, and I generally went along. Anyway, it was getting late, and I went to find him with a drink and to convince him to take me home. I found him in his office banging two guys over his desk."

Jesus Christ. "Damn. That had to hurt. I can't imagine." Without thinking, I leaned closer. Why anyone lucky enough to call Tai their own would even think about going elsewhere was beyond me. I'd pay good money for five minutes alone with his jerk of an ex. The guy had obviously done a number on Tai that was going to take some undoing.

"And I know what you're going to ask," Tai said. "Why did I stay after the first time?"

"I wasn't going to ask. Relationships are complicated. Most people wouldn't believe someone they loved would do that to them a second time."

He gave a thin smile. "That's partly true. I did want to believe him when he said it wouldn't happen again, but I was also a coward."

"I can't imagine—"

"Dad?" Leo tugged on my jacket, and Tai and I sprang apart. But Leo seemed oblivious to how close we'd been standing, too busy chatting with his new friend. "Can I have some money to get us ice cream from inside? Mark's mom says it's fine."

I glanced behind them to Mark's mom who nodded with a smile. "Sure." I dished out a ten-dollar bill, asked for the change, and got a loud laugh in return as they ran off.

Tai grinned. "Ten dollars doesn't go far these days."

"I'm showing my age, aren't I?"

"Maybe a little bit," he teased. "What are you? Thirty-three?"

"Five and counting."

"Mmm. Eight years older." He stared at me for a second, then glanced back at the water as another boat passed at a distance and the family on board waved out. He held his hand up in reply, then turned back to face me.

"The reason I didn't leave Dion, as embarrassing as it is to say,

93

is because he practically fucking owned me. As you know, he didn't want me to work. I had virtually no money of my own. Hell, he gave me a fucking allowance." He blushed bright red. "God, I can't believe I'm telling you this. He bought all my clothes. I lived in his apartment. He bought me the damn car I'm sleeping in. It's in my name, but it still feels like his and I hate the fact that I need it. My phone is even on his account."

"Which is why you don't want to use it."

"Exactly."

"Why don't you sell the car?"

Tai blinked slowly. "I might, yet. But it still feels like taking his money—like he'd have something over me. Plus, I need it to sleep in and get around. It wouldn't bring in enough to get me a room or anything. And it's only in my name because it's worth shit, and he didn't want the insurance to be in his name in case anything happened."

Bastard. "What about your other stuff? You must've brought things over from home. He can't own *everything*."

Tai shrugged. "I'm trying not to think about that. There's some photos and shit that I'd love to get back and a few clothes. But I wouldn't put it past him to have burned it all." He looked away. "I'll work it out. I'm just not ready to face it yet. Bad enough he knows I'm in Burlington."

My heart beat in my throat. "Are you worried?"

He shook his head. "Not in the way you're thinking. Dion's never been violent. Just controlling. And mostly because I fucking let him do all that shit. There was a pay-off, right? I should never have let it go on this long. I just didn't want to admit my family had been right about him. And I don't want to talk with him until I've got a plan. I'm worried I'll cave and go back because it's the easiest option, otherwise. I pretty much deserve the mess I'm in."

My hands landed on his shoulders before I even realized. "No one *deserves* to be treated like that. No one. Understand?"

He hesitated before nodding, then a wave from a passing vessel sent the ferry lurching, we both stumbled, and Tai kind of fell into my arms. I grabbed him tight around the chest as he fought to regain his balance. His hair flicked across my jaw and the rich scent of amber flooded my nostrils together with the cinnamon and maple from his daily cruller. I inhaled deeply and he went rigid in my arms, his hand locked on the railing.

"Emmett. You can let me go now."

"Dad?" Leo appeared at my side, a frown sliced into his smooth forehead.

I cleared my throat. "We nearly lost Tai over the side with that wave." I half laughed, half choked. "If I hadn't caught him, we might've been fishing him from the lake."

"Are you okay?" Leo spun to Tai, his confusion switching to concern.

"I'm fine, kiddo." Tai ruffled Leo's hair. "Your dad's got quick reflexes." He flicked me a knowing glance and heat rose in my cheeks.

"Okay cool. We're gonna go inside and read with Mark's mom, if that's okay?"

I took a step to the side and peered through the window to see the dark-haired woman wave from a seat just inside the cabin. I waved back. "Okay. But don't move from there, got it?"

"Got it." The two boys took off inside.

"Fish me from the lake?" Tai eyed me pointedly.

"Shut up." I turned back to lean over the side. "It wasn't impossible."

He grinned and leaned next to me, the wash of the large boat still messing with the ferry's previously smooth glide through the water. We were almost at Port Kent on the New York side of the lake. The quiet road that ran along the lakefront was dotted with colonial style homes and rougher bungalows—and between us and them, a rolling skin of blue-green water dotted with sail boats, all enjoying the gorgeous Saturday fall afternoon.

I kicked at the railing. "I meant what I said."

He tilted his head. "I thought we'd finished with that."

"You wish. But it's worth saying again. You didn't *deserve* what happened. Trusting someone to take care of you, to have your best interests at heart, believing they love you, isn't foolish or naïve. That's what a real relationship is all about. It wasn't your fault he was a shit-for-brains narcissist."

Tai barked out a laugh.

"And just so you know. Any man who doesn't see what they have in you and feels they have to go stick their dick into someone else, anyone else, isn't worth the shit on your shoes. You're beautiful, kind, smart, and you'll get through this because *that's* what you deserve. Not him. Not . . . *Dion*. You deserve to be appreciated." *Fuck.* I blinked rapidly and looked away, lowering my voice. "Sorry." *Too much. Way too much.*

Tai stared at me, his expression a mixed bag of surprise, amusement, wonder, and confusion. So yeah, *way too fucking much.*

The buzz of activity grew around us—people gathering their things and heading down to the car deck.

"You." Tai gently stabbed a finger at my chest. "Come with me." He turned and headed for the other side of the deck, disappearing behind a sign that said Crew Only.

I glanced through the window to see Mark and Leo still chatting up a storm, Mark's mother alongside. She smiled warmly, and I nodded as I followed Tai around the corner, hesitating when I got to the sign, then pushing on. He was waiting out of sight beside the service door. He fisted my jacket and spun and backed me up against the wall.

"This is such a bad, bad idea," he said, going up on his toes and hovering his lips a tantalizing breath away from mine. "But you are just too fucking irresistible, and no one has ever said anything like that to me, ever."

He hesitated, and I knew he was waiting for me.

It took me about half a second to close the distance and finally, oh god, finally feel the warm soft glide of his mouth over mine, so fucking sweet my knees almost buckled. His tongue immediately slipped along the crease of my lips and I opened like I'd been waiting for him for years, hungry for that first taste. Coffee from the ferry terminal, cherry from the preserves on the toast he'd made me share with him, maple cruller, and the mist from the crisp fall air that blanketed the lake.

He sighed into my mouth and pressed closer, aligning our groins, and holy shit, *everything* was awake and paying attention.

He was hard, so fucking hard—his dick nestled right alongside my own, just a single thrust to make sure I knew how he felt. And I couldn't help shifting just to feel more of him, which drew another groan and a deep sweep of his tongue over mine, just for a second before he pulled back.

I chased his lips but he kept me at arm's length, those dark brown eyes searching mine under a frown the size of the lake itself. He wiped a thumb across my lower lip, almost sadly, shook his head, and practically sprinted for the cabin. I slumped against the wall, my heart pounding out of my chest—shock, confusion, excitement, desire, all warring in my head, but mostly the last one. Because damn, if I thought I'd been in trouble before, I was fucking buried now.

I stayed for a few more seconds to let my heart calm and my dick settle, listening to the man on the speaker warn passengers to return to their vehicles.

"Dad?" Leo's voice rang out from around the corner.

I brushed myself off and walked calmly out to meet him.

"What were you doing in there?' He frowned, his eyes catching the sign above my head.

"Looking for the bathroom." As far as lies went, it wasn't bad, but it was a fucking miracle I got it out with a relatively straight face, what with Tai standing right behind Leo, watching me. He wore an uncertain expression, like he wasn't sure how I was going to react, and I wanted nothing more than to cover his mouth with mine and pick up exactly where we left off.

Bad Emmett. Bad, bad Emmett.

At the risk of exploding into a mess of confused emotions on a public ferry deck in front of my son, I wisely dropped my gaze and kept moving, sliding an arm around Leo's shoulders and steering him toward the lower deck stairwell. He accepted the idiot parent mantle I'd donned without question and loudly pointed out the bathrooms on the way down. I popped in to keep up the charade and threw Tai the keys to the truck. "I won't be a minute."

Tai shooed Leo toward the truck. "We should play I spy. I'm kind of a reigning champion at that." He waggled his eyebrows.

"Oh yeah? We'll see about that." Leo rose to the challenge and dragged Tai off toward the car.

Tai glanced back over his shoulder and we locked eyes—a million questions asked in that one exchange and not a single fucking answer.

7

TAI

What the hell was I doing?

The cool grass of the bank leached through my jeans as I watched Leo play in the freezing shallows of the Saranac River that bubbled past the picnic spot Emmett had chosen just a little out of Plattsburg. My jeans were rolled to my knees, my shoes stowed safely somewhere dry, while my wet feet desperately tried to suck the last remaining heat from the weak fall sun. To anyone observing our little threesome, the scene must've looked downright domestic. It sure as hell felt that way. Not least of all because I was loving every terrifying minute of it.

A damn picnic. Fuck. Me. This was some rabbit hole I'd stumbled down when I'd crossed that state line into Vermont. Dion was hardly the picnic type, and I was pretty sure the last picnic I'd been on was with my parents at Muriwai Beach back home, when I was about Leo's age. It had been my birthday, and my five older brothers had picked me up and thrown me in the sea for the privilege, and I'd lost most of my birthday cake on the sand when I finally surfaced and made it to shore.

My heart squeezed. I missed them more than I was willing to admit. And I still hadn't called my mum. I just couldn't. Not until I was set up and had something encouraging to share. Contact with home had been another thing I'd let slide while I'd been with Dion. Mum didn't like him much, or the life he'd led, and therefore, consequently the one I did, so it was simply easier not to talk.

Which meant telling her he'd finally fucked me over was going to be tough. It wasn't that she'd say I told you so, but there'd be that quiet, familiar, disappointed edge to her kind words of sympathy and encouragement not to waste my life and trust in how smart I was. Things I hadn't been ready to hear. But maybe that was changing too.

And that's why Emmett's words hit so hard. He'd been the only person, other than my mum, to see beyond what most people thought of me, and even more importantly, to tell me. My dad wasn't one to gush. And my brothers loved me but generally thought I was an amusing, nice-looking, waste of space. Pretty much what Dion and every other boyfriend I'd ever had thought as well. Mostly because I'd let them, even played it up at times. And yeah, it was past time to look at all that shit.

Saying I was a work in progress was like calling Gaudi's Sagrada Familia a small renovation project. Nothing was going to be solved easily, but for the first time I thought I was maybe ready to try.

I should never have kissed him. Emmett wasn't some hot guy in a club or a quick fuck in a back room. He was a good man, a dad, a guy who'd had his heart broken already in the worst way. And I was guessing pretty damn inexperienced with men as well. The last thing he needed was a fuckup like me screwing with his feelings.

But when he'd said that stuff about me, it was like something plugged in, and I was done pretending. I couldn't keep a lid on it any longer. He'd meant every word, that's what got me. It was in his eyes, his voice—earnest, indignant on my behalf, raging at the world, wanting more for me. All the things I should've been feeling for myself.

Although he wasn't right about everything. To a certain extent, I did deserve Dion, if only because I'd stayed way longer than I should have. But I was done with that now. From now on, I made my own choices and relied on myself.

Which brought me back to Emmett, and what the fuck was

wrong with me? I might not have a firm plan in my head, but one thing for sure, it needed to specifically *not* include jumping into bed with the hot veterinarian—for all sorts of important and eminently rational and sensible reasons.

Not the least of all being that niggly, troublesome feeling taking root in my heart that I just might fucking like the guy, and in ways that had nothing to do with those unruly blond waves, stark blue eyes, and body I could lick like an ice cream. And that spelled trouble I couldn't afford at the moment, not on top of everything else. If I could only get my recalcitrant dick to get on board with the program, we'd all be hunky-dory. But yeah, apparently not happening.

The rude slap of frigid river water to my face startled me from my funk in time to see Leo hare off in hoots of laughter, empty bucket in hand. I leaped to my feet with a shout and he squealed and ran for the safety of the bank, but I got to him first and scooped him over my shoulder while employing my best cackling bad-guy laugh.

"What dost thou say, mon liege?" I shouted to Emmett, who was staring at the two of us with a huge grin on his face. "Shall I soak this flea-ridden scrawny peasant for his boorish disrespect? Your wish is my command."

"No!" Leo hooted and giggled. "You wouldn't dare. Dad!"

Emmett laughed and ran across. "Now, let me think about this." His eyes met mine with a devilish smile. "So, *my* wish is *your* command, huh?" He smirked.

And oh god, my face could've fried an egg over hard in a second flat—every cell in my body clasping its mortified hands over its eyes with an audible groan.

Thankfully his gaze slid to Leo who was still giggling. "Mmm. It's a hard decision," Emmett said, tilting his head from side to side. "The water's not *that* cold. I think the ingrate would survive."

"I agree, my liege," I answered, doing my best to keep a straight face.

"No, Dad. You have to save me. It's the only chivalrous thing to do." Leo laughed.

Emmett frowned and leaned close to peer at his upside-down son. "Dad, you say? I have no memory of such a thing. Set him down so I can take a look."

I bit back a laugh. "Yes, sir." I set Leo on his feet and Emmett stood back with his chin in his hand and studied him.

Leo opened his arms and did a twirl. "See, Dad, it's me. Heir to all your land and money."

Emmett snorted. "Yeah, good luck with that. Mmm, I guess it *could* be you," Emmett conceded, taking Leo's chin and turning his head from side to side. "Yes, I see it now. An excellent nose and good cheekbones. You have to be mine."

I coughed loudly which earned me a deathly stare.

"I clearly need to reconsider my staffing choices," Emmett said, eyeing me up and down.

"So, I'm free?" Leo tugged Emmett's sleeve.

"You are."

"Yes!" Leo punched the air and immediately ran for me.

I spun and took off, just slow enough to make sure Leo could catch me which he did in seconds. Then, just as he tried to grab me, I scooted around him and headed back to the bank, falling in a heap on the grass with my arm across my face. "No, no. Save me, my liege. The peasant attacks me forsooth."

"Forsooth?" Emmett laughed.

I shrugged. "Hey, I'm doing my best here."

"Get up." Leo grabbed a stick and prodded me gently.

"Ow." I grabbed the end of it and tugged Leo forward.

"To the rescue." Emmett seized Leo from behind and then collapsed back onto the grass with Leo on top, both of them laughing.

I scrambled to a sit and watched their horseplay while rubbing my freezing feet which had turned an alarming shade of blue. They finally ran out of breath and fell back on the grass, panting and holding hands, face-up to the few clouds that now batted the sky.

I breathed past the sudden thickness in my throat and tried to ignore the way my heart flopped over in my chest.

"I'm sure, I heard someone say there was food involved in this excursion." I pushed to my feet and headed for the picnic basket and the blanket Emmett had laid out on the grass. Leo almost beat me to it, diving into the basket to see what his dad had packed.

"Leftover pizza!" he cried, in obvious delight, and I glanced Emmett's way.

He looked somewhat apologetic. "There are some homemade cookies to finish, just so you know. I'm not a total Neanderthal."

I threw up my hands. "Hey, I'm not complaining. I happen to love pizza."

Leo dished out the slices and my gaze slid sideways to find Emmett watching me with soft eyes and a small smile playing on his lips.

"Thank you," he mouthed over Leo's back.

I held his gaze for far longer than I should have, long enough to see his eyes dip to my mouth and a brief flush paint the pale skin of his cheeks. I took the paper plate of food Leo handed me and scuttled to safety at the back of the rug, leaving Emmett and Leo to divide the remains of the pizza between them. That first tangy bite of tomato had saliva pooling in my mouth, but it wasn't nearly as delicious as the wistful look Emmett fired my way before he started on his own.

Oh yeah, I was losing my fucking mind if I thought this didn't have hurt written all over it.

By the time we hit the ferry terminal for the crossing to Gordon's Landing on Grand Isle, we barely scraped on board with five minutes to spare, having spent far too long messing around with a Frisbee after our picnic. I enjoyed a game of catch with the best of them and appreciated a good win, but competitive didn't even begin to cover Emmett with a Frisbee in hand. It was all kinds of endearing watching the otherwise quiet, conflict-avoidant, distracted man become as ruthless as I'd ever seen, racking up points and calling fouls left right and center in our supposedly friendly game.

"You should see him play Monopoly," Leo whispered after his

dad had disqualified one of Leo's points because I'd lifted him up to catch it.

I watched Emmett make a high catch and do his little victory dance and thought, yeah, we were definitely going to play that sometime.

Except for the fact I'd be gone in a week.

So yeah, there was always that.

Safely on the other side of the crossing, the lush green pastoral flats of Grand Isle gave way to the spectacular Roosevelt Highway causeway, taking us over flat shallows glistening pink in the late afternoon sun, all the way back to the mainland. From there, we made a couple of quick stops at the Sand Bar State Park with its beautiful swimming beaches and the Lamoille River below Heineberg Bridge. Then it was back to Burlington, where, in response to Emmett's less than subtle offer to drop me back at my *accommodation,* I'd asked instead to be dropped at the clinic, saying I intended to call in at V and V on my way home.

His eyes called me out on the lie but he said nothing. By the time he pulled into an almost empty parking lot close to the clinic, it was almost seven, and Leo was laid flat in the back seat, curled up and looking gloriously guiltless and vulnerable in that way only sleeping kids could. But the sharp tug on my heartstrings still came as a surprise.

We sat in the truck with the engine still running and stared at each other over the massive center console, the presence of which saved me crawling into Emmett's lap to steal another taste of his lips, but it was a close call. Leo in the back seat was far more of a deterrent. It should have been awkward as hell, but it wasn't.

"I had a great day," I said, not trusting myself to voice how truly wonderful it had been. From being furious, hurt, homeless, and second-guessing every damn life choice I'd made, today I'd still been homeless, but the rest of it hadn't mattered, and I'd felt a sense of peace and certitude about my future that was new and encouraging.

Maybe it had been Emmett's kind words on the ferry? Maybe it had just been the chance to relax and be lost in beauty and fun for a few hours. Either way, the afternoon had been exactly what

I'd needed. And the kiss? Well, the kiss had been the icing on the cake. A lovely memory to take with me.

Emmett nodded at my thanks, his gaze flicking to the back seat. "Let's take this outside."

He switched off the engine and we moved to the rear of the vehicle, out of Leo's sight should he wake.

"I had a good time too, a great time." Emmett held my gaze. "I thought maybe it was wrong to ask you on something that was supposed to be a way for Leo and me to reconnect after the mess I've been making as a dad lately, but it wasn't. It was exactly the *right* thing to do. He needed this. *I* needed this. It was fun. And yes, we would've had fun on our own, but having you there made it better."

He looked around, then reached for my hand and squeezed. My gaze locked on where we touched. My heart thundered in my chest.

"Well, of course." My gaze drifted down. "I mean, I make everything better, right?" My rough voice betrayed the truth behind the poor attempt at a joke. The man was killing me.

"Don't do that," he said softly.

I looked up and wished I hadn't. Tender eyes, a deep blue-black in the shadow of the evening, caught mine and sent those butterflies swarming once again in my belly.

"Don't dismiss yourself like that. You *did* make today better, for Leo . . . and for me. Maybe especially for me." His thumb rubbed small circles on the back of my hand which he still held fast.

It was as though someone had kindled a tiny fire under my skin where he touched. "I think we should get things—" I held up our joined hands "—*this* out on the table. Use your words, Emmett," I said carefully.

He nodded. "Fair enough. I'm bi. And I loved Luelle with everything I had."

I took a second to digest that. I wasn't jealous, more relieved than anything. "Have you *ever* been with a guy?"

He nodded. "A couple, when I was younger. Just messing

around. Quick and anonymous. Nothing to write home about. I'm still pretty much a greenhorn with men."

"Thank you for your honesty." I cupped his cheek with my free hand. "I'm gay, in case you hadn't noticed. No women. Never any questions. Straight down the line, one hundred percent man-loving gay."

Emmett's cheek bunched against my palm as he grinned. "I had noticed."

"Mmm. Okay, so here's the deal as I see it. I like you, Emmett. Hell, I kissed you when I knew damn well I shouldn't, so I like you, a lot. But that's as far as it can go. Under different circumstances, maybe we could see if there's anything more to this. But the timing sucks, and you know it. I can do this job for the next week, maybe a few days longer if you need me, and I don't want to have to leave because we cross a line and one or both of us gets uncomfortable."

He stared at me, his thumb circling, circling, burning all the way down to my bones and straight into my soft-as-butter heart. "I know you're right." He turned his head to press a kiss to my palm, and I nearly fucking melted into a puddle right there in the middle of the Cherry Street parking lot. "But I don't seem able to turn off whatever this is and I don't understand it either. This isn't me."

"Yeah. I get it. This is a big step for you, Emmett," I said thickly. "And this wouldn't be just a quick hand job to satisfy your interest in men. You're not out, and I'm hardly the discreet option. You need to really think about this. And what is it with this bloody thumb thing?" I glared down to where he still held my hand.

He grinned and kept going, circles, circles, circles.

I didn't stop him.

"Does it make you uncomfortable?" he said, a soft challenge in his expression.

Yes. "No." I returned the look. "But you should know I'm not so easily seduced." *Liar.* "I'm made of much sterner material. I have scruples, and, well—" *Circles, circles, circles.* "—scruples . . . mostly those."

His thumb moved to the delicate skin under my wrist. "That's very . . . disappointing." He leaned close and I so fucking wanted him to kiss me.

No, I didn't. I pulled back. "Or at least a principle or two."

His thumb moved again, this time to the hollow of my palm, and the electrical socket that clearly resided there connected straight to my aching dick.

Zing.

Holy shit. Fucking thumb sex. Who knew that was a thing?

"Okay, maybe just one itsy-bitsy principle." I squirmed. "The one that says you touching me like this is trouble neither of us can afford."

He squeezed his eyes shut for a second, then opened them again. "I know. And I'm sorry. The problem is, I happen to like touching you. And I very much liked kissing you. But yeah, I take your point. We have to be sensible."

It took everything I had to pull my hand free and shove it in my pocket before it found its way to Emmett's trousers. "Sensible. Yeah. Like that's *ever* going to be written on my gravestone. But there's always a first time, right? Have a great day tomorrow with Leo. Tell him we'll rehearse again on Monday. I'll see you then." I turned to leave but he grabbed my arm.

"I know you're sleeping in your car," he huffed out.

I blew out a long sigh. "I am, and it's fine."

His brows dipped, annoyed. "It's *not* fine. Let me find somewhere—"

"No. Emmett, please." I patted his chest. "Honestly, I'm fine. It's only for another week. Don't do this. If it becomes *not* fine, I'll let you know." *Like hell.*

His jaw worked as he swallowed whatever argument he was about to add, and I wanted to kiss him for it. Frankly, I wanted to kiss him for most things, so that was hardly news.

"At least tell me you'll use the clinic facilities," he insisted.

"That I can promise." I gave him a warm smile. "And thank you, again."

He nodded and I headed across the street to the Marketplace

without a backward glance. I couldn't afford it. One look and I might've changed my mind about everything.

To hell with not having enough money to waste in a bar. After turning down Emmett, I'd fucking earned a beer. And so, I let myself be drawn by the smoky jazz that floated from the open door of V and V, grabbed a large beer and a quiet seat at the end of the bar, and tried to convince myself I'd made the right decision.

I flipped Dion's phone over and over in my hand as I sat. I needed to text Mum, to at least let her know I was okay, and I wasn't about to use Emmett's phone to do that, it didn't seem right. Plus, Dion already knew I'd been in Burlington so I didn't have a lot to lose there. I powered it up, ignored a ton of messages from the arsehole, and shot my mum a quick text. Said I was doing some traveling, was on and off my phone, and would check in with her in about a week.

It might've been arse-crack early morning in New Zealand, but she immediately answered with a few texts that reeked of relief and concern.

Where are you?

Is Dion with you?

Why not?

Are you coming home?

I gave vague answers to each about taking a break and seeing the sights, enough to settle her concern for a few days, and glad I'd made the effort to connect. And then, unable to resist, I gave in and checked the last few of Dion's messages.

I immediately wished I hadn't.

Get the fuck back here.

Come on. Jesus Tai, it meant nothing.

I miss you.

What am I supposed to do with all your shit?

If you don't call me I'm gonna burn it.

Like that was a surprise. Saved me working out how to get it back. I powered down the phone and seriously considered chucking it. But I couldn't afford another, not yet. I pocketed the damn thing and concentrated on my beer and scanning the patrons.

A big guy with tatts and a no-nonsense face looked to be in charge of the place. I'd have said he was a mean fucker up until he crossed to a guy with an English accent a couple of seats along from me. Brute and brusque suddenly turned to tender and loving as he cradled the man's face and whispered something I couldn't hear. Goddamn, fucking teddy bear. Once was a time a guy like that would've stoked my fantasies and been right up my alley . . . so to speak. Now? Well, my fantasies were filled with blue eyes, blistering smiles, and shaggy blond waves. Go figure.

They shared the briefest of kisses, and I snorted to myself about how wrong that first impression had been. My grunt earned me a withering glare from the barman with no small amount of threat behind it.

I threw up my hands in apology. "No offense meant. Just pretty damn cute. That's all I'm going to say." I added my best reassuring smile.

Tatts stared at me a few seconds longer, then nodded curtly and moved away while the English guy flashed me a slightly more welcoming smile, which I returned. Then I slumped in my seat to focus on how long I could make a single beer last and whether I could risk a quick wash in the bathroom basin before I left.

8

TAI

Ivy put her hand over the phone, glanced at her next client waiting, and whispered to me, "Would you mind setting up my room for me so I can get Sandra's pooch in right away. This guy won't take no for an answer." She indicated the phone.

I nodded, handed Sassy off to Ivy's lap and headed for The Groom Room. "Take care of her," I told Ivy. Sass was in to be spayed, and I was loving her up before she went under the knife.

As I passed through Ivy's cage room, I stopped to scratch the chin of a particularly adorable Labradoodle puppy, Morton. Look at me—knowing the name of an actual breed and everything. And I was finally beginning to get a handle on the whole dog wash caper, give or take the occasional over-exuberant sweetheart and the need for a remedial change of clothes. Emmett had foisted on me another advance wad of cash, and I was now on a first name basis with thrift-shop Claudia, having added to my stock of clothes and pimped out my car with pillows and another blanket.

The two-dollar T-shirt I'd donned that morning said, *Just Put Some Maple Syrup On It*, with a downward arrow. Ivy had taken one look and choked on her toast while Emmett had simply rolled his eyes and made himself scarce.

Achievement unlocked.

Plus, I'd secured a better place to park my car overnight—a quiet suburban no-exit road closer to the lake and with no time restriction between 7:00 pm and 8:00 am. I moved it there late at night and left early after a walk along the lakefront. The early morning ramble fed my soul in a way I wasn't prepared to question and was worth the shuffling around. On my first morning there, a low-lying, almost cloying milky fog hung like a solid curtain over Burlington Bay, dipping its skirts into the flat skin of the water. By noon it had gone, not a whisper of its presence to be found, and I grabbed it for the metaphor it was—about change and the possibilities that lay hidden.

I took Emmett up on his offer to use the clinic facilities, and Ivy's to make use of the washer and dryer. That meant my overall hygiene got a boost, and getting a negative result on my tests after Dion, had gone some way to relieving my stress as far as my health was concerned. In the evenings I usually grabbed a cheap takeout after I left the clinic, then nursed a coffee or a single beer in V and V while planning my next move. There was always music playing and more than enough eye candy—which had come as somewhat of a surprise—to make a solitary gay man smile.

California or Seattle were high on my preferred list of destinations, although Oregon would be cheaper to live. But the question remained about what I was going to do once I got there. I needed a career, or at least a better paying job. Jesus, listen to me—a *career*. My mother would weep for joy.

A barista job would keep me above water for a bit. I was good with coffee and the banter. Or maybe Emmett would give me a reference to help me pick up something similar.

A week in the clinic and I'd learned two things. One, I liked the camaraderie and the sense of accomplishment way more than café work, but I wasn't necessarily good at all the animal stuff, it just hurt my heart too much. I preferred cuddling to assisting Emmett excising their bits and pieces.

The second thing I'd learned was that I was actually surprisingly good at all the office stuff—the accounts, ordering, and organizational shit. *And* I liked it more than the vet tech side. But then I'd always been kind of particular about having things clean and tidy. I'd given Dion a heads-up on more than one occasion when I thought his club employees were slacking. And although he'd pat me on the head and tell me I shouldn't worry about stuff like that, he seemed to always follow up on what I said and made changes.

When the truth of that registered, it had given me pause. Dion had damn well known I wasn't useless, that I had an eye for that kind of thing, but he hadn't wanted me getting ideas. *Motherfucker.* And while I'd done Pete's café books for two years, I hadn't really thought anything of it other than a way to earn a bit of extra cash, certainly not that I might have a knack for it.

But reorganizing Emmett's appointment spreadsheets, finding those overdue accounts, sending out the reminders, and then seeing some of the money start to come in and the appreciation and relief in Emmett's eyes? Yeah, that was damn satisfying. This was Emmett's business. I might not be much help in the treatment rooms, but I'd achieved something behind the desk. And that got me thinking.

So, while I nursed my beer or coffee, chatted with Briar, or earned a nod of welcome from the gorgeously tatted Tanner behind the bar, I'd begun to put an idea together. I needed to see what my New Zealand education counted for over here, but then —holy shit, I couldn't believe I was even thinking this—*maybe* I'd look at something in the business management line. A certificate or degree or something.

My belly clenched at the very thought, and I hadn't got the words past my lips into the real world yet, but yeah, I was thinking about it. It was enough for me to feel comfortable calling home using the wine bar Wi-Fi and be honest about what had happened.

Mum answered straight away, and although it wasn't easy, I finally got the story out. Mum, bless her heart, wanted a few minutes alone with Dion and me on the next flight home, whereas Dad took a more supportive approach which kind of threw me.

Instead of his usual, non-committal 'find something steady' response, I detected almost pride in his voice as he'd told Mum to leave me alone. That I was a man and this was something I needed to do. That they had to trust me to find what I was looking for, and that coming home wasn't going to solve it for me. It hadn't in the past and it likely wouldn't now. That I needed out from under my brothers and from under Dion. That this was maybe exactly what I needed.

You could've knocked me over with a damn feather and I almost fucking cried on the spot. Because he was right. And it was exactly what I needed to hear to keep Emmett at arm's length. The last thing I needed while rebooting my life and getting back on track, was a complicated hookup.

But knowing it and doing it were two different things, and working together while dancing around each other and trying to ignore the mutual attraction in that tiny clinic space was doing my head in. Every time Emmett passed within a yard or I caught a whiff of that fresh woodsy soap he used, my antenna waved frantically and everything snapped to attention. It was mortifying, not to mention a fucking mystery.

I liked guys, obviously, and I especially enjoyed the lingering presence of an especially hot one in my vicinity, but none had ever affected me this way. With Emmett, my senses were attuned to every move, every sound, every cellular mitochondrial exchange he made, like a damn heat-seeking missile.

And he wasn't exactly making it easy on me. Brushing past my back or leaning in front of me to grab something he needed—the heat of his touch burning straight through my clothes. He may as well have branded his name on my skin and be done with it.

That he needed every single thing he so shamelessly sought in order to do his job, was beside the point. He was making it virtually impossible for me to ignore him.

The only upside? Judging by the looks I caught him sending me, he wasn't doing any better. If I'd stripped naked and burned my clothes in a pile on the waiting room floor, he couldn't have looked hungrier. The electricity zapping between us could've powered a small city for a year. And if we actually made it between a pair of sheets . . . damn, I couldn't even go there.

Another excellent reason to keep it my pants and my oversized jeans.

And what the hell was up with that? Did no one in this godforsaken place donate decent skinny jeans? I could get any damn color I wanted in a check shirt or fleece for five dollars, but not a single pair of ass-hugging jeans that I could wear to work and be proud of. It was number one on my to-buy list once I was flush.

With all these thoughts spinning hamster wheels in my head, I shut the cage on Morton and gathered his used towel from on top to add to the laundry. I spied another wet towel thrown in a cage and I took that too, then headed for the washing machine, which was nearly full. I shook out one of the towels and threw it in, then put the other in the hamper and set the machine going. To finish up, I tidied the grooming table and swept the floor. Ivy did more than enough to help me out, constantly bringing me food and babying me more than my own mother. I didn't begrudge helping her out when I could.

As if she'd heard my thoughts, Ivy stormed into the room, nostrils flared. "Lord, save me from that man. I don't give a rat's ass if his malamute's a prize-winning freak of nature, it doesn't get him onto my books this week when there are no appointments available. Do you know he wanted me to bump a regular—" She stopped mid-rant to appreciate the room. "Wow, you work fast. It looks great. Thank you." She pulled me in for a hug and the familiar scent of jasmine flooded my nostrils.

"You're welcome. Did you put Sassy back in her cage?"

"Yes. Emmett says she's next on the list."

Bugger. "I was kind of hoping he wouldn't need me for her."

She patted my arm. "He probably doesn't, not once the IV is in and she's out. He'll understand."

I shook my head. "I'm just being soft. It's all part of the job, right?"

She nodded in approval. "Good for you. Send Sandra in as you pass the waiting room, will you?" Then she suddenly grabbed my arm. "Tai? Where did Shamus go?"

I stared at her, then at the empty cages. Shamus was the cutest little jet-black Cavoodle puppy whose owner had left him for his very first groom.

"He was in the cage next to Morton."

My eyes locked on the cage I'd grabbed the bundled wet towel from. The wet *black* towel.

"Fuck." I spun and ran for the washing machine with Ivy hot on my heels, praying all the way to anyone who might be listening. *Please, no. No, no, no.*

I hit the pause button on the machine and began hauling its contents out one by one into the sink, spewing water all over the floor. "I know I shook it out first. I'm sure I did . . . fuck, what if I . . . ?"

Ivy stood with her hand on my shoulder. "Calm down. It was my fault for leaving him all cuddled up in the towel, but he seemed to like it. If you shook it out, he can't be in there."

"I know but—"

A muffled yap froze my frantic searching. "Where did that come from?"

"Not from in there." Ivy nodded at the machine as she upended the laundry basket onto the floor.

And there, looking pleased as punch with himself and none the worse for wear, sat a damp black bundle of fur, still wrapped in the towel and tail wagging.

I scooped him off the floor and cradled him to my chest. "Oh my god, I'm so sorry Shamus. I'm so, so sorry." I spun to Ivy. "I can't apologize enough. I just saw the towel and thought you'd left it there and I . . . shit. I'm such an idiot. I'll tell the owner it was all my fault."

"Shh." Ivy scratched the pup's ears. "What's there to tell? Nothing happened, and Milly's a friend. But yes, I'll let you tell her. I'm sure she'll just laugh it off. After all, it is kind of funny." She was clearly struggling not to laugh herself, but I couldn't see the humor.

"You might think it's funny now since we found him, but what if I'd put him in the machine—"

"Did you?"

"No, but—"

"Why not?" She arched a brow.

I sighed. "Because I shook out the towels like you said to make sure no grooming combs got thrown in and to get rid of most of the hair."

"Exactly. So, you didn't *nearly* do anything. You did exactly what you were supposed to."

I narrowed my gaze. "I threw your client in the laundry hamper, Ivy."

She grinned and lifted Shamus from the towel. "True. But think of all the pleasure I'm going to get retelling the story . . . over and over and over."

I could only admire her. "You're an evil woman."

She waggled her brows. "You have no idea."

Emmett stuck his head in the room and caught my eye. "Sassy's ready if you are?" His gaze flicked between Ivy and me. "What did I miss?"

"Nothing." Ivy winked at me and took Shamus back to his kennel.

Emmett eyeballed me. "You may as well spit it out. I'll get it out of her somehow."

"I doubt you'll have to try too hard." I scowled at Ivy's back. "Suffice to say, I screwed up, again."

Emmett rubbed his hands together far too eagerly for my liking. "Oh, I can't wait to hear this."

"Then find me later." Ivy closed the door on Shamus's kennel and dried her hands on her apron. "But I think Tai needs to make a 'stop and think' sign for the top of the washing machine, right Tai?"

"A warning sign?" Emmett turned to me. "Do I even want to know?"

"I hate you both." I threw the balled-up towel in my hand Ivy's way, but she ducked it neatly and kept laughing.

EMMETT

"This was a good idea." I stretched my legs out on the bench beside Tai and reached for one of the sandwiches he'd grabbed from the deli on our walk to the lake. The boardwalk hummed with workers chatting as they strolled and enjoyed the unseasonably warm and still October day. It was . . . nice, companionable, frustratingly friendly.

The Burlington-Port Kent ferry that we'd taken only five days before pointed its stern our way as it made its turn around the breakwater and headed across Lake Champlain. It was an unnecessary reminder of that blistering first kiss I'd shared with Tai and everything I was trying not to think about.

With Sassy successfully spayed and tucked in her warm cage to recover, Tai had suggested a walk to shake the morning off, and I'd eagerly agreed, unable to remember the last time I'd taken my lunch anywhere other than my desk, at least not since Lu had passed.

Ivy happily waved us off with a knowing smile, which I'd dutifully ignored. She meant well and just wanted to see me with a life beyond just the clinic and parenthood, but it wasn't as easy as that. Tai might be under my skin, in my shower fantasies, and nudging at my heart in ways I couldn't explain, but he was also right. It made no sense to start something when he was leaving, and the truth was, I'd never been a hookup kind of guy either. Boringly serious and monogamous all the way.

Maybe that's why I'd never pursued men in the same way I had women. It required effort. Women, I knew. Women, I had a plan in my head for. A way of approaching, of dating, a set of mutually understood "rules of engagement." Men? Who the hell knew how that worked? Not me.

Heaven knew I was out of my depth sexually. The only experience I'd ever had was quick and anonymous—which didn't ring my bell. I'd never entertained the idea of dating a man or being with a man long-term. But Tai was messing with my head about all of that. I couldn't pretend anymore that what I felt for him was simply lust. That ship had sailed after the weekend, and it was only getting worse. What I felt was different. Different and all kinds of complicated.

He sunk down on the bench next to me, stretching his legs, and when our thighs brushed together, I practically choked on my bacon and egg salad sandwich, sending chunks of lettuce and bread down the front of my jacket. *Jesus Christ*. I was a basket case. Tai slapped my back, harder than I felt was entirely warranted, and with a smirk on his lips.

"You okay?"

"Fine." I scooted across to put a bit more room between us and brushed off my jacket.

Tai gave no indication he noticed, just grabbed a second sandwich and started to eat. A minute later he asked, "So, has he texted yet?"

We were both staring out over the lake, the water dressed in smart navy blue and shimmering silver, still rolling from the wash of the ferry. Small waves broke in sharp whispers against the stones of the shore just yards from where we sat. All in all, it was pretty magical. I really needed to come down more often.

I broke my gaze to check my phone for the umpteenth time. "No. What if he missed out? Do you think I should text him?"

It was audition day at Leo's school and he and Tai had been rehearsing all week at the reception desk.

"Pfft," Tai scoffed. "He was reading those lines like a champ yesterday. They probably just ran over time, or he's playing with his mates at recess. Give him till we get back."

"But he said he'd sneak into the bathroom and text. What if he forgot his lines?"

Tai faced me with a broad smile. "We aren't talking Shakespeare here, Emmett. He had them down pat after just two days."

"Oh, right." I took another bite of my sandwich and continued to worry.

Tai cracked open the orange juice I loved and handed it over. "Here, drink. We didn't stop for coffee this morning. You need fluids."

I took it with thanks and emptied half of it in one swallow, trying to ignore just how damn touched I was by the fact he already knew what juice I liked and when I wasn't being careful with myself.

He watched me drink, then went back to his sandwich. "He'll be fine whether he gets it or not, you know that, right?"

I didn't, not really. "It's the first school thing he's shown any real interest in since . . . well, since Lu died. I just want him to be happy."

A warm hand landed on my thigh. "He's going to be fine, Emmett. He knows he might not get it; we've talked about that. He'll be sad for a bit but he'll be okay. He can help backstage. He's a great kid. His happiness doesn't depend on the opportunity to participate in an albeit dubious reinterpretation of a Lewis Carroll story. He has you, and that's far more important."

I shoved my half-eaten sandwich back in its bag and dropped it in my lap. "I'm being ridiculous, aren't I?"

Tai squeezed my thigh, which apparently had a direct connection with my ridiculous heart and sent my pulse racing in my throat.

"No, you're being a dad. And I might not know much about it, but I can recognize a good one when I see one." He took the bag from my lap, ferreted the remaining sandwich out, and handed it back to me. "Eat. You've got Malorie Walters coming in to discuss her overdue account when you get back. You're gonna need sustenance if her snotty return emails to me are anything to go by. She's turned down every payment option I've given her, including micropayments that would likely see her six feet under before even half the account was paid."

"Oh god." I forced down the lump of bread stuck in my throat and slumped on the bench. "Remind me how much she owes."

"Four and a half thousand. Her Chow had hip dysplasia and she opted for the most expensive implants. She paid some when she picked him up, but nothing since."

I groaned. "Jesus Christ. I remember the woman was a nightmare at the time. Nothing was ever good enough. I'm not sure we're going to be able to convince her to pay the rest."

"Then you put it out as a bad debt like we talked about."

I spun to face him. "A vet practice relies on word of mouth. I can't afford to have her bad mouth me in a town this size."

He took a deep breath and I could tell he was weighing his words. "A vet practice relies on people *paying their bills* to operate. You can't afford to let the Malorie Walters of the world take you for a four-thousand-dollar ride. And you have a bazillion clients who love you to spread the truth about how great you are."

I chewed my cheek, then nodded. "Okay, you're right." Because he was. My practice did okay, but this newly discovered debt was putting a big dent in my profit.

"And while we're on the subject—" He turned back to the lake and took a guzzle of water. "Your accounting software is older than God, Emmett, close to its last breath, and I don't think even he could resurrect it."

I snorted.

"What would you say about me looking into a possible upgrade? Just see what's out there for you to choose from. There's much smarter software that helps track your debt and trends and a lot more. I did some investigating when Dion upgraded his clubs."

I stared at him. "I can't afford something complicated."

He turned to face me. "I know. I've been in your books, remember? I thought maybe I could talk to Briar? See what the bookstore uses. And then I could call that vet tech in Colebury. See what they use."

My cheeks warmed. "Okay, sure. Just don't mention the debt."

He held my gaze. "Did you really think I would?"

No. "No, I didn't. Sorry."

His mouth curved up in a slow smile. "It's me who should be sorry. You're just protecting your business, as you should. Remember that when Malodorous Malorie tries to weasel out of what she owes you."

I barked out a laugh. "Malodorous Malorie? Well, I'm sure you'll protect me. You seem to be good at it."

He looked at me strangely, those dark eyes intent on something apparently only he could see. "You're damn right I will."

The force behind his words kicked the dust off old feelings that had been buried in my chest for too long, and I quickly glanced away.

Feelings about safe places and safe hands.

Tai cleared his throat. "Emmett, I—"

He stopped when my phone pinged with an incoming text. I opened it immediately and fist-pumped the air. "He got the part."

Tai whooped loud enough to draw a few stares, the genuine elation on his face making me want to pull him into my arms and kiss him until we were both breathless. Instead, I held up my hand for a high five which he met enthusiastically.

I fired off a congratulations to Leo and leaped to my feet. "Come on, let's go squeeze Malodorous Malorie's balls."

He grinned, grabbed my trash, and threw it in the bin along with his own. "She's not due for another hour. If you don't need me, would it be okay if I made a detour to Briar? I've only got a few days left and I'd like to ask about that software before I leave."

Oh. Right. A few days. "Yeah, yeah, of course. Good idea. It's funny right? Feels like you've been here forever."

He sent another of those strange looks. "Yeah. Yeah, it does."

9
TAI

Based on what Briar told me, the accounting software the bookstore used *could* work, but it wasn't entirely suited to a vet clinic. With that in mind, I planned to call Penley that afternoon to ask about their system. But while I was in the bookstore, after checking with Emmett, I ordered a couple of basic business strategy books aimed at vet practices in particular. It couldn't hurt.

"You doing his books for him now?" Briar raised a brow.

I avoided that perceptive gaze. "Just helping out. I used to do them for a café I worked for, so it's no big deal, and Emmett's pretty busy."

"Aha. Here's your receipt."

I grabbed it and headed out before he could ask anything more.

"The Booklover meeting is on Friday," he called to my back and then laughed. "I'll save you a seat."

It had become a standing joke between us.

"Cold day in hell, Briar." I waved backwards over my shoulder. "Cold day in hell."

Only when I was outside did I finally register the brochure in my hand that Briar had stuffed the receipt into. A pamphlet for Burlington University.

Sneaky little shit.

I made it to the clinic in record time, jogging to avoid the stiff lake breeze that had appeared from nowhere in the twenty minutes I'd been in the bookstore. In just a week I'd learned never to underestimate a wind off the lake. The weather in the town could be crazy. In its mission eastward, the breeze had whipped up a rainbow of fall leaves that danced up the sidewalk and collected in doorways like piles of crunchy red and gold cornflakes.

I kicked a mound of them from the entrance of the clinic and scooted inside, pulling at the zip on my jacket. "Damn, what happened to the temperature?" I hung my coat and turned to where Ivy sat behind the desk. The scowl she wore froze me in place.

"What happened?"

She flicked her head toward the waiting room.

"Hey, baby. Long time."

Fuck. I spun slowly until I was face-to-face with Dion, looking as handsome as ever in fitted black jeans tucked into black leather boots, a black sweater, brown-and-black check scarf, and a tan woolen knee-length coat that stank of money and more than likely other men's cologne.

The rest of the waiting room was empty, thank god. But it wouldn't be for long.

He reached for my hand, but I jerked it back. "Good to see you. Looking as beautiful as ever."

"You don't get to call me baby," I snapped. "And you sure as hell don't get to touch me. How did you find me?"

"It wasn't that hard. This is a butthole town. I asked in a few shops and I was soon pointed this way. Quite a little fan club you've got going." Dion glanced Ivy's way. "Can we maybe talk in private?"

"No. I've got nothing to say to you. Have a nice trip back to Boston." I turned and almost got to the desk when he grabbed my arm.

Ivy sucked a breath between her teeth, but I caught her eye and shook my head.

I yanked my arm free. "Touch me again and I'll have Ivy call the police."

"Damn right," Ivy practically growled.

Dion frowned. I rarely talked back to him when we were together, and I certainly never threatened him. It was undoubtedly one of the many mistakes I'd made.

"Come on. It's me, Tai. You surely can't think I'd hurt you."

My eyes rolled before I could stop them. "Maybe not physically. But you hurt me many, many times, Dion. In fact, I've spent the last week wondering what I ever saw in you and why the hell I stayed after the first time you cheated on me. You're a lying, cheating asshole and I'm well rid of you. So, in case you didn't hear it the first time, goodbye. Have a nice life."

"Okay, okay." He raised his hands and backed off a step. "I admit the cheating was unforgivable. I *was* an asshole, and yes, I took you for granted. I'm sorry. You didn't deserve it."

I stared at him, jaw clenched to stop from gaping. Dion never apologized, never admitted anything.

"And yes, you should probably walk away from me. That would be the sensible thing to do."

What the hell?

"But maybe it's not the *right* thing to do." He ran his fingers through his thick mop of lush black hair and pulled the cowlick down over his forehead in that way that always made me soft for him. "I know I fucked up, but I'm asking you to give me another chance."

Was he nuts? "I already did that, in case you'd forgotten, and you fucked that one up as well."

His head dropped and he looked almost despairing. "I know. I know. But I didn't understand how important you were until you weren't there anymore. You leaving was probably the best thing to happen to me. I've missed you so much. I needed that kick in the pants—"

In the fucking balls, more like it.

"—to wake me up to how I really felt." He took a step closer. "You know I love you, ba— Tai."

I snorted. "Well, of course, that makes all the difference."

Ivy choked on a laugh.

Dion threw her an irritated glance. "Look, I'm sorry it's taken me this long to get that I love you. But I do now. What happened last week won't happen again."

Was he serious? "No, it won't, Dion. Because I'm not coming back."

Dion took another step forward. "I haven't slept, Tai. Not since you left. I've been so damn worried. You know how hopeless you are in new places. Remember when you first got to Boston? I had to send friends with you just to make sure you got to the grocery store."

Son of a bitch. "You *sent* people to make sure no one flirted or talked with me. You didn't give a damn whether I got to the grocery store or not, only that I stayed away from other men. And while we're on the subject, those *friends* you sent with me to keep me *safe*? *They* were the ones you should've worried about. Every one of those friends has tried to kiss, grope, or fuck me at some point in the last three years."

Dion's eyes blew wide, which gave me all kinds of pleasure. *Fuck him.*

But I wasn't done. "So you might want to be careful who you call friend. And you don't miss *me* at all. You only miss getting to show me off and then take me home and fuck me. Have everyone know I belong to you. Well, I don't, not anymore. In fact, I never did."

His gaze narrowed and yeah, there it was. That familiar arrogance, conceit, and narcissistic entitlement finally breaking the surface. This man I knew only too well.

I mentally slapped myself. How had I ever found that arrogance sexy? How had I ever thought that being with him made me a more worthwhile person? That just because a successful man wanted me meant I wasn't a fuck up?

I almost winced as the scales ripped from my eyes. Because it wasn't just him I was seeing clearly. He might've treated me badly, but I'd let him. I'd let him because I *wanted* that reflection off him, even if it had been a lie. But it was a lie I didn't have to live with any longer.

His finger stabbed at me. "How the fuck do you think you're going to survive? You came here with a single fucking suitcase. You've got no money, no skills. Everything you have, I gave you. None of it belongs to you. All you can do is make coffee and fuck, moderately well—"

"He has a lot of skills."

"Butt out." Dion shook his finger at Ivy and I was done. I shoved him back. "Don't you dare talk to her like that. It doesn't matter what I do or how much money I make, *anything* will be a million times better than living with your sorry ass. I'll survive just fine."

"How?" He pushed back, getting right up in my face until I could smell the familiar spice of his Tom Ford cologne.

It almost made me retch.

"Do you really think a shit job like this is going to work for you?" He stared me down, but I held my ground. "What are you making? Ten bucks an hour? That wouldn't even keep you in lip gloss, sweetheart, and you're hardly the roughing-it type."

"No," I fumed. "That's you, not me. I can rough it just fine. I never needed all that shit you bought."

"But you never turned it down either, did you?"

My stomach turned. "No, and I'll be forever ashamed of that."

His steely eyes flashed. "Whatever. But I know you better than you think.'

"You don't know me at all." I raised my voice to match his. "You never did."

"And so now, you think *this* is you?" he scoffed. "This cozy little thing you've got going here with the hot veterinarian?"

My eyes popped. "That's not what—"

"Don't bother. One look at the man and it wasn't hard to put together. He's hot in that hapless, homely kind of way, I guess. Although I have to say, I wouldn't have thought he'd have enough going on in the sack to keep you interested. A little too . . . backwoods for your partying tastes."

I had Dion's shirt in my fist before I knew it, shoving him back into the display shelving. "Shut your mouth. There's nothing going on—"

Dion laughed and stroked my cheek. "Oh baby, you've got a crush. How sweet."

I leaped back like he'd slapped me. "Shut your mouth."

He came at me again. "But I'm willing to overlook that minor indiscretion. Payback and all that. I get it. Maybe I can find us a third who looks like the young vet, if that's your thing. Would you like that?"

My hands fisted but I managed to keep them at my side, just. This was Emmett's business. "Ivy, call the police."

"On it." She reached for the phone and Dion immediately raised his hands.

"Okay. Calm down, I'm leaving."

"What's going on out here?" Emmett strode into the room, followed by a client with her cat in a carry crate. By the woman's bug-eyed look, I knew they'd caught at least some of the conversation. Her eyes darted between all three of us, half-nervous, half-curious, and I wondered how long until word spread about whatever she'd heard.

"Go on, Phyllis." Ivy scuttled the reluctant woman out the door. "It's not for your ears. I'll email you the account."

"I repeat." Emmett stared hard at Dion. "What the hell's going on here, and who the fuck are you?"

Dion smirked and offered his hand. "I'm Tai's boyfriend—"

"Ex-boyfriend," I corrected. "And he's just leaving."

Emmett accepted Dion's hand, which kind of surprised and disappointed me at the same time. But then he used the grip to tug Dion closer.

"Well, Tai's *ex*-boyfriend, I suggest you go ahead and do what he says, right now, and stay the fuck out of my clinic." He held Dion in place for a few seconds longer, eye to eye, while my heart beat loudly in my chest.

Emmett was supporting me, defending me. He had my back, and I couldn't put into words what that meant, other than it felt good. Really good.

Dion freed his hand, stepped back, and brushed his coat off. "Don't worry, I'm leaving." Then he turned to me. "Your pet has some teeth. Who'd have thought? You better be sure about this.

Cos the offer closes the minute I leave here. I won't ask a second time."

"Good. That'll save me repeating my answer. Now fuck off."

Out the corner of my eye, I saw Emmett smile and warmth flooded my chest.

"I want the phone and the car back." Dion held out his hand.

I reached in my pocket and slammed the phone into his hand. "The car's in my name."

"I don't give a fuck. I bought it. It's mine. You want me out of your life, you give my shit back."

I stared at him, panic curling low in my belly. Without the car, I was screwed. I'd have nowhere to sleep and no way to get to a job and back if I had to. And the bastard knew it. It might be legally mine, but I'd always intended to give it back. I'd just hoped to hold on to it until I was in a better place.

"It's got my stuff in it."

"Then get it out."

Emmett interrupted, "What about Tai's things in your apartment?"

Dion's lip curled. "If he wants any of that crap, he can come and get it himself. Otherwise I'm throwing it out."

"Why you—" Emmett took a step forward, but I stopped him with a hand to his arm.

"There's nothing I can't replace," I told him. Then to Dion, "Throw it out."

He looked surprised.

"I'll drive you to get your things." Emmett's warm body pressed alongside mine. To Dion, he said, "*You* can wait in the mall, asshole. I won't have you in my clinic a second longer. When we've emptied the car, *I'll* bring you the keys. Me, not Tai, understand?"

He looked pissed but nodded.

Emmett turned to me. "But only if that's okay with you?"

It was. I'd said all I wanted, and if I didn't have to see Dion again, so much better. I nodded.

Emmett breathed a sigh and turned back to Dion. "Then as Tai has already told you, fuck off."

Mortified didn't even begin to cover it. I couldn't face Emmett after bringing such a shit show to his business. I also needed to work out what the hell I was going to do now that I didn't have somewhere to sleep. And so, after I cleared my car and Emmett handed the keys back to Dion, I found an endless amount of busy-work in order to avoid any and all conversation with Emmett. Cowardly? You bet.

I called Shamus's owner and fessed up to my near-miss disaster with him that morning and she, as Ivy predicted, laughed till she almost cried and then told me she'd lost Shamus for thirty minutes just a couple of weeks before, only to find him sound asleep under the blanket on the floor at the foot of her bed. A theme was emerging.

Ivy had, of course, offered me her pull-out sofa bed for the night while I decided what I was going to do, but I turned it down because . . . well, fuck if I really knew why, other than it seemed too close, too much to expect, too . . . easy. Of course, I regretted it five minutes later, but I wasn't about to go back and admit I'd been an ass. Besides, I'd said I wanted to do this on my own, and I did.

Ivy had tip-toed around me after that, which was so *not* Ivy and I wasn't sure what to think about that. Emmett had also left me alone, although the pointed looks he kept throwing my way made it clear I wasn't fooling him for a second. But I just didn't have it in me to talk about any of it. Whatever he and Ivy thought of me after seeing the jackass I'd spent three years with, I didn't want to know. Hell, I disgusted myself. God knew what they thought of me.

I'd thought life was a pack of complicated shit before Dion tracked me down; it had just got a whole lot worse. Not having a car crashed my options significantly, took away my safe base and my place to sleep. I might've found some balls at long last, but they were nowhere near hairy enough to face roughing it on the streets, not in a Vermont fall that seemed designed to freeze those fuckers right off you if you weren't careful.

But one thing was crystal clear. I didn't have the luxury of biding my time in Burlington for any longer than absolutely necessary, no matter how cute Emmett was. The attraction between us wasn't going anywhere. I needed to make a decision and get my shit together. And I had the inklings of a plan that might make my West Coast musings a realistic option.

My brother James had a friend in Seattle. I'd met the guy at James' wedding. David someone. We'd seen a bit of him and his wife while they were there and I'd got on well with them both. They were the only contact I knew, but just maybe they'd be okay with me couch surfing for a few days while I got myself organized. I'd have to check with James first, but it was a definite option.

I wasn't going home to New Zealand with my tail between my legs. Even in the middle of this hot mess, it still felt like I was on the cusp of *something*. Like I was hanging onto a bucking bronc as tightly as I could and I had to make the bell. This unholy shit was only eight seconds of my life on that damn horse, and I was determined not to lose my seat. Eight seconds that could define the rest of my life, and for once I wasn't going to fucking run.

And so I kept busy, kept out of Emmett's way, and kept thinking. I spoke to Penley at the other vet clinic and got the name of the software they used. It sounded much more suitable than the bookstore option. I got a price and emailed the information to Emmett, because I was too damn chickenshit to simply go and talk to him.

Malodorous Malorie arrived late, because of course she bloody did, all fifty-something years of her, buttoned up in a hideous cowpat green woolen suit that seemed determined to strangle her body, a silk shirt complete with ubiquitous jeweled scarf clip, and an expression sour enough to curdle milk. Emmett told me her husband owned three successful businesses in town and a couple of farms, and that as far as he knew, she could well afford to pay but was known to mess people around.

We traded blistering glances across the waiting room after I asked her to take a seat. We'd had more than one conversation over email and phone, and she clearly wasn't happy with me.

Screw her. I made her wait longer than necessary because . . . well, because she was a bitch who was fucking with Emmett, and I didn't feel a single ounce of guilt.

When I figured she'd stewed long enough and looked suitably pissed off and ready to scale the walls, I apologized sweetly for keeping her waiting and delivered her into Emmett's office. On Emmett's surprise invitation, I stayed and hovered in the background as they talked, printouts at the ready regarding every cent she owed.

She wriggled and blustered and threatened, but in the end, she paid, brushing aside our repeated offers for her to drip feed the payments over two years. Emmett was clearly uncomfortable with the whole confrontation, but he held his ground and I was so damn proud of him.

That nasty task done, I disappeared once again into the kennel area to clean the already spotless room, and Emmett let me. I wasn't sure how much rope he was going to give me, but all thoughts of trying to spin it out for the entire day vanished when running feet in the corridor turned into ten-year-old arms wrapped around my neck.

"How's Sassy?" Leo practically shouted into my ear, quickly followed by, "I got the part!"

EMMETT

I leaned on the kennel room doorjamb and watched Leo throw his arms around Tai's neck. He was vibrating with excitement, gushing thank yous and details about the audition. Still jabbering away, he turned his attention to a sleepy Sassy, feeding her all the same news through the mesh of her cage. Sassy begrudgingly opened one eye, blinked a couple of times, then closed it again. Not that it made any difference to Leo's chattering as he slid open the cage door and stroked her gently.

But it was Leo's effortless affection with Tai that had stolen the breath from my lungs and shoved a lump down my throat the size of Malorie's ego. It was running a loop in my brain that wasn't going away anytime soon. I tried to catch his eye but he was still avoiding any direct communication between us, and I got it. I did. He was embarrassed and hurt, and simply telling him he didn't need to be wasn't going to make it any easier.

I hated confrontation, which only made my instinctive reaction to that prick Dion kind of astonishing. I'd been all up in the asshole's face before it even registered what I was doing, and although I didn't want to dwell too long on the whys of that, I knew. What the hell Tai had ever seen in that manipulating bastard, escaped me. But then, guys like that knew exactly where to find people's weaknesses and pick away at them. And Tai's weren't exactly under wraps. A smart, gorgeous guy who didn't believe in himself. All Dion had to do was find that spot and start digging.

And I wanted to punch him out for just thinking it.

Case in point.

After all that, Malorie had been a walk in the park. I knew damn well she could afford to pay her account, but without Tai's pushing, I would've likely let it go, and I couldn't afford to do that anymore. The clinic should've been doing better than it was, mostly down to my slack oversight. I'd let things slide after Lu died.

A week with Tai at the desk had made things crystal clear. I needed to take back control. I needed help, but the right kind; a proper vet tech and a separate office manager. Oh, and apparently, a new accounting system. Tai was almost completely unaware of his natural talents.

After running out of steam, Leo closed the cage door on a sleeping Sassy and grabbed hold of Tai's hands. He spun him in a circle, their laughter quick to draw Ivy from the desk to see what the hell was going on.

She elbowed me none too gently in the ribs as we watched their antics. "Look at that."

I knew exactly what she meant. Neither of us had seen Leo like this in years.

She tugged at my sleeve. "Come with me."

I followed her into the nearest treatment room and she closed the door.

"You like each other," she said bluntly, keeping her voice low. "Don't even try to deny it. How you reacted with his ex tells me everything I need to know. And Leo likes him too. I don't want to know if anything has happened between you or not. But you're an idiot if you let him just walk out of here," she hissed. "And you know damn well, he will."

"Am I an idiot, though?" I fired back. "Because I don't know if that's right. If I were *out* and if Leo knew, then *maybe* I'd risk taking that step. But the idea of Tai and me is way too complicated. I'm not out. Tai's not hanging around. He's working for me as an *employee*—do you even understand what position that puts me in—and Leo could get hurt."

Ivy pursed her lips. "All of that's true. And keep your damn voice down. But there *are* things under your control. You could choose to come out if you wanted, totally up to you, of course, but you could. You could actually talk to Leo, just in general, without telling him anything direct. See where he's at in his thinking about sexuality and the idea of you even dating again—*anyone*.

"You could actually ask Tai if he's interested in staying; he's said nothing of his plans to me. And as for working for you? This isn't some corporation, Emmett. You could simply talk to the guy. Because, frankly, I'm not sure I can survive another few days in the pall of all this suffocating sexual frustration—you two making moon eyes at each other through thinly veiled snark and innuendo while trying to pretend you're not. And you're both shit at hiding it. So why not do us all a favor and take the guy for a drink *or something?*"

I snorted. "Tell me how you really feel."

"Which brings me to my final point on the matter."

Dear God. Queer dating advice from a gray-haired sixty-two-year-old straight woman? *Kill me now.* "I can't wait."

She shot me a withering glare. "Don't be sarcastic. All I'm going to say is that Lu died four years ago, son, and maybe it's time to rethink your whole strategy, because clearly staying in the closet isn't working."

I sighed. "But I'm also a father to a son who's lost his mom and who knows nothing about this part of me. Where do I even begin to have *that* conversation?"

She shrugged. "That's for you to figure out. All I know is that since that young man walked into this clinic a week ago, I've seen more of the old Emmett than I've seen in years. The man who loved life and couldn't wait to see what was around the corner."

A fist clenched in my gut. "Yeah, well look where that got me. That *naïve* guy never saw bad stuff happening; never imagined getting a call to say his wife was dead in a car accident; never imagined consoling his son through the nightmares that followed; never—" I couldn't finish past the lump in my throat.

Her arms wrapped around me. "But you got through, Emmett. And you got Leo through as well. I'm not saying you should take a chance with this particular guy—although I can't deny I like him, and you like him too—but that maybe it's time to start living again, or at least thinking about what that act of will might look like, and all of its possible variations."

She gave me a final squeeze and then headed back to her rooms, while I returned to the kennel room to watch my son chat with a guy I barely knew and yet who'd somehow spun this warm web around me that I couldn't shake. And after the confrontation with his ex, I knew Tai would be planning to leave. It's what I'd do. I could see it in his eyes, and in the way he was so carefully avoiding me. He had no place to sleep tonight, but he'd already turned Ivy down, and he'd do the same to me.

"Dad, can we go for Pizza at Tito's, please, please, please? To celebrate."

Tai snorted and waggled his eyebrows my way, and the shock of it, to have him look at me again, for any reason, filled me with warmth.

"Sounds like the perfect celebration," he said.

I narrowed my eyes in jest. "You're not helping." Then I looked to Leo who was practically bursting out of his skin. "Yeah, okay."

"Really?" Leo jumped up and down. "Holy sh—shipwrecks. On a Thursday? That's awesome. Tai's coming too, right?"

Fuck. My gaze jerked up to Tai, who'd suddenly gone pale, somewhat of an accomplishment considering the deep olive of his skin. "Yes, of course he can. He's the one who really helped, right?" I wasn't about to let any excuse pass to get Tai close to me again.

Tai's expression told me he knew exactly what I was doing and what he thought about it.

"Yes!" Leo spun Tai around again and I watched Tai's expression soften and warm. He went to his knees and pulled Leo against him. "You'd have been fine without me. I just helped get your ducks in a row, that's all. The talent was all yours, kiddo."

My heart squeezed as it always did when Tai called Leo kiddo, and even though Leo had to be used to it now, his eyes shone brightly.

"A lesson about talent we could all learn." I eyeballed Tai, who rolled his eyes in reply. "How many clients have I got left?" I checked with him.

"Glen Holden's spaniel is the last for the day," Tai answered.

"Good. We're going for pizza right after so you better be ready. Both of you. We'll come back and pick Sassy up afterwards, okay?"

"Yes!" Leo took off, no doubt to share this news with Ivy, leaving Tai and me alone.

"You didn't have to do that," Tai said quietly, his face a mask.

Oh sweetheart, you have no idea. "I wanted to. And you deserve to celebrate with Leo. He wants you there."

Something passed behind Tai's eyes that I couldn't read, and he dropped his head. "He's a great kid."

"He is." I tipped his chin up with my fingers and smiled. "Been a hell of a day, right, and not just the unexpected visitor?" I grinned.

He snorted. "Ivy told you, huh?"

Almost immediately. "I thought it was . . fucking hilarious." I broke into laughter and he walloped me on the arm.

"I could've drowned the poor little guy."

"But you didn't, because you did what you were supposed to," I pointed out. "Hell, I could hurt animals every day if I didn't stick to my routine checklists and do what I was supposed to. So, enough with the self-flagellation, on all counts."

Tai held my gaze. "Okay."

"Stay at my house tonight." The words were out before I knew it and I saw him wince.

"No."

"Please? You don't have anywhere to sleep. I won't allow it."

He cocked a brow.

Shit. "I'm sorry. I understand *why* you want to stand on your own, especially after meeting your asshole ex. What the fuck is it with that guy?"

"He's a narcissistic bastard. I think I understood that pretty soon after I arrived here. It just took a while to do what I should've done a lot earlier. I'll stay in a hostel tonight; it's fine. Briar gave me the name of one on that first day. And I need some space to think. I'll take what I need for tonight, but if it's okay with you, I'll leave the rest in your car, just to be safe. I can get it tomorrow."

"Sure."

He looked relieved. "Thank you. And I'm sorry, again. I wish you hadn't seen all that shit with Dion. I'm such an id—"

"Stop." I put a hand to his chest and felt his heart thump against my palm. He glanced down and I let it fall.

But he caught it and then held my gaze. "I'm sorry he came to the clinic. I should've known he'd do something like that when I didn't answer his texts."

"No," I said, barely able to focus past the warm feel of my hand in his. "He's a manipulative bastard. I can see exactly why you stayed, what he did to you. There's nothing to apologize for. And I was so fucking proud of how you handled him, what you said."

The corners of his mouth twitched. "Yeah?"

"Yeah." I turned my hand and threaded our fingers together. "Whatever made you stay with him, you're not that guy anymore. I suspect you haven't been that guy for a long time. Maybe this was just the right opportunity."

He stared at me for a few seconds and then leaned in and

brushed his lips over mine. "You're a good man, Emmett. Thank you." He untangled his hand. "Now can we finish this damn day and get some pizza?"

I laughed and clapped him on the shoulder. "You have the best ideas."

EMMETT

Tanner strode to meet me from the loading bay at the back of V and V, a wry smile on his normally taciturn face. "Thanks for coming." He clasped my hand in his.

I nodded. "No problem. As I said, I had to bring Leo, so can we make it quick?"

Tanner stuck his head inside the bar and called one of his staff. "Can you keep an eye on Emmet's car for a minute? Leo's inside."

The guy nodded.

Tanner clapped him on the back and headed inside.

"Thanks," I said in passing to the guy as I followed Tanner in.

For a Thursday night, V and V was pumping, most of the crowd focused on the singer at the mic.

Tai.

I drew a sharp breath, gripped by the mere sight of him. For all that Tai was clearly well on the way to being smashed, he still captivated every scrap of attention in the room, as always. With his head thrown back, smooth olive skin luminous under the lights, his black silky hair tumbling in a waterfall almost to his shoulders, eyes closed, and with his slim, tight body sliding in sinuous moves with the rhythm, he was intoxicating. Not to mention he was belting out a pretty damn good rendition of Crowded House's "Don't Dream It's Over," and I couldn't help the smile that split my face.

"He's something, right?" Tanner said from right next to me, jolting me back to reality.

I swallowed hard. "Yeah. Yeah, he is."

Tanner studied me with something close to amusement. "He's got a great voice and the crowd is enjoying it, which is the only reason we haven't taken him off yet, although we did turn the volume down." He chuckled. "Look, I know he's not strictly your responsibility—"

"No, that's fine." I still couldn't drag my eyes away. "You did the right thing." I took a minute to gather my thoughts, watching as Tai stumbled a little while attempting a circle of his stool. "Good lord, how on earth did he get into that state? We only left him two hours ago."

Tanner raised a curious brow.

"Leo, Tai, and I all went to Tito's to celebrate Leo getting a part in the school play."

"Oh. Right."

I ignored Tanner's stare.

"He started with a couple of beers and then someone bought him a shot, and that was that," Tanner explained. "There are a couple of us serving tonight, and I lost track of the number he'd thrown back or I would've stopped him sooner. Before we knew it he was at the mic and . . . well, you can see for yourself."

I certainly could. As could everyone else. Tai was going to be mortified come morning. "He's had a . . . difficult day. But you're right. He's got a great voice. I'm sorry if he's been a problem."

Tanner's gaze swept the room. "Nah, they've been pretty amused by it, to be honest. Plus, we don't get too many looking like him around here too often. A guy like that attracts attention. He's been good for business. I think a few of these guys were waiting to try their luck when he was done."

I gave Tanner a sharp look.

"Don't worry," he reassured. "I was keeping a close eye on things." Then he chuckled. "But the floors are going to need an extra mop to clean up the drool."

I looked around and yeah, there were more than a few sets of hungry eyes locked on Tai, male *and* female. My hackles rose with a stab of possessiveness I'd forgotten I was capable of.

"Jon even accompanied him on stage for a song before he had to go home," Tanner continued. "I suggested I call Tai an Uber at the same time, but he said he didn't have a home. That's when I called you."

I blew out a sigh. "Good call. And thanks for keeping an eye on him. I'll take over now." I felt Tanner's eyes on me.

"He's a good-looking man."

I couldn't look for fear Tanner would see the truth. "I guess."

He snorted. "Okay, well, I'll leave him to you, then."

"Thanks."

"No problem. I'm thinking he's in good hands."

I finally met his gaze. "He is."

"He spoke well of you."

"Me?" I gulped.

"Yes, you. Said you were a great boss, and that Leo was a wonderful kid. That Ivy was like a mother to him and the best groomer in the world." He snorted. "Of course, he was drunk as shit by that stage."

I glared at him.

He simply grinned. "But truthfully, he spent the first hour being sad as all fuck. Then when I asked him how the job was going, he lit up like sunshine. He likes the clinic, apparently. He likes you. And if he really doesn't have a home, maybe he'll consider staying in Burlington?"

How I wished. "He's just passing through. His life is . . . complicated, at the moment. He needs to find himself, I guess."

"Mmm. No law says a person has to do that alone, as far as I remember. We're a good community to have at your back. You of all people know that, Emmett."

I did.

Tanner turned to watch Tai again who was just finishing up his number. "Tell him if he wants to come back sometime on *actual* open-mic night, he can have another go. Preferably when he's sober."

I laughed. "I will. And thanks again."

"You need help to get him out?"

"Nah. I don't think so. Where's his jacket?"

Tanner grabbed it from a chair and handed it to me. "Tell him he's welcome here any time, and maybe we'll see you back *with him* next time."

My gaze narrowed. "I'm not sure what you mean. I just said he's not staying."

Tanner laughed. "Nothing to be upset about. Just that it's been a while for you, now. Life's crazy right? You never know what's around the corner."

He left and his words hung in my head like an executioner's blade of truth.

I, of all people, knew that life could rip something from you or drop something special at your doorstep with no warning. And that either way, you were generally ill-equipped to deal with whatever it was.

I was no more prepared for Tai's appearance in my life and the way he rattled my sexuality and my comfortable routine than I'd been when I'd first set eyes on Lu across that room, or the day I'd taken the call that took her away and imploded my world. And the fact I was even putting all of those things together should have shocked me far more than it did.

But watching Tai take a shaky bow while trying to get the mic back into its holder, I realized one thing: I was a lot more worried that he'd leave without ever getting a chance to know him better than I was about coming out.

Tai greeted me with a huge smile and open arms, which drew no small amount of amused interest from the audience, most of whose faces I knew at least in passing and some a lot better. More than a few were clients.

"Hey, Emmett. What you doin here?'

"Giving you a lift. Time to go, Neil Finn. Here put this on." I helped Tai fumble his way into his jacket and then wrapped an arm around his waist and led him from the stage.

"This is my wonderful boss," Tai said loudly, aiming to plant a kiss on my cheek but getting my ear instead.

My face flamed.

"He was great," someone called out from the back.

"Give him a raise," shouted another.

"Yeah, gimme a raise, Emmett," Tai slurred in my ear, and a strong waft of Jim Beam hit my nostrils. I almost reeled from the fumes alone. *Holy shit.*

Plus, hell yeah, I'd like to give Tai a raise. And if there was a shade brighter than scarlet, I think my cheeks had that sucker nailed.

I squeezed Tai's waist to keep him upright. "Say goodnight, Tai," I told him.

"Goodnight, Tai," Tai called to the crowd, and they hooted. He buried his face in my shoulder, laughing. "Get it, Emmett? You said say goodnight, Tai, and I said—"

"I get it. I get it." I kept a firm grip and led him to the door.

Half the audience was still laughing while the other half was clapping, at which Tai spun unsteadily and replied with a huge wave. "I'll be playin' allllllll week."

"He won't," I called over my shoulder as we stepped into the corridor and I manhandled him down to the loading bay.

I sent the bartender back to his work and propped Tai against the back door of the truck while I opened the front. Leo was still sound asleep on the back seat, thank goodness. Drunk Tai was pretty damn cute, but I wasn't sure Leo needed to see that just yet.

Tai caught sight of Leo and a grin broke over his face. "He's a great kid." He turned and patted my chest, then pulled free and swayed in the cool air, arms outstretched.

I reached to steady him but he reeled away. "Man, look at that." He looked up at the sky and turned slowly in place. "Lookit those stars. Ya know wha . . . ?"

He swallowed and cleared his throat and I looked for a nearby bush for him to throw up in.

"Emmett? I *said*, didja know what?"

I rolled my eyes while trying to time my lunge to grab him, but he kept pushing me aside. "What, Tai?"

He grinned like a loon, a very drunk loon. "I think Vermont stole all the fuckin' stars in the world. I think they're all 'ere."

I finally got my arm around his waist again and he fell against me, his face inches from my own. Another wave of alcohol fumes flooded my nose and my eyes watered. I shuffled him against my side and led him back to the car.

He dropped his head on my shoulder. "I like you, mister vet man."

I snorted against his hair. "I like you too, Tai. Now get in."

"Okeydokey." He practically fell into the passenger seat, somehow managing to whack his head on the console in the middle. "Ow. Damn. Who put that there?"

I hauled him upright in the seat.

"Dad?" Leo was propped on one elbow in the back seat.

Tai beamed. "Hey, kiddo. Sorry I woke ya." He reached through and patted Leo's head. "Go back to sleep."

"Okay." Leo snugged back down under the blanket, but not before adding, "Oh man, are you going to have an awesome hangover?"

Tai turned to me with wide, unfocused eyes.

I shrugged. "He's not wrong."

His face fell. "Fu— Damn. I'm sorry. He shouldna have ta see me like this."

"He'll survive." I waited for Tai to get himself back upright in the seat, which took a minute considering he missed the dash with his hand three times. But when he was done, I shoved a bucket in his lap that I'd had in my vet supplies in the back. "If you're going to throw up, do it in there."

"Yes, boss." He saluted, stabbed his finger in his eye, winced, and hugged the bucket tighter. "Where we goin'?"

"Home." I jolted at the rightness of the word on my lips. A quick sideways glance reassured me Tai had missed the slip, his gaze firmly focused forward.

We made it home without Tai losing his stomach in my car, so bonus. He managed to stumble out of his seat and across to my overgrown flower bed before that particular delight happened. Thank Christ for small mercies.

I left him to finish purging the rest of the Jim Beam while I lifted a sleeping Leo into his bed before returning to make sure Tai had discovered the back door without further incident. He was still out in the garden, only now he was lying on the damp grass, staring up at the stars like a kid in a candy shop while making snow angels, or grass angels, I guessed.

I watched for a minute, quite sure he had no idea I was there, then sighed and walked across to stretch out beside him, the grass a cold wet cloth on my back that sent a shiver through my body that I didn't give a fuck about. What the hell was I doing?

"It's so fuckin' beau'ful, ya know?" He sounded awed.

It was. "Like a cloud of angels in ball dresses, my dad used to say." Our breaths fogged, mingled, and rose skyward together.

"Fuckin' poetry, Emmett. Ya never see 'em like this in Boston." He sucked in a ragged breath. "Hated it."

I frowned. "Boston?"

"Yeah. Hated it. Missed home."

I took a second to let that sink in. "I thought you liked cities. Liked dancing. Liked the clubs?"

He turned his head to look at me, eyes still swimming in their sockets, but it felt good to be seen by this man anyway I could get it. Then his fingers threaded with mine and I froze. There was something in his alcohol-fueled, unguarded expression that answered every question I hadn't even dared whisper in my heart. It was far, far too much and not nearly enough.

I took a sharp breath but didn't pull away, the heat of his touch burning the length of my arm.

"I just like ta dance, Emmett. Doesn't matter where it happens. But I . . . like this too." He squeezed my hand, his gaze unwavering. "Shouldn't, but I do."

He turned back to study the stars, and I was certain he saw at least twice as many as me. But I couldn't take my eyes off him, the brightest one there was. He looked impossibly young and vulnerable, in that way people did when all their walls crumbled at their feet and the universe seemed trustworthy, if only for a moment.

Then he wriggled closer and rested his head on my shoulder, his fingers still threaded with mine, and my whole world tipped sideways in an overwhelming flood of emotion.

Without thinking, I turned and pressed a soft kiss to his hair that I doubted he even felt and counted all the reasons this fragile and ridiculous connection we seemed to share was impossible. But when Tai's eyes drifted closed and he gave a contented sigh and snuggled close against my side, every damn one of them melted away like the lie that they were.

TAI

Something soft brushed my cheek. I wrinkled my nose and floated back into the dream.

Another brush and a rough tongue.

What the—? I jerked awake and . . . froze, a thousand razor-sharp bells rattling against the inside of my skull. *Son of a bitch.* With utmost caution, I eased my cheek back onto the pillow and let out a pained groan.

Jesus Christ. I either had the hangover from hell or someone had been using my head as a whack-a-mole target. I guessed the former, but then this was Vermont. I'd learned pretty quick that shit got real here in the weirdest of ways. Any state that boasts a graveyard complete with headstones dedicated to the 'dearly de-pinted' ice cream flavors of Ben and Jerry's is not a place you take for granted or turn your back on. And I kind of loved it for that.

Risking complete brain annihilation, I peeled my eyes open one at a time and squinted in the cruel strip of light that attempted to stab them to death. But before I could focus on where the fuck I was, blessed dark descended again. However, with the relief came a worryingly familiar purr—

I cocked one eye open and blew fluff from my nostril. "Sassy," I hissed. "Get your butt out of my face." I gently pushed her but she didn't go far, stretching over my legs to settle behind my knees instead.

Then it suddenly hit me. Sassy. *Emmett and Leo's* Sassy. *Holy shit.*

I blinked rapidly, but it took a few seconds for my vision to clear and bring Leo in sharp-ish focus. He was perched on a coffee table a couple of feet away, chewing on a piece of toast and swinging his legs.

He smiled and held out his plate. "Want the other piece? I usually have jelly, but Dad gave me banana today."

I took one look and nearly lost my stomach there and then. Through some miraculous feat of control, I didn't know I had, I pushed the plate back from under my nose and struggled to a sit, dropping my feet to the floor while suddenly realizing I was missing my shirt. My hand drifted south. And my jeans. *Fuck.*

I pulled the blanket over my lap. "No . . . but thanks. You have it."

He shrugged and kept chewing while Sassy crawled onto my lap with a soft whine and resettled. I remembered her surgery the day before and stroked her chin. "You feeling like trash too, huh?"

"She slept with you all night," Leo said, then took another bite of his toast, the smell of warm banana coiling like a sour ribbon in my stomach. "She was gone from my room when I got up to pee, and I found her here."

Oh. "She did, huh?" My gaze traveled the room, bits and pieces of the previous night coming back to me in all their mortifying, technicolor glory, including lying on the grass with my head on Emmett's shoulders talking about fucking stars and . . . well, a lot of stuff I shouldn't have.

If only half of it was accurate, I'd made an epic arse of myself.

"She must've thought you were lonely," Leo added.

Out of the mouths of babes . . . or cats, as it happened.

I stole a longer look around the room. We were obviously in the heart of Emmett's home—open-plan family living with noises coming from a kitchen somewhere to my left. I didn't dare look. I could smell his body wash, like he'd imprinted on me. All freshly showered and reeking of care. But as yet, he was leaving me alone, and I could kiss him for that one thing alone. Except I wouldn't, because I couldn't be trusted, apparently.

The house felt old in that well-worn, loved-up way that vintage houses did. The furnishings all soft golds and creams, deep-cushioned couches, a large screen TV, throw pillows galore, and just enough disarray and clutter to make it comfortable.

Then I looked again.

Perhaps a little *too* much disorder. A dusting wouldn't have gone astray, the piles of magazines were only this side of toppling, and the mullioned windows had witnessed enough sticky fingers to give Martha Stewart a panic attack.

"You threw up in the garden," Leo informed me, following that mortifying statement with a wide grin that promised a shit load of teasing.

And, holy shit, I'd forgotten that bit.

"Dad shoveled it into the garbage can this morning."

Oh. My. Fucking. God.

"He didn't think I saw." Leo smiled in a decidedly predatory way. "But I did. Man, you must be feeling bad. Are you sure you don't want some toast?" He shoved the plate under my nose again with a wicked gleam in his eye.

I shoved it aside and leveled him with a glare, then closed a hand around his knee and squeezed.

He squealed—the sound cleaving through my head like a Band-Aid ripped off my brain. Then he dissolved on the floor in front of me, gurgling with laughter.

"Dad! Dad! Tell him to stop." More squeals and I thought I might need surgery to realign my nerves, but Leo's glee did all kinds of wonderful things to ease the guilt ravaging my heart.

He should never have seen me in that state.

I let him go and he uncurled on his back on the floor, panting but still laughing.

"From what I heard of that, you deserved every second." Emmett made an appearance in the room, his smiling eyes catching mine, then drifting over my naked chest where they paused for a few long seconds.

The heat in that one look sizzled on my skin and dangled in my heart.

"It's a low blow hitting a man when he's down," he teased Leo. "Remember when you tried it on me after I had too much champagne at that last Christmas of Nana's?"

Leo sat and crossed his legs in front of him. "You grounded me for a week."

"And you were lucky. Snow in my bed before breakfast wasn't funny."

I stared at Leo. "You put snow in his bed?"

Leo nodded enthusiastically. "It was awesome."

"Wow, I'm impressed." I held my hand up for a high five and Leo connected.

Emmett looked between us and shook his head. "Wow. Good to know where I stand. Shower, then school, Leo. Off you go."

Leo took off laughing, which finally allowed me to sink down into the couch and pull the cushion over my face.

"That bad?"

I felt the couch dip beside me and merely nodded.

A hand brushed my forehead. "Here, ibuprofen and green apple tea. Best hangover cure ever. You can add a cruller from The Maple Factory when we get to work."

My stomach gurgled in disagreement, but I took the pills and tea and got them both down, eventually. "I'm so sorry, Emmett," I mumbled into the material. "I screwed up. I seem to be doing that a lot lately."

He pulled the cushion from my face. "You had a bad day. Everyone's allowed a few of those."

I shook my head. "It was only going to be one beer before I headed to the hostel, but . . ."

"I know." Emmett rubbed gentle circles on my back. "And it's fine."

"But Leo—"

"Has seen it all before." Emmett pulled a face. "I had some rough nights after Lu died. I wasn't a saint, nowhere near it. But be prepared. He'll be merciless in teasing you."

I snorted. "Not like I don't deserve it." I shuffled around to face him. "Thanks for rescuing me last night. I feel like such an idiot."

"You're not. And you're welcome. Tanner says you can go back anytime. You sing pretty well."

Blood rushed to my cheeks. "Oh my god. I sang a bunch of Crowded House songs, didn't I?"

He nodded.

"Son of a bitch. They always come out when I've had too much. What a train wreck. I'll never be able to show my face there again."

Emmett laughed. "Nah, it was sweet."

"It was ridiculous and embarrassing, is what it was." I took a second to gather my thoughts then locked eyes with him again. "Look . . . about last night. I think I said some stuff—"

"Don't." He eyed me sternly. "Don't apologize. Don't take that away from me. It was . . . nice. I know you were drunk, but it was sweet and I want to hold on to it for a while."

God, this man. Through the haze of alcohol, I unfolded the memory of being curled against him, the warmth of his body alongside mine. Which reminded me—

"I appear to be minus my clothes?" I cocked a curious brow his way and a bright flush instantly stained his cheeks.

"They were soaked . . . from the grass," he stumbled. "Mine too, as it turned out."

"So, you undressed me, Emmett?"

"I did." This time he smirked. "But I closed my eyes, so your virtue is intact."

"Oh, I feel so relieved."

"They're finishing in the dryer now," he continued. "You can use my bathroom if you like. Upstairs at the end of the hall on the left. I've put fresh towels in there. I'll leave your clothes outside the door when they're done. We'll leave in about a half an hour."

I followed Emmett's directions and headed upstairs, taking my time to study the line of family photos filling the hall, my headache still banging against my skull like an out of rhythm drum.

They looked a happy family, a thought which pleased and saddened me at the same time. A couple of images caught Emmett looking at Lu while she was focused elsewhere, and the depth of his feelings for her was written all over his face. The few photos from their wedding day radiated joy and promise, and my heart squeezed for what they'd both lost.

I ran a finger across the wide smiles they both wore. It filled my heart with an odd hunger that bore the slight sting of impossibility at its edges.

A family.

Something I'd never considered; never thought I'd wanted; never thought would be possible. Now? Yet another question to add to the burgeoning list fucking with my head. But I was immensely glad Emmett had found that kind of love and was sure in knowledge he'd find it again. He deserved it. And Leo deserved a chance at another parent as special as Lu.

"She was pretty, right?" Leo appeared beside me, wrapped in a towel and looking fucking adorable.

"She was. You look just like her."

"Dad says that too." He ran his hands over the glass, then blew the dust off it. "He also said you remind him of her sometimes."

What? I almost fell sideways. "Me? He said *I* reminded him of your mother?"

"That's what Ivy said." Leo took the wedding photo down and held it up next to me. "You don't look like her, so I think he means that you laugh a lot. You make us all smile."

I couldn't form any words, still stuck on the fact that I reminded Emmett of his dead wife? *Was that why he was attracted to me?*

At a gut level, I hoped not. I hoped it was more.

I cleared my throat before I answered. "No, I didn't realize that."

"Well, you do." He hung the photo back on the wall. "I can still remember her laugh if I really try."

I rested my arm around his shoulders. "That's a wonderful thing. I can tell she loved you so much, just by these photos."

He touched the glass over his mother's image. "I know. I can still feel her . . ." He put a fist to his chest. "In here."

He left to finish dressing, leaving me a shattered mess and wanting to call my mum. I dragged myself into Emmett's bathroom, ignoring the unmade bed and clothes on the floor that shouted his name. The room smelled of him, the clothes hammered me with memories of the night before, and the bathroom carried the scent of his body wash. By the time I was finished in there, I did too, and I wasn't complaining.

True to his word, Emmett had left my clothes outside the bathroom door and I made it downstairs in twenty minutes. Emmett shooed Leo to the car, but when I went to follow, he stopped me with a hand to my arm, his expression nervous.

"Hear me out first," he said. "I'm not going to argue or try to talk you into anything you don't want to do."

My nerves ratcheted up.

"But the simple fact of the matter is, I don't want you sleeping in a hostel."

"Emmett—"

"Hear me out."

I closed my mouth.

"I have a studio above the garage. We've *never* used it except for storage, so it's a mess. I haven't been up there in years. But it does have a bathroom and a tiny kitchenette. It's yours if you want it, for as long as you're in town."

"Emmett." I glanced through the window to where Leo waited in the car. "I appreciate the offer, but you know as well as I do, it's the worst idea."

He nodded. "You're probably right. But I still want you to use it. We're adults, Tai. And I won't have you sleeping in a hostel when I have a perfectly good, independent space you can use. It's only for a few days, right? Surely we can handle that."

I screwed shut my eyes and scrubbed a hand down my face. A warm room. A bed. A safe place to think. Just a few days. Just until I had enough to get that bus ticket to Seattle and leave with a bit of a cushion in my wallet. I'd call my brother tonight and get David's number. I had a plan. And Emmett was right. We were adults. We could do this.

I opened my eyes and nodded. "Okay. Just for a few days."

EMMETT

I swung an arm, hit the phone with my hand, and sent it flying to the floor where it continued to blare. "Goddammit."

I scrambled out of bed and down on my knees to try and find the damn thing before it woke Leo. Light flashed between the bedside table and the bed and I snaked a hand through to retrieve it.

Eleven thirty.

Shit. One hour's sleep. And calls at this time of night were never good news for a vet, especially a sleep-deprived one.

Then the name of the caller finally registered. Jasper. *Shit.*

I shuffled onto my ass, put my back against the mattress, and answered.

"Oh, thank god." Jasper's panicked voice shouted down the line. "I can't get him to move. You've got to help him. I can't do this, Emmett. I can't lose him too."

"Whoa, whoa." My heart lurched in my throat. "Slow down and tell me exactly what's wrong. Is it Gus?"

"Yes! I put him outside to do his business before I hit the sack, but he never came back, and he wouldn't come to my call. It took me five minutes to find him. He was just lying on the ground, panting, and all this saliva pouring out of his mouth. And his stomach . . . shit, Emmett, it's all blown up. I can't get him up."

Fuck, fuck, fuck. "Is he still outside?"

"Yes. I couldn't lift him. I need you to come, Emmett, please. I can't lose him."

I thought quickly. "Look, wait a second. You're going to need to get him to the clinic. I could come there, but we'd just be wasting time. Do you think you can get him to your car?"

"I . . . shit. I don't know. I can try."

"Get a blanket or something strong and roll him onto that. Then drag him to your car."

"Okay, yeah I can do that. I'll call next door. Harrison or Finn will help me. Anything else I should do?"

Pray. "Just get him to the clinic as soon as you can. Maybe one of the guys can drive you?"

"I'll get him there somehow. Just go."

I called Tai, but the call went straight to voicemail, so I left a message and glanced up at the dark windows above the garage. I'd have to bang on his door on the way out, because I was going to need his help, not to mention his strength. Gus weighed 130 pounds, and Jasper was going to be a mess. I couldn't have my friend in the room trying to help while I tried to save his dog's life. I needed to be on my game, and his understandable fear wasn't going to help.

Next, I called Ivy, and then woke Leo to get ready so I could drop him at Ivy's on the way. I threw on some clothes, my heart pounding in my chest. If Gus had dog bloat like I thought he did, we were in for a long night. Bloat was more common in larger dogs, and a Giant Pyrenees fit the bill perfectly. Painful, distressing, and fatal if not treated quickly.

Leo appeared, yawning and wearing his jacket inside out. "Who's sick?"

"Gus." I sent Leo back to his room for his school bag, and seconds later the phone rang in my hand and Tai's sleepy voice came down the line. "Sorry, the phone was still in my jeans' pocket."

I tried not to picture those heavy-lidded eyes, rumpled face, and sticky-up hair, knowing he was just a short walk away, tucked in a bed above my garage. He roused immediately when I explained why I was calling, but I had to move quickly. I told him to take Lu's old car and meet me at the clinic. I couldn't afford to waste time when I needed to drop Leo off at Ivy's on the way.

Fifteen minutes later I was unlocking the clinic when Tai ran up behind me, his labored breaths blowing steamy puffs of fog over my shoulder in the frosty thirty-seven degrees.

"Talk to me as you go," he gasped. "Tell me what I need to know and what you want me to do."

I took him at his word, explaining what was likely wrong and what it would mean as I turned off the alarm, flicked on the lights, and headed for my small operating room. I threw equipment onto the table and began prepping oxygen and X-ray and all the other paraphernalia I was likely to need while Tai got to work on my shopping list of requirements.

"So, this bloat in dogs? Is it like what cows get?" Tai grabbed some blankets and threw them in the warmer for post-op care.

"Yes. Or gastric dilatation and volvulus, GDV to be more technical. It can kill a dog within an hour."

"Shit." He returned to the table where I was still setting up for surgery. "What next?"

I was frankly amazed at his calm. Amazed and impressed as hell. "There should be a list of the paperwork Jasper's going to need to fill out in that protocol folder at the front desk. Get it ready for when he arrives. There'll be resuscitation forms as well. He'll have to decide what he wants if things go to hell in here."

Tai stared at me with wide eyes. "Fuck."

"Pretty much. Then get a kennel ready."

"I'm on it." And he was gone.

It seemed there wasn't much Tai couldn't cope with, and my heart did a ridiculous flip with something pretty close to pride.

A few minutes later, the slam of the front door ricocheted through the clinic.

"Emmett?!" Jasper's voice rang out loud and frightened, and I rushed out to find him and Finn grappling to hold Gus in his sheet sling.

"It's bloat, isn't it?" Jasper was white as a ghost. "I know what that means, Emmett." His wild eyes pleaded.

I took one look at the huge Pyrenees and schooled my expression. He was out of it; chest heaving, drool running like a river from his mouth, eyes rolled back with the whites showing. "I can't be sure, but yes, it looks that way. Bring him around back." I ran ahead to clear the way.

Tai appeared from the kennel area and followed us into the room. Once Gus was up on the table, I caught Tai's eye and asked him to take the men out to the waiting room.

"I'm not going anywhere," Jasper shot back. "He's all I have."

Tai put a hand on Jasper's arm and the man's face crumbled.

"Come on." Finn tried to nudge Jasper out the door. "We're no use here."

But the look Jasper fired him said he wasn't going anywhere.

"Hey." Tai moved in front of Jasper, keeping his hand on Jasper's arm. "If you want Emmett to save Gus, you have to let him work with the least amount of distraction. That's Gus's best chance of getting through, understand? We know you love him, Jasper, but you can't be with him, not for this. Not if you want Emmett to do his job the best way he knows how."

Jasper stared at Tai like he'd only just realized he was there. Then he glanced at me and I nodded. "He's right. Let me work. You have to trust me on this."

Jasper drew in a shuddering breath, then let it out slowly. "Okay. But I'm waiting out there. You come and get me as soon as you can. No fucking around, promise?"

"I promise."

Jasper turned back to Tai. "So, you're the famous Tai."

Tai frowned and glanced my way.

I shrugged. "Small town. Tai, this is my good friend Jasper and his friend and neighbor, Finn. Now get them out of here. There's a mess of forms you need to fill in. Then make yourself comfortable in the waiting room. This could be a while, but we'll keep you informed every step of the way, okay?"

Jasper nodded. "I trust you." He buried his face in Gus' thick mane of hair and whispered something to the dog that included Jasper's husband's name, Michael. Then he let Tai walk him back to the waiting room. Finn followed after flicking me a wide-eyed look. We both knew if Jasper lost Gus, there was no telling how he'd take it.

"Tell Tai I'll need him back here, ASAP," I called to Finn as I got the X-ray machine ready.

"Will do." He turned and fired a pointed look my way. "Seems like a nice guy."

I rolled my eyes. "Yeah, yeah. Thanks for your help. Now scat."

Tai was back in under a minute with the news that Jasper would make any resuscitation decision on the spot since he was here. Not the best solution but there wasn't much I could do.

With Tai's help, I got an IV line in place, drew blood, took X-rays, did a cardiograph, and a few other things in record time. Gus remained pretty much unresponsive, his breathing labored, his body systems slowly shutting down. It was going to be a close call with no guarantees, and I could tell by the look on Tai's face that he was nervous as hell.

But he never said a word, just kept working.

I needed to feed him every little thing I wanted him to do as I intubated Gus and prepped him for surgery, but Tai followed my instructions to a T and never needed telling twice. Before long we were working as a team and he was beginning to anticipate. He even fired a couple of sassy salvos over my bow, which were exactly what I needed to keep the tension manageable.

"You think you can use suction?" I asked through my mask as I was about to open Gus up.

His eyes danced in reply. "Baby, I was born to suck."

I laughed and pointed to the suction machine. "Then turn it on and stop being a fucking tease."

"I thought you'd never ask." He switched the machine on, got ready with the Yankauer suction handle, and waggled his eyebrows. "Let's do this."

I ignored the tightness around his weary eyes and the slight shake to his hand that told me he was only human. It was a lot to ask of anyone.

The operation took longer than I expected. Not only had the stomach bloated and then rotated on itself, but that had affected the blood supply to the spleen as well. I'd needed to resect a section that was looking necrotic, but eventually I got everything re-situated as it was meant to be, Tai helping with suction and passing instruments and swabs as best he could. Not perfect, but it was good enough, and way better than I could've expected.

The next step was to surgically tack the stomach permanently in position so it couldn't twist again—something that was prone to happen after a first incident, like a weak spot.

We survived a couple of scares when Gus's blood pressure had bottomed out and his heart needed a bit of drug encouragement to remember what it was supposed to do, but we got there. And at some ungodly hour, with Jasper's help, we finally carried Gus through into his kennel, loaded him with warm blankets, and prayed. He wasn't out of the woods yet, but at least the surgery was done. It was the best I could hope for under the circumstances.

I explained all of this to Jasper and then left him with Tai while I cleaned up. A half hour later, Tai had convinced a greatly reassured Jasper to go home and get some sleep. We would look after Gus.

"You promise me you'll call if *anything* happens." Jasper's eyes flashed. "And you'll keep a real close eye on him, right?"

"I promise." I pushed through all that prickle and pulled him in for a hug. "You did your part and I've done mine. Now, Gus has to fight for it himself, but he's got a big heart, Jasper. You need to get some sleep. Leave him with me."

"And me," Tai said firmly, looking my way. "What? You didn't think I was going to leave you here, did you? Who'd make sure you ate or got some rest?"

"But—"

"No," Tai snapped. "I'm staying. This conversation's done."

I blew out a sigh. Like I had a tired fuck left to give. The man was worse than a mother hen. "Fine, whatever." I waved a hand in the air. "I'll take cheese on that toast then."

Tai's lips curved up in a self-satisfied grin. "Your wish is my command."

Our eyes locked and my heart skipped just a lick in my chest.

Jasper's curious gaze flicked between us. Then he surprised the hell out of me by yanking Tai in for the briefest of hugs. "Thanks," he said hoarsely, thumping Tai on the back. "I really appreciate it."

I smothered my smile at the stunned look on Tai's face and addressed Jasper instead. "Come on, I'll walk you out. If you don't hear from me, Gus is fine. Come back after seven and you can stay all day if you want. He's going to be here for a couple of days, at least."

Jasper mumbled his thanks, and after a final tentative stroke of Gus around all the tubing and dressings, he let me walk him to the front door.

"I like him," he said.

My eyes jerked up. "Who?"

He flicked his head over his shoulder. "Tai. I like him. That's all I'm going to say."

A slow smile spread over my face. "Yeah, well, that makes two of us."

TAI

While Emmett saw Jasper out, I managed to find the blow-up mattress in the storeroom and had it set up in five minutes flat. It wasn't a single, but it wasn't that big either. When Emmett arrived back, I hustled him into the shower while I threw some blankets on the mattress, switched the sandwich maker on to heat, and checked on Gus.

When Emmett was done, I dove in for my own clean up while he whipped us up some cheese toasted sandwiches and a drink. Then we sat around his office desk and ate in silence, the video feed from the kennel room showing Gus quiet and settled. With each bite, my spirits sank from the high I'd been on ever since the surgery to a deep biting low. Yes, the surgery had been successful. And yes, I was so damn proud of Emmett saving Gus. But I'd felt more hindrance than help, and both Gus and Emmett had deserved more.

"You okay?" Emmett studied me from the other side of the desk, and I realized I'd stopped eating, sandwich still in hand.

"Oh." I laid the sandwich down on the plate and wiped my hands. "Just tired, I guess."

His expression softened. "Come on, let's go check on our patient one last time, and then we can try to get some shut-eye. You take the mattress and I'll crash in the waiting room."

Like hell. "No way. I'm quite capable of sleeping on that waiting room bench. I'm smaller than you."

He opened his mouth to argue, caught the warning in my eye, and closed it again. Clever man.

"Fine," he grumped.

"Fine." I bit back a smile. "Now, let's check Gus."

The big Pyrenees was still completely out of it. He would be for a while according to Emmett who left me to go grab another IV bag. I studied the big dog. His breathing was even and he was warming nicely, not that my assessment was worth much. I ran my fingers through his heavy coat and talked to him softly, explaining that his dad was missing him and he needed to get better quick. And that everything was going to be all right.

Gus's big body shuddered and I nearly jumped through the roof. Then a long rumbling groan ran up his throat, and he sighed and settled again. I wiped the sleepy crust from his eyes, my hands shaking like a leaf. Jasper had been a whisper away from losing him; I'd known by the way Emmett moved when Gus had bottomed out. He'd been on to it, and professional, and ran all his procedures like a star, directing me to do exactly what he needed, no raised voice, no panic. But he'd been scared. There was no hiding that.

Jasper had lost his husband some years before—Emmett had told me as he'd worked. That's how they'd become friends, getting drunk one night and sharing their grief. I'd listened, laser-focused on every word, thinking of the anguish on Jasper's face with Gus in his arms and the look in Emmett's eyes when he talked about Luelle. In that moment, I realized one thing. Aside from my family, I'd never loved like that. Not an animal, not a person, and certainly not Dion. And I'd wasted three fucking years to understand that.

I ruffed the thick hair around Gus's neck and leaned in close. "Hey, big guy. Maybe you and Jasper can teach *me* something. First lesson: give your love to someone who's going to keep it safe, right? Well, you're safe with Jasper, baby. Good for you."

Gus shuddered and coughed and my eyes jerked to his chest, but he was still breathing. So, that was okay, right? Wasn't it? He coughed again. *Shit.* How did I know if he was okay? The IV bag was almost empty. Where the hell was Emmett? Should I turn it off? *Fuck.*

Another cough.

A fist closed inside my throat and my heart kicked up. "Emmett!"

"What's wrong?" Emmett rushed in with an IV bag and went straight to Gus.

"Where were you?" I turned on him.

"Warming the bag in some water, why?"

"It's Gus." I scuttled away to give Emmett room. "He shook and then c-coughed and the b-bag was empty . . ." I stammered, stumbling to my feet so Emmett could change the bag. "I . . . I didn't know if he should do that. Should he? I thought maybe his throat was swelling or something. I didn't know. I didn't know—"

I was crying before I knew it—hot, fat, rolling tears messing up my face and fucking with my determination to get through this night without making a complete fool of myself.

"I'm sorry. I'm sorry." I stepped back toward the door. "He just looked . . ."

"He's fine." Emmett lifted the blanket back over the huge dog. "He's just coming out of the anesthetic. The shaking and coughing and groaning, it's all part of it. I should've told you. There's nothing to worry about."

"I . . . shit. I didn't know. Sorry. I'll go get . . . something." I spun on my heels to leave. I didn't belong there. I had no freaking idea what I was doing other than making more work for Emmett who looked ready to collapse from exhaustion.

I didn't make the door before arms enfolded me from behind.

"Hey, hey, hey. Where are you going? What's going on?" Emmett's breath brushed hot against my neck. "If you're worried about Gus, I'm hopeful he's going to be okay, but we're going to keep a close eye on him."

"You." I spun in his arms and scrubbed my wet cheeks with the heel of my hand.

"Me?" He frowned, his blond hair hanging in dark, damp locks, a few errant ones plastered to his forehead.

I reached up and tucked a few wayward strands behind his ears and patted them in place. "Yes, *you*, Emmett. *You'll* keep an eye on him. *I*, on the other hand, have no idea what the hell I'm doing, and I'm so sorry for that. You'd have done a lot better asking Ivy to help and left me to babysit Leo. I don't know why you didn't." I tried to free myself, but his hands landed on my shoulders and held me in place. I dropped my head and studied the floor instead.

"What on earth are you talking about?" His fingers tipped my chin, forcing me to look at him. "I didn't ask Ivy because I wanted *you*, I *needed* you. And I knew you'd manage just fine, which you did. I would've had to talk Ivy through a lot of the same stuff as I did you. She hasn't helped with this kind of surgery before either, and I needed your strength. I couldn't have done this without you."

I arched a brow.

He grimaced. "It would've taken me far too long, and we'd likely have lost him."

I glanced at Gus, who looked quiet and peaceful, and let Emmett's words sink in.

"You did an amazing job for a guy who's mostly only had to help with cat and dog neutering so far."

I bit back a smile. "There was that one boil thing."

He grinned. "*And* the boil thing."

His hands stayed hot on my shoulders. "You impressed me tonight, and that doesn't happen easily."

My eyes sought his. "That's kind of you to say, but . . ."

He cradled my face, and without thinking, I turned my cheek into his palm and his thumb brushed my lips—once, twice—the feel of his hands on me burning every neuron on its journey south.

"It's the truth." He leaned toward me and I held my breath. "It was a big surgery and not always successful. It's stressful. With animals that sick, you never know if you can save them. And this?" He brushed a thumb across my damp cheek. "This is normal. Part of the adrenaline crash. But you were . . . *are* amazing, and so much more capable than you think you are. Forget what that asshole said, because I know he did a number on you."

I couldn't answer, not just because it was true, but because there were still too many days I almost believed Dion was right.

Emmett's lips set in a thin line. "Fuck him, and anyone else who's ever said shit like that to you. In the last week with me, you've been more helpful than I could possibly have expected. And not just helpful. You found where I was leaking money and you're doing something about it. You've used initiative, charm, and street smarts to handle my more difficult clients. And I've laughed more at work in the last week, than I think I have in the last year. So, don't you dare think you're not capable. I don't know what the future holds for you, Taika Samuels, or where it lies, but you've got everything you need to succeed inside you, and don't let anyone tell you any different."

I stared at him. How did he do that? It wasn't like I didn't know those things about myself, because I mostly did. I hadn't always lived them, but I kind of knew them. But Emmett somehow grabbed them by the roots and tugged them into the light. He saw them. He saw me. And it had been so fucking long since anyone had seen me like that.

He was breathing hard, his face hovering only a few inches away, but I didn't move. I wanted him so badly I was almost vibrating. I could taste it—a scorching spice that sizzled on my tongue. We were so close, just a lick away, but this had to be Emmett's decision.

His breath ran hot over my skin, his gaze dipping to my

mouth, our foreheads touching. The clean scent of soap and apple shampoo flooded my nostrils and almost took my knees from under me. I wanted to bury my face in his neck and set up camp.

My tongue flicked over my lips and a shudder passed through him. He lifted his head and pressed a kiss to each of my eyelids before brushing his nose across mine, my name carried on his breath in a long exhale.

"Tai."

I'd never felt so fucking turned on in my life with my clothes still intact.

And then his lips were on mine and I couldn't, wouldn't fight it any longer, melting into the kiss, the kiss that was always going to happen. I sighed into it, giving myself over to whatever he wanted, it was all fine with me. The world could take a hike. Nothing mattered except *this*.

His tongue dove between my lips for a deeper taste, his fists clutching the back of my shirt, hauling me up and against him like he was scared to let me go. He needn't have worried. I wasn't going anywhere. With my arms wrapped around his neck, I met him stroke for stroke, our tongues tangling in a complicated dance of advance and retreat as we tried to get our fill.

He groaned and growled, his mouth hard and voracious, leaving no doubt he was as fully into this as I was, and I fucking loved it.

Always the damn quiet ones.

A line of kisses was peppered along my jaw to my ear before he nibbled on the lobe, and I soared another notch or two on my hell-yeah meter.

"Fuck, that feels good." I angled my neck to give him better access, and he ran with it, nipping, licking, and sucking the curve of my shoulder, his heavy stubble delicious and rough on my bare skin. Then he peeled my T-shirt to the side so he could reach the tip of my shoulder before making his way back up to sink his teeth into the flesh just below my ear. Hard enough to leave a mark, it drew a sinful moan from my lips.

"You are so damn beautiful." Another kiss to my jaw. "I've been losing my fucking mind wanting to touch you, to do this."

He kissed my nose. "But I have no fucking idea what I'm doing here, so feel free to instruct me." A kiss to the other side of my jaw, and I was awfully damn close to creaming my jeans.

I pushed him back and sucked in a breath. "Just a second." I held him in place. "You need to know I got tested . . . after I got here . . .after Dion. I'm negative, but still, you should know."

Emmett's eyes flew wide. "Shit, I didn't even think to ask. I'm so crap at this. I should get tested again too. I mean, I did, after the last time. I was negative then, but I'll get tested again anyway."

I stroked his cheek. "I know you will. And you're not crap at this. Just things to learn, right? Always check."

"Yeah, lots to learn. Lots I *want* to learn. But you're negative, right?"

"I am. But you decide how far you want to go and I'll follow along. So, just keep doing what you're doing." I cupped his cheek. "There's no wrong move here, Emmett. And just so you know, I feel exactly the same. I might've had a few more men in my time than you, more than a few, but this is starting to feel awfully like I'm out of my depth, *way* out of my depth."

His mouth curved up in a slow, sexy smile. "Is that right?"

I wagged my finger at him. "Don't get cocky. It's very unattractive."

He snorted and leaned in for another taste, but I held him back. "You sure Gus is okay?"

He smiled indulgently. "I'm gonna take that as a sign you want me to check again before we get carried away?"

"Is that what we're doing here?" I searched his eyes for . . . something, some kind of handhold to grab onto, to float a hope on. "Getting carried away?"

He grinned and kissed me hard. "I certainly fucking hope so. Stay right there, because I'm not done, nowhere near."

He took a minute to give the sleeping dog another once over while I stood like a fool and watched him, the debate in my head running circles until I finally kicked it to the curb. Enough already. I had no idea what I was doing, but I did know that if I didn't run now, I was screwed.

I didn't run.

So, yeah. There was that.

Emmett finished his check and then immediately crowded me against the row of cages. "Now, where were we?" He nuzzled into my neck and began another line of kisses around to the dip at the front of my throat. A little tongue and suction there and my balls started to sing. My head fell back against the cage and he licked a swathe back up to my lips and—

Oh yeah, totally screwed.

"You taste like sunshine," he whispered against my ear, then nibbled that tender spot just beneath. "How the hell do you do that?"

I smiled against his lips. "You talk a good game there, Mr. Veterinarian. I bet you have all the girls swooning." I said it jokingly, but there was a wariness to the words even I could hear —a direct reminder that I wasn't his usual *go-to* gender.

He nipped my lower lip and leaned back to look at me. "Eyes here." He pointed to his, and I raised mine.

"There's only one person I'm interested in *swooning* right now," he said evenly. "And unless my foundational animal anatomy lessons were all wrong—" He dropped a hand and squeezed my dick through my jeans, drawing a filthy groan from my lips. "—you sure as hell aren't any girl. What's more—" That hand kept squeezing and stroking my dick as I tried to focus on his words. "—I wouldn't have it any other way. I want *you*, Tai, exactly as you are. I might not be experienced, but I'm not pretending, I'm not experimenting, I'm not simply curious. I've known I'm bi for a long time. Lulu knew it. Jasper knows it. Even Ivy knows it, now. And I want *you*. Just you. Only you. Is that what you need to hear?"

Yes. No. Yes! Because I'd been thinking exactly that. That maybe he was just curious. That my presence had fired a simmering question in the back of his mind. His solid denial both reassured and panicked me in equal measure. A quick, curious fuck, I could handle. It might sting my ridiculous heart, but I could do it. More than that? Knowing Emmett wanted me, eyes open, and maybe even hoping, just like me? That scared the ever-living hell out of me.

But not enough to back away. Not enough to do what I should to protect my heart.

"Let me help you with that?" He tilted my jaw up with his fingers till my gaping mouth closed.

I narrowed my gaze. "Think you're funny, don't you?"

He brushed the hair back from my eyes. "No. But I think I surprised you. I think I caught you off guard. You thought you had this whole thing figured out, didn't you? Well, Mr. Samuels, news flash. You don't get to decide what I feel or where I am in my sexual awakening. You only get to decide if you want to be part of the ride."

I leveled him with a glare. "Who are you and what have you done with my quiet, slightly absent-minded veterinarian?"

He grinned, spun me around, and walked me backwards until I hit the wall where he caged me in. "Oh, he's still here. But there's an awful lot you *don't* know about me, Tai, including the fact that I like sex, like it a lot, always have." He brushed his lips over mine. "And I think I might just love it . . . with you."

Damn. He had all the fucking words.

Another teasing brush of lips crossed mine, and I made sure to snag one in my teeth for a nibble before letting him go.

"And just so you know—" His blue eyes burned dark and hot on mine. "—I can be exceedingly focused in that particular arena, when I choose to be."

Goddamn my thudding heart. The lamb was a fucking lion. My toes curled in my socks, every nerve went on high alert, and I'm pretty sure I squeaked.

"That's excellent news." I cleared my throat and ran my finger-tips over his brow, more to distract *him* and give *me* a chance to catch my breath than anything else. His eyes sunk closed at my touch, and I tapped his forehead to open them again. "But I feel it would be remiss of me not to ask for a quick . . . demonstration." I pulled my lower lip between my teeth and watched his pupils darken further. "Just to be sure."

His lips met the underside of my chin. "How very . . . thorough of you."

I yelped as his teeth nipped firmly, then groaned and rubbed myself up against him to make sure he continued.

"I'd like to say that quick isn't my style," he whispered in my ear, then pulled back so I could see him. "But right now, I'm a half turn to the left away from something I haven't done since I was fifteen."

You and me both, sweetheart. "Which is also good news cos I'm right there with you. Let's save indulgence for round two."

He frowned. "Round two?"

"Is that a problem?"

His pale skin flushed to his hairline. "None whatsoever."

"Then come here." I slipped my arms around his waist and drew him flush against me, finding that hard edge I craved, tucked behind those annoyingly closed buttons. I ground shamelessly up against him while he moaned and covered my mouth with his, arching his back to meet me thrust for thrust until we were both panting.

"Fuck, that feels good. But I'm close." He pulled back as if unsure what to do next.

I flipped our positions and pulled him sideways until he had solid wall behind him. Then I looked him in the eye. "Tell me what you want. This goes as far as *you* want, any way *you* want, understand?"

He frowned. "What about you?"

I laughed. "Really? Baby, right now, I'll take anything I can get, and it'll be goddamn amazing."

He raked his fingers through my hair, tilted my head back, and took my mouth in a fierce kiss. Then he cradled my face and looked me in the eye. "In that case, I want to see these gorgeous lips wrapped around my cock before I explode."

I couldn't keep the grin from my face. "My fucking pleasure."

EMMETT

Baby? God, I liked that way more than I should from a man I'd known little more than a week. And as Tai fell to his knees and set about unbuttoning my jeans, I took a second to really look at the man who'd somehow turned my neat little world upside down.

Just *how* upside down? The fact I was getting a blow job in the kennel room of my veterinary practice said it all. How the fuck was this my life? I wasn't out, and he wasn't staying. And we damn well shouldn't be doing what we were. But fuck, I wanted him. And above everything else, I really fucking liked him.

My jeans and belt hit my ankles, and I had to push back against the wall to hold me up as Tai's talented mouth descended on my cock. Hot, tight, slick heaven—his tongue circling the head, playing with the foreskin, dipping in and out of the slit, teasing, promising.

Then he took me to the back of his throat, swallowed, and—

Holy fuck. My head thumped back against the wall and I nearly came there and then. I shoved his head away and slammed the flat of my palm against the wall a couple of times, the sting just enough to bring me back from the edge.

"Something wrong?" He licked those plump, glossy lips and grinned.

I narrowed my gaze. "Maybe keep the big guns under wraps

for a bit. Let me enjoy it for at least a minute before I embarrass myself, please?" I begged.

He chuckled, grabbed hold of the base of my cock with one hand, and keeping his eyes on me, he licked up the length and swirled the flat of his tongue across the head once again. He looked so damn sexy. I'd never been given head like this, so deep, so filthy so . . .

"Fuck, that's hot." I couldn't take my eyes off him.

Another long swathe. Another sweep across the head, drawing the top two inches of me inside his mouth to suckle on, light and lazy, on and off, flicks and licks. Not enough to push me over. Just enough to blow my fucking mind. He knew exactly what he was doing, edging me in the best possible way. Damn, he was good.

Then he dropped his hands behind his back, looked up at me, and winked.

My pulse quickened. I knew what he wanted, but I'd never . . . "You want me to . . . ?"

He nodded.

So damn trusting. I thrust gently, not too deep, watching him closely. But he simply rolled his eyes, grabbed my ass with one hand, and yanked me closer, sinking me deep into his mouth, gagging a little, eyes watering, but holding me tight to keep me in place.

Well, okay then. I took him at his word, pulled back, and thrust, deeper this time, eyes slamming shut with the rush of heated bliss. And in seconds I had a rhythm going, slow but deep, just how I liked it. He moaned, vibrations humming around my cock, adding another dimension, dialing up the pleasure. I cupped his head to keep him still and watched my depth, checking he was okay. He moaned, his hand falling from my ass to unbuckle his jeans, freeing himself so he could stroke off and just . . . damn.

That was new. "Show me."

He leaned back so I could get a better view and I was transfixed. God, he was gorgeous. He caught my gaze and that was it. Eyes half-lidded, watching mine as he swallowed me down, his free hand working himself as he feasted on my cock, and I just couldn't fucking hold it any longer.

The buzz hit the base of my spine, and a wave of pleasure crashed through my body. I grunted, once, twice, thrusting deep as I spilled every drop I had down the back of Tai's throat, and he swallowed every mouthful, hungry eyes still watching me.

He pulled off, groaned, and licked his lips like I'd fed him damn chocolate. Then he leaned back on his heels so I could watch him finish. *Like fuck.* I had my jeans up and was down on my knees before I knew it, my hand wrapped over his. He smiled and stroked himself faster, dropping his head back with a loud groan, and spilling through his palm and mine, onto the floor with a full-body shudder as the pleasure lit up his face.

I kept my hand over his until he was done, kissing his lips, his cheeks, anything I could reach. And when he wobbled on his knees, I grabbed his hand to steady him, lifted his fingers to my mouth, and licked them clean, then my own, as he watched slack-jawed.

Yeah, I'd never been shy about sex or hesitant in bed, and I enjoyed the fact I could surprise him. I might be a novice with men, but I knew what I liked. And everything Tai, was apparently, very definitely, what I liked.

"You look very pleased with yourself," Tai muttered, and let me help him to his feet before pulling up his jeans, but leaving them undone.

"Considering I just had an epic blow job, that would be putting it mildly," I replied, doing up my own jeans, before grabbing a nearby towel to throw on the floor.

He tilted his head. "You're a bit of a dark horse, Emmett Moore."

I brushed my thumb over his slick lower lip and lifted it to my mouth. His dark gaze followed. "I think you like that about me, Tai Samuels."

He ran his eyes over my face and smiled. "Maybe. But you do realize we had an audience, right?" He turned and tipped his head to the line of cages where three sets of feline eyes, a single, slightly disconcerting chameleon one, and the somewhat manic gaze of an out-of-sorts hamster glared back in the dimmed lighting. "I'm feeling very judged."

170

I pulled him close and nipped his ear from behind. "The only judgment that matters is mine. And I give you oh . . . at least a six out of ten."

Which earned me an elbow in the ribs and an ass shoved back into my groin. "A six, huh? And this is based on your vast experience with men giving you head?"

"Hah. Touché." I slid a hand down to cup his soft dick tucked back into his briefs.

He hummed and thrust into my palm.

"I wish to change my score. A definite ten."

"Mmm, good decision. Your dick might live to fuck another day." He wriggled once more and my cock perked up even with nowhere near enough gas left in the tank to get me past first gear. A man could dream.

I grabbed his hand, and led him to the mattress tucked just behind a mound of dog food sacks, out of sight of all those prying animal eyes. "We need to get some sleep."

"Together?" His expression was guarded.

"Together," I said firmly. "If you think I'm letting you out of my sight after that, you must be crazy. But I'd kind of like to see *all* of you first, if that's okay?"

He licked his lips. "More than okay. I'm all yours."

And my heart tripped in my chest.

I took a deep breath and tugged him closer. He came willingly, and then stood as I stripped him slowly, studying me through those deep brown eyes. I wanted to know what was going on in that head of his, but I didn't want to ask. Didn't want to break the moment.

When he was finally naked, I took a few steps back to drink my fill. And yeah, that took some time, because just like that beautiful face, the rest of Tai was stunning. Acres of soft olive skin wrapped up a slim, tight body just a touch shorter than mine. Sleek muscles defined but not pumped, a flat stomach with an elegant slender cock—every inch of his body, lean and smooth, not a hair in sight . . . anywhere. That had to take some work.

It was kind of surreal. All those years of knowing I liked guys, and I'd never really pictured this moment—a guy in my arms, in my bed—albeit an air mattress on the floor of my clinic. And on top of it all, a guy I really liked and who seemed to like me. I appreciated a handsome face, could get excited at a tight ass and a ready smile, but nothing like this, nothing . . . deeper.

But then again, the Tais of the world were a little thin on the ground in Burlington, Vermont, so there was that. I took in the beautiful curves and tight lines of the man standing in front of me, and my spent dick valiantly tried to acknowledge its ongoing interest with an approving nod.

"You are so fucking beautiful."

Tai's cheeks stained a deep shade of brown, and his smile was almost shy, so at odds with that sassy vibe he wore like armor. He shook it off and struck a dramatic pose instead. "So, I pass inspection then?" Thick lashes batted over those deep brown eyes.

"I have no fucking words." And it was true. He took my breath away.

He waved a hand in my direction. "Your turn."

"Oh, right." I was suddenly struck by nerves. "I don't look anything like—"

"I can't wait to lay my eyes on you, Emmett." He sashayed my way, wicked intent in every roll of those hips. He slipped my still unbuttoned jeans to the floor and lifted my T-shirt over my head. "Mmm. Look what you've been hiding all this time."

He rubbed his smooth cheek across the thick blonde hair on my chest, the only place I really carried it. The rest of me was pretty average, in every regard.

"Damn, that feels good," he purred, threading his fingers through the tangle. "Look at us. We're beautiful together."

I looked, noting the deep olive of his skin against the paleness of my own. His thick black hair threaded through the fair curls on my chest, fine slender fingers running over my soft body. There was no doubt he was beautiful and that we struck a startling contrast, but as for me . . .

"You're gorgeous, Emmett." He licked a swathe across a nipple before drawing it into his mouth and I hissed.

"Fuck." I mentally counted to ten.

He caught my eye with a wicked smile. "I certainly hope so,

but not right now. I don't think either of us have it in us, but let's hold that thought." His fingers found the band of my briefs and pushed them down, his body dropping with them, holding them while I stepped out. Then he rose, his tongue licking one long swathe from my knees, alongside my valiant cock, and all the way up to my throat.

I wrapped my arm around his waist and pulled him in for a hard kiss. He melted against me, and my hand dropped to clasp that silken ass and—

Froze.

Holy shamoly.

"What the—" I spun him by the shoulders so he faced the other way and took a step back. He gave a cheeky wiggle of his butt, and I dropped to a squat to check out a piercing I'd never seen before.

"Don't move." My fingers traced a line of three brushed silver dots sitting low on his sacrum, leading down into the crease between his cheeks, the lower one held a heart hanging free just tantalizingly nestled into the crease itself.

"It's a valley piercing," he said over his shoulder. "You like?"

Did I like? Was he fucking crazy?

"I don't care what the hell it's called," I answered shakily. "It's driving me wild, and *like* doesn't even begin to cover it. Damn, that's hot." I traced the line again and he shivered, so I leaned in and placed a chaste kiss at the top of the line, letting the tip of my tongue dip just into his crease before sliding out again. The groan he gave was all kinds of dirty, and I marked this particular part of Tai's anatomy for some dedicated investigation at a later date.

I rose to my feet and pulled him back against me, my lower belly registering the cool run of his metal piercings. "I'm putting a bookmark right here," I told him.

"It's all yours." He let his head fall back against my shoulder and I foolishly hoped for more than his words likely meant.

But for now, we needed sleep. "Come on. Get on that mattress."

He pouted dramatically but dropped down and I covered him with the blanket. Then I checked on Gus who was a little more responsive but still sleeping. I slowed the IV right down and got two bottles of water from my office fridge before joining Tai.

The mattress creaked and groaned under our combined weight and we looked at each other and laughed.

"Soooo romantic." Tai raised his water bottle and touched it to mine. "A freaking air mattress in a kennel room."

"I don't need romance, only you. Come here." I tugged him close so I could curl my body around his and wrapped an arm over his waist. He tensed for a second and I wondered if I'd crossed some line; then he relaxed.

Okay then.

I nuzzled my lips against the nape of his neck, and he lifted a hand back to cup my neck and keep me there.

"That feels amazing."

My palm brushed his nipples and he arched up, the back of his head finding my shoulder, putting the soft nub of his ear next to my lips. I pulled it into my mouth and he groaned loudly. I nipped and let it go.

"You take my breath away, Tai Samuels," I whispered in his ear. "You're so damn irresistible."

He spun in my arms and put a finger to my mouth. "Shh, enough."

My gaze fell into his as he tapped at my lips. Then he dropped his finger and replaced it with a brief kiss. "You're a snuggler, Mr. Moore. Who'd have guessed?"

"Guilty as charged. Lu grumbled all the time because she generated heat like a furnace."

"Well, I'm not grumbling." He brushed a lock of hair from my eyes. "But Man on Man 101, for future reference, most hookups *don't* snuggle." His gaze flickered for a second, as if the idea of me with someone else didn't sit well, and foolish hope bit at my heart. "But it might be that I've never had a boyfriend who was really into it, I guess. If Dion got cozy, it was because he wanted my ass." He gave a thin smile.

Fucking hell. "Well, they don't know what they missed." I wrapped a leg over his hip and locked him in place. "You have an eminently snuggle-worthy body, just to be clear."

"Good to know." He ran his fingers through the hair on my chest. "Tell me about Lu."

TAI

He tensed at the question, but I kept playing with all those delicious strands of gold and he slowly relaxed. I loved hair on a man's chest, but I'd never been with a guy who had it to spare. Most of the men in the club scene groomed themselves to within an inch of their waxed lives, just like me. But any worry I might've had about what Emmett thought of me all smooth and silky burned to cinders in the hunger I saw in his eyes when he looked at me naked. It was a miracle I wasn't ash on the floor.

Fingers threaded through my hair as the tension bled from his muscles.

"Lulu was a spitfire." He laughed and I smiled against his chest. "The first time I saw her was at a party. I was smitten right away, but she didn't want to know me. She had no intention of falling for *anyone*—independent as they came. Man, did she put me through the mill trying to win her over. Six months until I even got a date. But it was worth every minute."

Persistent. Good to know. "Seems you don't pick the easy ones."

He ruffled my hair. "Now, where'd be the fun in that?"

I tried not to read too much into the comment, but it was hard not to. I turned and rested my chin on my hands, atop his chest. "I'll assume Lulu was your pet name for her? I notice Ivy calls her Lu."

"Yeah. Most people call her Lu. And in her own words, 'Luelle sounds like a fucking Texas bitch, and I could wring my bloody mother's neck for saddling me with it.'"

I snorted. "Gotcha. Spitfire." And I decided in another life, Lu and I could've been friends.

"Seems clichéd to say it, but it was pretty much love at first sight, at least for me. She took a little more convincing as I said,

175

but man, I loved her. We had a great life. And then when Leo came along unexpectedly—"

I arched a brow and his cheeks lit up.

"Yeah, yeah, I know. A bloody vet, right? Not like I didn't know how it all worked. But the best-laid plans and all that . . . plus Lu and the pill didn't always get along that well, so we were pretty condom dependent. Enter Leo." He chuckled and planted a kiss on my forehead.

I walked my fingers up his chest and neck to his lips and stroked his cheek. "Can I ask how the car accident happened?"

He held my gaze and ran a finger down my nose. "She took my car to the grocery store on a Saturday afternoon to get ingredients for a dinner we were having with friends. She never came back. A guy in an SUV ran a red light and slammed into her door. Leo was home with me, thank God. He was six. The other driver walked away without a scratch, but Lu was trapped in her seat. She was dead before the ambulance got there . . ." His voice quavered and stopped.

I rolled on top and straddled his waist, our naked cocks soft and snuggled together. The mattress sank alarmingly but held, and I leaned forward, my forearms on either side of his head, and took his mouth in a long, slow kiss, butterflies flicking through my chest. There was just something about kissing him, I couldn't explain. He gave into my touch immediately, eyelids fluttering closed, both hands cupping my ass, a sigh breaking loose into the kiss.

I kissed him until his body stopped shuddering, then pulled back and brushed the end of my nose all over his face, noting the damp on his cheeks. "Jesus, Emmett, how did you survive?"

He blew out a sigh. "I had Leo," he answered as I came to a stop and hovered above him. "There was no choice. He needed me, and so I sank into the role of only parent and avoided dealing with my own grief for . . . well, for too long. But you can't run from that shit, and it caught up with me about a year later when I crashed. I had to get a relief vet in for six weeks so I could get my head back on straight."

"So fucking brave." I rested his cheek on his chest.

"Not really. Ivy was amazing. I couldn't have done it without her. I saw a therapist and began to open up all those feelings, you know? Mostly, I just fucking cried. Leo did too. He and I began to sort through her things and got her memorial stone organized—something I'd put off for too long. I fought my parents from wanting to come and rescue us, something they're still trying to do, as you know, and then cried some more. There was a lot of crying, in case you missed that part."

"Oh, baby." My heart broke for him. I lifted my head to his shoulder and his arms folded around me. "I don't know how you did it."

He kissed my head and ran his hot hands up and down the hungry skin of my back, hovering over the valley piercings and just dipping into my crease, more comfort than interest. But I scooted up a little so he could reach any damn thing he wanted and a finger slid in and came to rest.

"I don't think I told you," he said. "But our dog, Didi, was killed in the accident as well. She was a mixed breed with some beagle somewhere, and she got thrown from the back seat, straight through the front windshield."

My head jerked up. "Jesus. So, you guys lost *two* of your family."

He gave a weak smile. "Yeah, and we could've done with Didi's help in trying to cope with Lu. But to lose them both? That's maybe what hit Leo hardest. He lost his mom *and* the dog he loved. And I wasn't much help to him in the early days."

"I don't believe that." I gave him a stern look. "Help doesn't have to *do*; it can just *be*. You were there. You're his dad. That's everything."

He snorted and rolled me sideways onto the mattress, tucking me into his side with my head on his bicep. I melted against him, enjoying the feel of his body wrapped around me. Stubble grazed my forehead before a kiss was planted there again, and he lifted a leg over my hip to make sure I wasn't going anywhere. I'd never had so much sweet affection in my life, and my heart reeled dangerously.

"You're pretty smart for a club bunny, you know that?"

I poked him in the ribs. "Well, don't hold your breath. Any minute now I'm gonna break out into a rendition of 'It's Raining Men,' and it'll all be downhill from there." My hand drifted over the firm curve of his arse and down the hard muscle of his thigh to hitch his leg higher. Then I slipped my thigh between his and rested it there.

"Is that why you don't have a pet? It seemed kind of strange for a vet."

He nodded. "I just haven't been quite ready to go there until now. You helped with that."

I tilted my head and smiled up at him. "Sassy?"

He grinned. "Leo loves that damn cat."

"What about Lu's parents?"

"They live about two hours away in Newport. I see them every month or so. They come here, or we go there, mostly the former, because the clinic's open most Saturday mornings. It was hard for them when Lu died. We're both only children, so Lu's were kind of left hanging. At first, I think Leo reminded them too much of Lu and they struggled to spend a lot of time with him, but they're good now. A little conservative, perhaps, but their hearts are in the right place. And both sets of grandparents take Leo at some point during any school breaks. All in all, I'm pretty lucky."

"What would they think about you being bi?"

He was quiet for a moment, which said a lot.

"To be honest, I don't know, and that's probably why I've never come out to them. Plus, it wasn't like I had to. Lu and I met pretty young, after all. The coward's way out probably, and I do regret it, now. It would've been much easier to come out with Lu there supporting me. Not much anyone could've said then."

I tweaked his nose. "Nope. Nothing cowardly about it, at all. People come out when they're ready. There's no timetable or rules, and fuck anyone who says there is."

He looked at me with soft eyes. "Thank you. But Lu being killed *did* make things more complicated. They'd have been shocked anyway, just because I don't think I've ever given them reason to ask the question."

"Unlike me."

He tweaked my nose. "But now, with their understandably over-protective attitude toward Leo, and me being a single dad and all, I'm just not sure how they'd react. Lu's parents are pretty churchy, although mainstream. And mine? I think Dad would probably be okay; there's not a prejudiced bone in his body. But my mom? It's not that she's homophobic, I don't think. It's more that she's so up in my face about my life and what she thinks is best for Leo, as it is now. God knows what she'd do with the idea of me being bi or the idea of maybe another *man* in Leo's future, as opposed to a woman."

"And Leo would be caught in the middle," I added. Fact, not question, because it was true.

"And then there's that."

"How do you think Leo would react?"

Emmett blew out a sigh. "I'm hoping he'd be okay. I don't know if he told you, but Cody's dad is bi, and Jon recently moved in with his boyfriend. Cody appears really open and happy about it, so I'm hoping that's rubbed off on Leo. We've had a talk about Jon and Brent, just to check in. Leo was pretty noncommittal other than saying he liked Brent and everything was fine. I guess I have to take that at face value and hope it's encouraging."

"It's a lot better than the alternative."

He shrugged and slid to his back. "I guess. But it's hard to read Leo sometimes. He seems really upfront and blunt, and he is about the stuff that doesn't really matter. But when something's important to him? He keeps those things pretty close to his chest."

A crease formed between his brows and I wanted nothing more than to kiss that sucker off, and so I got up on my elbow and did just that before staring down at him. "Leo loves you. He idolizes you."

A dopey grin erased the frown. "I like it when you kiss me."

"Don't change the subject." But I kissed him again anyway. "I think Leo just worries about you. He made sure I knew your favorite foods and to check that you ate lunch."

Emmett blushed a bright red. "Shit. Don't remind me. He's a mother hen when he wants to be. It's my own fault. I dropped the ball after Lu died. We didn't eat well or keep up with the house, and I'm still trying to get back to all that. In those first few months, Leo sometimes had to wake me for work. I simply couldn't get my head around it all, you know?"

I didn't, but I could imagine, and my heart broke for him all over again.

"Then Jasper and I had a big pity party and downed a bottle and a half of Jack at the same time, about a year after Lu died. He was grieving hard for Michael as well. We made an oath to check up on each other and kick butt when it was needed. Things got better after that."

"He's a hard man to read. He doesn't exactly say much."

I laughed. "He says enough."

The room fell to silence, and a slow smile spread over Emmett's lush mouth. He was just so effortlessly sexy. Nothing contrived or engineered. No hours spent at the gym or day spa or shopping. Just oodles of pure natural masculine sensuality completely free of attitude or intent. And the sexiest thing of all? He didn't have a single fucking clue about it. You couldn't teach that; you couldn't learn it. I was just lucky enough to be one of the few people who got to see it close up.

"Kiss me."

He pulled me flush against him and covered my mouth with his in a slow, leisurely kiss that went on for minutes, days, weeks, who the hell knew? I was so lost in the press of warm skin and the hypnotic slide of his tongue as it slow-fucked my mouth that everything else slid away. Everything but the feel of Emmett as he covered my body and slipped under my skin, anchoring at a spot somewhere deep and perilously close to my heart.

I tried to remind myself, this wasn't mine to have. *He* wasn't mine to have. It was just a moment and I was going to enjoy it for what it was. But it was no use.

His hand glided over my hip, chasing those piercings as it passed, and we lay there kissing lazily until exhaustion caught us both, and my cheek fell against Emmett's chest.

He gave a contented sigh. "You feel good in my arms," he

whispered into my hair. "I haven't slept the night with anyone since Lu died."

I tried not to react, not to let him see what those simple words did to me or the burning question that lay on my lips. I wanted it to be because it was me, not just the pleasure of a warm body. But I shook the question loose and let it go. It didn't need an answer. I had nothing to offer a man like Emmett. But I could offer this.

I snuggled against him. "I'm not going anywhere."

Not tonight.

13

EMMETT

I had a man in my arms.

Holy shit.

I had a *man . . . in my arms.*

I waited to let the idea sink in, which didn't take nearly as long as accepting the fact that I fucking loved it. No panic, no regret. And not because it was a man, but because it was *this* man. My only encounters with men had been juvenile lust and curiosity. But not this, not Tai.

I watched him sleep, the breath moving in and out of his chest, the defined bow of his dark lips, the smooth wash of olive skin that swept down his slender back to the swell of his ass before it disappeared under the covers, and a sigh broke my lips. A swathe of black hair hid one eye and I lifted it aside, exposing those sharp cheekbones, so at odds with the softness of his smile and gentle heart. I wanted Tai. Craved him. And I really fucking liked him. I pulled the covers over his shoulders and sighed.

It was . . . A. Lot.

My stitched-up heart was ready to date again, there was no denying it. But a guy had never really been a serious option— whether from habit, comfort, or plain old chickenshit fear. But it sure as hell was an option now.

But Tai was leaving sooner rather than later. And even if he stayed around for a while, what the hell did I have to offer a guy like him? Tai was a damn tulip and I was more your garden variety Brussels sprout, with a baby sprout I loved more than anything; I wasn't going anywhere. Tai might've hit some speed bumps in life, but he was savvy, and made for brighter lights than either Burlington or I could offer him. He'd lived a fast life in Boston. What the hell would he do in Burlington?

Gus coughed and Tai stirred briefly but didn't wake. A band of weak light sliced into the room from the skylight in the corridor, adding a sharp edge to the nightlight. And the clamor of migrating snow geese, like the baying of hounds, drifted over the clinic from the lake, shaking the last of the night's peace from my head.

I checked the clock on the wall. Six thirty. I blinked rapidly, wanting to scratch my eyes from their sockets, their tired surface rough and itchy. I'd wrapped the spare blanket around me and checked on Gus three times as Tai slept, and the dog had remained settled. On the last check, I'd even managed to fit him with a cone since he was awake enough to worry his wound. But still no bowel sounds, so the IV stayed in place.

After each check, I'd crept back on board the ridiculous mattress and got my arms back around Tai. He rolled into my embrace without so much as a whimper of protest. I told myself we took up less room on the wobbly thing that way.

And there'd been one time when I'd woken up cold and alone, the spare blanket missing. I'd been about to get up when I caught Tai's soft voice talking to Gus. Hidden behind the mound of dog food bags, Tai was telling Gus all about New Zealand and his family. How much he loved his brothers and how they drove him up the wall. How much he missed his parents. How Gus should go visit one day. How Gus would like it there although he'd have to get used to the accent. That the girls were really laid back, apparently, although he couldn't talk from personal experience, but he guessed that crossed into doggy girls as well.

And so it went on.

Tai said he'd visit Gus at home when he was better, if he was still in Burlington. That he'd make sure I gave Gus all the good drugs. Then back to New Zealand and how many sheep there were, but how Gus would have to leave them alone. That Kiwis took their sheep seriously. How there were no nasties to kill you there; no snakes, no killer spiders, no big predators, zip.

How maybe Tai might get a dog one day just like Gus, although Gus wasn't to get a big head about that. And an awful lot about how Gus just needed to damn well fart. That yes, it was gross, and dog farts were apparently the worst, although Tai was willing to overlook that in the interim. But until Gus farted, he couldn't eat and get better, and Tai needed him to start eating . . . please.

The entire conversation was punctuated by the occasional soft whine from Gus who appeared to be enjoying the company and the soft lull of Tai's voice. Then, after fifteen minutes or so, Tai had crawled back onto the mattress, pressed a gentle kiss to my lips, and then snuggled against me to fall asleep.

I'd kept my eyes closed and tried to ignore the flutter in my chest, but sleep hadn't come quickly. And when it did, it was full of images of dark-haired beauties with soft lips, light stubble, and big hearts.

"I can feel you staring at me." Tai opened his eyes and stretched, all that tempting skin luminous in the dull glow of the nightlight.

He rolled to face me and I pulled the covers over his shoulders to keep him warm. "There's a lot to stare at." I tucked a lock of that dark silky hair behind his ear and he ducked his head, hiding a pleased grin.

His hand landed over my heart, his cheek on my chest. "Mmmm. How did you sleep?"

"On and off. You?"

"The same." He drew lines through the hair on my chest with his fingertip, still not looking up. "You felt good against me all night. Warm."

I pressed my lips to his hair. "Glad to be of service." My fingers found his chin and tilted it up so I could kiss him properly, but he pulled back.

"Saving you from yourself," he explained. "I have it on good authority my mouth would give a sewer a run for its money in the morning. Dion had no trouble fucking me at daybreak, but kissing was definitely off the menu."

What the hell? The more I heard about this guy, the more I wanted another five minutes with him. And do what? Slap him with a plastic head cone?

Maybe. Those fuckers had to hurt.

"I'm making a rule."

He looked up at me.

"That bastard's name is not allowed to be spoken in our bed."

Shit. Our bed.

Tai's eyes widened slightly, but he said nothing. And it was on the tip of my tongue to apologize, but then I thought, fuck it.

"Agreed?"

He held my gaze and nodded.

"Good." I covered his mouth with mine, not hesitating to slide my tongue inside. He groaned and pressed up against me, already hard, making us a matched pair. My hand cupped his ass, fingertips catching the valley piercing and spiking the memory of him standing naked in front of me, which had me grinding against him. He wriggled deliciously in my grasp, humming his pleasure into my mouth. I doubted things got any better than an armful of horny Tai first thing in the morning.

The mattress dipped and groaned obscenely and he smiled against my lips. "If that was you, I'm impressed," he said, peppering my face with kisses. "Gus could learn a thing or two from that."

I slapped his ass. "Sassy tart. Get on your feet."

He scrambled off the mattress so fast he tripped and nearly face-planted on the floor, and I had to grab his hand to steady him. He pulled me up and slid effortlessly into my arms like a well-rehearsed dance move, capturing my lips in a fierce kiss. It could have felt strange, awkward even, but it was neither of those.

Then Gus groaned and we both froze.

I peeled back from Tai's lips to check on Gus around the bags of food, but the big dog was merely shifting position. He turned unsteadily and collapsed on his other side, the move was accompanied by the less than dulcet, bubbling expulsion of colonic air.

Tai's face appeared over my shoulder and we burst out laughing. In seconds the room was dubiously redolent with the promise of breakfast for the poor animal.

"Woo-hoo!" Tai fist-pumped the air. "And yeah, okay, that was weird."

I chuckled and tugged him back behind the dog food, turning him to face the wall, arms stretched above his head. "Don't move."

"Oh, I can get bossy." He wiggled his ass as I ran my mouth the length of his body from nape to the dip between his hips. He made every filthy noise I'd ever imagined, and some I hadn't, until I was kneeling with all the beautiful curves of his ass filling my vision.

It was worth a pause to take it all in, and his butt cheeks twitched as I lightly ran a finger over each, the clench of that smooth dark skin under my fingertips, the ripple of goosebumps trailing in my wake.

"Yesssss." He pushed his hips back and I slipped a hand between his thighs to spread his legs. "Do it."

I had every intention.

A soft kiss to each cheek to start, then it was straight in to get that sexy fucking line of metal under my tongue. I'd been fantasizing about it all night, feeling it against my leg, my dick, my hand. And now here it was, and I was so fucking turned on, I could barely breathe.

I teased him for a bit, my tongue dipping barely into his crease before flicking back out, then back lower, brushing his hole, then out—Tai's moan muffled, his fist shoved in his mouth. His hand fell and cupped the back of my head, keeping me right where he wanted me, a weighty groan of pleasure rumbling in his throat.

"Jesus, Emmett. Just fucking do it. You're killing me."

I licked back up, jangling the little heart as I passed on my way to his waist, the sound cranking my shit big time.

He hissed. "If you're gonna tell me you're done, your balls are mine, mister."

I smiled against the cool of his skin, then licked back down to his ass cheek and sank my teeth in just enough to leave a mark.

"Fuuuck," he muttered. "Damn, that's . . . holy shit, I don't know what that is, but goddamn, you better keep doing it." He went up on his toes and arched his back to get my mouth back where he wanted it.

And this time I was ready. I spread his cheeks and dove in until his legs shook like jelly and the lewd sounds falling from his mouth had me so damn close to the edge, a puff of wind from the wrong direction would've ripped that orgasm right out of me.

Keeping my tongue where it clearly belonged, I slipped a finger alongside and then two, and then I pulled back to watch my fingers slide in and out of his glorious ass.

Tai's curses became increasingly creative. Then he looked down and captured my gaze, riding my fingers, mouth open, pupils black as pitch. I reached around his hip and fisted his swollen cock with my free hand, and his head fell back, his body rocking in and out of my fist, driving my fingers deeper into his ass, his skin hot, all those damn noises taking me to the brink.

One glance down to find my cock leaking all over the floor, and I was pretty sure I could come hands-free from the show Tai was putting on alone. But yeah, a third hand would've been just dandy.

Tai shuddered and I crooked my finger, aiming again for that sweet spot inside, and on the next stroke he tensed, arched his back, and exploded into my hand with a loud grunt, pumping between my fingers, legs shaking.

I stroked him through until he pushed my hand away and spun around.

"Get up," he said, dropping to his knees.

It took me a second to figure it out—too enthralled by the sight of a naked trembling Tai at my feet, his come still slathered on my hand. But once I did, I was on my feet in a flash, and a half dozen strokes were all it took before I unloaded, half in his open mouth, the rest all over his face.

And holy fucking shit. That was a first.

I hauled him to his feet and into my arms, taking his mouth and plunging my tongue deep inside. He trembled and snaked his arms around my waist as I cradled his face and licked him clean.

"That was . . ." He buried his face in my shoulder. "Goddamn, I don't know what that was."

"Me neither." We rocked in each other's arms and said nothing. Seconds passed, a minute, maybe more, until—

"Jesus, what the hell are we doing here, Emmett?"

And just like that, the world crashed in.

His warm breath rolled over my skin, his face still crunched against my shoulder. "I'm not here to stay. My life is a mess. I have literally nothing to my name. This makes no sense, and neither of us need the hurt."

"Neither of us?" I pulled him down to the mattress and laid him flat, grabbing some of the sheet to clean us up. "So, you're saying *you* could be hurt here too? Because that means something, Tai. It means I'm not in this alone."

He nibbled nervously on his lip. "I know it means something. And do I really need to answer that?" He blinked slowly and took a breath. "But it doesn't change the fact that I'm not staying. It only makes it more imperative that we stop and think."

"Riiiight." I nodded sagely and straddled him. "Excellent point. How very . . . sensible of you."

"Well, *I* thought so." He eyed me warily.

"Mmm." I cupped his jaw and stared into those troubled eyes. "There is, of course, *another* sensible option."

"Mmm. Why do I think this isn't going to be sensible at all?" His eyebrow arched. "Go on then. Tell me."

I took a deep breath, because this was it. My last chance to walk away.

He waited, eyes locked on mine like he knew.

I let the breath out of my lungs and opened my heart. "Option number two is the one where you *don't* go in four days or a week or whenever. Option two is where you *stay* for a while. The one where we get to know each other, date a little, under the radar, of course—"

"Meaning, I'm your dirty little secret?" He merely raised a brow, but the sting was there in his eyes, and I winced for putting it there.

"*Meaning,* we give it some time to see if this *thing* between us has traction. And it's also the option where if it does, I come out."

His mouth fell open. "You can't come out just *for me*. I can't be responsible—"

"I won't be doing it just for you. I'm going to come out anyway, very soon. You'd just be influencing the timing, that's all."

He didn't look all that reassured. "What about Leo?"

Good question. "Leo is the *only* reason we'd keep it quiet at all. I'm hopeful when we're ready that he'll adjust pretty easily. Besides, he likes you."

"He likes me because I'm a *friend,* your *employee,* an issue you're neatly stepping around, by the way. And I doubt that's gonna hold when he realizes I'm your . . . floozy." He waved a hand in the air and left it at that.

"Floozy?" *God, he was adorable.* I laughed until I registered his scowl and cleared my throat instead. "Look, we can take it one step at a time. I'm not asking you to marry me. Just stay around a bit longer and see what happens."

"Marry—" His frown reached epic proportions. "Nope, I can't even go there. This is such a bad idea."

"Stay." I rested my elbows on either side of his head, putting our faces only inches apart. "Stay because I like you, and because I think you like me. Stay, because I haven't felt this attracted to someone since . . . since Lu. Please, just stay. Give us a chance."

His gaze slid away. "You'll realize you were wrong. That it was really only sex, and then you won't know what to do about me, and it'll get . . . awkward. You're surfacing from grief, Emmett, and a long dry spell, and I'm here, and I'm a guy, and—"

"Don't," I snapped.

"Don't what?" He worried his lip.

"Don't cheapen this. Don't pretend that's all you felt last night."

He didn't answer for a long minute. "I didn't say *I* felt that way. I said you might come to realize that for yourself. You hardly know me, Emmett."

"It's not just sex for me either. And I want to know you."

His eyes bugged. "I can't."

"You barely thought about it."

"I don't have to."

"So, you're just going to run?"

His jaw set. "You don't get to judge me, Emmett. You don't know me. I'm barely two seconds out of a fucked-up relationship, and you want me to what? Stay and play house so you can see if you want to risk coming out?"

How had we gotten here? "It's not like that."

"Isn't it?"

I held his glare without flinching. "No, it's not. And what's more, you know it. You're throwing up roadblocks because you're scared. Well, I am too. But you're right. I have no place judging you, and I'm sorry."

His expression softened, if only a little.

But I wasn't giving up. "I know you're fresh out of a relationship. I know you have all sorts of shit to sort out. And I know this is awkward as hell while you're supposed to be helping me in the clinic, and I don't want you to feel pressured. I'll help you find another job, if that makes it easier. Or we just take sex off the table. But I can't ignore the feeling that if I let you leave without even trying, I'll regret it. And if that means I don't get to touch you again, so be it. I'll be happy with getting a coffee or two, a meal, some hiking, a chance to get to know each other."

That stubborn determination in his eyes flickered. "You'll keep advertising for help?"

Yes. I nodded.

"And you'll help me find another job if it becomes awkward, or even just if I want to?"

My heart soared. *Please say yes.* "I will. Come on, admit it, it's a good idea. I need help, and even if I find someone, they might not be able to start right away."

"Emmett—" He cupped my cheek.

"And you need the money, regardless of what you decide to do, and this gives you more money in your pocket and more time to work out what you want."

"Emmett, I—"

"Please, just think about it," I appealed to him. "And we'll keep it strictly hands off until things become clearer."

He side-eyed me. "Have you lost your freaking mind? Keeping our hands off each other has about as much chance of success as me buying a flannel shirt, ever."

I waggled my eyebrows. "Speak for yourself. I mean, I understand where you're coming from." I waved a hand over my body. "The temptation is real, right? But I think you'll find I have a lot more self-control than some."

His eyes widened. "You did not just say that. Are you serious?"

"Deadly."

He chewed on that luscious bottom lip as he mulled things over. "Okay, I'll stay another couple of weeks." He side-eyed me. "But we keep our hands off each other. Loser buys maple crullers for a week."

A grin split my face. "You're on. And just for the record, I think you'd fucking rock flannel."

"Never. Gonna. Happen. And this"—he pointed to where I still straddled him, our soft dicks nestled together—"is hardly keeping our hands off each other. Just saying." He shoved me off and was reaching for his clothes when—

"Emmett!" Jasper's voice rang through the clinic at the same time the glass in the front door rattled under a fist. "Open up!"

"Shit." Tai grabbed his clothes and flashed me a wicked grin. "I'll be in the shower."

I rounded on him. "Chicken shit. He's going to know, you realize that?"

Tai shrugged. "He's your friend. You explain it." His gaze swept the room and he grinned at the mess we'd made. "Good luck with whatever lies you're planning on telling." He spun on his heels and headed for the bathroom, that pert ass mocking me every step of the way.

"Emmett!"

Shit. I did the best I could, threw a blanket over our mess, and headed for the front door.

Jasper took one whiff of the room, a long look at my thoroughly debauched state, the clothes I'd hastily donned, the pile of bedding shoved into the corner, and the sound of the shower running, and rolled his eyes. "You've got to be kidding me."

My back straightened. "I have no idea what you're talking about. Go talk to Gus. He's not out of the woods yet, but I'm happy with his progress. His bowel is waking up, and we'll try him on a little food later. He needs to stay another day, but hopefully you can take him tomorrow."

Jasper sagged a good half dozen inches as relief swept through him. He sucked in a shaky breath and knelt beside Gus's cage, the Giant Pyrenees stretching his head out for a scratch, seeking comfort. Jasper murmured something to the huge dog, his voice trembling.

I rested my hand on Jasper's back. "That's exactly what he needs. You stay where you are, and I'll get my day started."

Jasper nodded and wiped his cheek. He reached for my hand and squeezed it. "Thank you. You've no fucking idea what this means to me. He belonged to us both, you know?"

I squeezed back. "Oh, I think I know exactly what it means. You and I have lost enough, right? We don't need to go there again."

Jasper nodded and wiggled his ass onto the floor beside Gus. Then he opened the cage door and pulled the dog's head right onto his lap.

"Coffee?" I asked him.

"Thanks." His gaze swept the room and landed back on me. "You know you're not fooling anyone. The room smells like se—"

"Don't," I snapped, then winced. "Sorry. I just . . . look, I know everything you're going to say, but I like him, all right? It's ridiculous and inconvenient and could blow up in my face just like you think, but . . ."

Jasper sighed. "You like him? Like, *like* him?"

My head dropped and I slumped against the wall. "I do. In fact, we've just talked about it. He's going to stay on a bit longer so we can get to know each other, see how things go. We won't say anything to Leo or anyone else just yet, not until we work out if it's going anywhere."

Jasper gave a low whistle and watched me with a sad, almost wistful expression in place. "I hope you know what you're doing. I know you don't need reminding, but it's not only *your* heart you're playing with. There's Leo as well, and Tai's what, a half-second out of a bad relationship with a prick of an ex?"

I frowned. "How did you—"

Jasper snorted. "You didn't think that would stay a secret for long, did you? Phyllis came out with you from the treatment room right in the middle of it, remember, and she's the wife of one of my clients, so . . ."

"Fuck. This damn town."

"Yeah. So maybe remember that. Tai's already staying at your house, and if I can feel the sparks between you, others will too. You've got Tanner and Briar curious as well."

"Shit."

"Tongues are going to wag."

"I know. I know. And if it was only me, I wouldn't hesitate to be open about us. I'm so tired of having a secret that wasn't ever really meant to be one in the first place. I couldn't give a fuck what people thought. But with Leo . . ."

Jasper's expression softened. "I understand. Just don't take too long to come to a decision, yeah?"

"I know. But I also don't want to scare Tai off. I've got a kid, Jasper. That's a lot for anyone to consider in a new relationship. If he decides to pull out, it's easier if Leo doesn't know. This isn't exactly dipping my toe back in the dating pond, you know. This is taking a full running jump and sinking like a fucking stone."

Jasper snorted. "Is anyone really ever ready? And if he runs, then he was never the one, was he?"

"Maybe. But who said he would be the one running?"

14

TAI

I put my back to the steaming needles of hot water, resting my forehead on the tiles.

What the hell am I doing?

Bad enough I was staying in Emmett's freaking garage studio and working in his clinic, but now I was apparently heading into the closet to try dating the guy. I must've lost my damn mind. He might not have been thinking of coming out just for me, but his attraction was sure as hell forcing his hand sooner than he might have liked, and I didn't feel good about that on any level.

Not to mention, I was barely free of a fucked-up relationship, had nothing to my name, and the last thing I wanted was to end up beholden to anyone else to keep me afloat, especially another man who wanted to—holy crap—date me. And reliant was starting to feel exactly what I was in danger of becoming. Emmett paid my wage, had given me a place to sleep, lent me a car and a phone, and none of that felt right.

We needed to talk.

I switched off the water and caught the soft murmur of voices from the kennel room next door. What the hell Jasper had to be thinking of me and what Emmett and I were doing, I had no idea, but it couldn't possibly be good. And there was no way he'd have missed the clues. He was probably in there trying to talk some sense into Emmett while I showered, and I could understand why. I was a hot second from doing that very thing myself.

What I really needed to do was stop being a selfish prick and get the hell out of Dodge. Head west and get my shit together. Make a life. Stop messing with Emmett's and let him go on being a good dad to Leo and let him find someone a damn sight more sensible and less messed up than me.

I grabbed a towel and scrubbed myself dry, ignoring every cell in my body telling me to run, because I couldn't get past just how much I liked Emmett. Only ten days and he'd wormed his way under my snarky skin and set up shop. Ten days and we were drawn together like magnets. We couldn't be in the same room without finding ourselves next to each other.

And there was no way that bet was going to survive more than a couple of days. I wanted Emmett, wanted him any way I could get him, and I was pretty sure he felt the same. And together, the sex was explosive. Kind of a surprise, to be honest. I'd had my fair share of good sex, even great sex. But last night had rocked me, even worried me at some level.

I had feelings for Emmett. Inconvenient, awkward, unexpected feelings. I wasn't in love with him, not yet. But I knew it could go there if we tried this *thing* between us. I cared for Emmett. I felt safe with him, and I knew he cared for me. That on some level, I was important to him. And I knew I unsettled his world as much as he did mine. That kind of power was heady, potent, something you could get used to. But I also knew he was as lost as I was about how to go about finding out if it was real.

I'd never had any of that with Dion. I'd thought I loved him, but I never felt I moved him, never felt he saw me. And that's why I'd said yes to staying, when everything in my head screamed that I shouldn't.

And that's why Emmett and I needed to talk.

"Tai, Tai, Tai, are you finished?" Leo bellowed through the door. "Dad said we can go to The Maple Factory for breakfast. Hurry up."

My mouth turned up in a huge grin. "I'm coming. Two minutes."

And then there was Leo. What the hell was I doing starting something with a guy who had a kid? I wasn't dad material. Hell, I was barely boyfriend material. The last thing I wanted was to hurt Leo. He'd had far too much of that in his young life already. And yet here I was, selfishly willing to fuck up not one life, but two.

So yeah, Emmett was right wanting to keep us under wraps for as long as possible. When he finally came to his senses and realized I wasn't what he wanted long-term, at least Leo wouldn't be caught in the crossfire. I could patch my own heart with time. Leo needed to be safe.

I checked myself in the mirror and opened the door.

"Good morning, Tai." Ivy shoved a cup of coffee in my hand and looked me over with a keen eye. "Good work last night."

I narrowed my eyes. I had a sneaky feeling she wasn't referring to Gus.

Her lips turned up in a cheeky smile and she blew a few locks of pink hair out of her eyes. "You might want to shove that boss of yours in the shower now that it's free," she said. "And throw that bed linen in the wash. Leo's eyeing it for a blanket fort."

"Shit." Definitely not referring to Gus.

I shoved the coffee back in her hand and ducked into the kennel room. Two minutes later I had everything in the wash and Emmett on his way to the shower while Jasper and Leo fussed over Gus.

"We need to talk." I shoved Emmett into the bathroom and stood in the doorway.

His face fell. "You've changed your mind?"

I blinked hard. It would've been so easy to just go with it and say yes. "No." *Goddammit.* "But we still need to talk."

He looked relieved. "About what?"

"Keep your voice down." I leaned my head into the kennel room where Leo was regaling Jasper about the audition and the play. I lowered my voice to a whisper. "I can't have you giving me everything."

His brow creased. "What do you mean?"

"The studio, the phone, Lu's old car, everything. I can't do that again. I won't freeload—"

"You're *not* freeloading," Emmett hissed. "You're allowed to accept help."

"It might not seem that way to you, but it's important to me, Emmett. I have to play my part in *whatever* this is we're doing. I can't just be along for the ride. How will you ever see me as an equal if the only reason I'm making it through is because of your generosity?"

"Move this from the bathroom to the office," Ivy snapped from behind me.

I hadn't even heard her sneak up.

"I'll keep Leo busy if he comes out." Her gaze flicked between us. "Don't make me regret this."

Emmett's eyes blew wide. "Did you tell her?"

"Of course not." I fisted Emmett's shirt and pulled him down the hall and into his office. "Did you tell Jasper?" I fired him a pointed look and his ears burned hot. "I thought so. Don't worry, I'm not angry. Just don't get pissy when you run your own rules as well. But just so you know, even someone with their eyeballs hanging out and half a nostril could read the signs this morning."

"Really?" He looked shocked. "I mean, I expected Jasper to pick something up, but . . ."

I shut the door and Emmett pulled free of my grip. He brushed himself off and perched on the edge of his desk, wearing a hungry, feral look that almost boiled my blood. The man was killing me.

"You look delicious enough to eat." He pulled me between his knees and ran his nose up my neck. "Fuck, you smell good. I've been wanting to do that since the minute you came out of that shower."

And there it was. My dick was ramrod hard in two seconds flat. I pushed him away, stepped back, and stabbed a finger his way "You were a tasty pair of lips away from losing that bet there, mister."

"Shit." He stared and shook his head. "How the hell do you do that? Make me forget everything else except getting my hands on you? It's sorcery, that's what it is."

I brushed my shirt off. "It's a gift, what can I say? Now listen up."

He sighed. "Okay, I'm listening." He reached up and tucked a lock of my damp hair behind my ear. "But you're pretty damn cute all riled up like this."

I turned and pressed my cheek into his palm, and . . . froze. *Damn.* I'd almost kissed him. I looked back to find a smirk plastered on his face. *Fucker.* "You did that deliberately."

"You'll never know. Now come on, Leo will be looking for you in two minutes. He wants pumpkin spice donuts. Talk."

"Yuck." I stuck out my tongue. "What is it with you guys and Halloween, sticking pumpkin and spice into everything you can get your hands on? It's crazy, not to mention disgusting, and an affront to perfectly delicious baking and drinks that never did anything to hurt you."

He laughed and I wanted to kiss him. Mind you, I always wanted to kiss him, so there was that.

"Just you wait till the last weekend in April when the sugar season is running and the Vermont Maple Festival takes off. There is no food off-limits from the addition of maple syrup. Read my lips. N.O.N.E."

I didn't answer, knowing the likelihood of me still being around for that was close to zip.

He touched his finger to my lips and smiled softly. "Have some faith."

I was trying.

"Which leads me back to our talk." I eyed him sternly. "I need to carry my weight. I need to pay rent of some kind. I need to *keep myself.*"

"But—"

"Or I leave."

He stared at me, chewing his lip. "Okay. But you don't have much money you can access. Dion made sure of that."

"Not right now, I don't. But I can pay *something.* Take a little from my wages and I'll keep a running total of what I owe you.

Then, whether I stay or leave, I'll pay it back. And if I decide to stay longer, I find my own digs, understood?"

He sighed. "Understood. But how about you clean and maybe paint the studio toward the rent instead. Then maybe I can lease it out later."

That worked. "Agreed. I can wield a paintbrush, kind of. But I don't want any more handouts. And I don't need much to live on. I can feed myself, and I'll get a cheap secondhand phone."

"But you have the old one I gave you. It's a legitimate necessity for your work."

My turn to chew on my lip. "Okay, I'll give you that. But just while I'm here."

He tipped his head in agreement.

"Did you know her message is still on the voicemail?"

Emmett's eyes widened; then his expression turned soft. "Shit, I'd forgotten."

"I was going to record my own, but thought I'd better check what was there first, and yeah."

A crease dipped between his eyes. "Is that a prob—"

"Not for me." I answered honestly. "She sounds . . . lovely. I just thought you should know."

He swallowed and said nothing as if he wasn't sure what the right answer was.

"I don't mind if you don't," I said, and I meant it. If this thing between us was to have a snowball's chance in hell, neither of us could pretend Lu wasn't still a big part of their lives.

"I don't mind."

"Good. Ask Leo if he feels the same way."

"I will."

"But I'm not using her car, not unless it's an emergency, like last night. I can walk or catch a bus, but I'll accept a ride to work if that's okay?"

"Okay. But I'm giving you a raise."

"No—"

"Hear me out. I intend to replace Carolyn with a receptionist *and* a vet tech. I should've done it years ago. It's an expense I can't avoid, and like you say, it might even help build the practice.

Currently, you're doing both of those jobs *and* you've brought in a lot of money chasing those debts, nearly ten grand so far. I'm paying you more, no argument."

Tricky fucker. "All right. But don't think I didn't see what you just did."

He preened. "Nothing you can do about it though, is there?"

"Don't get cocky. I've got years of bitch on you. You have no idea."

He flashed a shining smile that made my knees wilt. "Don't do that."

"Don't do what?" He pulled me closer and ran his hand around my waist.

"That." I punched a finger at his chest. "That thing you do with your eyes. Like you want to eat me alive."

"Mmm." He nuzzled my hair. "What an excellent idea. Where should I start?"

"Don't. I can't resist you when you . . . mmm, oh yeah, that works."

His lips ran down my neck sending a cascade of shivers rippling down my spine. Then his mouth met mine, his tongue slipping inside, the rush of that familiar addictive taste, and I melted against him.

For two seconds.

Then I shoved him back with a wink and a smile. "You lose, motherfucker."

His eyes sprang wide. "Why you little . . . You did that on purpose. You seduced me."

"Moi?" I blinked my lashes furiously. "I have no idea what you mean. It's like witchcraft. You weave this spell over me and the next thing I know you're kissing me. *You.* Are. Kissing. *Me.* As in, you lose the bet, baby." I checked the clock. "Huh. You barely lasted an hour. Must be some kind of world record."

I held out my hand and clicked my fingers. "Pay up. Crullers every day for a week, remember. And if all they have is pumpkin fucking spice ones, I won't be responsible for my actions."

He slapped twenty dollars in my palm. "I thought you were all about independence."

I patted his cheek. "There's independence and then there's the awesomeness of kicking your butt and gloating. Don't swim with the sharks if you can't handle the bite, baby. Told you I'd win."

"Mmm. Well, if the bet's over—" He hooked a finger in my waistband and pulled me close. "Then there's nothing to stop me doing this."

The kiss was hard and voracious, curling my toes in my socks, and I groaned and pressed against him, wanting a lot more. He stood and cupped my dick with his free hand and I plumped against his firm grip, fisting his shirt, looking for any friction I could get.

Then suddenly he was gone, and I was left teetering in place, smacking my lips like a goldfish. The door opened behind me, and I spun to catch his shit-eating grin.

"I'd offer to help you with that—" He indicated the bulge in my jeans. "But I'm all out of witchcraft." He turned into the hallway. "Hey, Leo, Tai's ready."

Shit. I scrambled to pull my shirt over my fly and grabbed Emmett's coat from his chair to hang in front.

Emmett waggled his eyebrows. "Catch you later, darlin'." And then he left.

Bastard.

15

TAI

And so it began, this two-week slow dance between us—box steps and lock steps, reverse turns and heel spins, dips and dos-à-dos. Yeah, my mother was a big ballroom dancer and I learned a lot watching her favorite shows, although my interest primarily lay with those tight outfits the men wore.

But the little tango Emmett and I had going on was a close reminder. Working closely together in the clinic, learning each other's moods and habits—the way Emmett's left cheek twitched when I pushed him a little too hard or how his blue eyes grayed when he'd forgotten to eat. The fact he always lost his keys at work, and the warm smile that did strange things to my heart when he began handing them to me for safekeeping every morning at the desk.

The way his whole face lit up when Leo arrived every day from school. That he was hopeless at keeping his desk tidy and even worse with mine. That I had to ban him from my pen drawer, and that Post-it notes on his computer screen worked better than my nagging. And how the sappy notes I hid in his coat pockets and the inside of his treatment room cupboards made him blush and earned me kisses.

I hid a lot more.

That he liked to press me up against the closed door of his office every morning before the day began, as if he needed to get

202

his fix for the day. And how he would ghost his hand over my arse at the slightest opportunity, and I made sure to give him plenty. That he loved when I straddled him on his chair or rested my hand on his thigh in the car if Leo wasn't there. That he liked us touching, anyway, anyhow, and as often as we could, even though we mostly stuck to our original agreement—keeping it light. Kissing, the odd grope and taste, but nothing more.

I liked it all. I loved it. The sweet promise it held. I knew he wanted me, that given half a chance, he'd throw me over his desk and fuck me senseless. And god, how I wanted that. But this seductive slide into friendship was too damn delicious to ignore.

How did I not know that? The blistering tease that set my heart skipping like a damn teenager. And Emmett was so good at it, so . . . relentless. I thought of Lu and his months of pursuit and sent a quick thank you, wherever she was.

"If he gives me a chance, I'll take care of him," I promised her.

And it was getting impossible not to want more with him. The *let's see how it goes* trial had turned into, at least for me, a *yes, please*, and *more*, and *oh god, I'm falling for him*, certainty.

I hoped he felt the same. In fact, I was pretty damn convinced of it, based on the way he fired up all possessive and adorably territorial when a cute guy with a miniature schnauzer stared flirting with me at the reception desk. He'd shooed the poor owner into the treatment room and dismissed my cheeky offer of assistance with an audible growl. I'd waltzed back to my desk feeling tight in my jeans and light in my heart.

And not a single job candidate in sight, which to be honest, I found hard to believe. I kept asking and Emmett kept telling me that no one suitable had applied. I'd pushed Ivy for the truth, but she'd simply iced me out with a knowing smile and asked if I really wanted to know.

I didn't, but then I didn't know what to do with that either. Emmett and I hadn't talked about how long we'd give this thing between us, and it seemed we didn't want to.

And so, the dance went on.

We had all day at work and sometimes evenings as well, the full-immersion test.

And I fell hard and fast.

Pouring over the accounts in his office, developing a budding business plan, arms brushing, the heat of his skin branding mine with the words *eat me*. Yeah, maybe that last bit was in my head.

Or the trip out to Jasper's to check on Gus, with Emmett and I singing along to a seventies rock station—Emmett badly. The man had a voice like a chainsaw with none of the charm, and I loved him a little bit for it. Gus was back to demolishing his food and chasing down cottontails with not a chance in hell of catching a single one.

And then there was Emmett's gaping mouth at my new addition to the clinic—a signboard in the window, the first quote being *It's all fun and games until somebody ends up in a cone.*

He might have rolled his eyes, but he'd been damn impressed with the number of people who'd dropped inside just to say how much they loved it, then bought something for their little darlings while they were there. Or how later, he'd crowded me in the bathroom to ravage my mouth and slide hungry hands up under my shirt and all over the hot skin of my back.

Two days later I upped my game, and after consultation with Emmett, we ran a new sign: *No Hump Wednesday: 10% off spay and neutering for the next week.* Five bookings came in the first day.

And then there was the afternoon we spent bitching and arguing while trying to upload the new accounting software I'd ordered—Emmett stubborn, stabbing his finger at the screen while I fought with him and some fuckwit online help desk as Ivy watched on, amused. Increasingly irritated with each other, then a kiss to my head, one to his lips, and laughter, lots of laughter. And sharing a drink that night when we finally got it working—a cool wind on the deck, fire pit blazing—Leo practicing his lines at my side, complaining about one of the Alice actors hanging around him too much. Emmett and I sharing knowing glances over the fire, Leo leaning against my leg.

Hopes and wishes.

Sharing lunch over his desk or down at the lake; watching Vermont draw her pretty fall cloak over her shoulders and shrug against the cooling temperatures. The fresh scent of a cold wind blowing down from the north. The soft rush of leaves swept and cleaned as Burlington tidied house for the snow.

The secret smiles we shared over pets while owners talked in our ears about fleas and neutering and god knew what, completely unaware I wanted to climb their beloved vet like a tree and shove my tongue so far down his throat he'd still be looking for it next year.

The scent of pumpkin and spice that hung heavy over the Marketplace like a reassuring blanket. I'd gotten used to it. Finding my way around the cutesy provincial feel; the costumes, the banners, the hanging streams of colored lights, but finding no place for the pumpkin and spice martini Tanner tried to convince me I'd love.

Discovering V and V had a short memory. Finding a song to offer in apology at the open-mic night Emmett dragged me to— him clapping enthusiastically from our table with Jasper alongside looking bemused. Finding more than one pair of curious eyes watching us. Finding the desire to wrap my arms around Emmett and claim him almost irresistible.

And finding the walk to my studio each night increasingly endless. But I'd kept to the plan. I looked after myself at night, and I rarely entered Emmett's house unless Leo invited me—a movie, a dinner or two at most. We separated after work and met the next morning at his car. It was a miracle my right hand wasn't chaffed to the bone with the additional workouts.

We tidied the studio together and he bought paint at my request. Then the three of us spent the weekend painting the tiny space. Leo had his own corner to work on, which we redid the second he lost interest. Between coats, I jollied them both back into the main house and supervised a fall cleanup. Guilt clouded Emmett's eyes, which I was having none of. I got rid of every last worried wrinkle of it with a blistering kiss in the kitchen while Leo organized his LEGO in the lounge.

Leo proved a whizz with a dusting cloth, if a little short to reach most of the places that mattered, while Emmett whined and dragged his sorry arse about every little thing I asked him to do. It was like working with a sulky teenager, and it was all I could do not to drag him into his bedroom and paddle that delectable pair of buttocks, something I added to my growing list of fantasies.

I made a mental note to get the man a damn house cleaner before I left.

Left. A feat that was becoming increasingly harder to imagine, and I was getting worried about Leo. What had seemed so sensible at the start to protect him was now starting to feel more like we were lying. I'd been so sure Emmett would discover he'd made a mistake with me and would change his mind, that at first it didn't seem to matter how we spun it. But what was Leo going to think if Emmett talked to him now?

It was time.

We needed to talk.

We needed to decide.

"This is it." Leo emerged from the dressing room of the pop-up Halloween costume store, hands on his hips. With the big event only a week away, the selection had been pretty much picked through already, but there were still enough left to spark Leo's imagination.

For some reason he had wanted me and not his dad to help him choose this year's outfit, and I was still puffed up about it. Emmett had been fine with the decision, too fine, in fact, with a distinct note of relief added in. And after an hour of looking, I got it.

With a pounding behind my eyes that a couple of ibuprofen wasn't going to touch, a crick in my neck to match the one in my back, and a pile of costumes in our rear vision mirror, I waited . . . and waited for Leo to make up his mind.

Several kids had come and gone from the other two cubicles while Leo still vacillated—deciding, then changing his mind so many times my brain had whiplash.

I pinched my chin and pretended to study him. In truth, it helped me keep a straight face because the kid was freaking adorable—a descriptor I was pretty sure he wasn't aiming for—

and I wasn't convinced I'd survive any more superheroes, skeletons, freaky lumberjack serial killers, or 'knife through the head' masks.

"It's perfect." I twirled my finger and he did a spin.

"You think so?" He brushed at the fake smears of blood covering the black-and-white striped, zombie convict outfit, complete with cap and shackles. "It's better than the warlock one Dad made me wear last time. He promised I could choose my own this year."

Ah, so that's why I was the choice of consort. I bit back another smile wondering what the hell Emmett was going to say when he saw the gruesome outfit, but then I remembered he'd given me no guidelines and just told us to have fun. Silly man.

"Well, I think we've outdone ourselves." I smiled and stood behind him as he fussed in the mirror. "You're going to be the terror of the Marketplace come Halloween. I'll get the paramedics on standby for all the people you're gonna scare."

"Coooool." He puffed out his chest and rattled his chains.

"Just like that." I smiled and bent down to whisper in his ear. "Now can you hurry it up and let Grim Reaper junior get in here before his dad decides to try out that scythe on me." I shooed Leo into the change room and gave a nod to the scowling man waiting next in line.

Fifteen minutes later I followed Leo into the clinic, his costume securely tucked under his arm.

"Grandma!" He dropped his parcel and flung his arms around the waist of a fifty-something woman with shoulder-length brown hair and bright blue eyes. She cut a trim figure in jeans, ankle boots, and a stylish jersey.

Even without the *grandma* giveaway, I'd have known Emmett's mother in a hot second by their matching eyes.

Emmett stepped forward to introduce us. Karen and Joseph Moore. We shook hands and then stood awkwardly. Thank god for Leo, who hadn't stopped jumping up and down.

Emmett's gaze locked on mine, eyes widening slightly as he got a better look at my lightly made-up face. *Be careful*, it said.

I hardly needed reminding. His dad looked friendly enough,

but Emmett's mother conjured all the reassurance of a smiling piranha.

"So, you're Emmett's new receptionist?" Karen Moore regarded me with a cool look. "My son conveniently omitted telling us Carolyn had left him in the lurch. It was lucky you were able to step in so quickly."

I caught Emmett's eye as he mouthed the word "Sorry."

"No, I was the lucky one," I countered and watched her eyes narrow. "I needed a few weeks of work, and Emmett was kind enough to take me on. I think I've been more of a hindrance than help, to be honest. I didn't know much about animals when I started."

"But he's a quick learner," Emmett stepped in. "And he's been whipping my accounts into shape, as well. Not to mention he's got a good eye for marketing. Did you see our new board in the window? That was all Tai's idea."

I groaned, remembering the new quote I'd stuck there just that morning. *The only balls your dog needs are the ones he fetches.*

"Yes, we saw." This time the smile was genuine. "Very amusing. I'm sure people love it."

"Mom and Dad were in Montreal for a few days and decided to travel back home via here as a surprise for Leo," Emmett explained. "They're staying the night with us but will be heading off early since Leo goes on his school camp tomorrow night." Emmett gave particular emphasis to the last bit and there was no hiding the wicked gleam in his eye.

And I was with him one hundred percent. A whole freaking weekend to ourselves. Some seriously dirty shenanigans were in the offing, and I couldn't fucking wait. I doubted we'd be coming up for air before Leo's Sunday afternoon pickup.

I'd learned about the trip just after deciding Emmett and I needed to talk about what we were doing, and when, or if, to tell Leo. But I really wanted this weekend to not be under a cloud. *Really* wanted it. So, I'd decided not to have that little talk we needed to have until Sunday morning at the earliest. If this was the last time I got to have Emmett on my own or feel his hands on my body, I was damn well going to make the most of it.

"But they'll be back next week for Halloween," Emmett said to Leo, now. "Grandma's going to cook dinner after the Marketplace trick or treat street on Friday. She's already asked your other grandparents to come." He glanced my way with an expression that had apology written all over it.

"Yay!!" Leo jumped up and down. "*Everyone* will be there."

I swallowed hard and turned to Emmett's parents. "What a great treat for Leo."

"Well, we love our boy."

"I'm sure you'll all have a wonderful time."

Leo's gaze jerked up to mine. "But you're coming too, aren't you Tai?" Then to Emmett's mother. "Right, Grandma?"

My gaze flicked to Emmett and I was sure he read the panic there.

"Oh, I'm sure Tai has better things to do." Karen smiled my way.

"No, he doesn't," Leo said bluntly. "And he lives with us. He has to come."

Karen and Joseph's brows both hit their hairlines at the same time.

Fuck.

"He *lives* with you?" Karen faced Emmett, clearly thinking she'd misunderstood.

If only.

To his credit, Emmett never wavered for a second. "Yes. Tai's using the studio in the garage while he's in town."

"We all helped paint it." Leo struggled to rip the tape off the bag that held his costume and I bent down to help. "And then he made us clean the house and Dad sucked at it."

Karen eyed me with interest. "Is that right?"

"That Emmett sucked at cleaning?" I threw back. "Yes. Absolutely. It was just something to do in between coats."

Karen looked less than convinced. "I've been trying to get Emmett to give that house a serious clean for over a year. Seems he's kept a *few* things from us lately."

Emmett rolled his eyes, making no effort to be discreet. "Mom, I—"

"I'm going to book him a regular cleaner before I leave." It was out before I thought about how it might sound.

Karen's jaw dropped.

"You are?" Emmett frowned, then bit back a smile.

Karen regained her composure and spread her hands. "Well, it sounds like you know our boy, and actually, it's not a bad idea. What do you think, Joseph?"

But her husband had yet to take his curious eyes off me, and I'd felt the burn of his interest since I'd walked in. It might've been the pink Sugar Mama tee shirt I wore or the obscene amount of lip gloss I'd applied before leaving the shop to protect my lips from the biting wind off the lake. Or maybe even the eyeliner Claudia had loaned me so I had just the right amount of fierce to face down those parents in the costume Olympics.

But regardless of the reason, I couldn't have shouted out "proud gay man" any louder if I'd donned a fruit crown and started singing "YMCA."

"Well, I guess we'll have you to thank for a clean house next Friday for Lu's parents." Karen studied me closely. "So, of course you'll come to dinner. I insist."

Dear god. Kill me now and be done with it. I turned to Emmett and pleaded with my eyes.

He simply smiled. "What a wonderful idea."

I was going to kill him.

My eyes shot daggers, but he brushed them aside with a single bat of his lashes.

Bastard.

"Look what Tai helped me pick." Leo finally got his costume out of the bag and held it up.

"Oh." Emmett glanced my way and winked. "Much better than last year. How very . . . gruesome of you. What do you think, Dad?"

Joseph Moore laughed. "It's perfect. Terrifying and yet oddly cute at the same time."

I wanted to kiss the man.

Leo patted Emmett's hand in a consolatory way. "Last year's was okay, Dad, but it was time to step up my game."

Emmett snorted. "Absolutely. Did you thank Tai?"

Leo turned and gave me a big hug. "Thanks. You were awesome. Next year we'll do even better."

Next year.

I swallowed around the lump in my throat and hugged him back, acutely aware of Emmett's parents watching, and feeling like we were about to kick a hornet's nest.

16

EMMETT

Leo jiggled in his seat on the bus as if he had a million caterpillars down his pants. They all did. Three busloads of them. Energy levels through the roof. Lids popping on bubbling brains that were only a few ticks south of an imminent surge of teenage hormones. A box of dynamite, minus the match. Something the teachers and parents along for the ride appeared to understand only too well. Still only Friday afternoon, and they looked like they'd fought a few battles already.

"We'll take good care of them," Leo's teacher called from the bus that held Leo's class. He looked more than comfortable with the chaos, in contrast with the parent volunteers whose fear showed in the whites of their eyes.

"May the force be with you," I shouted and the rest of the gathered parents laughed.

Leo's teacher snorted. "We're definitely a Yoda or two short of enough wisdom with this bunch, so I'll take all the help I can get." He closed the door and the bus eased out of the school parking lot, windows jammed with excited faces and waving hands, Leo included.

I watched until it disappeared around the corner, trying to ignore the curl of worry in my gut that every parent experienced when their kids were out of sight. I smiled and shook it off. Nothing was going to ruin this weekend with Tai.

I turned to him and dropped my voice. "Get in that fucking car before I out myself to the entire parent population of Leo's class and drop right here to suck your damn brains out of your cock."

His gaze jerked to mine with a saucy look, and he flicked back his hair. "You can try, sugar."

I watched him waltz that cute ass away with a smile on my face. He might talk a good game, but I knew Tai was as desperate for this time together as I was. I'd closed the clinic to any Saturday appointment—something I'd rarely done since Lu died. We had no overnights, and all the recent surgeries had been given an alternative clinic to call if they needed it. Gus was doing well, sutures removed and eating like a horse, and Jasper had a smile on his face.

So, there it was.

Two days and two nights alone with Tai. If I thought about it too much, I was going to blow my nut before we even got back to the house. The last two weeks had been exquisite torture. Having Tai in my space, at home and at work, getting to know each other —laughing, fighting, and not nearly enough kissing for my liking.

Watching him with Leo brought an ache to my heart that had taken a bit of time to work through. I'd wondered at first if it was because I thought it should've been Lu, but after a few days I realized it was simply wistful recognition that a change was happening—the past moving into a new present, even a future, be that with Tai or someone else. But as the time passed, it was impossible to deny that I wanted the chance for it to be Tai.

He simply did it for me on so many levels, and not being able to touch him as I'd wanted to only heightened everything else I liked about him. His quick wit and sassy smile. His honest-to-a-fault, take-no-bullshit attitude but with a huge heart to balance the snark. And I was falling so goddammed fast, I was breaking speed limits. Then again, it had been the same with Lu. I wasn't someone who had his head turned easily, but when it happened, it hit hard and fast.

But there was still Leo to think about *and* my damn parents, Lu's as well. Leo liked Tai, but as Tai said, that was *friend* Tai,

Dad's *employee* Tai. What the hell was he going to think about having a bi dad? What was he going to think about *boyfriend* Tai? Or, fuck me, *stepdad* Tai?

Because yeah, as crazy as it sounded, I could see us heading that way.

As if he knew what I was thinking, Tai's hand landed on my thigh and squeezed. "You all right there, baby?"

God, I loved it when he called me that. "No. Not even close. Ask me in about two hours when I've sampled your appetizer."

He leaned across and pressed a kiss to my cheek. "My appetizer, huh? I like the sound of that. But—" He hesitated. "Just to be clear, we don't have to do anything you're not ready for. We can have a nice weekend, go for a drive, watch some movies. If it's too soon or you're worried about Leo. If you're having *any* second thoughts."

My gaze darted sideways. "Are you?"

His gaze remained steady. "Not a single one."

I pulled up at the lights and returned his look. "Me neither. I don't need an out." My hand covered his. "I want this, Tai. There's nothing I want more than to spend every second of this weekend with you. But even if we weren't going to fuck, I'd want it just as much, so I don't want you to feel pressured either. But I also know we have to talk, soon, about what comes after—"

"You don't need to make promises you're not sure you can keep." He looked away. "I don't need them. I'm yours this weekend, regardless." He stared ahead. "We can have this time, and then I can still leave. Another two weeks and I'll have enough money, *and* you should've found a replacement, if you'd just be sensible about it."

Heat flooded my cheeks.

He flipped his hand and threaded our fingers together. "I know damn well you've been turning down perfectly good candidates. And as flattering as that is, you need to stop. Even if I stayed, we both know I'm not cut out for the vet tech side. You deserve better—"

"That's not—"

"It *is* true. I love animals, but I don't like the surgery part or how desperately sad some of it is."

And I knew that. Tai had learned quickly and could do whatever I asked of him with direction, but I saw how affected he was by the more difficult side of the job. He was great with the owners, but the animals could rip open his heart.

"My brother's friend in Seattle has offered me his spare room for as long as I need it. I'm going to be fine, Emmett. I have an out. You don't have to protect me or worry about me."

The lights turned green and I began moving. None of what he said felt right.

"I appreciate everything you've done for me, but I'm going to be okay whether I stay or not."

"Are you done?" I freed my hand to turn the vehicle into the driveway and brought it to a stop. Then I shifted so we were facing each other. "Well, are you?"

He frowned and nodded.

"Good, because I need you to listen up. I'm not simply doing you a favor. I'm not worried about you. I'm not protecting you. And I'm *not* Dion. So, stop treating me like I might be."

He blanched. "I didn't mean—"

"I'm not going to suddenly grow tired of you or want somebody else or need to control you or what you do. I'm not that guy. You're a grown man. I know you can look after yourself. And yes, I know you'll be fine. I have zero doubts about that. Would I *like* to have the right to worry about you and want to protect you? Damn right, I would. I'm falling hard for you, Tai, and I'm not going to pretend otherwise. I want to try to make this work, for real, *and* with me out of the closet. *That's* where my head is."

His eyes popped. "Really?"

I reached across and tucked a lock of hair behind his ear. "Yes, really. So, let's talk seriously before the weekend's done, make a plan. I thought I'd give Leo Halloween and dinner with his grandparents first, just in case. I don't want them arriving with something going on. I don't need the grief. Then I'll talk to him as soon as they've left next Sunday."

"What about your parents, and Lu's?"

"They can think what they like. They'll be okay if Leo is. If he's not okay? Well, we'll deal with that then."

Tai stared at me, eyes wide. "I can't believe you really want to do this with me?"

I brushed the back of my fingers down his cheek and cupped my hand around the back of his neck. "I can't believe you'd even look at someone like me twice. I'm so fucking lucky. I'd be crazy not to want this with you."

Tai leaned across the console and kissed me. I tried to hold him there but he wriggled away.

"But just so you know," he said, keeping his eyes on me, "I'm falling for you too, Emmett. All handholds gone, ropes hanging free, we're in this free fall together."

My heart settled in my chest. "Thank Christ for that."

He smiled and cupped my groin. "You wanna take this discussion inside, baby?"

I arched into his hand. "I thought you'd never ask."

After a brief to and fro about which bed to head for, I shut Tai up with a kiss, grabbed his hand, and hauled him inside the house and upstairs to my bedroom.

"Don't look," I told Lu as I raced past our wedding photograph in the hall.

"Are you sure about this?" Tai continued to sound worried. "You said you haven't had anyone in your bed since Lu. I don't want—"

I spun to face him, caging him against the wall. "That was metaphorical. This is not the house we had and it's not *our* bed. I got a new one last year."

"Oh, I thought—"

"Mmm." I nuzzled up the side of his neck. "How about you let me do all the thinking and you just feel." I paused with my cheek alongside his, eye to eye, so fucking lost in him. Then I slid my hand under his sweater until I reached the burn of his skin and his eyelids fluttered closed. I kept moving, up over that sleek stomach, his hard nipples grazing my palm, the smooth satin of his skin sparking little fires in my brain and drawing a low groan from his lips as he turned to nip my jaw with his teeth.

Then I slid my hand around to his back and over his jeans to cup his ass and pull him tight against me. "You have no idea how much I've wanted to do this, feel this." I turned and pulled our groins flush, the hard length of him slotted next to mine.

"Oh god." He fumbled with the buttons of my jeans until he could shove his hand inside to wrap around me. "I know exactly how much you've wanted it."

He squeezed and I bucked against him, my fingers dipping down the back of his waistband to the top of his crease over those piercings. Close but not close enough.

His lips moved alongside my ear. "I want you to fuck me, Emmett. Good and hard. I want to know you were there. I want to feel you thick and desperate for me, so far inside you can pitch a tent in my heart. I want you to fuck my head into the damn headboard so I leave a dent. Can you do that for me, Emmett? Can you?"

And holy fuck. I was going to need better medical insurance.

"Yeah, I can do that." I ran my tongue down the curve of his neck and bit down.

He surged against me. "God, yes."

I bit harder, not caring if I left a mark. I wanted to. I wanted him.

Then I pulled off to catch my breath. "Bed. Now." I grabbed his wrist and dragged him laughing into the bedroom.

I was in so fucking deep. This wasn't just sex—it hadn't been from the first time I'd touched him. If I wasn't in love with Tai already, I was skirting the crumbling edges with a blindfold on, because being with him filled my heart in ways I'd almost forgotten were possible. Ways that gave meaning and light to an ordinary life, *my* ordinary life. Ways that scared the shit out of me, because I knew the stinging, gut-wrenching pain of losing it. The emptiness when it was ripped away. And I wasn't sure I'd survive a second time. All this, and we'd shared each other's bodies only twice. How was that even possible?

Tai stripped and was laid across my bed in seconds, arms wide, a coy look on his face. "Come and fuck me."

Dear god. I wanted inside him more than I could say, was deeply aching for it. But I didn't want to rush and miss a second of it either. I took some deep breaths, slowed, and let myself fall into the feel of him in my room, in my bed, and soon to be in my arms—let all of who he was slip under my skin and fill me up.

A frown dimpled his brow as he felt the shift, but then his lips curved up in a slow, sexy smile. He understood. "Any way you want me, baby. I'm all yours."

I stripped under his watchful gaze as he slowly stroked himself. He was so damn hard . . . for me, and I still couldn't believe it. That he wanted *me.* I stepped out of my briefs and trailed my fingertips from his toes to his chest—long lines of dark copper skin over tight muscle, lean and fit.

Something I . . . wasn't. There was no hiding the difference between us.

He caught the flicker of concern and stretched to run his fingertips over the soft swell of my stomach. "You do things to me I can't explain," he said, bending forward to press a kiss where his fingers lingered on my non-existent abs. "I want you. I love every gorgeous, sexy inch of this body. The softness, the care, the way it folds around me and makes me feel safe. Will you give it to me, Emmett? Can I have it today?"

God, this man. I pushed him flat and pressed my finger to his lips. "It's yours. You can have it all, any way you want."

He shuddered and sucked my finger into his mouth, rolling his tongue around it, eyes locked on mine, daring, laughing, and sexy as fuck.

I crawled onto the bed and straddled his hips, our rigid cocks sliding together, checking each other out, getting friendly. Then I lowered my body over his and took him in a hard kiss, sweeping into his mouth to claim exactly what I wanted.

Arms curled around my neck, legs around my waist, and hungry groans filled my mouth as I grappled with a sexy armful of this amazing man who'd stolen my heart. We kissed, urgent, then lazy, then insistent again. Smiling against each other's lips, laughing and teasing while our cocks rubbed gently together, ramping things up.

He nipped my lip and pulled away. "I'm not gonna last, baby. Tell me what you want."

And just like that, I faltered.

"Hey." He cradled my face and forced me to look at him. "What's wrong?"

I stared at him, so damn beautiful in my bed. "I don't want to . . . disappoint you," I confessed. "I've never—I mean not with a guy. Lu and I did a little playing around but . . ."

His hold became firmer. "You could *never* disappoint me, Emmett, ever. Anything you want to give will be more than enough. If you played around with Lu, you've got the basics. But this is your choice, all the way. If it's too much, there's lots of other options we can enjoy. You'll blow my mind regardless."

And just like that my nerves settled. This was Tai. I was safe. "I don't need other options," I told him. "I *want* this. But fair warning, if I last more than a few seconds inside you, it'll be a fucking miracle."

He flashed me a wicked grin, then ran his hands down over my shoulders and back to grip my ass. "I guarantee I'll be right there with you." Those dark eyes bored into mine. "I am so fucking turned on; you have no idea. Now get that gorgeous cock of yours into me and send me flying. And just for the record, I don't need much prep. I like to feel it. You have supplies?"

I reached into the bedside drawer and threw lube and a brand spanking new packet of condoms on the bed, my face aflame.

"Excellent." His eyes danced and he ran his fingertips down my face. "I love these blushes. They're like little reminders of how special this is, how I get to be your first in lots of ways. Now come here."

I was so gone for this man. We kissed a little more to sink into that urgency again, but when I reached for the condom, he slapped my hand aside, wanting to suit me up instead. Then he slicked a fuckton of lube in and over *everything*.

"Lesson number one." He caught my eye and winked. "Less prep—more lube. Lots and lots more lube." Then he laughed, flung himself back on the bed, and spread those gorgeous legs, wiggling his hips and just daring me. It was fun, flirty, sexy, and totally focused on me. And it blew my fucking brains out my ears.

TAI

I couldn't tear my eyes from Emmett's face. He looked like I'd offered him the moon, and I couldn't remember the last time *anyone* had looked at me like that. Like I was more than a pretty face, more than a good lay. Our bodies moved like puzzle pieces that fit, and as desperate as I knew we both were, he kept us slow, languid, and silky smooth. Like he wanted to treasure every second. And when his finger finally found my hole, I arched into the feel of him, his hard length racked up against mine, the connection between us stealing the breath from my lungs.

And he never stopped kissing me. Kissed me as he slid a lubed finger deep inside and over my prostate, sending licks of electricity zinging through my body. Kissed me as he added another and finger fucked me for longer than I needed, telling me how beautiful I was, how hot, how tight, how amazing. Talked until I slapped his shoulder and threatened bodily harm unless he got with it.

He kissed all the way from my mouth to my leaking cock, licking for a taste and then kissing back up again. And then finally, he kissed me as he pushed through the tight band of muscle and slid his dick deep inside me in one thick breath-sucking push, until he was fully seated. Until that tipping point of pain and pleasure that I craved, filled me up to my fucking eyeballs.

And as I held my breath and adjusted, he kept kissing—soothing, cursing how tight I was, how I was killing him, humming with need . . . for me. He wasn't small and he filled me tight as all hell, but it felt so fucking amazing. And then suddenly, I was there.

"Damn, that's good," I told him, slapping his thigh. "Wreck me, sweetheart. Take me to town."

He grinned like a kid on Christmas morning and it made me so damn happy.

I thought he'd haul up onto his knees, but he stayed down, his lips back on mine, peppering kisses between deep, long strokes—eyes open, marveling, watching me, angling his thrust to get the expression and sounds he wanted—catching that sweet spot. Emmett might not have done it with a guy, but his instincts were spot on, and I soared as he almost split me open—everything I'd asked for.

I fought the urge to close my eyes and just sail with the feeling, but he was close, we both were, and I couldn't look away. I couldn't miss a second of him going over inside me.

A few more thrusts and he pulled up onto his knees to watch himself shuttling into me with something like wonder on his face, pupils black as night and so fucking sexy. Two more strokes and he ripped a cry from my throat. I shot over my stomach and shuddered with pleasure from the bone-deep orgasm I only got from a deep fuck bordering on rough.

But it was only as I watched Emmett follow me over, head thrown back, eyes clenched tight, feeling his cock pulsing deep inside me, did I realize I'd come without a single touch. *Well, damn.* Hands-free. That was a first.

Tension eased from his body and Emmett collapsed on top of me, gasping for breath as he rocked down slowly, still buried deep inside me. I wrapped my arms around him and wondered and worried, but most of all I hoped. And on top of that, I prayed.

I knew sex. I knew it bookend to bookend and every damn page in between. Hell, I'd probably written one or two of them, or at least updated the references. But this was so very much more. If it wasn't love, I'd eat my fucking rainbow flag. And when I opened my eyes to find him staring right at me, I knew he felt it too.

He dropped his head on my shoulder and I put my lips next to his ear. "Score?"

He snorted and mumbled, "Fifteen out of ten."

"Mmm." I ran my fingers up and down his back. "I think we could definitely do better with practice."

"Jesus Christ," he groaned but didn't raise his head. "I'm going to need a fuckton more vitamins."

EMMETT

The second time I woke with Tai in my arms rocked my world as much as the first. It shouldn't have felt as right as it did with him in my bed, in my house, my son's room only yards down the hall, my wife's photos on the wall just outside my bedroom. But it did feel right. It felt pretty damn perfect, if I was honest.

The first-round escapades in bed had been followed by a second in the shower, where Tai's hand had wrapped around mine as I jacked us both off, while he hooked my leg over his hip and fingered my ass in spectacular fashion. I knew I'd want him inside me before long, a thought that both excited and terrified me in equal measure. But I wanted that deep connection with him. I needed it in a way I couldn't explain.

After the shower, a thrown-together meal of whatever we could find in the fridge and a half-assed attempt at looking interested in a movie was quickly followed by another round of lazy blow jobs back in bed and a long meandering conversation about absolutely nothing—both of us simply enjoying each other and not wanting to face any hard questions. That time would come.

At some point around midnight, with ample frosty moonlight slicing the room and stippling the ash-gray cover wrapped up to our chins, Tai had drifted off in my arms. The angles and shadows of his face softened as his dreams took him and I watched him go, planting occasional kisses on his forehead and wallowing in the heat of his body next to mine like a banked fire.

It was an apt description of the man.

Sleep had taken me not long after, and when I woke in the early hours covered in a sheen of sweat, a smile broke over my face to find Tai wrapped around my body like a fiery limpet. I rolled him over and spooned in behind, pulling him tight to my chest. He turned his head to kiss me, not really awake, and then burrowed his face back into his pillow. A soft murmur escaped his lips and cracked open my heart as I tried to make sense of the words I was so sure I'd heard. But the doubt didn't stop me nuzzling into his hair with my hushed answer. "I love you too."

He'd never moved.

But that was hours ago, and nighttime whispers didn't always make it into daylight. I needed to be patient.

Not to mention, I had plans.

The cool gray light so typical of a Vermont fall morning softly lit the bedroom with the promise of a clear day, and I was pumped.

I nudged Tai's sleeping body.

"Go away," he groaned. "My arse has a do not disturb sign on it."

I snorted and slapped it. "It's a beautiful day."

"Congratulations. Now leave me alone. I need sleep. You fucked me out."

I snaked my hand around his waist to wrap around his morning wood. "This says different." I stroked him firmly and he wriggled back against my groin. I was hard in an instant.

"I've created a monster," he grumbled but turned slightly so I had better access.

I smiled against his back and pressed a line of kisses up his spine. "Just say the word and I'll stop."

He grunted. "Or we could try these words. Take me now." A condom and lube hit me on the face as he shoved them over his shoulder, and I laughed. "Is that a hint?"

His hand disappeared under the sheets and around to his ass. "No, this is," he said.

I lifted the covers to find him opening himself up.

"Get inside now, or I'll finish it myself," he threatened, arching with pleasure.

I was suited up in record time. And after making sure he was good and slick, I slid inside all that tight, welcoming heat and took us both home.

And when we were done and lying in each other's arms, only then did I allow myself to wonder if he remembered the words we'd exchanged in the night.

"I have a surprise," I told him.

The corners of his eyes crinkled with mischief. "You've decided you're straight after all?"

I laughed. "Like hell. You're the best fucking thing to happen to me in a long time."

His eyes lit up with pleasure. "Excellent answer. Okay, so what's this surprise then?"

"It's a secret. But it involves packing an overnight bag. You do that while I get breakfast going."

He looked over my shoulder to the clock. "It's seven o'clock in the morning, you jerk. This was supposed to be a sleep-in."

"It was." I slapped his ass and threw the bedclothes back. "Come on. You're not a Boston club bunny anymore. No more late nights and lunchtime brunches with sunglasses. You're in Vermont now, baby. This state wakes up at dawn. Up and at 'em."

He narrowed his eyes and tugged the covers back over his body. "You're an evil bastard, Emmett Moore. What the fuck is wrong with you people?"

I whipped the covers to the floor again and lost my breath for a minute as I registered the mess in our bed with him in the middle of it, fucked out, sated, and all floppy and happy. I wanted to see him that way every damn morning I could.

"You take the shower first. Be downstairs in twenty minutes," I ordered. "We have things to do, places to go."

He slapped a hand to his forehead. "Fuck. Me." A sly grin stole over his face and he spread his legs, tugging that plump lower lip between his teeth and wiggling his hips. "You should really join me to save water."

And fuck, if that wasn't tempting.

I threw his jeans at him and left the room with my fingers in my ears.

TAI

The ambling climb to Sunset Rock above the pretty township of Stowe had come as a bit of a shock to the system. I'd done roughly zero physical activity since leaving the dance floors of Boston, something I clearly needed to remedy. About a hundred yards up the trail, we'd taken a moment to turn and admire the collection of roofs and the pretty church with its fairytale spire spread out below us. It was a picture book vision, set on a forested backdrop, all painted with the fiery colors of fall.

It had stolen my breath.

The whole day had been like that and I had one man to thank for it.

Emmett.

At the top of the one-and-a-half-mile trail, we snuggled on the blanket he'd stowed in his backpack, toasted each other with sparkling water, and ate crackers and cheese as the sun set. Cringeworthily clichéd and fucking glorious.

After his planned day of sightseeing, we were both happy to simply drag the blanket over our shoulders and sit in silence to enjoy the peace.

I had to pinch myself. A month before, I'd been on the bones of my butt, an asshole boyfriend in my rear vision mirror, and a life going nowhere. Now, I was still on the bones of my butt, but that butt was currently seated next to a man I was infinitely unworthy of but who, for some reason, liked me. A man who set me on fire with his touch, whose son brought a smile to my face, and who was increasingly becoming more important to me than I knew what to do with.

Totally fucked to the very soles of my happily tap-dancing feet didn't even begin to cover it. It had been one of the best days I'd had in as long as I could remember.

Emmett had refused to give me a clue as to what he'd planned for the day, other than it was an overnight adventure, and I'd vibrated like a little kid with excitement as he bundled me into the car to be driven who knew where. As he drove, we'd talked about anything and everything, including Leo, with Emmett sharing a lot about Leo's early life and his relationship with his mother. I'd greedily lapped it up, wanting to know everything.

We'd left Burlington and headed east into a sea of thick forest, a bright canvas of brilliant red, gold and green that went on forever. That you could go online and find where the best colors were that day or week and plan your road trip around them came as no surprise, not in Vermont. Vermonters were nothing if not passionate about their state.

Emmett had done exactly that, trying to ensure my perfect first foray into the mountains during fall. He'd succeeded, especially with the gorgeous chocolate-box cabin he'd rented just out of Stowe, on Taber Hill Road—its fire laid, a box of food and other goodies on the table, and champagne in the fridge. The main bed was in the lounge to make the most of the fire, while there was a smaller bedroom with its own bathroom at the back. It was romance on a scale I simply couldn't get my head around.

I just knew I wanted more of it, a lot more.

Before we got to the cabin, he'd stopped for lunch at the cutest little diner in Waterbury Village and we'd feasted on thick chowder with crusty bread and a cold beer—all set amongst an explosion of pumpkins and harvest paraphernalia that I was developing a surprising affection for.

I figured it was the Vermont equivalent of desensitization—a month of gradual exposure to the enthusiasm of seasonal Vermont and I was being rendered immune. Another year and I'd likely be filling the vet clinic window with jack-o-lanterns myself.

We'd spent the afternoon sightseeing around the area and driving to places like Gold Brook Covered Bridge and Moss Glen Falls, my mouth perpetually unhinged at the drop-dead gorgeous scenery. New Zealand was a stunning country but it wasn't the only one. However, I deftly avoided Emmett's determination to induct me into the delights of the Vermont Ski and Snowboard Museum by telling him we needed to leave something for next time. He bought it. The man was adorable.

When we'd had enough of driving, we headed for the fairytale cabin, unpacked, and then lazily made out on the bright patchwork quilt that covered the king-size bed—had I mentioned cutesy? The hot tub went on the list for later, after we'd driven the short distance back into Stowe to make the Sunset Trail before dusk when it closed.

I snaked an arm around Emmett's waist and leaned my head on his shoulder. "Thank you for today. I don't have enough words for how special it was."

"I'll have you turned into a Vermonter before long." He buried his nose in my hair, something I noticed he did a lot.

I found his lips and indulged myself. "Is that right? Well, if I start sprouting chest hair, wearing plaid, brewing beer, buying an axe, or looking sideways at anyone who hasn't lived here for at least twenty years, I expect you to put me out of my misery."

He laughed and pulled me close. "Aw, I promise I won't let it get that bad. First sign of any plaid and I'll take to you a big city somewhere so you can detox in safety." He tipped my chin up for a kiss. "I like you just the way you are."

My ridiculous heart tipped in my chest and I almost said the words. But he kissed me again and that seemed better, safer. We stared over the treetops into the deep blue of the darkening sky for a little while longer until I started to shiver.

"Come on." He got to his feet and held his hand to help me up. "There's a hot tub and a bed with our names on them. But that quilt has to go. It feels like my grandmother's bedroom."

"Ew. Don't even think it." I grabbed his hand and let him pull me up. "My nana used to get all six of us in her bed before breakfast to tell us all about our Maori ancestors and tribal stories. And that woman never had sex. I know this as fact because it would've upset the entire balance of the universe. Her kids must've come via immaculate conception, although I'm not sure even God would've been that brave. She had more wrinkles than a Shar-Pei, could clock a lie at fifty yards, and my grandfather thought the sun shined out of her . . . well, a place she likely didn't have either, considering she was a goddess, or a witch, depending on the day."

Emmett snorted. "That was . . . oddly specific. I think I'd like to meet your grandmother someday."

I rolled my eyes at him. "Well, hopefully not soon. She died just before I left. I'm surprised you didn't hear the rent open between heaven and hell the moment it happened, each vying for the right to her soul."

Emmett cupped my face in his hands. "God, I love you."

Holy shit. I froze with my mouth half-open.

His eyes flew wide. "Shit, I'm sorry," he stumbled, planting kisses all over my face. "It just slipped out. Not that I don't mean it, because I do. I just shouldn't have said it. It's too soon, right? It's only been a month. I'm sorry." He pulled back and stared at me as if assessing the damage.

My mouth closed, then opened, then closed again, words failing me, my heart tripping in my chest, threatening to burst out of my ribs.

"Please don't run," he said softly, brushing his lips over mine. "I won't push, I promise—"

"Shh." I finally found my voice and cradled his face. "I love you, too. I've known for a bit, I think."

He rested our foreheads together. "I love you, Tai Samuels."

I grinned like a loon. "I love you Emmett Moore."

He crushed me to him. "We're in big trouble, aren't we?"

I blew out a long sigh and kissed just under his ear. "Up to our freaking necks, baby. Come on, let's get outta here."

Rather than staying to eat in the town, we decided to take all the newly shared feelings, and the highs that went with them, back to indulge in the goody box Emmett had ordered for the cabin. After that, we'd boil ourselves red as lobsters in the hot tub and then fuck each other senseless.

And that's pretty much what we did.

Best. Day. Ever.

EMMETT

We woke to a light dusting of snow that turned the cabin and surrounding forest into a freaking winter wonderland. The little log structure was set well back from the quiet road, and it felt a million miles from civilization, not just down the road from pretty little Stowe village with its coffee shops and tourist traps. Snow wasn't unheard of in mid-October, and although beautiful, the leaves never looked as good once the snow hit them, so I was glad Tai had seen them before.

Having said that, my home state was really turning it on for us, and I couldn't be happier.

Tai was ecstatic.

He insisted we drag the quilt *and* our breakfast out to the chairs on the deck so we could enjoy the experience like tourists. Like the fool that I was for him, I followed without a word.

Twenty minutes later we hauled our chattering teeth back inside, stripped off, and headed for the hot tub to finish our toast without losing our toes. One thing led to another, and we landed back in the shower with me buried balls-deep in Tai's world-class ass, and him slamming his hands on the wall and shouting as he painted the tiles. I made a mental note to rate privacy high on the list for any future vacations and to maybe shift Leo to the bedroom at the far end of the hall.

His bus was due back from the school trip at four-thirty, and with just under four hours to drive, we couldn't linger. We headed back to Burlington via the coffee shop in Stowe and a few side trips along the way, including a cider mill just out of Waterbury.

Talk came easy, answers didn't. If I said I loved Tai once, I said it a dozen times in a dozen different ways. But Tai was less . . . free with the words.

I let it go. He'd been through a lot, relationship-wise, in a very short time, and it had to be messing with his head.

"Have you thought about what you might like to do, work-wise, since you're staying?" I asked him as I drove. We'd been talking about the clinic and where I saw things heading there. I still wanted a vet tech but I completely understood why Tai didn't want that role. "What if I change the clinic reception role into an office manager? You're really good with that side of things."

He looked at me with disbelief. "An office manager?"

"Yes." We were about a half hour from Burlington and still had plenty of time to unpack before heading to collect Leo. "I think Ivy's ready to dial down her business though, and I'm not sure where that leaves me."

"Why don't you buy her out?" Tai suggested. "You could run her grooming service in conjunction with the practice. That leaves her an easy out when she's ready to hang up her clippers. You can always employ a new groomer at that point and pay them a salary. The two businesses feed into each other. It'd be a shame to lose it."

I grabbed his hand in mine and kissed his knuckles. "See. You're good at this shit. You've got a natural business mind. I'm not saying you should work at the clinic, though. You could work anywhere. But I saw the way your eyes lit up when you found all those invoices and then got the money rolling back in. You're a masterful little shit."

He grinned and slapped my arm. "And don't you forget it. I've been reading those veterinary business books I got for you. The ones you haven't even opened yet." He eyed me pointedly and my cheeks warmed.

"Not *yet*."

"Riiiight. Anyway, there's a whole lot of stuff you aren't claiming on your taxes. You could be saving a fortune."

I couldn't help but laugh.

"What?" A crease formed between his eyes.

"Look at you. I like it when you're trying to save me money. It's . . . sexy."

He laughed. "Lip gloss and numbers huh? Who'd have guessed?" He slid our joined hands into my lap, and yeah, I'm not going to say that didn't feel good. Maybe there'd be time before Leo's bus got back—

"Yes," he answered with a laugh.

I frowned. "Yes, what?"

"Yes, to everything that just went through that dirty little mind of yours when I nudged your dick. We'll make it quick."

"Not too quick."

We scraped into the school parking lot with just under ten minutes to spare after Tai had dropped to his knees in my kitchen to deliver me a spine-tingling blow job. This was after he'd chased me out of his studio when I tried to grind on his ass while he was unpacking.

Worked for me.

We garnered a few interested looks from the other parents as we waited. Newcomers stood out in Burlington, but the gossip mill was fast and I had no doubt most of those gathered knew Tai worked at the clinic, at the very least, and were probably wondering what he was doing with me after hours.

I smiled and waved to those I knew, and Cody's mom came across for an introduction and a brief chat. She eyed Tai with interest and asked a few questions, having no doubt heard about him from Cody and Leo. Tai shuffled on his feet but held his own. Then the buses arrived and everything took a back seat as the doors opened and vomited a million tired and sleep-deprived ten-year-olds into the waiting arms of their parents.

Leo looked as bedraggled as the rest—tired but hyped enough to chatter nonstop all the way home, regaling us with stories about games and fights and hikes and horrid vegetables they had to eat, while Tai peppered him with questions and listened indulgently to the long-winded replies.

With Leo's help, I managed to talk Tai into staying for dinner and then spent most of it ogling the man I loved as he continued to laugh and chat with my son while sending me sexy looks and playing footsie under the table.

How was this my life? And did I really get a second chance at all these feelings again, and with this man?

Leo helped Tai with the dishes and then lasted all of thirty minutes before we found him sound asleep on the couch. Although he was almost too big, I decided to risk my back and carry him to bed. Tai followed us upstairs, turning Leo's covers back so I could slide my sleeping boy in for the night. Tai then found Sassy and deposited the cat beside Leo's pillow before we switched off the light and stood there watching him sleep for far too long.

It was achingly familiar and comfortably domestic and filled a hunger in my heart that had been denied for too long. I threaded my fingers through Tai's and kissed the side of his neck. Then I walked him to his studio door at the top of the garage stairs but didn't go inside. Instead, I slid my arms around his waist and pulled him close.

"I had the best weekend I can remember in a very long time, and I have you to thank for that," I whispered against his lips.

He hummed and slid his thigh between mine. "Me too. And I know I haven't said it as often as you have today, but I do love you. I want to make sure you know that."

"I do." I had no doubt. Tai might not be saying the words, but they were in his eyes every time he looked at me.

"Good. But I also know Leo comes first," he said flatly. "As he should. And until we know how he feels, I just . . . well, I don't want to get ahead of things. And I need to remind you that I'm coming into this with nothing to offer, except me. I'm no more together in my life than I was a month ago, and that still doesn't sit right with me."

I cradled his face to make sure he was looking right at me. "You're wrong about that. You're a lot more together than you give yourself credit for, so maybe you need to think about that. I understand why you feel that you don't have much to offer, but none of the things that you're referring to are really important. I don't need anything more than you, not a single thing."

He turned his lips into my palm and pressed a kiss there, his eyes misting in the faded glow of the single light above us. "Thank you."

But I wasn't finished. "And yes, Leo's feelings are important, absolutely, but mine are too. I also deserve to be happy, Tai. I deserve more than to simply lose myself in work and a son I'm crazy about. I deserve to be loved too, *this* kind of love, and you do as well. And I deserve to be proud of who I am, no more hiding. Please trust me on that."

He stared at me for a long moment and then nodded. "Okay. I trust you. Let's do this."

I let out the breath I'd been holding and took his lips in a hard kiss, wishing I had him in my bed, *our* bed, or at least I wanted it to be.

But I was determined to make it happen. And the first step to that was talking to Leo.

The next week couldn't pass fast enough.

18

TAI

The week dragged. Waiting until after Halloween to talk with Leo was the best thing for him, but it was hell on us. Leo's reaction might turn out to be positive, like we hoped, but if it didn't go to plan, neither of us wanted that shit show happening just before Emmett's parents descended.

But knowing it was the right thing to wait did nothing to stop the curl of worry in my gut about not getting it over with sooner. Two huge things were about to happen, both of which were going to rock the foundations of Emmett and Leo's world.

First, Emmett was going to be an out and proud bi man and he was inviting me into his life as his boyfriend.

And second, Leo was going to have to adjust to having a bi dad and to having me in his life in a way he wasn't prepared for.

Emmett might not be thinking that far ahead, but I knew only too well that neither of those things was going to happen without repercussions and push back—parents, students at Leo's school, clients, maybe even Leo's grandparents. I wasn't just another man in Leo's life, I was a visibly gay man dating his father. There would be no hiding me away or passing me off. And as okay as I was with myself, people and kids could and would be cruel, and I'd bet money that both of them would cop some comments.

Telling Leo, and hopefully getting him on board, wasn't going to be the end of anything, just the beginning.

I was terrified of hurting Emmett *or* Leo. Or not living up to what they deserved. And I wasn't going to do anything to make that kid's life any more difficult than it needed to be. He'd been through enough.

And so, we waited. Ivy picked up on the vibe and cast worried glances between us. Emmett said she'd bailed him up in his office to ask about the weekend, and he'd confessed how we felt about each other. She'd been delighted but then whacked him on the arm for waiting too long talk to Leo. Said we were playing with fire.

We were.

Jasper had called in to pick up some deworming tablets for Gus and was cool but not unfriendly with me. I got that he was protective of Emmett and that was fine. But it did nothing to reassure me. After sharing a coffee, Emmett sported damp eyes and Jasper had been a little pale. I watched them hug but didn't ask. It wasn't my place. And Emmett had disappeared back into his office immediately after.

Everyone had an opinion, it seemed. And that was before the grandparents were even factored in. I viewed the approaching weekend with a dread I couldn't shake, and I thought Emmett did too. But neither of us mentioned it, content to get through the workweek as best we could while stealing kisses behind closed doors and trying to stay positive.

The only bright point? The cutest pair of boxer puppies brought in for their first vaccinations, and I got to be the meat in a wriggling boxer puppy sandwich for nowhere near long enough. They were freaking adorable, but not even they could match the sappy look on Emmett's face as he'd watched me roll around with them on the floor.

I scraped together the best pout I could muster while telling the puppies very loudly how much they'd love living with Emmett and Leo, what beautiful boys they were, and how they'd be soooo good for Leo—teaching him all about responsibility and obligation and all that important stuff.

The puppies' owner couldn't stop laughing, while Emmett merely gave me his biggest eye roll to date. But the way he'd dragged me into the bathroom as soon as the puppies left and kissed me until I couldn't breathe made messing with him totally worth it.

None of it, however, helped alleviate my nerves. And by Halloween I'd tied myself in enough knots, you could've stuck a plant in my arms and sold me as a macramé hanger. But I'd had a couple of wins along the way, including foiling every one of Emmett's earnest attempts to get me to accompany them to trick or treat street. Point to me. I wanted Leo to have memories of Halloween trick or treating without me in them, just in case

Instead, I was headed back to Emmett's house to await my doom—aka sitting around the dining table with both sets of Leo's grandparents, neither of whom were aware that the father of their beloved grandchild was in fact bi and merrily fucking his lodger's brains out in style, and on a regular basis. Nope. Not awkward at all.

The fact that Ivy had also been invited to the family dinner was the single positive in the looming debacle. I'd need her help to distract attention from the way Emmett seemed unable to glance my way without frothing at the mouth and looking like he wanted to devour certain parts of me whole, or at least lick them to death, very slowly and very thoroughly.

And yes, those images had taken up altogether too much space in my brain over the past week, and I might have added the odd swish to my hips and nibble to my lips just to fuck with Emmett's head. The T-shirt I'd put on the day before had said it all. *Let's get sticky in Vermont.* I'd picked it specifically to rile the man up and made sure to do a slow reveal in the clinic when we'd arrived.

Ivy had snorted coffee all over the reception desk and Emmett had taken one look, glared, and disappeared into his office. Mission accomplished. But although I was totally on board with Emmett's lusty appreciation, the man's poker face sucked, something that was likely to get us into trouble. Mostly because I couldn't help responding in that reflex way that didn't bear thinking about, especially with his parents around.

"Are you sure you've got a big enough treat bag?" Emmett eyed the massive red velvet pillowcase I'd given Leo, thanks to

Claudia in the thrift shop. We'd come to the clinic, partly to escape Emmett's parents who were busy with dinner preparations back at the house, but also to check on a dog who was overnighting after having his broken tail removed.

Leo's head bounced up and down. He hadn't been able to sit still since he'd donned his costume in the clinic bathroom ten minutes before. "Tai says it's better to be safe than short on candy."

Emmett cringed. "Yeah, but Tai doesn't have to deal with the sugar high, does he?"

I grinned. "That's what dads are for, right?" I handed Emmett Leo's coat in case it rained as the forecast warned. "Ignore your father and have a good time with all your grandparents. I hear there are face painting booths, food stalls, and a fire truck you get to look inside."

"Really?" Leo's eyes lit up.

"Really. And if you save me some candy, I'll put aside some extra dessert for you tomorrow, if you want it."

"Promise?"

"Cross my heart."

In the middle of our high five, the clinic door opened and both sets of grandparents spilled into the waiting room.

My heart jumped in my throat.

Let the games begin.

Georgia Foster approached with her hand extended. "You must be Tai," she said warmly. "Leo has told us all about you."

"He has?" I shook hands and gave Leo the hairy eyeball. "How many lies did you tell?"

"None." Leo slid his hand into mine, something that didn't go unnoticed by any of the grandparents if the raised eyebrows were anything to go by. "I told Nan the truth. You suck at Scrabble and have terrible taste in clothes."

I suddenly remembered the T-shirt I was wearing and I'm pretty sure I blushed. "So, really, really big lies." I shoved him playfully and he shoved me back.

Georgia laughed and turned to her husband who was studying me intently. "This is my husband, Craig," she said.

We shook hands.

"I see the sign stayed." Emmett's mom nodded to the window with a hard-to-read expression on her face.

Shit. I'd meant to change out the quote. But there was no denying *Fifty Shades of Spay* had a nice ring to it.

"Well, I think it's a great idea," Georgia interrupted whatever Emmett was about to say to his mother. "We need as many smiles as we can get, right?" She fired me a wink and I could've hugged her.

I had one ally, it seemed, and possibly Emmett's dad as well. He didn't say much, but I sensed he was giving me the benefit of the doubt. I wondered how long that would last when he knew about Emmett and me. One thing for sure, Karen Moore still wasn't happy, even if it was only regarding how close I was with Leo.

"I'm going to let you guys go and have all the fun." I squeezed Leo's hand and let him go. "Karen, tell me what I can do to help back at the house before you get back."

She looked surprised. "Oh. Well, I've put everything in the oven and set the timer, but if you could keep an eye on things and maybe turn the vegetables once, that would be very helpful. We'll be back before they need to come out. Thank you . . . Tai." Her gaze darted to Emmett and then back to me.

"You're very welcome, and I'm sure I can manage that," I told her, ignoring Emmett's eye roll. "Ivy can check I do it right when she gets there. I'll see you all later." I caught Emmett's eye and tried to put as much into that one look as I could. *I love you. I wish I could be with you. I'll make you proud. Have fun.*

I'd almost made it out the door when Emmett's voice rang out. "Hey, don't forget your car keys." He threw me Lu's set, which still carried the lime-green heart-shaped disk with her name on it.

Fuck.

All sets of eyes landed on me and I hoped my expression left Emmett in no doubt that he was a dead man walking. We'd needed two cars today and . . . yeah, that hole we were digging ourselves just got deeper.

He smiled innocently.

Dead *and* buried.

I fisted the keys and got out of there as quickly as I could.

———

Leo took the clean roasting pan I held out and got busy with his tea towel. "And Cody wore this cool purple Joker outfit," he chattered on. "With the green hair and everything." Full of smiles and loaded with sugar, he hadn't slowed since they'd gotten back from the Marketplace.

But then again, everyone was in a good mood—enough that I'd even started to relax myself. Ivy was quieter than usual but clearly enjoying the family banter. Even Karen had been friendly and thankful for the work I'd done to help with dinner.

Maybe there was hope after all.

"Brenda Peters wore the same costume as Cody, but hers sucked cos her mother had dyed an old wig and it came out yellow not green," Leo prattled on. "But she made Brenda wear it anyway."

"Don't say sucked, Leo," Karen said from the dining table in the next room where everyone else was seated. "It's not a nice word."

"Sorry, Grandma," Leo called over his shoulder, then rolled his eyes at me.

I slid him a wink. "I bet everyone loved your costume."

Leo's grin split his face. "It was the best. No one else had one with the manacles. And Cody's mom squealed when I crept up behind her."

I snorted. "I bet she just loved that."

Emmett appeared at my shoulder, the heat of his body reaching across those careful inches left between us. "Go and sit down. I'll finish here." He turned and put his back against the countertop to face me.

I narrowed my gaze. "I'm perfectly fine, thank you."

He leaned in and whispered, "You're hiding."

"Exactly. And you're not helping."

"Go. You too, Leo. You've been a big help."

Leo whooped and was gone in a flash. I took a little longer, making deadly sure Emmett knew exactly how much I'd make him pay for his meddling.

He laughed and flicked me with the wet tea towel.

The price went up.

I'd been seated less than a minute when Ivy's foot nudged me under the table and I looked up to find her expression pinched and gray. Even her shock of pink hair appeared faded.

"I think I'll head home," she said in a strained voice, and my heart jumped in my throat. "I'm not feeling the best."

I was at her side in seconds, along with Emmett. "What's wrong?" I felt her forehead, but if anything, she was cool rather than hot.

She pushed my hand aside. "I'm fine. Just a bit of indigestion. I'll feel better once I can stretch out in bed."

A deep crease formed between Emmett's brows, and I knew what he was thinking. Ivy was rarely sick and reluctant to let you know if she was. Something was up. "I'll call a doctor," he said.

"No," Ivy snapped. "I said I'm fine, and I am. I just need to go to bed. Stop fussing."

"I'll drive you—"

"No, I will," I interrupted Emmett. "Stay with your family. I'll make sure Ivy's okay, but if I'm not happy—" I fired Ivy a determined look. "I'll take you to a doctor myself, no argument."

It took a minute for Emmett to agree, but in the end, he nodded. "Call me when you get there."

"Hey, still here," Ivy protested, punching me on the arm. "I can take care of myself, and I'm quite capable of driving."

I pinned her with my best don't-mess-with-me glare until she finally looked away. "All right," she grumbled. "Drive me if you want."

"What an excellent idea." I kissed her cheek. "I wish I'd thought of that." The comment earned me another punch and a chuckle from everyone else.

"Take the Ram." Emmett shoved his keys into my hand. "It's slippery out and it's already on the street." He saw us safely down the back steps and then took my arm out of sight of everyone inside. "Drive safely."

I stole a hidden kiss. "I will."

He turned and folded Ivy in his arms. "No playing hero, okay? Call me if you need me. Promise?"

She nodded against his chest. "I promise."

Emmett and I shared a worried look.

"I'll stay for a bit to make sure she's okay," I told him. "Now go inside, it's freezing out here." I watched him go and then linked my arm through Ivy's. "Ready?"

She smiled weakly. "Ready."

We made our way around the corner of the house and slowly down the slick driveway, past the other cars. Emmett's truck was one of only a couple of vehicles parked on the quiet dead-end street.

By the time we got to the passenger door, Ivy was noticeably puffing and I decided there and then that we were going to the hospital, regardless of her protest. She could argue with me on the way. I popped the locks and helped her inside, making sure she was securely belted in. Then I pulled out my phone and made my way around the back of the truck so I could discreetly let Emmett know the change in plan without Ivy hearing exactly how concerned I was.

But before I could hit dial, a hand landed on my shoulder and spun me around.

"Well, well, well. Look at you."

Fuck. Dion. I jumped backwards only to find myself jammed against the truck's tray and canopy. "What the hell are you doing here?"

He caged me in with an arm on either side. "I have to give it to you, Tai, you move fast. Cozying up with the vet in under a month? Who knew you had it in you? Then again, you do like to be looked after. How long till you can get him to move you out of the garage and into his bed for good? Then again, maybe he's the careful kind. You didn't get invited to the family trick or treat thing, after all, did you?"

Bile poured up the back of my throat. "You've been watching us, me? Have you been here the whole time?"

He snorted. "Don't flatter yourself. I came back a couple of days ago. Thought I'd given you enough time to come to your senses and get bored with the vet and this asshole town. Now, it's time to go."

"Get lost." I tried to shove him away, but he turned and backhanded me hard across my face. The pain exploded in my head and I staggered back against the Ram, momentarily stunned and shocked to my core. I'd honestly never believed he'd hit me.

Think again.

"Tai?" Ivy's panicked voice called from the front seat. "I can't see over the back. Who are you talking to? Are you okay?"

I blinked hard, trying to clear the stars from my brain. "Stay—"

Dion's palm closed over my mouth. "Tell her it's just a friend." He dropped his hand slowly.

"You touch her and I'll fuck you up, understand?"

Dion's lip curled. "Tell her."

Like there was a choice. I wasn't risking Ivy for the world. "I won't be a minute, Ivy. Just talking to a friend. Stay there."

Dion stroked my cheek. "Aw, baby. We're a lot more than friends."

It was all I could do not to throw up in his face. "We're nothing. *Less* than nothing. So, you can just fuck right off. I'm not coming back, Dion. We're finished."

His expression hardened. "Stupid boy. We're nowhere near finished. Did you think I'd just let you walk away after everything I've done for you? We had a good thing going and your ass isn't easy to replace. It's time to stop playing house with the good vet and come back where you belong."

I swallowed hard, my saliva sharp with the iron tang of blood. "Get it through your thick skull that I'm not going anywhere with you. And if you don't fuck off, I'm calling the police."

"You're not calling anyone." He knocked the phone from my hand and fisted my jacket. "You and I have unfinished business."

Like hell we have. I jerked back and lunged sideways, the

twisting motion loosening Dion's hold just enough to let me ram my elbow into his face. Blood arced up from his shattered nose, catching me in the face, and he screamed and immediately let go.

For a second, I froze, stunned by the fact the self-defense lessons I'd taken all those years ago had actually fucking worked. But I managed to shake my head free while he was still reeling and jammed my knee as hard as I could into his balls.

He bent double and spewed on the road. And I prayed he'd never get his pathetic dick up again without remembering me.

"Tai!" Ivy's door flew open.

I yelled at her to stay in the cab, but when I turned back, Dion was right there. He spat blood and then his fist connected with my jaw in a sickening crack.

I stumbled and tripped on the gutter, landing on my back on the wet grass, the weak streetlight swimming in my eyes. Everything rang in my head, pain ricocheting through my neck from the impact as I rolled to my side and tried to scramble to my feet. Then Dion's boot landed under my ribs and sent me sprawling again.

"You fucking piece of shit." Dion wiped his nose, still running thick with blood. "Who the hell do you think—" Slammed from the side, Dion crashed to the ground with a heavy thud.

Emmett. Air whooshed from my lungs and I tried to scramble out of the way.

"Get your fucking hands off him." Emmett crawled on top of Dion, pinning him to the ground. Dion scrambled to get free, but Emmett had the weight advantage, raining blows as the man grunted and groaned beneath him.

"Emmett, stop." I shot out a hand to try and stop him. "Enough, okay?" I choked. "It's enough."

He deflated immediately, scrambling off Dion and over to me.

"The police are on their way," Ivy called from the Ram's cab. She looked white as a ghost in the streetlight.

"Are you all right?" Emmett ran his desperate hands over my body and I nodded.

"I think so."

"Oh, thank god." He crushed me against his chest.

"Ow, ow, ow." I jerked back as my bruised jaw connected with his shoulder.

He instantly let me go and turned my face to the light, his eyes narrowing. "Fuck. Did he do this? I'm gonna fucking kill him." He spun, only to find Dion had already scarpered to his van. The engine cranked and Emmett made to chase, but I grabbed his shirt.

"Let him go. They'll find him."

"I've got his plate," Ivy called as Dion fishtailed it down the street, bringing neighbors to their windows.

Emmett fingered my jaw, then gently brushed his lips over mine. He lay his cheek alongside and I felt the dampness there. "Don't ever scare me like that again. I couldn't . . . I thought he was going . . . just don't, okay?"

"I'll . . . fuck, that hurts." I could barely form the words through the stinging ache in my jaw. "I'll try not to."

Emmett's eyes filled. "God, I love you so fucking much." He pressed his lips to mine and kept them there.

"Emmett?" Karen's voice shook.

"Dad?"

Shit, shit, shit. Leo.

"Fuck," Emmett whispered against my lips.

He sat back on his heels and turned to Leo who was standing less than a yard away. Leo's shocked and confused expression said everything.

I tried to shake Emmett's hand free of mine but he clung to it, the gesture earning every last shred of my hopeless heart. But this wasn't the time. "Let go. He needs you, Emmett. I'll be here. And get someone to take Ivy to the hospital."

"Dad?" Leo's gaze flicked between us. "What's going on? Were you kissing Tai?"

"Leo, I—"

"You said you loved him. I heard you! Are you— Is he—" Tears rolled down Leo's cheeks. "What the hell, Dad?"

Emmett jumped to his feet and went to draw Leo into his arms. "I was going to talk to you—"

But Leo lurched back. "No. You're not gay, you're not! You don't love him. You can't! What about mom?"

Emmett blanched, his face distraught. "Leo, I loved your mom—"

"No!" Leo shouted. "Don't lie. I don't want him. I hate him! I hate you!" And Leo was gone, bolting back into the house, the slam of his upstairs bedroom door saying everything that needed to be said.

Emmett's shattered gaze landed on me.

"Go to him." I pushed the keys of the truck into Emmett's hand. "Don't forget Ivy."

Emmett nodded, kissed me once, ignored his stunned parents as he asked Georgia and Craig to get Ivy to the hospital, and then took off after Leo.

Which left me lying on the wet grass, battered by my ex-boyfriend, my pseudo current boyfriend busy in the house consoling his son who hated the sight of me, while his parents stared at me, gobsmacked, like the homewrecker they clearly thought I was.

And as the sirens drew closer, it was really hard to disagree with them.

19

EMMETT

I'd barely made it to Leo's room when the police arrived and everything was put on hold until they were done interviewing. In the meantime, I hadn't said a single word that I wanted to my son. I'd only caught a glimpse of his bereft, tear-stained face before leaving him again to talk with the police. Luckily, Leo hadn't seen any of the violence and the police were happy for him to remain in his room, but I was beyond desperate. I *needed* to talk to him.

My dad, god bless him, helped Tai into the house where he'd sat ominously quiet and refused to meet my eyes, other than a single look to warn me off when I tried to take a seat alongside. Cold packs to his face hadn't stopped the bruising starting to bloom on his jaw—a mottled tapestry of red and white with dusky undertones that would be impressive tomorrow.

He'd refused the coffee my father tried to force on him, wouldn't talk to anyone except the police, and fear ripped through me. I was desperate to get my hands on him, to know what he was thinking, but it had to wait.

The interview process didn't take as long as I expected, helped by the cops finding a security camera on the neighbor's house opposite with a good view of the street in front of mine. The footage was pretty clear regarding what happened, and that made things a lot simpler. What wasn't simple were the increasingly confused and incredulous expressions on my parent's faces as they listened to Tai and I explain the background. Like I could give a fuck by that stage. Leo was the only thing on my mind.

When the interviewing was done, Tai insisted on going back to his studio. He pulled me aside. "This needs to happen between you, Leo, and your family first. Having me around right now isn't going to help."

I knew he was right. As much as I desperately wanted him at my side, I needed to first talk with Leo and my parents. Alone. And I wasn't going to expose Tai to any ignorant barbs or lashing out. But it didn't stop me from worrying. I had no idea what terrible thoughts were running through Tai's head as he waited alone in his studio, but I could guess, starting with him thinking this was all his damn fault.

Well, fuck that.

The whole thing was a fucking mess.

The detectives were heading for the hospital to talk with Ivy, and also with Lu's parents. They were less than happy about the truck being driven from the scene with possible prints on it, but I hadn't even thought about that at the time. I'd just wanted Ivy taken to the hospital quickly. I had to hope they had enough with the camera footage and eyewitnesses. I told Lu's parents to call if the police took the car and they needed a ride. The hospital was running tests, but according to Georgia, Ivy was doing okay.

And then there was Leo.

The betrayal in his expression and the words he'd said—I could barely breathe at the memory. And of course, he'd immediately assumed I was gay and, with that, had a whole lot of questions about Lu and me. My heart broke. I'd let him down. I'd fucked up badly not telling him sooner—not giving him credit for the amazing kid that he was. He was so very wrong in his thinking about Lu and me but in order to make sure he understood, I had to damn well talk to him.

The minute the detectives left the house, I headed for Leo's room, but my mother had other plans.

She was on me the second the door closed. "What the hell were you thinking?"

My hand shot up. "Don't! Just . . . don't." I kept moving.

She grabbed my arm. "We deserve to know—"

I spun on her. "No, not right now. I'm not willing to hear *anything* from you right now. Not until after I've talked to Leo."

"You should've thought of that bef—" She read my expression and swallowed whatever it was she was going to say.

"Karen . . ." My dad rested a hand on her arm. "Sit down." She flashed him a killing look but did as he said.

My dad flicked his hands at me. "Go, talk to your son, then come back."

I bolted up the stairs like my life depended on it, and to a large extent, it did, at least the one I hoped to build. Leo's closed door gave me pause and I took a few seconds to get my thoughts together. Then I knocked.

There was no answer.

I knocked again and then eased the door open and . . . froze. The room was empty.

Tai's door slid open just seconds after I hammered and I knew he'd been waiting for me. He looked shattered—red-rimmed eyes and a battered, swollen jaw. I hauled him into my arms, not giving a single fuck about my parents waiting at the bottom of the stairs.

He sagged against me for a second, then caught sight of my parents watching and pulled away. "Emmett, I can't—"

"Leo's gone."

His eyes blew wide. "What?"

"When I went up to talk, his room was empty. We've searched the house, but he's not there."

"Fuck." Tai raced inside to pull on his boots and jacket. "Have you tried calling him?"

"It goes straight to voicemail." Then it hit me. "Shit. We left his bag in the truck when we went to the Marketplace, and then he came home with my parents. Fuck. Fuck!"

Tai grabbed my shoulders and pressed a kiss to my lips. "We'll find him. Have you tried Cody?"

"His mom's apartment is a couple of miles away and Leo's bike is still here, but it's worth a try."

Tai stepped away to let me call. "It doesn't sound like he was planning to go far, then," he said.

Ashely's phone rang a few times and then went to voicemail. I left a message and hung up.

Tai tipped my chin up. "It's gonna be okay, Emmett. Let's go find him."

Tai followed me down the stairs to where my parents waited and I caught the sour look my mother shot his way. I cowed her with a glare. "You stay in the house in case he comes back," I told her, so fucking done with her attitude. If I didn't find Leo soon, I was going to lose my damn mind.

She opened her mouth to protest, but my father stilled her with a hand on her shoulder. "Go inside, Karen."

She bit back whatever comment she was going to make and headed inside.

"We should do a quick check of the street and then call the police," my dad said.

I nodded, even as my knees crumbled beneath me. I grabbed for the handrail as I went down, but Tai got to me first, and the next thing I knew I was in his arms, my whole body shaking. I couldn't lose anyone else. Leo had to be okay. Why hadn't I just told him about us? What the hell was wrong with me?

Tai ran hands up and down my back, his voice calm. "Shh. It's going to be okay. He's just angry and upset. He hasn't left you; he's not that kid. He's gone somewhere to think, and he's smart. He won't do anything foolish."

I sucked in a shaky breath and stepped back. "You're right. He *is* smart. Thank you." I pressed a kiss to his lips, then turned to my father who was watching us closely. "Dad, can you check the cars and garage, and then up that path into the woods at the back? You remember that fallen tree about fifteen yards in that he sometimes plays on? Tai and I will check the street."

"I remember." My father tightened the grip on his flashlight and started with the cars in the driveway.

I grabbed Tai's hand and pulled him toward the street. "You

take the cul-de-sac, and I'll work my way to the intersection. Bang on doors if you have to. I can't think of anyone he'd go to on the block, but you never know."

The street was little more than two hundred yards long and it didn't take us much time. There were no kids Leo's age on the street, and like Tai, I didn't think Leo was simply hiding from us. He was hurt and shocked and he'd left to think. I wouldn't believe he was just trying to scare me.

"Stop it." Tai slipped his hand into mine when we met back in the driveway. "I can see your head spinning. This isn't your fault."

I stared at him. "Tell me you're not blaming yourself."

His gaze slid away.

"Yeah. I thought as much."

He looked crushed, the angle of his face against the weak streetlight only serving to highlight the swelling of his jaw. Several neighbor's windows shined bright in the night, their occupants watching us through the glass.

I stroked his cheek. "I'm sorry. I didn't mean . . . I just . . ."

He grabbed my fingers and faced me with a determined look. "Don't. We need to find Leo first, then we can talk, okay?"

All the breath left my lungs. "Okay. But just know that I love you, nothing's changed about that." I brought his knuckles to my lips.

His eyes softened. "I love you too. But I think we both know everything's changed. How about you try Ashley again."

I did, and once again it went to voicemail.

My dad ran breathless from the backyard. "I took the path all the way through the woods to the next street, calling all the way, but he's not there."

Tai squeezed my hand. "It's time to call the police."

My mother ran toward us from the house. I saw the minute she spotted our joined hands. But when Tai went to pull away, I held on tight. *Don't you dare.*

"I let Georgia and Craig know." She stood beside me, rubbing my free arm while ignoring Tai. "Georgia's going to stay with Ivy, but Craig's coming back to help."

"Do it." Tai nodded at me.

But before I could make the call, my phone rang in my hand and Ashley's name lit up the screen. Tai saw at the same time and our eyes locked.

"It's Cody's mum," he told my parents.

My heart jumped in my chest as I fumbled to answer. "Ashley?"

"Emmett. What's wrong? I was watching a movie in bed and my phone was out in the kitchen, sorry. Do you need me to take Leo?"

My heart dropped. *Fuck.* "Leo's missing. I hoped he was with you." *Please, please, let him be safe.*

"With us?" She paused. "Why would he be—"

"Can you please just check?" I tried not to shout.

"Of course."

I was grateful for Tai's arm around my waist and noticed my dad had his around Mom.

Seconds later, Ashley was back.

"Yes, he's here," she almost yelled down the line. "Leo's here. Oh god, I'm so sorry, Emmett. I didn't know."

The phone juggled precariously in my hand as I fell into Tai's embrace. He grabbed it, asking Ashley to wait while I got my shit together.

Tears coursed down my cheeks. Relief. Hope. "Oh my god, he's okay. Tai, he's okay."

"I know, baby, I know." Tai stroked my hair as I wept.

My mother cried softly beside me, muffled against what I assumed was my dad's chest. "Thank you, God," she whispered, and I was right there with her. She reached for my hand, which was at Tai's back, not to pull it away but just to hold on, and it felt good.

My dad patted my shoulder. "He's safe, son," he said. "He's safe. Now take a breath and go get him."

I got myself together and took back the phone.

Ashley explained, "He got Cody's attention with the old stones-at-the-window trick. I was in my bedroom and Cody

252

sneaked down to let him in. I didn't hear a thing. I'm so sorry, Emmett. If I'd known—"

"It's not your fault, Ashley. I'm just happy he's safe. How did he get there? His bike's still at home."

She breathed out a shaky sigh. "His skateboard. He said his bike light doesn't work."

Fuck. I dropped my head to my chest. He didn't use his board often, but I should've thought of it.

"What happened Emmett?"

"Can you hang on a minute?" I looked to Dad who was waving to catch my attention.

"We'll let the neighbors know," he said, pushing my mom in front of him up the path. "And Georgia and Craig. You do what you need to. Tell Leo we love him."

They left and Tai pulled me under the shelter of the stairwell, out of the drizzle which was rapidly turning to rain. He dried my face with the sleeve of his coat and zipped my jacket. I grabbed his fingers with one hand and then leaned close with the phone between us so he could hear.

"Okay, long story short," I began. "An ex-boyfriend of Tai's turned up tonight and there was a bit of a scene. He hit Tai and I went to help—"

"Is Tai okay?"

"Yes, a bit banged up, but he's fine." I fell into Tai soft gaze and felt the warmth of his hand on my back, calming my heart as the rain sheeted on the driveway in front of us. "Anyway, I ran to help and . . . well, I was so worried about Tai, and then Leo . . . well, he saw me kiss Tai, and yeah . . . he didn't know we were . . . like that."

There was silence on the end of the line for a good few seconds. "Like that? You and Tai? Emmett, you're . . . bisexual?"

Tai caught my eye and I leaned close to kiss his forehead.

"Yes, I am. Lu and a couple of other people knew, but I've never been out to my parents or anyone else."

More silence. "Okay. I can see why that might be a bit of a shock for Leo."

I grunted. "You think? Anyway, he said some things, yelled

them, actually. He seems to think I'm gay, and so now he's confused about what I felt for Lu because I never got the chance to explain anything before the police came—"

"The police?" She hesitated. "Oh, Emmett."

"Yeah. Then when they left and I went to talk to him, he was gone."

"Shit. Well, at least he came here. Listen. I've got a suggestion, if you're okay with it."

Anything. "I'm listening."

"How about you come and talk with him for a bit, but don't take him home. Leave him with Cody and me for the night. No one knows better about having a bisexual dad and ex-husband than us, right? By the looks on their faces when I went in, they've been talking already. It might do Leo good to keep going, and then I'll drop him back in the morning."

It was a great idea, and Tai nodded as well.

"Thanks, Ashley. I'd really appreciate that. I'll come now." I hung up and collapsed on the step with Tai at my side.

He rested his head on my shoulder. "And just think, the day's not even done yet."

I snorted and lifted his head to take a better look at his face. He automatically fingered his jaw and winced.

"Sore?"

"Like a bitch," he admitted. "But I'll survive." His expression was carefully neutral but he couldn't hide a flicker of concern.

"Are you worried Dion will come back?" I pressed him.

He shrugged. "Not really. At least not tonight. He'll be too busy fretting about his fucking nose. Damn, that felt good." He chuckled and my heart lightened just a little. "His vanity will make him get that fixed first. And I think we gave him a bit of a scare. The cops are letting Boston know, right, so all we can do is wait. Maybe the van will get picked up."

"Doesn't seem like the kind of vehicle he'd own."

Tai shook his head. "It wasn't his. He'll have got it off a mate." The silence stretched.

"You should go to Leo." Tai got to his feet.

"Come with me."

"We both know that's not a good idea. Leo needs *you* right now, not me. Talk to him, then let's see where we are. You've got a lot of talking to do over the next couple of days." He nodded to the house. "It can't be easy for them either, and we don't know how any of this is going to pan out, not yet."

I glanced at the house and nodded. "But *we're* still okay, right?" I brushed the backs of my fingers across his cheek. "I still love you. And I still want us to be together. We'll get through this."

He didn't answer for a second and my heart plummeted.

"I want that too," he finally said. "Let's just see what happens."

I hated his answer, but I couldn't argue with it. And so I pressed a final kiss to his lips and ran through the rain to Lu's car.

Tai

When Emmett's taillights finally disappeared around the corner, I collapsed against the wall of the garage with my heart in my throat, sick to my stomach. Because it didn't matter how Emmett tried to spin it, none of the shit show tonight would've happened if I hadn't wormed my way into their lives.

Leo felt betrayed and angry. Emmett's parents were confused and upset. And Emmett had outed himself in spectacular fashion when he hadn't intended to. Not to mention, I'd brought my bastard of an ex into their wonderful safe world and exposed them to a nasty side of life that Leo, for one, could've certainly done without.

What the hell had I been thinking? That someone like me could have a family like this? Like my brothers or my parents? A nice little everyday domestic dream—helping Emmett run his business, taking Leo to school, walking our damn dog, making sure Emmett ate lunch. What the fuck was wrong with me? Just because I wanted it, craved it, didn't mean it was mine for the taking. Nothing was ever that simple.

I looked to the house where the back-porch light lit up the rain like a glittering curtain and sighed. There was nothing to do but wait. Wait to see how Emmett's talk with Leo went. Wait to see what his parents thought, what Lu's parents thought—likely none of that good. Even if they coped with the whole bi thing, I was hardly going to be their first choice of partner for Emmett, *or* Leo, not after tonight.

One thing for sure, I wasn't about to face any of them until Emmett had talked with them first. I started on the stairs to the studio and made it halfway before the raised voices caught my attention.

"What the hell was he thinking?" Karen's voice sailed through the partially open family room window to where I stood on the stairs.

I should've moved, but yeah.

"Did you know anything about this *thing* he has with this *man*?" she continued. "I knew something wasn't right. Having him staying here, at the house. Emmett's not like that. And he was having way too much to do with Leo, and the business as well. Joseph!"

"Of course, I didn't know anything," Joseph scoffed. "Do you really think I'd risk my balls not telling you if I did?"

"Don't talk to me like that. Is he telling us he's gay? He can't be."

"I think we need to let him tell us in his own words."

"Emmett should be dating. It's been four years. This is just because he needs *someone,* and this *man* is right under his nose. It's pretty damn obvious that *Tai's* gay. Who knows what he did to get Emmett's attention?"

"I doubt Tai did anything at all. You know it doesn't work like that."

"Do I? How do I know that? If he was gay, then why wouldn't he have said anything to us?"

"Don't push this, Karen."

"Why shouldn't I? Our grandson's hurting. The whole thing is a mess. That man was Tai's ex-boyfriend, *fighting* on Emmett's front lawn. What kind of person has a boyfriend like that? We had the police here, for heaven's sake. And Leo saw it all. He ran away, Joseph. Now tell me *any* of that was good for Leo. So, why shouldn't I push to protect him? You were always much easier on Emmett than me."

"And for good reason. He's a grown man, Karen. He doesn't need us to tell him how to live his life."

"He has a *son, our* grandson. We have a right to have a say in how he's raised."

"Do we?" Joseph shot back. "And even if we did, I think Emmett's been doing a pretty good job so far."

"He needs us here, Joseph. If we'd been here, none of this would've happened."

I left them arguing and disappeared up into the studio to find Sassy on my bed.

"How did you get in here?" I collapsed beside her, and she flicked her tail across my aching face.

"Ow. I hope that wasn't your final opinion," I said and ran my hand down her back. "I know I fucked up."

She meowed and shifted to knead her claws into my leg. "Stop that." I pushed her away and she set about washing her butt instead.

I snorted. "Okay, I get the message."

I watched her clean as Karen's words sank into my brain. She was right about one thing: what a fucking mess. Emmett's mom might be a piece of work at times, but most of it came from the right place. She wanted to protect her son and grandson, and I could hardly argue with at least some of it. Leo *shouldn't* have witnessed what he did, any of it. Emmett and I had royally screwed up and Emmett's parents had a right to be angry.

I sucked in a breath and got to my feet, sure of only one thing. Right now, I needed to not be anywhere near here. I needed to leave Emmett and his family to pick up the pieces. Maybe I'd have a place in Emmett's life after that, maybe not. But having me a stone's throw away from everything about to go down in that house wasn't good for anyone, especially Leo.

I shoved my few belongings in a bag, then wrote a note for Emmett and put it on my pillow. After that, I called for an Uber. I had plenty of money for a night or two in a motel, a bus ticket to Seattle, and a start at the other end until I got a job.

I slipped Sassy in through the back door of the house without drawing attention to myself and then made my way out front to wait for my ride. The family room window was closed, the curtains drawn and light on, but all was quiet. I leaned against the wall of the garage and took a long last look at the house I'd hoped to have a future in.

The gnawing ache in my heart threatened to bring me to my knees and I didn't even try to bite back the tears.

EMMETT

"Take as long as you need." Ashley shooed Cody into her bedroom and the television volume went up.

I needed to find a way to thank her when all this was over. *Over.* God, how I wished.

Leo had yet to meet my eyes, sitting as far away from me as he possibly could at the opposite end of the couch, his jaw set in anger.

Damn.

I took a deep breath and wondered where to begin, sending a prayer to Lu if she could pull a few strings here.

"I loved your mother with all my heart." It was as good a place as any to start.

Leo's gaze flicked to me for just a second, then away.

"From the minute I saw her, I was smitten. There was never anyone else. She brought sunshine into my life, and we were so happy together. I couldn't have loved her more. And then you came along and I found that, in fact, I could. Things just got better."

Leo turned his head a little, so I knew he was listening. It broke my heart to glimpse his tear-stained face and the pain in his eyes and to know that I was the one who put it there.

"I would've done anything to not lose her that day, Leo. Your mother meant everything to me. She was the best wife and mother we could ever have had. I'll always love her."

He blinked furiously but said nothing, and I almost smiled. He was so like his mother that way. Mule-headed stubbornness.

"I'm not gay, Leo." I waited for that to register.

He frowned and studied his hands fisted in his lap.

"I'm bisexual. Just like Cody's dad. I've always known that I was, and your mother knew as well."

His gaze darted again to my face, but this time stayed there.

"I never told my parents, but I *should* have told *you* sooner, and I'm sorry I didn't. It wasn't fair or right for you to find out like you did, and I apologize. We both apologize."

"Were you ever going to tell me?" His voice was small and nervous.

But at least he was talking and a shudder of relief ran through me. "Yes, I was. This weekend, in fact, after your grandparents left. I wanted you to have a fun time on Halloween *before* we talked, just in case you found any of it hard."

He turned to fully face me and then scooted back against the cushion, his legs curled under his hips. He was still wrapped up in a defensive ball, but he was finally engaged. "What did mom say when you told her?"

I smiled and fell back on the couch cushion. "She didn't say much at all, actually. You see, it was never a big deal for her. She just hugged me and told me she loved me."

He thought about that for a minute. "Why didn't you tell Grandma and Grandpa?"

"Ah. Well, that was a bit different. I've never been quite sure how they'll react, and I'm still not. I haven't talked to them yet. Talking with you is far more important." I kept my eyes steady on his so he'd see the truth.

He nodded, adding a tiny smile that was worth the whole fucking world.

"And since I never met a guy I wanted to date before I met your mother, I chickened out, I guess. I told myself I didn't need to risk it."

"But you want to date Tai?"

Oh, my precious child, that and so much more. "What would you think if I did?"

He chewed at his lip. "I don't know."

At least it was honest. "What you said back at the house—"

"I didn't mean it when I said I hated you," he blurted. "Or . . . Tai . . ." He said that a bit more quietly.

I nodded. "That's okay. We caught you by surprise. I understand, and so does Tai. But just because I like Tai, or even if I'm in love with him, doesn't mean I didn't love your mother just as much. That's part of being bisexual. I can fall in love with a man *or* a woman, and I was deeply in love with your mother."

He kept chewing on his cheek. "Are you in love with Tai?"

Fuck.

"I heard you say it," he dared me, and I knew I couldn't lie.

"Yes, I am. I'm in love with Tai."

Leo's eyes filled and I reached for his hand. He let me take it and I thanked every saint I could remember for the privilege.

I scooted closer, but not too close.

"I fell in love with your mother really fast, in just a few weeks. And I have with Tai, as well. Maybe that's how I'm made. Love hits me hard and fast. But I've never loved anyone else. Just your mom, and now Tai. But things are still very new between us. And being in love with someone doesn't always mean you decide to stay together forever. That's why we were waiting to tell you. I hope he's the one for me again, and maybe for us as a family. But we need to learn a lot more about each other first. We need to date and to give you time to get to know him better as well."

The frown on Leo's face hadn't left completely but it wasn't angry anymore.

"It's a lot to take in, and it's a big change for me as well. We plan to take things really slow. Make sure it's right for all of us, and that includes you. Your happiness means everything to me, Leo. I won't risk that. But I love Tai."

He tilted his head and studied me. "Does he make you happy?"

I didn't have to think and there was no reason to pretend otherwise. "Yes, he does."

Leo said nothing for a minute and I left him to think. "He's funny, and he laughs a lot, like mom."

Air whooshed out of my lungs. "He does. I like that about him."

Leo squeezed my hand. "Me too."

It was such a small thing but it changed everything. And in that single gesture, I knew Leo and I were going to be okay.

"I'm sorry I ran away." He shuffled over to sit right alongside me, and I wrapped my arm around him and pulled him close. "I guess I wanted to scare you, but I'm sorry."

I could barely talk past the lump in my throat. "You did scare me. I can't lose you, Leo. I can't lose you too." My voice broke and he scrambled onto my lap and wrapped his skinny arms around my neck. "I'm sorry, Dad. Don't be sad."

I crushed him to my chest and shook with the tears. "I'll always be sad if I hurt you, Leo. Just don't run away again, please. You can always talk to me, even yell at me, but just don't run away."

His wet cheeks pressed against my neck. "Okay, I promise."

We rocked in place for long enough I thought I'd squeezed all the air from Leo's lungs. I probably came close by the urgent way he wriggled to get free and pushed back to sit on my thighs.

"I'm not going to ask what you feel about Tai and me dating right away. I want to give you time to think about it, okay?"

Leo's forehead creased further.

"Ashley said you can stay the night here with Cody, if you like. That way you can talk to him about things. Would you like that?"

In truth, I wanted nothing more than to take him home and to know he was tucked up safe in his own bed. But this was the better option for everyone if Leo wanted it.

Leo nodded.

"Then that's what we'll do. Now, we've kept Ashley long enough. She said she'll drop you off in the morning. Can I have a hug? It's okay if you don't feel like it."

Leo immediately flung his arms around my neck, and my

heart flipped. "Thanks, Dad." He pulled back with a worried frown in place. "Is Tai okay? That guy hit him."

"He's sore but he's okay. You can see for yourself tomorrow."

A smile broke over his face. "Tell him I'm sorry about what I said."

"I will."

He scrambled off my lap and ran for Ashley's bedroom where Cody was watching television with his mom, which allowed me a minute or so to wipe my eyes and stitch some steadiness back into my heart before she appeared.

I said goodbye, along with a truckload of thanks and promises to talk again when things settled. She gave me a knowing look, a huge hug, and wished me well.

The first thing I did back in Lu's car was to call Tai, but it went straight to Lu's voicemail. I frowned and tried Georgia's phone to check in on Ivy instead.

"She's fine," Georgia reassured once she'd pried all the information she could from me about Leo. "They think it was angina, although she'd settled by the time we got here. They're going to monitor her for a few more hours, possibly overnight, and she'll have to get an angiogram next week sometime. Depending on the results of that, she might need a stent in one of her arteries. We offered to stay, but Ivy insists we go back to the motel. We've told her to call us, not you, when she's ready to be discharged, and we'll see that she gets home."

"That's kind of you, but I can come—"

"No," Georgia cut me off. "Ivy was very clear on that. Once we knew Leo was okay, we told her what had happened, and she said she'd catch up with you tomorrow. She wants you to stay with Leo, Emmett. The police have dusted the back of the truck for prints, so as long as you don't mind us borrowing it until tomorrow, we'll be fine."

"Of course. Take it. And thanks for helping out. About what happened tonight—"

"It's all fine, sweetheart," Georgia soothed. "Lu told us years ago that you were bi, not long after you met. She probably shouldn't have said anything, but you know Lu."

I did. And the news didn't surprise me at all. She and her mother had always had a very close relationship.

"She knew we'd never breathe a word unless you said something yourself. Craig and I both like Tai, by the way. You don't need to worry about us."

Relief coursed through me. "Thank you. That means a lot. I wished I'd talked to you when Lu was still alive, and I'm sorry about that. But I'm not sure my mother feels quite so generous about it all."

"Well, that's her journey, and she'll get there in her own time, I have no doubt. You just keep your eye on the prize: that grandson of ours and the man you seem to have fallen for. We'll talk tomorrow."

I pocketed the phone and after a second attempt to call Tai went straight to voicemail, I headed Lu's car toward home, anxiety curling in my gut. I'd expected Tai to be waiting for news about Leo. Why wasn't he? I put my foot to the gas.

The minute I pulled into the driveway and saw Tai's studio was dark, I knew. I raced up the stairs, threw open the door, and almost dropped to my knees when I saw his bag was gone. Then I caught sight of the note on his bed and my stomach clenched.

No.

I grabbed the note and sat on the edge of the bed, my hands shaking.

You can stop panicking!

I haven't taken off. I wouldn't do that to you. But I think we both need a little time. You need to put some of that into your family, and I need to think about what it is I really want to do moving forward. Your mother hates me, by the way, not that I blame her. Tonight was hardly my finest hour. We both fucked up and now we have to face the consequences. I want to know about your talk with Leo and I'll call, I promise. I just need to get situated. And even if Leo is okay about us, he's going to need time to adjust to the idea. I'm still in town. I'm not going anywhere, not yet, and never without talking to you. Thanks to you I have enough money to see me through for a few days, so don't worry. Trust me. I love you more than I can say. Tai

Shit. Shit. Shit. I threw the note on the bed and kicked the bedside trash can clear across the room.

I called Tai's phone again but nothing, Lu's voice taunting me on voicemail.

"Tell him to pick the fuck up," I bitched at her. "Goddamn, this motherfucking crapfest of a fucking asshole day."

A text came through and I almost dropped the phone in surprise.

Are Leo and Ivy okay?

I shook my head and snapped one back.

Yes. Now pick up the damn phone.

I'll call soon.

Fuck! I re-read the note, and then stormed from the studio back to the house where the family room lights still blazed.

"What did you say to him?" I slammed the back door shut with enough force to rattle the plates in the plate rack.

My father jolted upright from next to my mother on the couch, almost knocking both their coffee mugs from the table. "Say to who?"

I was in no mood for bullshit. If there wasn't smoke already coming out my ears, there damn well should've been. "To Tai. What the hell did the two of you say to him?"

My dad glanced at my mother in confusion. "We said nothing. He never came inside after you left."

My mother's gaze flicked to the window and back. "We thought it best to leave him be, until you got back."

What the hell? Unbelievable. "So, you decided it was fine to leave him up there on his own, feeling guilty for everything that happened, not to mention having to deal with being assaulted by his ex and almost having his damn jaw broken?"

They exchanged nervous glances. "Well, we thought . . ." My

mother hesitated. "Your father wanted to check on him, but he had asked to be left alone earlier . . . so, I didn't think—"

"That's exactly right. You *didn't* think! And if you didn't say anything, why does he think you hate him?" I flung Tai's note at my mother. She held it between them to read and blanched.

My father's eyes closed. "Shit. He must have overheard. Sorry, son."

"Overheard what?" I demanded.

"Sit, Emmett, please."

"No! What did Tai overhear?"

"He must've heard us arguing," my father explained with a pointed look at my mother who was busy staring at her hands. "About tonight. You have to understand, it was a shock, son. And when Leo ran off as well—"

"It's my fault." My mother rested a hand on dad's arm and found the courage to look at me. "I was angry with you, with him. I said some things I shouldn't have, about how he might've influenced you—"

I drew a sharp breath and shook my head. "How could you—"

"I'm sorry, okay?" Her eyes locked with mine. "If it makes any difference, it's not about you being gay—"

"I'm not gay. I'm bi."

Karen waved a dismissive hand. "Bi. Whatever."

"Karen." My father's tone carried a distinct warning. I could've hugged him if I wasn't so fucking mad at them both. But Dad had always been the fair-minded one and at least he listened. My mother simply reacted.

"I'm sorry . . . again," she backtracked. "Look, I know I'm doing this all wrong. It doesn't matter—"

"But it does," I argued. "It matters because I loved Lu. I was *in love* with her. It wasn't a sham relationship. It wasn't a cover, and it's really, really important that Leo understands that. So yes, the terminology matters, Mom, and you *need* to get it right."

She stared and I saw the light bulb finally fucking going off in that brain of hers.

My dad nodded quietly. "Yes, I think we get that now."

"And this was never how I planned to tell you both."

"So, you *were* going to tell us?" My mother could pout with the best of them.

"Of course, but *after* I'd talked to Leo."

"What about Lu?"

"She knew. But I didn't know she'd told her parents."

My mother's sharp intake of breath said it all, and I couldn't find a fuck to give about how much the sound pleased me.

"Why didn't you tell *us*?" she pressed.

I rolled my eyes. "Because I didn't know how you'd react. Case in point." I spread my hands and she flushed. "It wasn't a deliberate slight, Mom. I knew I was bi from the time my hormones came on board, but it took me a while to come to terms with it. Plus, coming out isn't exactly straightforward, there's no plan to follow, no right time or place. And then I met Lu, and it just didn't seem necessary to take the risk. But I should have. I know that now. Especially since Lu didn't bat an eye when I told her. But you don't get to judge me. I get to choose where and when I feel safe coming out, not you."

It was easy to see she didn't like my answer, but to her credit, she accepted it. My mother wasn't mean, just too damn used to getting her own way.

My father spoke up instead. "We understand how difficult it must've been to think about telling Leo. And us—"

"But—"

"Shh, Karen. Let me finish."

She fired him a sharp look but closed her mouth.

"And you've been an excellent parent to Leo since you lost Lu. We trust you to know what's best for you both—"

He clamped down hard on my mother's arm as she sat forward.

"—and who you fall in love with. Because we heard you outside. You love this man, right?"

"I do. He's the best thing to happen to me since Lu."

My dad smiled, a single beaming smile. And even my mother's expression softened, although it was fleeting.

"And Leo likes him too, I understand."

"He does."

"Please, tell us how it went with Leo." My mother finally freed herself from my father's grip, her expression one of genuine concern. Regardless of what she thought about Tai or the two of us together, she loved Leo with everything she had.

I sank into the chair opposite and scrubbed a hand down my face. "It went okay, I think. Once we got over the fact I wasn't gay, but bi—" I fired her a pointed look. "—and that I really had loved Lu, then we were able to talk. He's going to need some time, but I think he'll be okay. I left him with Cody and Ashley. It's the best place for him tonight. Cody's dad is bi and living with his man, and Cody has a great relationship with them both."

My mother's eyes bugged. "Jon is bi?"

I grinned. "Yes, he is." I studied my mother and thought *to hell with it.* "Do you really not like Tai?"

She balked at the bluntness and didn't answer right away. Then after she'd bristled long enough, she sighed and grew a little smaller on the couch. "I hardly know him. It would be ridiculous of me to say I didn't like him, right?"

I merely cocked a brow.

She huffed. "Yes, all right, I admit I could've handled it better."

My dad snorted, which earned him a sharp elbow in the ribs.

"But if you love him," she said, watching me closely, "and he makes you happy, then there must be something very special about him, and I'll make sure to look for it."

And with that one statement, I knew we'd be okay.

She smiled somewhat apologetically and my dad pulled her in for a hug.

"One thing I've learned about your mother in forty years of marriage," he said, "when she gets things wrong, she doesn't do it half-assed. More often than not, it's an epic shit show."

Mom whacked him on the chest and he laughed, tipping her chin up for a kiss.

I wasn't willing to be quite so conciliatory and stayed in my seat with just a nod. "I'd appreciate you giving Tai more than just a chance, Mom. I intend to make us a family if he'll have us, and if you want to be part of that . . ." I left it for her to finish.

She held my gaze and licked her lips. "Understood."

"So, what are you going to do about *this*?" Dad handed the note back to me.

I stared at it and felt my eyes well again. "I don't know. This isn't just about tonight. I don't think. I've had a feeling I might've swept Tai along in all this, and I think he needs to decide how much he wants me in return. I know he loves me, but he has to decide if he's willing to fight for that."

My father gave a nod of approval. "Well, you certainly seem prepared to fight for *him,* and I couldn't be more proud of you." He pulled my mother to her feet. "We'll be in bed if you need us."

I stood for a hug and even accepted one from my mother. We'd get through the awkwardness as we always did, with time and way too much talking for my liking.

Left alone, I stared at the empty room and groaned. It had been a day. And with the chances of me getting any sleep pretty dead in the water, it wasn't likely to finish anytime soon. My gaze was drawn to the dark studio above the garage. I pulled out my phone and tried again. Still nothing.

"Oh, for fuck's sake." I grabbed the keys from the fruit bowl, left a note on the table, and locked the back door behind me. Then I headed for the studio and lost myself in the intoxicating smell of Tai's sheets—from the last time we'd snuck some time together.

I'd barely closed my eyes when my phone buzzed beside me on the pillow.

I jolted upright at my first glimpse of the name on the screen. Tai.

"Hey." It was one word, but the shattered exhaustion behind it hit like a punch to my heart.

"Hi." The shake in my voice surprised even me. "I was so fucking worried that you wouldn't call."

"I said I wouldn't do that to you."

"I know, but I didn't expect you not to be here when I got back either, so . . ."

"I'm sorry. It took longer than I thought to find a room and get sorted. Bloody Halloween. How did it go with Leo?"

"Good, I think. He's still unsure, you know? Not against the idea of *us*; I need to be clear about that. But just working through things. He's staying the night with Cody. And he said to tell you he's sorry for what he said."

There was a long pause before Tai answered. He'd needed those words from Leo, and I was happy to give him time to digest them. "I'm glad he's okay," he said. "Tell him I'm sorry too. Tell him I miss him . . ."

"Why don't you come home and tell him yourself?" *Please, come home.*

He ignored the question. "How's Ivy?"

"She might need a stent, apparently, but she's okay. She's been told to slow down."

He snorted.

"That's what I said. Why did you leave?" I pushed a little. "I know you overheard my parents arguing, but I thought we were okay? The day was fucked up but—" *I love you.*

He sighed, and I caught laughter from a TV show in the background. "I guess I felt overwhelmed by it all—us, Leo, your parents, Dion. It suddenly felt wrong to be there. There's so much going on in my head, and then when I heard your parents . . . Don't hate me for leaving. I just needed to get away from that for a bit. There's a lot to think about."

"Is there? I kind of thought we'd done quite a bit of that already."

Silence. I could've slapped myself. I had to tone it down. Tai needed to want this as much as I did. But I hated this awkwardness between us.

"My mother apologizes, by the way. They both said they'd like to get to know you."

He snorted. "Let me guess. That was your dad talking, right?"

I chuckled. "Well, you can't have everything. But to be fair, you don't really know them either, do you?"

He hesitated. "That's true. I might have to talk to the police again tomorrow."

"Do you want me to come?"

"No. They said they'd contact you if they needed anything more from you guys."

"Okay. Tai, please, I just want you home. I'm sleeping in your bed."

More silence.

"It's the closest I can get to you. I can still smell you, smell us. I want you back in my bed, in my life."

"I'll call tomorrow, I promise. I'm sorry. I don't want to hurt you."

Goddammit. "I know. Tomorrow then. I love you."

"I love you too."

I hung up but kept the phone in my hand, staring through the grubby window of the cheap motel out into a deluge of rain. Giant puddles patchworked the parking lot reflecting the bright green and pink motel sign, its letter M flickering on and off like a scene in a bad movie.

Cue the arrival of the bad guys.

Oh right, that was me. At least according to Emmett's parents, I suspected.

I hadn't lied. It *had* taken me a while to find a room, what with the long Halloween weekend, but I'd also ignored Emmett's calls for a while once I had. I was desperate to know how the talk with Leo went, but I'd been too scared to hear the disappointment in Emmett's voice that I'd left.

He and Leo would be fine with or without me, but I'd also meant what I'd said. I wasn't running away. But I couldn't stay in that studio any longer, either. And I wasn't sure Emmett would understand why. So, I'd left before he could argue with me, because I was pretty sure I'd have caved without much of a fight.

I just needed some time to nut things out without the specter of his parents and Leo only yards away. Everything had happened so fast, not just the day, but the whole month. I still worried I was riding on someone else's coattails, even if it was Emmett's, and I'd promised I'd never do that again.

Fucking Dion.

I cupped my aching jaw. The motel owner had taken one look at the bruising and given me the side-eye, standing at the door clutching her dressing gown across her chest for a minute before finally letting me in. I looked like I'd gone a couple of rounds in a fight club and lost, emphatically. The only upside, I was pretty damn sure Dion looked a whole lot worse about now.

Him turning up at Emmett's house had rocked me and was another reason I needed to really think about where I was headed, and why. I'd left Boston to be my own person, to leave that insecure version of me behind and find a place for myself in the world, standing on my own feet.

But was I really doing that?

A flash of lightning jolted me back from the window, the whip crack of thunder close on its heels followed by a rolling grumble. An image of Emmett curled up in my bed tore at my heart.

Home.

He'd asked me to come *home*. Like I belonged there. I wanted to. I just wasn't sure if I should.

An image of Leo wrapped up in a blanket and discussing big important things with Cody slipped into my head. Getting his brain around what had happened with his dad and me, making decisions that might frame his life to come.

I grabbed my phone and fired off a quick text. When Leo got his phone back, I wanted him to know I'd been thinking of him and that I had his back, regardless.

Hi Leo. I'm really sorry if I hurt you. I never meant to. Your dad is a good man and he loves you more than you'll ever know. You're a great kid and I'm so lucky to have met your family. I just wanted you to know that.

Another flash of lightning. I slammed closed the curtains and took a seat on the worn carpet, leaning back against the scrappy bed with its bleak musty odor.

I stared at the phone in my hand, Lu's phone. *What the hell was I doing?*

I took a deep breath and made the call.

She picked up on the second ring. "Son?"

One word from my mother's mouth and the tears came.

"Tai? What's wrong, honey? Talk to me."

As if I could fucking stop myself.

Everything gushed out.

I babbled my way through a month of pain, joy, hope, fear, and confusion. I talked about Dion, leaving Boston, Emmett, Burlington, the clinic, Leo, everything. Mum listened to it all and never said a word, other than to tell me she was putting me on speakerphone so my father could hear as well. I didn't care. They were bookends for the package of unconditional love I'd been lucky enough to be wrapped in my entire life. I wanted them to know.

And when I finally ran out of steam, the ensuing silence wasn't awkward or judging, just safe. I pictured their eyes meeting across the dining table in my family home, the place Mum always sat to talk. Maybe one of my brothers was there, all of them so perfect in their jobs, their lives, their families.

"I know what you're going to say," I broke the soft quiet. "I've been such an idiot—"

"Stop right there," my mother interrupted. "That's not at all what I was going to say, or even close to what I'm thinking, so don't you put words in my mouth, Taika Rewena Samuels."

I sat straighter on the floor. I'd been full named. "Sorry, Mum. But I know I'm always screwing up—"

"Who told you that?"

I couldn't help the snort. "My teachers? Your family? My brothers? Like every one of them, all of my life."

"Pffft. Your brothers don't know their arses from their eyeballs half the time," she scoffed. "It's easy to take the high road when you've known what you wanted since before you could walk. But that was never you, Tai. And that's not any discredit to you, either. You've always taken the long route; it's how you're made. You couldn't be told anything, not that it stopped us from trying, but maybe that wasn't a good thing. We should've done less telling and more listening, and I will always regret that. When you followed that bastard to Boston, I knew we'd made a mistake."

I jolted in place. My mother never swore.

"We saw he had you all dreamy-eyed and that he was messing with your head. You've always wanted to belong, Tai. Right from the first day we dropped you at kindergarten and you came home crying because the older boys teased you for wearing that pink T-shirt we couldn't get you out of. You belonged at home, in your family, but you never seemed to see it or believe it."

It was true. "I didn't feel like I fitted, not like the others."

"Well, you did. But that doesn't mean to say you knew that. And when you came out, it was like you had to show the world you didn't need anybody, but you still did. Deep down you did. Then your brothers settled down and you were left still looking for something, still hunting, and that's how that bastard got at you. He offered you something you were looking for, but it was a lie, Tai, and if we'd been better parents, we could've maybe stopped it. This isn't just on you, Tai. We all played a part, your brothers as well, and I'm so sorry."

My mouth opened and closed like a damn fish as I struggled to digest her words. Not because I disagreed—hell, I'd realized most of it for myself over the last month—but to hear Mum acknowledge it blew my fucking mind. All my life, I'd fought to claim a space for myself without really bothering to find out what I wanted that space to be. I'd chosen to simply rock the boat and do the opposite of my brothers for no better reason than I could. Dion was just another example.

"No one can tell you what to do, and we wouldn't if we could," my mother continued. "But I will say this. Be careful of dismissing something good just because you're scared or because you've got some idea of how things *should* be, and this doesn't fit."

"But I have to make my own way, Mum. I have to stand on my own feet. I can't roll through life anymore, just cruising behind someone else. I can't have another Dion in my life."

"Then don't."

"It's not that easy—"

"And you're only just figuring this out?" She hooted and my father's laugh boomed in the background.

"I'm glad you find this so amusing," I grumbled.

My mother composed herself. "Oh, you have no idea. But if you think you're the only son of ours we've had a version of this talk with, then think again."

Well, that was news.

"Do you think I'm weak?" she asked bluntly.

Was she serious? "No!" Holy shit, there was no one stronger than my mother.

"Do you think I rode on your father's coattails because he earned more than me?"

"Of course not." My mother was the hub of our family in nearly every way.

"Do you think your father believed I brought anything less to our relationship just because I had no idea what I wanted to do when we first met?"

"But you were training to be a teacher."

"No. Not at first. When we first met, I was working in the office of a campground. It was two years before I decided I wanted to teach. Having nothing when you go into a relationship isn't a problem if you're honest and talk about it. Not unless you make it into one." She paused in a pointed silence.

Message received.

"*Or* unless you have no intention of pulling your weight and balancing the scales. Is that what you're planning to do?"

"No. Of course not. I have some . . . ideas."

"Oh really? I think we'd like to hear about those. You know, Tai, relationships are never perfect, but they should always be places where both parties grow. They're organic. They change as the people involved change. They aren't cookie-cutter or set in concrete. What you start with isn't always what you end up with. The trick is finding the right partner who understands that and encourages you. I know you want to run because this all feels too risky, too close to the bone after Dion. You don't want to be reliant on someone again, even for a while—his house, his things. Only you can decide if you can trust him, and yourself. To make sure you find a way to balance things between you."

I thought of Emmett's encouragement, his delight in my skills and how I might put them to use. Always having my back, always supporting, never controlling, never any strings attached.

"We can't all be in the same place at the same time, son, and this man of yours isn't perfect either. I suspect there are aspects of him that you tend to, that you encourage him to develop? You have wonderful attributes too, Tai. Balance doesn't have to be about equal jobs, equal income. There are lots of ways to balance a relationship. Do you make a difference in his life?"

I thought of Emmett's overwork, his poor self-care, my time with Leo, and smiled. "Yeah, I think I make a difference."

"Of course you do. You're our son. Now, your dad has something he wants to speak to you about. But if, after everything, you decide you might want to come home, we'll get you back here as soon as we can."

Thirty minutes later I slid the phone onto the nightstand and clambered up on top of the blankets to try and get some sleep. There was no way I was getting in those sheets.

It was a lot to take in. A lifetime's way of thinking to change, and I wasn't sure how successful I'd be since I'd bounced around for so long. But maybe I didn't have to get it right straight away.

Maybe this was something I could grow into.

Maybe with someone who'd be patient at my side.

22
EMMETT

The sudden slash of light jolted me from sleep and my eyeballs jabbed like angry porcupines at the back of my lids. I hadn't gotten more than a couple of hours sleep, and I cursed my mother for not letting me claw back at least a few extra minutes, breakfast or no.

I jammed the pillow over my face to block her out and drank in Tai's scent one last time before I attempted to pry myself awake. "Go away. I'll be down soon."

The bed dipped alongside and a finger traced a path down my arm. "I'd prefer to stay, if you'll have me."

I threw the pillow to the side and Tai's beautiful face came into view—battered and bruised, but just as wonderful as the first day I saw him.

He cupped my face and his forehead crunched into deep furrows. "I'm sorry I didn't have enough faith, not in you, but in me." His mouth curved up in a slow smile. "I *always* believed in you. I just wasn't sure I could live up to that myself, and I didn't want to hurt you or Leo."

I grabbed his hands, my heart pounding in my throat. "*I* believe in you—"

"Shh. Hear me out."

"Not until you get down here next to me. I need to fucking hold you. What time is it anyway?"

"Seven." He shrugged off his jacket, kicked his shoes to the side, and crawled alongside me on the bed.

I hauled him close, running my nose through his hair and over his smiling face, being careful of his bruising, absorbing the fact that he was back in my arms. He chuckled, and I shifted on my hips so I could kiss him. Long, deep, and not nearly enough. He tasted so fucking good, I didn't want to stop, and by the time I pulled back, we were both breathless.

"I couldn't wait," he said, keeping us eye to eye, only inches in it. "The police called at six to say they'd arrested Dion at the ER in Middlebury. He was getting his fucking nose fixed. They'll be charging him today."

"That's great news." I kissed him again and again.

He hummed against my lips. "I've missed you."

"I can't believe you're here." I hauled his shirt up so I could get at some skin, splaying my fingers over his hot back. "You need to get a restraining order."

He nodded, shuffling closer, arching his hips into mine, and I pushed back. "Oh, fuck." He ground lightly against me. "I . . . damn, that feels good." He kept grinding. "I intend to. I won't have him turning up here again, not with you and Leo. Shit. Keep going."

I kissed him hard, scrambling with the zipper on his jeans till I got it open.

"Ugh, stop." His hand clasped around my wrist. "Wait. I need to say some things first."

"Really?" I pouted. "Now?"

He smiled. "Really. And yes, now."

"If you must," I grumbled. "But make it quick. I need you."

He stared at me with something like wonder. "You should be angry with me."

I took a deep breath and thought about my answer. "I was, at first. You leaving like that hurt, I'm not going to lie. I wondered if I'd got it all wrong. If I wasn't enough to hold you —single dad, busy life, inexperienced with men, a bit soft around the middle. Not exactly high on anyone's sexy list. But then I spent half the night terrified that I'd never get the chance to hold you like this again, and so now I'm just fucking thankful."

He shook his head and leaned across to kiss me, his lips warm and soft, moving against mine in that familiar dance we'd perfected. "I'm sorry I put you through that. And every one of those things you mentioned is exactly why I love you, exactly why I find you sexy as hell. I'm particularly partial to that softness around the middle you seem to dislike, and I'm hoping to see a lot more of it."

He cradled my face and kissed me on the nose. "I've spent my life feeling like I never measured up, Emmett. To my brothers, at school, to my boyfriends. A pretty face, a good fuck, but not much more. I think that's why I fell so hard for Dion. He made me feel special, at first anyway. Turns out he was a total fuck up, but we all know that story."

"That wasn't your fault."

"Maybe not. But the way I thought about myself opened the door to his manipulation. If it wasn't him, it probably would've been someone else. My mum pointed that out."

"You spoke to your mother? About us?" I didn't know whether to be flattered or horrified.

"I did. It was . . . enlightening." He chuckled. "She wants to meet you and Leo."

My heart did a little flip. "So, you really meant it? You're going to stay?"

He wriggled closer and I relished the length of his body next to mine, the warmth soaking into my skin. He was back. I threw a leg over his thigh just in case he changed his mind.

"I am. But there are things that need to go along with that."

Anything. "Just say it."

"You might not like them."

"I'm a big boy."

"You are." His brown eyes slid into black and every cell in my body reacted. "But getting back to the point. I barely had time to take a breath between leaving Dion and meeting you. That's part of what happened last night. I felt, still feel, I'm not bringing enough to the table in this relationship."

"But you—"

He put a finger to my lips and I shut up. I'd wanted him to fight for us, and he was, in his own way. He was laying down his battle lines and I needed to listen.

"I know a lot of that comes from me not wanting to repeat the whole Dion debacle, and yet I also know you're nothing like him. But it's still going to take a while for me to stop worrying that I've simply switched one freeloading relationship for another. I need to do something more proactive to change that. I need to start building a stronger future. I'm capable of more—you opened my eyes to that."

"You absolutely fucking are. You have so many skills."

He sighed and his eyes fluttered closed. When they opened again, their irises shimmered in the weak morning light. "See, that right there is why I love you," he whispered the words. "No one believes in me like you do." He stared at me with a shy but determined look I'd never seen before. "I want to look into going to university, here in Burlington, get myself a degree."

I could barely breathe. "In business?"

He shrugged. "Maybe. I don't know. I love the idea, but I don't want to rush it. I want to make sure I know all my options. In the meantime, if it's okay with you, I'll take that office manager position at the clinic, but only if you promise to get a vet tech as soon as possible."

I nodded enthusiastically. "I promise."

"*But* . . ." He eyeballed me. "*If* for any reason I feel that's not working for me or for us, I want you to be okay with me looking for something else."

I had zero problem with that. "Agreed. One hundred percent. And I'll be floating the idea of buying Ivy out now that she's been told to slow down. So, you'll be busy with two businesses, if you want?"

He simply nodded.

I chewed on my bottom lip and he saw and waited. I knew it was a risk, but I had to ask. "About college, the cost. The clinic could always help—"

"No. I have a plan for that."

He did? "You do?"

"Yes. Don't look so surprised. As it turns out, my mum and dad offered to help with the fees. Not all. I'll obviously need a big loan as well, which I *will* organize myself." He eyeballed me again. It was like he knew me or something.

My desperate need to look after Tai and his equally determined need for independence was going to take some negotiating. But I could learn to keep my mouth shut and he could learn to accept a little bit of help, I was sure of it.

"It was something my parents said they regretted not telling me," Tai explained. "They'd helped all my brothers through university, and I'd just assumed that help was ear-tagged for education. But Mum said I could've used it for any equivalent endeavor. If I'd needed it for starting a business and not a degree, I could have had it, but I never knew. They're going to deposit some for me when I open a new account next week. It's not a lot, but it will help me feel more independent."

"I'm so fucking pleased for you." I tipped his chin up carefully so I could press my lips to his once again and threaded my fingers through that beautiful silky hair. I slid my tongue along the seam of his lips seeking entry but he pushed me away with a hand to my chest.

"There's one last thing."

God, help me. "Of course, there is. Go on."

"I can't live here."

My heart sank. "But—"

"Emmett, listen to me. I don't want to be all up in Leo's space while he's getting used to this idea of us together, not to mention his dad being bi. I'm going to get a small place as soon as I can, and we're going to date like normal people."

I fisted his shirt and pulled us nose to nose. "There is nothing remotely abnormal about what we're doing. It's just different."

He laughed. "Maybe so, but Leo deserves to be able to take his time."

Dammit, he was right. "I concede you might have a point. Are you done now?"

His gaze turned sultry. "Why? You got somewhere you need to be, baby?"

"Damn right I have." I slid a hand down his back, into his jeans, and over the curve of his ass. "Can I fuck you, sweetheart?"

His mouth curved up in a slow, sexy smile. "Oh, I must have forgotten to mention that particular note in my catalog of requests. Silly me. Right at the top of this list is the requirement for that gorgeous cock of yours to be in my arse as often and for as long as possible, or the entire agreement shall be deemed null and void."

"Mmm," I kissed along the soft curve of his shoulder. "I don't think there'll be any problem meeting that particular objective." I pulled his T-shirt gently over his head, then disposed of his jeans and briefs with equal speed.

"Shit, the door." I turned to leave the bed but he pulled me back.

"I locked it when I came in."

I eyed him with a smile. "You were very sure of yourself."

The smile dropped. "No, I wasn't. Not really. But I was hopeful."

I nuzzled into his neck. "So was I."

Fingers danced over my clothes until they joined his on the floor, putting us naked in each other's arms as fast as possible.

And I could finally breathe again.

"I love you, Emmett, and I love Leo," he whispered against my lips.

"Then don't ever do that again." I peppered kisses down his chest and put the last on the tip of his cock before I lifted my gaze.

He was watching intently, pupils blown all to hell.

"If we're doing this together," I said evenly, "we do *all* of it together, good and bad, no lone rangers, agreed?"

"Agreed." He wiggled his hips enticingly. "Now, less talking, more sucking."

I rolled my eyes. "Like I was the fucking hold up." I took him down the back of my throat in a single swallow and reveled in the filthy groan that fell from his lips as he bucked into my mouth and fisted the covers. I rolled his hard dick over my tongue, sliding up and down its length, relishing every familiar sensation.

"Damn you, Emmett." He gripped a fistful of my hair and angled my head so he could thrust deeper. "You're getting too fucking good at this. I'm not gonna last."

Tears and saliva wet my face as I strained with the fullness of him, but I didn't give a shit. I was exactly where I wanted to be. I swallowed around his length and a new run of expletives fell from his mouth. I savored every sacred taste as he arched and moaned. Tai in my bed, in my arms, down my throat, any and every way I could have him was something I'd never take for granted.

I knew he had to be close when a tube of lube smacked me on the back and a condom hit my cheek.

"Hard and fast," he growled. "Now."

I suited and slicked up, swallowing him again while jamming two fingers up his tight ass with little more than a passing hello, and then crooked my fingers onto—there.

He arched with a loud groan and froze, panting, his fingers wound in my hair, the sharp sting of his hold hitting my heart like a kiss.

I fucking loved it when he lost control.

And then he moved, fucking himself on my fingers as I added a third. I knew how much he loved the burn and stretch, the wider the better, and an image of those limit-testing toys we'd talked about ordering flashed into my mind.

I slapped his thigh. "Turn."

He was over in an instant on all fours, staring back at me over his shoulder, his expression every fucking wet dream I'd ever had. How was I this lucky?

I took him at his word, pushing inside in a single thrust and giving him only the briefest time to adjust before setting a punishing rhythm. His hands crawled up the wall till he was nearly upright, and I put an arm around his chest to pull him tight against mine. He turned his face and the kiss was filthy, wet and awkward, and I loved every messy second of it.

Then he broke away and dropped his elbows to the bed, which

put his ass on full display, and an even better view of my cock shuttling in and out of his hole. And damn, if it wasn't the sexist fucking thing I'd ever seen. I slid a finger alongside my dick, watched it get swallowed up, and almost came on the spot.

He had to be close, grunting and surging with every thrust, but I needed more leverage. I backed off the edge of the bed, pulling Tai with me until I could stand. And then I really went to town, fucking him hard as he furiously stroked himself, his face pushed into the mattress, dropping muffled groans and curses with every drive of my cock. And then we were there, the buzz of sensation cresting, and I suddenly needed his skin on mine, as much as I could get. I fell forward, draping my sweat-slick body over his, planting kisses on his shoulder as the surge came, and I exploded into his ass like a fucking train.

He came seconds later, crying out and ramming his ass back to take me deeper as he shuddered his way through his own orgasm before we collapsed on the bed in a messy heap of sweat and muscle and boneless jelly legs.

"Holy crap." I pulled out and ditched the condom before falling to my back, gasping for air and a cool waft of air.

He laughed and rolled over, flinging a hot arm over my chest. "Damn, that was good."

I pushed his arm away. "God, you may as well be on fire."

He turned to face me, still laughing. "I know, right? That's what you do to me."

We lay there for a minute, his fingers threaded with mine, simply staring at each other.

I blew softly on Tai's face. "So, are you ready to face them?"

His expression tensed. "Do we have to? Can't we just hide in here? Your mother scares the shit out of me."

I turned and bit him not so lightly on the neck.

"Ow, what was that for?"

"Because you're so freaking adorable. Come on. I'll protect you.

"I am *not* adorable." He pursed his lips together. "I'm fierce and a force to be reckoned with."

I laughed and tweaked his nipple, which earned me a withering glare. "Of course you are." I ruffled his hair. "Sooo fucking adorable. Besides, Leo will be here any minute, and I have a feeling he's going to want to talk to you."

Tai's eyes widened. "Shit. Emmett, I'm not sure I can—"

I stopped him with a kiss. "Of course, you can. I don't know what Leo's going to want to call you in the future, but regardless of what it is, if we're a team, then you'll be a parent by any name. Welcome to the danger zone, babe."

His eyes nearly bulged out of his head.

"As I said." I grinned hugely. "Fucking adorable."

23

TAI

7 WEEKS LATER

"Max, stop! Max, no! Emmett, grab him!" I shouted.

Emmett spun at my frantic shout just as Max tore into the house right on the tail of Sassy. I had no fear for Sassy's safety, but our pocket rocket of a boxer pup already sported a scar on his shoulder and a notch in his ear from previous encounters, and I'd really rather not have Emmett spend another Saturday afternoon repairing yet more damage.

Max was cute as all hell, but he lacked a single self-preservation bone in his entire body, and Sassy, the little minx, knew it. She teased and goaded the poor puppy until she got the rise she was looking for and then ran for her life, drawing Max inside where she could corner him in a room and have her wicked way with him. And the damn puppy fell for it every time.

I hadn't even talked Emmett into the idea. Max had simply arrived on Leo's bed the weekend following Halloween, and since then he'd become a fitting hub for this newly developing family thing we had going on.

Family.

Yeah, somehow in the last couple of months, the three of us had become a family. I still needed to pinch myself.

"I've got him." Leo appeared, cradling Max in his arms.

"Sassy's so mean to him." He deposited the puppy unceremoniously onto the lawn and headed back inside to whatever he was doing.

"That puppy needs to use his brain." I dropped to my knees as Max arrived at my feet, his little butt all a wiggle. He instantly flopped onto his back so I could scratch his tummy. "You have to learn to ignore the nasty-wasty pussy cat," I told him.

"Nasty-wasty?" Emmett crouched beside me and added his fingers to the mix. I didn't think Max could wriggle any harder but I was wrong. "This is the pussy cat currently sleeping in your studio with you, in your bed, up against your naked body, every damn night while I pine away all alone in the house?"

I turned and rested my chin on his shoulder, batting my lashes furiously. "You sound just a little jealous there, babe."

He kissed me on the nose. "Damn right, I'm jealous. I almost wish Leo hadn't insisted you remain in the studio when we talked to him. It was really nice that he was okay enough about the two of us to want you to stay, but it would've meant a ton less sexual frustration knowing you weren't only fifty yards away. Not to mention an entirely separate and *private* place for us to escape to."

Max wriggled free and took off back into the house in search of Leo, while Emmett got to his feet and pulled me up and into his arms for a hard kiss.

"Mmm your lips are cold," I licked across the seam and he let me in for a taste. I could never get enough of him. "Besides, I think we've done pretty well, considering, and your office has never looked so clean." I winked. "Plus, we'd have missed coming up with all those creative ways to get off."

He threw me a sour look. "Ivy has already warned me about using the office, new lock notwithstanding. We're on thin ice there. And if you're referring to last night, we're gonna have a conversation about that."

I pulled my bottom lip between my teeth. "Promises, promises. Besides, I was merely getting ready for bed."

"Aha. With your studio window directly opposite mine, curtains open, candles going, and stripping so fucking slooooowly until you were naked as the day you were born, and then jerking off for me. You're lucky Leo was sound asleep."

"His bedroom faces the other way and it was after midnight. I trusted you to check."

"I know you did."

"Besides, you came like a train after watching me get off."

"I did. It was so fucking sexy."

He cradled my face in his gloved hands, his cheeks pink in the icy air. "I love you so much."

He melted my heart on a regular basis. "I love you too. You and Leo."

"Speaking of which . . ." Emmett turned as Leo bounded out of the back door and called us over. "It appears we've been summoned."

I narrowed my eyes. "What's this about?"

"I have no idea." He gave a wry smile.

"Why don't I believe you?"

Come on." He grabbed my hand and tugged me toward the fire pit, which we'd fired up that morning so we could sit outside and enjoy the clear but crisp pre-Christmas day.

Emmett pulled me into a seat alongside him and bundled a blanket over my knees while Leo rolled a small tree stump across and then flipped it on its back to stand on it. He pulled a piece of paper from his pocket and glanced at Emmett.

I caught Emmett's nod.

"What's going on?" I asked Emmett, my heart pounding in my chest.

"Shhh." He squeezed my hand harder. "Just wait."

Leo cleared his throat and I gave him all my attention. He looked so damn cute in the Christmas wool beanie my mother had bought him—just a few locks of dark hair escaping around the edges—a thick jacket and bright pink puffy gloves—my idea, of course.

"Hear ye, hear ye."

I cocked a brow at Emmett, who smirked. He knew exactly what was going on, the bastard.

"Tai!" Leo scolded. "Pay attention."

Oops. "Sorry. Go ahead." I waved my hand at Leo. "Forsooth."

Emmett chuckled and leaned close. "I don't think that means what you think it does."

"Shut up." I squeezed his fingers till he winced.

"Dad!"

I snorted.

"Sorry," Emmett apologized.

"On this day before yuletide," Leo began, reading earnestly from the paper in his hand. "I, Leo Moore, on behalf of Emmett Moore, Lord of Burlington—"

"Always wanted to bang a lord," I whispered out the side of my mouth, drawing a choked cough from Emmett.

"—and ruler of all you see—"

"That includes you," Emmett whispered back.

"In your dreams."

"—do formally ask Taika Samuels, envoy from the southern lands, to move into the Moore castle and become . . . family." Leo's gaze landed nervously on mine. "Please, Tai?"

"What?" I spun to Emmett who was staring at me with such love, and then back to Leo, still anxiously waiting my answer. My hand flew to my mouth, big fat tears rolling down my cheeks.

"Come here," I called Leo over and he jumped off the stump and flew into my arms, burying his face in my shoulder. "Are you sure?" I asked him, although my eyes were on Emmett, who nodded, his eyes glassy with emotion.

"Yes!" Leo screamed in my ear. "Dad helped me write it, but I was the one who asked." He pressed his lips to my ear. "I think he was waiting for me."

"I think he was." I hugged Leo tighter. "Thank you. I'd love to be a part of this family."

"But you have to promise me something."

My heart skipped, hoping this wasn't a separate bedroom thing. "What?"

"Not too much kissy stuff in front of me. It's gross."

Emmett laughed.

"Define too much?" I eyeballed Leo, still trying to register the enormity of what had happened. We were going to be a real family. This was it.

His brow crunched as he thought about it. "A little is okay, I guess. And I'll probably get used to it. I'll let you know."

I nodded sagely. "I can live with that."

"Can I call Cody now?"

"Sure kiddo. How about you hug your dad first?"

Leo flung his arms around Emmett for a brief hug, then tore into the house to finesse his sleepover plans with Cody.

As soon as he was gone, I straddled Emmett's thighs and took his mouth in a fierce kiss, delving deep with my tongue to taste every single crevice before pulling off, breathless. "You knew about this and you never said?"

Emmett smiled and tucked a lock of hair into my tangerine beanie. "He's been planning it for a week."

I held his face in my hands, forcing him to look at me. "And you're sure about this? Like really sure? Like promise-to-the-stars-and-back sure?"

He laughed. "Never been more sure about anything."

I peppered his face with kisses. "You are so getting laid tonight, mister." I started another round of kisses only to be interrupted by Gus loping around the corner of the driveway closely followed by Jasper.

"Damn. That man has the worst timing." I whispered against Emmett's lips before getting to my feet.

Leo ran from the house to greet them and caught Emmett and me still face-to-face. "Ew, yuck. Not in front of the kid, remember?" he said, pretending to gag. Then he gave Gus a huge hug, with Max jumping up and down beside them. Max had taken a particular liking to Gus, and the huge dog tolerated being hassled with the patience of a saint.

"That goes for the rest of us too," Jasper grumbled. "We can do without all that sappy stuff, right, kid?" He held his hand up for a high five and Leo obliged.

Although it was all said in jest, I knew Jasper sometimes struggled with Emmett and I being a couple. I kind of hoped he'd look at us and see a chance for a different future for himself, but who knew? I'd learned quickly the man was as stubborn as a mule. We got on surprisingly well considering we were pretty much like oranges and apples at nearly every level.

I slid into the chair alongside Emmett as Jasper bent to say something to Leo I couldn't hear. Leo nodded enthusiastically and then raced back inside.

"Congratulations." Jasper smiled. "Someone warned me it might be official moving-in day." He held up the shopping bag he carried. "I thought a craft brew might be in order, you know, to prepare you for all that heavy lifting to get Tai's clothes the last fifty meters from the studio to your bedroom, Emmett. Not that I think there were that many left to move."

"Funny guy." I poked my tongue out and he laughed. "And how did you know?" I turned an accusing eye on Emmett.

"Don't look at me." Emmett threw up his hands. "Leo let the cat out of the bag. You're lucky you said yes, or it could've been embarrassing."

"Like there was ever going to be any other answer."

I flicked a finger from Jasper toward a chair. "Sit your soft arse down by the firepit."

He moved toward the chair, discreetly checking his rear end in the reflection of the patio door as he passed. Then he turned and flipped me off. "You're full of bullshit."

I grinned. "Only for you, Jas."

"And don't call me that."

"Whatever you say." I batted my lashes, drawing the smallest of smiles. The man loved me, I was convinced.

Emmett twisted the cap off his beer while Jasper pulled a soda out for himself and one for me. We clinked bottles.

"Cheers to new beginnings." Jasper's gaze flicked between us.

"Cheers to good friends," I answered. "And thanks."

"You're welcome." He took a long guzzle and dropped his hand to scratch Gus who was busy ignoring Max.

I stretched my legs to the warmth of the fire and rolled the cricks out of my neck.

"How're things at Leo's school?" Jasper watched the logs spark and burn in the pit. "I heard the play last week went well."

Emmett blew out a sigh. "It did. Leo was brilliant. And it helped in a way. He got some nice comments from some of the other kids, especially the girls which didn't hurt. But it's going to take a while."

I reached for Emmett's hand, because yeah, it hadn't all been plain sailing. Once word got around that Emmett was dating another man, the teasing and bullying had started, and not just from Leo's fellow students. He'd been left off a few birthday party lists and given the cold shoulder by a couple of his friend's parents.

The teachers had been great and jumped on anything they witnessed or were told about. Letters had gone home to parents about inclusivity in general, and a whole sensitivity program had been implemented.

Emmett and I had visited the school several times, presenting a united front, but in the end, it was Cody and Leo's other friends who'd stepped up and turned the tide. After all, Cody had been through it himself. Picking on one kid was easy. Picking on a group of five or six? Not so much. It hadn't solved everything, but it did help ease the sting, and Leo was slowly learning to cope. He shouldn't have had to, but there wasn't any point just wishing it away.

In the middle of the worst of it, he'd pushed back at both of us for putting him in that position, and I could hardly blame him. I felt guilty as hell, but we did as we'd promised and faced it as a team. And once Leo understood that we were going to fight it together as a family, including his friends, things settled.

The arrival of my mum and dad for a visit a couple of weeks before had also helped Leo, who'd quickly fallen under my mother's spell. The woman was a born mother, something Leo had been missing for a while, and although I was slowly learning how to juggle the whole boyfriend/parental role figure, my mom was a fucking star.

Even Emmett's mother had been charmed. Our relationship was still a work in progress, but after my parents' visit, Karen's approach had softened considerably. She'd even called me son, at least once, anyway.

Miracles happened.

Mum had also brought over a ton of photos which helped cement my decision not to return for any of the stuff I'd left at Dion's apartment, if it was even still there. He'd pled down to assault in order to avoid an attempted kidnapping charge, and a restraining order was in process. I'd been offered police assistance to get my stuff back, but in all honesty, apart from my clothes which would do nothing but remind me of his sorry arse, Mum's visit and the photos had given me all I needed. Everything else could be replaced. Emmett had protested, of course, but in the end, I'd gotten my way.

I'd waved my parents off with a truckload of regret, but not before they made Emmett and me promise to visit New Zealand, maybe even for next Christmas.

Next Christmas.

I could barely get my head around the idea that this was my life. A life with a man and a kid I loved more than I thought possible.

"So, I hear you guys have the house to yourselves tonight." Jasper wriggled his feet closer to the flames.

"Hell, yeah we do." Emmett waggled his eyebrows my way and my cock twitched. One look was all it took and the bastard knew it. I couldn't get enough of him, and it was getting worse, not better. Not to mention the package I'd ordered from the online store was still hidden away in Emmett's wardrobe. We'd been waiting two weeks for the chance to open it.

Jasper snorted. "You need to move that poor boy's bedroom to the far end of the hall before you scar him for life."

"We're tryyyying," I dropped my voice. "But Leo wanted the new one painted first, so that's our holiday job. Top of the fucking list. If I swallow any more of my pillow, I'm going to sprout fucking feathers."

Jasper almost choked on his soda and glared my way. "The concept of oversharing is clearly lost on you, isn't it?"

"Go on, you love it," I teased, which earned me another scowl. Then my phone buzzed and I pulled it out.

Emmett laughed when he saw who the text was from. "Briar,"

he told Jasper. "Tai's going to his first Booklover meeting tomorrow night."

Jasper's lips twitched.

"Don't you start." I narrowed my gaze, which only increased Jasper's amusement. All my fancy footwork to avoid joining the romance book club had come to a crunching halt when I'd taken my mum inside the bookstore to meet Briar. She'd thought it was a wonderful idea. And in truth, I was actually looking forward to it, not that I'd let anyone know. Briar and I had become good friends, and without him, Emmett and I would never have met.

"I've bribed Ivy to go with me." I smirked. "If it all becomes too mushy, Ivy's going to plead tiredness and ask me to take her home."

"Has she found a replacement for The Groom Room?" Jasper nudged Gus off his feet.

"Yeah. Some young guy from Buffalo," Emmett answered. "His family lives here and he wants to move back. He's starting after the holidays."

"Good, the woman needs to slow down. I hear you're buying her out."

Emmett nodded and hooked his leg over mine. "We're gonna let this new guy start first and then look at maybe March for the business change-over. My vet tech starts in January, so she'll be on top of things by then. That way Tai can start his winter semester courses at Burlington U in February without worrying about a change in the clinic books at the same time."

"I'm ready." Leo charged outside with his overnight bag in his hand and ran across to me. "Can you take me now, Tai? Cody's mom said she'd take us to a movie if I can get there soon."

Jasper glanced between us with a knowing smirk and got to his feet. "How about I drop Leo on the way. You two stay there and . . . finish that *moving in*." He winked and grabbed Leo's bag. "Come on, Gus, I don't want you exposed to what's about to go down. Catch you guys later."

Gus rolled to his feet and loped after his owner and a jumping-out-of-his-skin Leo out to Jasper's car. We barely got a wave.

For a few seconds after they left, we sat there and said nothing.

Then Emmett turned to me.

"You hear that?" He cocked his head.

I listened. "Nope."

"Precisely." He slid off his chair and held out his hand. "That, baby, is the sound of an empty house and the promise of twenty-four hours of uninterrupted privacy."

"Damn, I believe you're right." I put my hand in his and he pulled me to my feet.

"It is also the sound that comes *just before* the ripping open of a certain package waiting upstairs in my bedroom with your name written all over it."

I pulled him flush against me, running my freezing hands under his jacket and over all that hot tempting skin. He flinched but didn't move. I nuzzled into his neck and drank deep of the scent of all things Emmett: wood smoke and fresh Vermont air, ripe with a hint of vanilla from my candles, and always that background edge of the clinic.

"And your point?" I wrapped my hands around his neck and covered his mouth with mine. The feel of him pressed against me rocketed my dick to attention and I kissed him till I had to breathe.

"My point, baby—" He stared deep into my eyes, pupils large as saucers. "—is that I have an urgent need to be in *our* bed, in *our* bedroom, with *our* toys in *your* ass as fast as possible, so we can get this new adventure of ours off to the fitting start it deserves."

"I'm all for fitting starts." I nipped his lower lip. "I'm moving in, sugar. Brace yourself."

He nuzzled against my ear. "Have I told you how much I love you today?"

I grinned against his cheek. "Not in the last thirty minutes. Come on, I'll race you."

THE
END

ACKNOWLEDGMENTS

I want to thank Sarina Bowen and her team for this amazing opportunity to be part of an incredible group of authors working on expanding her True North World. It's been loads of fun and a huge privilege. Thank you all!

As always, I thank my husband for his patience and for keeping the dog walked and out of my hair when I needed to work. And my daughter for all her support.

Getting a book finessed for release is a huge challenge that includes beta readers, my wonderful editor at Boho edits, proofers, cover artists, and my tireless PA. It's a team effort and includes all those author support networks and reader fans who rally around when you're ready to pull your hair out and throw away every first draft.

Thanks to all of you.

Made in United States
Orlando, FL
07 November 2022

24286094R00167